EXTINCTION ACADEMY

SPARK
BOOK 0: SERIES PREQUEL

AND

FLAME
BOOK 1

Also by Andrew D. Connell

Crown of the Pharaohs
A Sean Livingstone Adventure (Book One)

Ark of the Gods
A Sean Livingstone Adventure (Book Two)

The Spearhead of Creation
A Sean Livingstone Adventure (Book Three)

Also available:

Crown of the Pharaohs (Special Edition)
Includes the prequel novella:
Monsters, Myths, and Microchips
A Sean Livingstone Adventure (Book Zero)

andrewdconnell.com

EXTINCTION ACADEMY

SPARK
BOOK 0: SERIES PREQUEL

AND

FLAME
BOOK 1

ANDREW D. CONNELL

EREBUS BOOKS

Extinction Academy: Flame
Copyright © Andrew D. Connell 2023
1st Print Edition, May 2023
Published by Erebus Books

Find out more about the author and upcoming books online at andrewdconnell.com

ISBN 0-6458133-0-3

ISBN 978-0-6458133-0-2

For Mum and Dad.

EXTINCTION ACADEMY

SPARK

BOOK 0: SERIES PREQUEL

I grip the hilt of my knife to settle my trembling hand and peer about the dimly lit space. The surrounding crowd of cadets stare straight past me, all struck with the same wide-eyed terror. This place isn't nicknamed *Extinction Academy* because we train alongside genetically resurrected dinosaurs to fight an alien threat – it's because many of these cadets won't make it past their first bonding.

Some of us are moments away from a gruesome death, so if I survive the next few minutes, I'll be doing well.

I've spent my entire life within the metal walls of the Union academy. All I know is a regimented routine of physical training and intense theory, but after 18 years, I'm finally here, standing in this grimy departure bay alongside several hundred cadets the exact same age as me. Nobody speaks as we stare at the well-worn metal door, anxiously waiting for it to open.

I try swallowing the nervous lump in my throat. It doesn't budge.

We're about to confront creatures that ruled the world 100 million years ago, but unlike regular academy training, there will be no metal bars or electrified fences separating us from the carnivores. We all must find and bond with our own unique dinosaur. Any cadet skilled (or lucky) enough to do so will move onto the next phase of training with their prehistoric companion. Some will be eaten, others maimed, and if you're injured bad enough, you don't return to the academy. Nobody knows what happens to them.

Live, die, or disappear, our fate is about to be decided.

I glance at the metallic bracer locked around my left wrist. My name, gender, and birth code, ZAYLA, FEMALE [BETA-8311], appears on the screen. Every cadet wears the same gleaming band displaying their unique identification. Once we're released into the jungle enclosure, our bracers will illuminate with one of three colours, specifying the zone in which to find our designated species, then unlock and drop off.

The Bonding isn't a random free-for-all. Our trainers have been watching us, secretly grading our interactions with different species, providing no clues as to what class of dinosaur they selected for each of us.

There's one thing I know for sure – it won't be a placid herbivore. Those poor creatures are used to feed the voracious carnivores.

Until we complete a bonding, that's what we are too. Food.

The immense door rumbles to life and several anxious cadets look around for an escape. Those are not disciplined. Or focused. They'll die first.

I concentrate on my breathing. Deep and steady breaths. Annoyingly, I can't control my trembling as the whine of well-used gears reverberates through the departure bay and the door finally descends.

A pair of panicked cadets back up and clumsily push to the back of the crowd. They're wasting their time. There's nowhere to go.

A blinding shaft of light spills over us and everyone shields their eyes. With light comes a blast of air, thick and humid, and the door disappears into the floor, exposing us to a primeval landscape.

We are now overlooking a grassy clearing that leads down to a verdant valley. The silhouette of a dormant volcano looms in the distance, rising from the mists hovering over the jungle. The entire landscape is set within the walls of a megalithic artificial enclosure. The lush wall of trees conceals a jungle teaming with life.

Two cadets rush forward. The moment they step out of the departure bay, their wrist bracers illuminate with a colour: one red, one blue. Moments later their bracers unlock and fall to the ground, leaving them to progress without it. More cadets follow, anxiously eyeing their bracer. Some bracers glow with a yellow light.

Blue means you head to the centre of the enclosure, atop the volcano's caldera, where the largest and lethal carnivores roam. Yellow designates the middle zone, red the outer. Each zone is home to a different species and military class of dinosaur.

Unless you're aiming for the command ranks, you don't want blue.

The cadets on either side of me scramble forward, carelessly bumping me as they pass. Our barracks were separated for the Bonding, so I don't recognise anyone around me. The Union doesn't want friends working together.

Don't look for your friends during the Bonding; they are a distraction – one that will get you killed. That's what our instructor drilled into us. Doesn't matter to me, I don't have friends anyway and prefer being alone.

It's my turn to leave. I don't want to be left with the nervous stragglers milling behind me, whose fear can be smelled from miles away. I race into the clearing and anxiously watch my bracer. *Come on. What's going on? What's my colour?* It doesn't activate immediately, like everyone else's did. Maybe it's broken. I wave my arm around, as if that will solve the problem. My forearm tingles with static electricity and the bracer pulses with a blue glow.

My heart skips a beat.

The girl standing next to me looks up from her yellow bracer and glimpses mine. Her petrified look eases. We both know blue is worse than yellow. Way worse. With a half-smug look, she darts off without saying a word.

My bracer goes dark, then snaps open and drops off, clanging against the discarded pile at my feet. My heart is racing now, pounding against my ribs like a drum.

Cadets have scattered in all directions and disappeared into the jungle. Like me, some are heading for the volcano in the central zone. *Why am I standing here? I should be running.* I start down the hill into the valley, keeping a close eye on the dense vegetation closing in around me. Distant roars echo through the enclosure. The dinosaurs can smell us coming.

I can't help glancing up while navigating the steep descent. The netting that encloses the central zone is becoming visible, stretching from the jungle floor to the artificial dome ceiling. It's a gigantic aviary separating the outer and inner zones. Silhouettes of pterodactyls and quetzacoatluses circle through the mists. The pterosaurs are a stark reminder: Spend too long in the open and the next thing you'll find yourself hanging from one of their beaks.

'Whoa!'

I lose my footing in a pothole and tumble. My world spins out of control.

Crunch!

I land face-first in a pile of freshly turned dirt and sit there, stunned. *I should know better.* The slightest distraction can be deadly. I pick myself up and brush off the soil. It was no pothole – the flattened grass and deep indentation in the ground is a footprint created by a dreadnoughtus, one of the biggest sauropods that ever lived. These long-necked, long-tailed herbivores tower over jungles with pillar-like legs that snap trees like twigs. These titanosaurs might be simple leaf-eaters, but they comprise the brute force in the Union's dinosaur army.

Desperate screams sound from the hilltop behind me.

An icy chill shoots down my spine.

A pack of four human-sized utahraptors encircle the last two cadets to exit the departure bay. Their vivid yellow skin is flecked with black spots and patches, like a leopard. They stalk through the grass with measured steps, methodically closing their deadly circle.

The first raptor pounces, baring the sickle-shaped claw adorning its hindfoot. I turn away, unable to watch as the cadet's hideous scream is swiftly silenced. *At least it was quick.*

If I don't keep moving, I'll be next.

I continue down the hill into the valley and several cadets burst out of the bushes to my left, almost making me fall over again.

'Keep running!' one of them screams.

The trees behind them shake violently. Leaves shower from the canopy. The solid tree trunks creak and snap, then burst apart as if a bomb went off. Splinters of wood shoot into the jungle ahead of me, piercing the palm leaves like darts. A dreadnoughtus thunders from the shadows, forcing the trees aside with the power and weight of a cargo ship. Its body is at least twenty paces behind me, but its smallish head is already hovering far above me on the tip of an impossibly long neck. The beast honks and grunts, unhappy at being startled by us pesky humans. It's not trying to eat us – it's just marking its territory.

I plough through the first line of trees and into a gully cut deep into the jungle. It leads to a narrow rock ravine, forcing the other cadets to fall in line behind me. Down here, the sunlight barely reaches the ground and the air is thick with moisture.

Each thunderous footfall from behind sends tremors through the ravine. Loose stones bounce down the cliff faces.

My legs are burning, but I keep up the pace. Just a bit further and the dreadnoughtus won't be able to fit between the ravine walls.

I sprint across the mossy stones faster than I should. One misstep and I could break an ankle. Or worse. The walls narrow to a point, littered with fallen boulders and rocks. I clamber across the wet stone, slipping and sliding all over the place, breathing just a little too heavy. *Is it fear or exhaustion?* I can't tell.

I slide down the far side of the rock fall into a secluded, ankle-deep stream. Exhausted, I hunch over and catch my breath, relieved the dreadnoughtus has left us alone. The three cadets, two boys and a girl, slide down the rocks and join me. None of us speak. We're all bent over, gasping for air. The boys look like any other in the academy with their buzz-cut hairstyles and camouflage fatigues. The girl flicks her auburn ponytail over her shoulder and paces through the stream, one eye on the jungle, the other on us. I subtly read their embroidered name patches: JAKE-4756, NATE-0847, and BETH-1549.

Jake, the larger of the two boys, straightens and eyes us over. He appears to be sizing us up, wondering what to do next. *Even I know we're dinosaur bait if we stick together.*

'I'm from Theta barracks,' Jake says. 'What about you guys?'

'Kappa barracks,' Nate replies.

Beth keeps pacing. Her delayed response evokes an air of frustration. 'Sigma.'

I keep my mouth shut. They don't seem that interested in my answer anyway. *Story of my life.*

'Anyone else heading to the blue zone?' Jake asks.

'Not me,' Beth says. 'I'm designated here, in the red zone.'

Nate sighs. 'Would've helped if you finished bonding with that dreadnoughtus, told it to back off.'

'As if I had a chance with you idiots running through the jungle like that. You put us all in danger. What the hell were you thinking?'

'I can't stop and wait for you. I'm trying to get to the middle zone.'

'Yeah, that makes sense,' Beth says dryly. 'Just because you've been selected for stealth and special ops doesn't mean you can walk all over us grunts. Without us, you and your dinosaurs would be useless.'

'Without us you'd be dead the moment you set foot on Daxma-5.'

'Okay, that's enough,' Jake says, raising his hands. 'Nate and I were taking the high route to the middle zone. We didn't mean to interrupt you. Everyone just take a minute, relax. Raised voices attract unwanted visitors.'

Jake is doing his best to diffuse the tension. He seems nice. Suddenly he looks at me with questioning eyes. I freeze. My breath catches in my throat.

'What about you? What zone are you heading for?'

I know I should answer him. That would make me look normal. *I'm anything but normal.* For someone who avoids social interaction, this is my worst nightmare – a small group of people I don't know all looking at me, waiting for me to speak. My face feels hotter, my hands sweaty. My heart gallops back to full speed.

Beth reaches for me in a consoling way. 'Are you okay?'

I instinctively flinch and she backs off with a puzzled, offended expression. My face feels ready to explode with embarrassment.

Answering a simple question is a normal reaction for most people, but for me, it's absolute torture. I can feel my pale white cheeks glowing like plump red tomatoes, and the awareness of it makes my involuntary embarrassment even worse. Now my face feels twice as hot. If I don't answer now, I'll go supernova.

'Blue,' is all my airless lungs can muster.

'Blue!' Beth blurts out. 'You're heading for the apex predators. That means you're in line for a command position.'

Beth is right. Given a chance to think about it, the less it makes sense. *How can I command a platoon when I can't even talk to people?* Did my bracer malfunction? That's impossible, the Union don't make mistakes. My bracer displayed the correct information: ZAYLA [BETA-8311], Code Blue. The one thing I can count on is my photographic memory, a trait that can be a blessing or a curse.

'You're heading into the same zone as me,' Jake says. 'We can help each other. If you want.'

This time, I make a deliberate decision not to answer. As nice as Jake seems, his company is likely to get me killed.

'We're not here to team up or make friends,' Nate says.

Beth glares at him. 'Why are you hanging around us then?'

'Excellent point,' Nate says, disappearing into the mists downstream. 'Good luck surviving the night. If you make it that long.'

Beth shakes her head, 'Pft! Just 'cause he's been assigned to special ops, he thinks he's a league above the rest of us – even those vying for command.'

I watch Jake carefully. He doesn't take Beth's bait, even though he's in line for command. This minor squabble is the least of our problems. It's easy to see why he's been chosen to command an apex predator, he's strong, measured, and in control of his emotions. Me, on the other hand...

A huge splash erupts downstream, sending water over the entire area.

Jake grabs his knife and spins around. 'What was that? It felt like a landslide.'

Beth takes a cautious step back. 'It's impossible to see through the mist.'

'Looks like the entire hillside moved.'

Nate is nowhere to be seen as droplets patter in the stream around us like rain, wetting my face. The three of us stare into the mist, anxiously awaiting signs of life. Nothing. I desperately want to see Nate running back to us, safe and well, but in my gut, I know that's not the case.

A snout materialises from the mist, flat and broad like a crocodile but as wide as a truck. The never-ending snout emerges from the swirling grey. Stained yellow teeth bigger than my forearm are nestled into each side.

'That's no landslide,' Beth whispers.

The cavernous nostrils exhale a powerful breath and a smear of scarlet rushes over the scaly dark-green skin. Nate's limp body dangles face-down out one side of the maw, arms flailing through the stream in a trail of blood, his tiny frame looking like a toothpick in comparison to the monstrous creature.

'It's a deinosuchus!' Beth gasps. Her voice wavers between terror and excitement. 'If I can bond with it, I'll have one of the strongest dinosaurs ever.'

I admire Beth's bravery. The deinosuchus has the strongest bite force of any dinosaur, almost three times the power of a T-rex. It's basically a gigantic prehistoric crocodile.

The entire snout emerges from the mist, extending the length of a bus. The dark reptilian eyes blink its double eyelids and the unsettling squelch echoes upstream. Those soulless vertical pupils narrow on us, indicating the deinosuchus has found its next selection of bony morsels.

Beth waves us away. 'I don't want any distractions this time.'

Jake gives me an uncertain glance. *Does he want me to go with him?* Once again, I don't respond. He doesn't wait for an answer this time and sprints off into the jungle.

'Go!' Beth hisses, raising a hand to the back of her head.

She's about to activate her neural transmitter. With any luck, her implant will link with the one implanted inside the deinosuchus brain. A successful link depends on two things, proximity and focus, but the slightest distraction can break the mental connection.

I sprint in the opposite direction to Jake and head for the cover of the jungle. I leap over the embankment and scramble up the incline until I'm out of sight. Nestled between two large tree roots, I plot my escape route through the area. A couple of rocky outcrops and a large tree give me points to aim for.

I look back, keen to see how Beth is doing.

I've never seen a bonding take place and my curiosity has got the better of me. I should keep running, but I can't help myself, knowing I'll have to do the same thing when I reach the blue zone.

Beth stands in the middle of the stream, head down in concentration, deep into a mental wrestling match with the deinosuchus. If she can telepathically link with the dinosaur for 30 seconds, she will complete the bonding.

That bond lasts a lifetime... Or until one party dies.

The deinosuchus creeps forward with plodding steps, each one slower than the last. I think it's working.

I hold my breath. *Keep concentrating, Beth. You're almost there!*

Beth raises her hands, blindly reaching for the scaly snout. If they touch, the link will be locked in and nothing can break it. The deinosuchus draws closer, one methodical step at a time, as if walking in a trance. They're so close to touching, she's going to make it.

CRUNCH!

Several trees crash into the stream as a pair of startled stegosaurs stumble across the water. They must have been running from something bigger. Beth loses concentration and raises her head. I can see the whites of her terrified eyes. The deinosuchus opens its jaws and lunges forward, scooping Beth up before she can even scream. The startled stegosaurs spin about and lash their spiked tails at the deinosuchus.

That's it! Time to get out of here.

A hot breath blasts the back of my neck, whipping my ponytail over my shoulder. A deep, hungry-sounding growl fills my ears.

Oh no!

I remain crouched in the shadows, frozen with terror. I peer over my shoulder, moving only my eyes. Mottled yellow skin flecked with black fills my peripheral vision. The pack of utahraptors from earlier has tracked me down. There's one right behind me. Two will be on each side, closing in for the kill and a fourth will be hiding in the undergrowth ahead of me, waiting to pounce if I try to escape.

I have seconds before I'm disembowelled and devoured. Raptors relish warm blood and prefer to consume their victims while they're dying. I've seen them do it to countless prey.

I'm not going out that way.

My hand is on my belt, right next to my flare. I can't withdraw it. The slightest movement will make the raptor behind me attack which means the flare must be activated in position. I slowly shift the palm of my hand over the casing.

A guttural growl fills my ears.

I grit my teeth. *This is going to hurt.* Using the palm of my hand to grip the flare cap, I slowly twist to release it.

Another hot raptor breath saturates my hair. It reeks with a putrid metallic odour, the blood of its last victim.

I subtly release the cap from the flare cannister. This next part must be completed in one swift movement. I squeeze the palm of my hand as tight as I can and wrench the cap off, miraculously catching the activator string between my index and middle finger.

The flare ignites.

FZZZZZZZT!

My shadowy alcove between the tree trunks erupts with stark white light as the searing pyrotechnic sets my pants alight.

The utahraptors squeal and scatter.

I somersault blindly through the undergrowth. The flare burns through my pants and sizzles my skin like bacon on a grill. Each second is an eternity of agony. I suddenly become airborne and land with a splash back in the stream, but the flare continues to burn me underwater. I tear it from my belt and toss it onto the adjacent bank. Half blinded by the dazzling light, I squint over my shoulder. No raptors, just an embankment strangled by giant roots. I drag myself towards the shadows and nestle into a watery alcove.

I'm scared to look at my leg. The pain is so intense. I've never felt anything like it and feel like vomiting. Thankfully, my med-kit remains attached to the opposite side of my belt, undamaged. My trembling fingers struggle to open it. I pull out a painkiller pen, expose the needle, and plunge it into my upper thigh. The relief is instant.

I close my eyes, rest my head back, and slow my breathing.

A shrill screech draws my attention across the stream. The pack of utahraptors has chased down the dying flare and are now circling the strange object, snapping and barking at the glowing tip as if it's a living thing. The light finally dies and one of the utahraptors smells it, then tentatively uses its clawed toes to roll it over. The pack raise their heads and sniff the air, looking for me. It won't be long before they pick up my scent from across the stream.

I edge deeper into the alcove, squeezing between the roots. My injured leg catches on one and I wince, swallowing my scream. The surge of pain stubbornly subsides and I peek at my wound for the first time. A large hole is burnt through my pants; beneath that, my skin is charred black with a pinkish-red crater the size of my fist glistening in the middle. Without the painkiller, I'd be writhing in agony from the third-degree burn.

The utahraptors bark at each other then leap into the stream and head in my direction. The lead utahraptor has picked up my scent and alerted the others.

I look about. There's nowhere to go. I'm trapped.

The raptors wade effortlessly through the waist deep water, reptilian eyes focused on me in the shadows.

I slip the knife off my utility belt, the last thing I own to fight them off. *A hunting knife versus multiple twenty-centimetre claws? That's not an even fight.*

The utahraptors enter shallow water and fan out, approaching my hiding space from multiple angles. One of them sprints around and leaps over the roots to land on the hillside above me. I hold out my knife, hands trembling, ready to defend myself. If I'm lucky, I'll take one of them with me.

The pack leader stops in front of the roots, tilts its head, and assesses my shiny metal blade. It hisses and pokes its head towards me, sniffing the roots with an air of caution. Its clawed toes can't reach me here.

I tighten my grip on the knife, ready to drive it through the raptor's skull.

The utahraptor suddenly raises its head, freezes, and its predatory stare turns into a glazed, unfocused stare downstream.

I keep the knife pointed at the raptor and press my heels into the muddy stream bed, forcing myself further into the roots and sodden wall of soil. The pack of utahraptors has stopped dead in their tracks, as if someone hit the Pause button. Then I realise another cadet is attempting to bond with them. I can't believe my luck! Raptors are one of the few species bonded as a pack, with the majority being a one-on-one partnership.

A female cadet appears downstream, one arm outstretched towards the lead utahraptor. She stares intently into its eyes and cautiously approaches. They meet. Gently, the girl places her hand on the raptor's snout and the beast shudders, then snorts and shakes its head.

The girl takes a nervous step back and frowns with concern.

I'm wondering the same thing she must be. *Did it work?*

The utahraptor leaps off the roots above me and splashes into the water behind the cadet as the pack surrounds her. For a tense, fleeting second, I'm convinced they're going to strike. Then the leader drops his head, offers it to the girl, and the other raptors follow. Tears of relief glisten in her eyes and she affectionately caresses the heads of her new companions.

The leader raises its head and barks.

The girl acknowledges him and approaches my hiding spot, searching for me in the shadows. 'Come out of there.'

I don't move.

'It's okay, they won't hurt you now,' she says, patting the lead raptor as it comes up beside her. 'He told me you were there.'

I lower the knife and edge out of the muck. My injured thigh stings with the slightest movement. The cadet offers her hand and helps me stand while the raptors watch over her shoulder like curious pets. I note her name patch: ELENA-8735.

'Thanks,' I say, tottering on my leg.

'You're injured.'

'I'm okay.'

'You don't look okay. Can you walk?'

I nod, more to convince myself than Elena. I'm not confident I can manage.

'What zone are you designated to?'

'Blue.'

Elena's eyes brighten. 'Impressive. You're going to bond with an apex predator. Allosaurus, gigantosaurus, maybe even a tyrannosaurus. If you make it that far, I'll need to salute you next time we see each other.'

I force a chuckle, dismissing her comment. I can't picture myself as a leader. That's the last thing I want.

'I owe you one,' Elena says. 'You distracted the raptors, gave me a chance to bond with the pack. We can cover you up to the yellow zone.'

My first impulse is to decline her offer, but I haven't had the best of starts. The deinosuchus and stegosaurs resume their fight downstream. Their thrashing tails flatten trees and kick up a shower of water, reminding me of the dangers to come. I focus on the misty jungle upstream. There's at least three kilometres to the yellow zone boundary, then another five to the inner blue zone. Considering my injury, I can use as much help as possible. I resign to Elena's offer with a nod.

Elena smiles. 'We'll hang back, give you some space. I'll treat it as a training exercise. I want to give my assets a test run.'

The utahraptors grunt enthusiastically and jostle about, eager to please their new master. They behave like well-trained dogs – not that I've ever seen a real dog.

'Thanks,' I say, limping off.

The utahraptors splash through the water behind me. By the time I glance over my shoulder, they're gone, leaving just ripples in the stream. They criss-cross through the jungle on either side of me in pairs. I can't see them, only a rustle of leaves as they zip stealthily through the foliage. Utahraptors are masters of being unseen until they want to be seen. By the time I turn around again, Elena is gone, just like her pack. *She'll make a good soldier.*

My leg remains stiff for the first few paces, but it eases up. The painkiller is finally kicking in. I have one more left, and no flare, which leaves me with my knife and my med-kit. I'll hold off using my last painkiller as long as I can.

For this event – some call it a graduation – every cadet is given the bare minimum of supplies. It's designed as our ultimate test and focuses on two things: survival and bonding.

Elena's comment repeats through my mind as I move closer to the embankment: *If you make it that far, I'll need to salute you next time we see each other.* I have no idea why I've been flagged for a command position. My personality doesn't match the criteria. Commanding a platoon requires self-confidence and social interaction – two areas in which I desperately lack. I'm a loner in the academy and prefer my company to others.

I wasn't always this way, though.

In part, I blame my photographic memory for my issues. I can easily recall every bad thing someone has ever said or done to me. It's a burden, and makes it hard to maintain friendships. I'd be better off if I didn't hold grudges, but I find it difficult to forgive people. It's rare for someone to show me an act of kindness.

I should have thanked Elena for saving me, but I suppose it doesn't matter. I won't forget her face. If I survive the bonding and see Elena again, I'll make a point of thanking her.

Considering my solitary personality, I'm better suited to the stealth and special ops division. Why was I chosen for command? Maybe the selectors wanted me based on other traits. I know how to look after myself. I just proved that. My picture-perfect memory helped me ace all my theory classes. But I've got a feeling it's about my dinosaur preferences. Growing up in the academy, I was drawn to the biggest and baddest carnivores. Even as a child, I was more interested in a carcharodontosaurus or majungasaurus over a triceratops or sauropelta.

I remember standing over the carnivore pens as a young girl, throwing bloody chunks of meat to the juvenile tyrannosaurs and being fascinated by their innate brutality – how they ripped the meat apart using their jaws and feet. Most girls at that age gravitate to the herbivore pens, happy to dangle branches over the railing to the cute leaf-eaters. Not me. I was excited by the rush of blood, the savagery.

This morbid fascination led to an incident I try not to think about, and something that shaped my life in the academy. But considering my dinosaur preferences, I understand why I was drawn to the apex carnivores. They embody confidence and power – traits I lack.

THUMP!

The noise reverberates through the entire valley. Ankle-high waves rush upstream against the current and wash over my boots. I spin around. A few hundred metres back, a stegosaurus lies on its side, the armoured plates along its back hanging snapped and broken. The deinosuchus stomps into view and munches down on its soft, exposed belly as the surviving stegosaurus escapes into the jungle, calling for its mate with a distressed roar.

I need to get out of the stream. It's too open and makes me an easy target.

My leg refuses to move properly as I clamber up the slope. It feels like my charred flesh has hardened and might crack open if I flex it too far. But I don't have a choice – I must keep moving. My protective circle of utahraptors stays hidden in the dense vegetation. It comforts me, knowing they're there, flanking me as I haphazardly trudge onwards. I hope the jungle levels out soon and gives me an easier run to the yellow zone.

There's plenty of dinosaur species lurking between here and there, some of which the utahraptors can't save me from.

As if on cue, the bushes to my left shake. Branches snap and crunch. A tree trunk cracks and crashes to the ground, pulling down a shower of leaves and tangled vines that blocks my way forward. I'm in no condition to outrun a predator, especially around the length of the tree. I look around for my backup but the utahraptors are nowhere to be seen.

I'm not sure their absence is a good thing...

A tank-sized ankylosaurus (an *anky*, as we call them) emerges from the debris and lumbers by, completely ignoring me. It must be at least 8 metres long, one of the biggest ankylosaurids I've ever seen. This heavily armoured dinosaur could fend off any predator, irrespective of size and bite force. Its broad head, stumpy horns, and beaked mouth appear relatively harmless. The armoured plates and bony rings protecting its neck look strong enough to bear the weight of a dreadnoughtus footstep but it's the massive clubbed tail that makes it so formidable. That thing has the power to punch a hole in the enclosure walls.

To my right, a cadet steps out of from the shade of a large fern and stares into the anky's gentle dark brown eyes.

I freeze, careful not to interrupt their delicate bonding. One swipe from that chunky tail would send me flying all the way back to the departure bay.

The cadet raises his hand, drawing the mighty creature in.

The anky obediently lowers its head and nestles its enormous beak between the palms of his two hands as they both close their eyes and stand still. The anky's heavy breathing slows to a calm, steady rhythm, and falls in perfect sync with the cadet's.

I never realised the bonding could be such a soothing experience for humans or dinosaurs. It's not something we learnt in the academy. To our Union instructors, it's all about making the bond and preparing for war.

The cadet opens his eyes, looks at me, and nods in appreciation. I nod back.

The anky shuffles around and buries its head under the fallen tree. Its unwieldy tail flattens several conifer saplings in the process. With one almighty shove, the anky flips the immense trunk into the air and it sails aside, clearing my path ahead. *Wow! That's impressive.*

'Thanks.'

The cadet salutes me. 'Good luck.'

The thrill of our encounter drives me on. I'm starting to see how cadets and dinosaurs can work together and look out for one another. I wonder what species I'll bond with. Until today, I had no idea what regiment of dinosaur I was even aiming for. It's a lot to take in. Six species of apex predators are assigned to the command regiments, the biggest of them being the spinosaurus. It's the largest carnivore that ever lived. But that's not what sets it apart from academy favourites, like the T-rex and allosaurus. It's that the spinosaurus was just as lethal in water as it was on land, which for me makes it the ultimate predator.

The thick ceiling of jungle leaves finally separate, allowing a welcome burst of sunlight to warm my face. It feels good. Far above, I can now see the dome's circular opening, stretching as wide as the caldera. This is the main source of natural light and the only view of the outside world from within the enclosure. The penetrating beams of sunlight create glowing pockets of light in the rainforest, and the air is more humid here. I've almost reached the top of the gully. My burst of positivity and adrenaline help to mask my aching leg. No need to use my extra painkiller yet. The longer I hold off, the better.

The incline becomes a gentle slope and I move quicker, although awkwardly – something between a hobble and a jog.

The yellow-green wall of ferns ahead is aglow with inviting sunshine. The fronds are so bright, they look like they're on fire. I increase my speed, eager to make it before my luck changes. The yellow zone feels closer than ever. One of the friendly utahraptors darts past me, grunting. *He's warning me.*

I stop just in time.

A 2-metre-tall pachycephalosaurus charges past me, barrelling headlong with its bony cranium down in attack mode.

THUMP!

A cadet springs from the clump of ferns ahead and becomes airborne, as if launched by a rocket. He screams all the way, arms and legs waving around. He crashes into the upper branches of a tree and hangs there limply, caught in the vines.

I spin around and find the utahraptor watching me from behind the trees.

'Thanks!' I gasp. *I never thought I'd be thanking a raptor.*

The rainforest opens into a flat grassy paddock that leads directly to the yellow zone. The electrified net encircling the area stretches in both directions, as far as I can see, and is fixed to a fortified fence with reinforced metal access hatches set every 500 metres apart. The nearest hatch is a quick sprint away, directly ahead.

Finally! I'm almost there.

Close to my position, a cadet bonds with a dreadnoughtus. Normally these gigantic sauropods stand higher than the trees, almost five storeys tall, but this one has dropped its long neck so its head almost touches the ground. The cadet places his hands on the dread's head to complete the bonding.

I sprint for the hatch, eyes trained on the metal handle, trying not to think about what's waiting for me on the other side.

My mission to bond with a dinosaur is about to get a lot harder. And deadlier.

I leap into the hatch's access area, press my arm against the scanner and the chip in my forearm vibrates and glows in response. The magnetic locks securing the metal hatch release with a heavy *clunk*. I turn the handle with both hands and push the metre-thick door open, then leap through and close it behind me, wary of any unwanted visitors following me through. The locks snap back into position, sealing it shut. There's no scanner to open the hatch from this side. This is a one-way journey.

I wonder how many cadets have made it this far.

The grass is longer on this side of the fence, standing waist-high in places. Ahead, about 100 metres, is a dense forest of redwoods and pines. The towering trees create a different environment than the rainforest I just passed through.

It's easy to forget this is all part of an enclosure. It looks like there's an open sky above, but in fact, the entire central area is covered by an electrified net too small to distinguish from this distance.

I gaze ahead. The long grass makes me nervous. The yellow zone is brimming with clever pack hunters. Three species bother me: the troodon, sinocalliopteryx, and coelphysis. The trio of agile carnivores barely stand taller than a metre, but are experts at moving in large numbers and sneaking up on their prey. They could be hiding in the grass right now. I wouldn't know about it until they were swarming all over me, their tiny teeth ripping the flesh from my limbs.

I hate small dinosaurs.

This zone is also home to another two species of raptors, the velociraptor and megaraptor. These cunning pack hunters are bigger, faster, and stronger than the utahraptors in the previous zone. They could also be hiding in the grass, crouching out of sight and ready to pounce. A fully grown velociraptor can jump over 10 metres from a crouching position, and once they're in the air, there's no escape from their sickle-shaped hind claws.

A threatening shadow passes over the grass.

WHOOSH!

I duck as a gust of wind whips through the grass.

Far above, a pterodactyl loops around, eyeing me over its extraordinarily long beak. In here, the majestic and elegant pterosaurs rule the sky. A fully grown adult's wingspan stretches over 9 metres, and on the ground, they stand as tall as a tyrannosaur. Their awkward and lanky bodies can waddle about, using the elbows of their folded wings as extra legs. But they rarely land, since doing so would expose them to ground-based predators.

I have no idea how any cadet could bond with an animal that spends most of its time in the sky. *How do you even get close?*

The pterodactyl circles around again, swooping lower this time, targeting its beak on me like a giant spear.

I spring from the grass, ignoring what might lurk ahead. If I don't get to the cover of the forest, the pterosaur will skewer me like a shish kebab. The painkiller is wearing off, making my charred leg stiff and painful. The burnt flesh feels like a heavy clump of mud stuck on my thigh and slows me down.

The pterodactyl bears down on me, whistling through the air like an engineless aeroplane. The noise reaches an ear-piercing crescendo until it's all I hear. I don't dare turn around. The safety of the redwoods is just metres away. The surrounding grass goes dark.

I'm not going to make it...

I dive sideways as the pterodactyl swoops in. My last-ditch manoeuvre seems to work – for a moment. The pterosaur's beak catches my lower leg and lifts me off the ground. Next thing I'm upside down, staring down at the grass, rising higher by the second.

RIP!

I inexplicably drop free. Somehow, I right myself mid-air and land on my butt amidst a soft bed of pine needles.

The pterodactyl screeches and soars over the redwoods and momentarily disappears.

I anxiously inspect my leg, expecting a deep gash. Nothing. The pterodactyl merely caught me by my pants, shredding them from ankle to knee. Unfortunately, my other leg isn't doing as well. My charred thigh is now cracked and bleeding. Fresh blood will attract more predators. I tear off a strip of my tattered pants and grit my teeth as I tie it around my thigh to stem the bleeding.

It takes a while for the stabbing pain to subside. Sitting there, staring at my torn pants, I realise how lucky I was. I should have known better than to stand outside the hatch for so long. The slightest hesitation can be fatal. I was only waiting there for a few seconds, but it was long enough. Sitting here is no different. I need to keep moving.

I roll over on my good side, keeping my burnt leg as straight as possible. The less I bend it, the better. Using the trunk of a tree as support, I hoist myself back to my feet. Blood rushes back to my leg and pounds in time with my labouring pulse.

The forest is growing darker by the second. More time has passed than I thought. The sun has reached the western tip of the dome, meaning daylight will fade within the hour. I don't want to spend the night out here, but there's no way to make it to the blue zone before sunset.

That's the way the Union selectors designed the zones. Only the most resourceful and resilient cadets will make it to the central zone on the first day. You would have to have run the entire way from our opening departure bay, a near-impossible feat without being reckless, or incredibly lucky.

Regardless, I have to find a safe place to spend the night.

The fringe of the forest is flat and obstacle free, but further inside, where the shadows are deepest, the landscape slopes upwards to a soaring cliff. Atop this 200-metre wall of stone lays the blue zone, concealed inside a sprawling, bowl-shaped caldera. The ancient volcanic crater keeps the giant carnivores from moving outside their area.

I sigh with resignation. The climb will be tough on my leg, but given a bit of luck, I might chance upon a supply drop. Several drop pods are randomly scattered throughout the three zones to assist us, containing food and a comprehensive selection of medical supplies. Amongst them is a healing gel that can seal my wound and numb the pain. It's just what I need. If I don't stem the ooze of blood, the tyrannosaurs will smell me coming from kilometres away. *They're probably licking their lips right now.*

The forest is dead quiet. The blanket of pine needles and fern leaves masks my footfalls. *Thank goodness.* I use the giant redwood trees as cover and move as stealthily as I can from one thick trunk to the next.

'ARGHH!'

A blood-curdling scream pierces the silence.

I press against the fibrous bark of a redwood trunk and slide down into the shadows. The scream wasn't far from here – maybe 500 metres to the west. The unfortunate cadet must have entered another one of the hatches further along the zone wall. That's unlucky, and fatal.

I wait for another noise. Nothing. After what seems like forever, I rally on, stomach rising to my mouth with fear and driven by nervous energy.

My goal is to reach the base of the cliff, find a hiding place within the rocks, and recuperate for the night. I haven't seen another soul since entering this zone. If any living cadets are nearby, they're giving me a wide berth.

That's wise. I'm a walking buffet with this bloody leg.

A shadow catches my eye, 100 metres to my right. I drop into the shadows again and swallow my breath. The humanoid shape appeared to mimic my movement. *Am I being hunted or followed by a cadet?* Crouching there, my nerves catch up with me and I can't stop myself from trembling. Gruesome images of teeth, claws, and spurting blood flood my mind. I lose focus and hyperventilate. *I'm breathing too loud.* I close my eyes, slow my thoughts, and fight each panicked gasp, managing to get my breathing under control. I wait a little longer, eyes closed, listening for the slightest noise. There's nothing. I take a settling breath and dart for the cover of the next tree.

I see the shadow again, closer than before. It's big, bipedal, and sports a distinctive spiky mane. *I'm being hunted by a megaraptor!* It won't be alone, and considering how close it's tracking me, means I'm already surrounded. My legs refuse to move. I'm incapacitated by fear, too petrified to draw breath.

A soft whistle sounds from above.

I look up and find a male cadet sitting on the branch overhead. My heart bursts with excitement as he reaches down and offers his hand. I grasp it and he yanks me up with so much power, I hit my head on the branch and scrape my forehead. Half stunned, I loop my legs around the branch and hug it tight.

'Don't stop!' he whispers, tugging me higher. 'Keep climbing.'

I scramble onto the massive redwood trunk and climb after him.

CRUNCH!

A grey-black megaraptor with vice-like jaws hangs from the branch I was on moments before, its glistening teeth buried deep into the bark. The carnivore snorts through flared nostrils, excited by the smell of my blood as its grey reptilian eyes devour me with an insatiable gaze. The raptor frantically scratches the tree with its clawed toes in an attempt to reach me. Shredded bark litters the ground below and three more megaraptors emerge from the shadows and circle the tree.

I follow the stranger to a safer height. We circle the trunk, climbing the ample limbs like the rungs of a ladder, and don't stop until we're as high as a dreadnoughtus.

The cadet stops and peers over me to the forest floor.

I glance down in time to see the megaraptors disband and sprint away. Their disgruntled snorts echo through the woods.

I'm so glad raptors don't climb trees.

'It's safer to stay high, but not too high,' the cadet says. 'There're plenty of pterosaur nests in these treetops. The quetzalcoatal nests are up on the ridge. They prefer the rocks.'

I nod, too overwhelmed to respond immediately. But I force myself to say something. He saved me, after all. 'Thanks,' I mutter.

'No problem. My name's Kane.'

I've never seen Kane before. He's not from my barracks, or any of the others we trained alongside. His friendly face and kind blue eyes are imbued with a sense of safety and security. I like the feeling. For the first time in a long while, I look forward to the company of another person.

'No need to hang around here like a pair of primates all night,' Kane says. 'I've got a much more comfortable place to rest.'

Kane climbs up another couple of branches and crawls out onto a precarious-looking limb that bows under his weight. He lowers himself down until he's hanging by his hands. *What the hell is he doing?* Kane suddenly drops off the branch.

I cover my mouth and stifle a gasp.

Kane falls a couple of metres and lands in a giant nest. I hadn't noticed it before now, concealed amongst the foliage on the adjacent tree. He motions me to follow and I shake my head. *He's crazy. There's no way I'm going to hide out in a pterosaur nest.* One close encounter is enough for me.

Kane waves me over again.

I shake my head with more conviction this time.

'It's okay,' he whispers across the space. He picks up a piece of broken shell and shows it to me. 'It's an abandoned nest.'

Looking more carefully, I see he's right. The edges of the nest are falling apart. Pterosaurs keep their nests pristine and this one looks like it was abandoned a while ago. Just like modern-day birds, pterosaurs won't return to a nest once it's been disturbed by predators.

Kane coaxes me to climb out onto the branch. 'Come on. You can do it.'

Of course, I can do it! This is the easiest thing I've had to do all day.

Heights don't bother me. Never have. I climb up and onto the branch. It doesn't bend as much with my lighter build, making my drop a few centimetres further than Kane's. I lower myself down and hang by my hands. This is going to hurt my leg. I take a deep breath and let go.

Kane breaks my fall and we tumble back into the nest.

The thatched wall scrapes my injury. I wince in agony and double over, clutching my thigh, sucking up the excruciating pain. It stubbornly subsides and I look up, eyes blurry with tears, face burning from straining so hard.

Kane takes a painkiller pen from his med-pack and offers it to me.

I'm tempted to take it but I can't, I've already had too much help today. I don't want to survive the Bonding by the grace of others. That's not how war works.

'It's okay,' I say, shaking my head. 'Save it for yourself.'

Kane leaves his hand there, the offer is still open. He lets a few seconds pass, then returns the pen to his pack. Wisely, he doesn't push the matter. I'm not in the mood to refuse his generosity a second time.

My leg returns to an acceptable level of pain and I ease back against the wall of thatched sticks and vines, realising I've never been in a pterodactyl nest before. It's big, easily five to six metres wide and the base is surprisingly soft, padded with pine needles and dry grass. The wall is sturdy and tightly woven, rising just above waist height. Broken eggshells litter the nest. I press down on one. It's harder than I thought and takes quite an effort to break.

'These eggs didn't hatch,' Kane says, pointing to the dried blood around the nest. 'They were probably eaten by a quetzie. They're the only predators able to reach a nest like this.'

The quetzalcoatlus – or *quetzies*, as cadets call them – are the largest flying dinosaur that ever lived. They don't normally hunt pterodactyls, but if food is in short supply, they attack their nests. The nutritious eggs are perfect food for their young.

We're safe for now, as the nest is hidden beneath a couple of fallen branches. I take a deep breath and relax for the first time in hours.

I notice the tiny rips in Kane's uniform. 'What happened to you?'

'Oh, this,' he says, poking a finger through the holes. 'Ran straight into a herd of troodons. Little buggers. You can kick 'em away like footballs, but they keep on coming. Got out of there before they swarmed.'

'That was lucky.'

'What happened to your leg? I don't know of any fire-breathing dinosaurs.'

I chuckle. 'I ran into a herd of utahraptors. Used my flare to stun them and escape.'

Kane nods, looking impressed. 'Good job.'

'Would've been better if I'd got the flare off my belt first.'

'You're alive. That's all that matters.'

I nod solemnly. Kane has a point. I've seen enough cadets meet a grisly end today. I'm glad I'm not one of them.

'What zone are you designated to?' Kane asks.

'Blue.'

'Makes sense. You know how to look after yourself.'

'What about you?'

'Yellow. That's why I've picked this vantage point. I can stalk my targets in safety, wait for the right time to attempt a bonding. I saw you come through the hatch. I thought you were a goner when the pterosaur swooped in for the kill. As soon as I saw you heading into the forest, I climbed down to help. The megaraptors that came after you killed a cadet outside the next hatch. You're not bleeding too bad, but it would've been enough to attract them.'

'Have you seen many other cadets make it through this zone?'

'A few. Most head straight for the ridge. I assume they're hunting apex carnivores, like you, but I doubt any of them will make it by nightfall. They'd be crazy to attempt the cliff climb in the dark.'

'What species are you hunting?'

'Megaraptors, if I can. Otherwise, I could settle for a pack of velociraptors. Both species are vicious enough. I just prefer bigger dinosaurs.'

'Me too,' I say. A smile creeps up from the corner of my mouth. I don't try to hide it. Kane seems nice. Shame there's no one like him in my barracks. 'What barracks are you from?'

'Omega.'

'Omega! I had no idea there was an Omega barracks. There're more cadets in the academy than I thought.'

'You never told me your name.'

'Zayla-8311. I'm from Beta barracks.'

'It's nice to meet you, Zayla. You're a Beta-stage birth, second generation. I've never met anyone from Beta barracks. That makes you 23 hours older than me.'

'I've never met anyone outside Beta, Alpha, and Gamma barracks.'

'They like to keep the 24 barracks separate until the Bonding, then mix us all up. Last month, it was Alpha and Sigma barracks. This month it's us: Beta and Omega.'

'What's your birth number?'

Kane gives me an odd, surprised look. 'I don't have a birth number.'

'How's that possible? Every cadet has a birth number. We were all cloned from our deceased parents after the Daxma-5 massacre.'

'I don't know – maybe they stopped assigning us numbers.'

'Why?'

'I'd rather be known by a name than a number. Wouldn't you?'

Kane is right. None of us have surnames, just a birth name and batch number. The only family I've ever known is the Beta barracks. I have 999 brothers and sisters, all the exact same age as me. I've only met as handful of them, as we're broken down into smaller units and separated amongst different buildings.

I can't wrap my head around the fact Kane has no birth number. It doesn't line up with the way the Union works. Everything about the academy is so precise and organised. Why wouldn't the Union stick with the same numbering and naming convention for every cadet and barracks?

'You can see the Union selectors,' Kane says, pointing through the treetops. 'Their viewing windows are visible around the rim of the dome.'

Thin strips of light run along the top of the outer wall, just below the dome opening. From this distance, the selectors appear as small as ants, scurrying about, busying themselves, observing and assessing our every move. I've never visited the world outside the academy, or my barracks. We've been taught everything about Earth and the war we're training for, but little about what goes on behind the scenes in the Union. A great deal remains hidden from us. Kane and his Omega barracks have added yet another layer of mystery.

'Get some rest,' Kane says. 'I'll take first watch.'

It's hard to think about sleeping, but he's right. Few cadets will rest tonight. We need to conserve as much energy as possible. I thank Kane with a nod and roll onto my side.

Should I trust this stranger? Doing so goes against my better judgement.

It's not like Kane can steal much from me. All I have left is my knife and a painkiller pen. I lay there, eyes half open, trying not to fall asleep. Sleep makes me vulnerable. Exposed. As hard as I try, it's impossible to resist closing my eyes.

4

I wake with a start and sit up in the darkness, heart racing, gasping short rapid breaths. My mouth is dry and my jaw aches. I've been grinding my teeth in my sleep. I slow my breathing and settle down. It's now the middle of the night and Kane sits across from me, his face just visible in the moonlight. The shadows exaggerate his features and hide his eyes in deep pools of black.

Kane leans forward and his eyes glisten in the moonlight, giving his ghostly appearance a friendly, protective quality. 'Are you all right?'

'Of course,' I respond, more defensive than necessary.

It's impossible not to raise my emotional barrier, but Kane has just seen me at my most vulnerable. My recurring nightmare has been a problem throughout my academy life, and a source of ridicule from cadets in my barracks. Truth is, I've never told anyone about my dream.

'I understand,' Kane says, as if reading my thoughts. 'Bad dreams are a part of life for most of us.'

The knot in my stomach eases. Kane has an uncanny knack of disarming me. As soon as I put up a defensive wall, he breaks it down. I barely know him, yet I feel like I could tell him anything. Not that I would. Regardless, he has a sincere, charming way about him. If he lived in Beta barracks, we might be friends.

'Do you have nightmares?' I ask.

'Sure.'

I'm not one to pry, yet I can't help myself from digging deeper. 'What are they about?'

'The Wraith, like most of us. I dream about dinosaurs too, even though we've grown up living with them. I dream about going to Daxma-5, fighting the war on an alien planet. I suppose your dreams are similar?'

'Kind of.'

Kane waits for me to continue. At first, I don't intend to, but I feel as though I owe it to him. He's been open and honest with me – saved me from the megaraptors and shared his hiding spot for the night. I could die tomorrow without ever telling anyone about my nightmares. I'm compelled to unburden myself from the images that have haunted me since I was old enough to comprehend them. Chances are, I'll never see Kane again and if I'm ever to speak my dream aloud, the time is now.

'You don't have to tell me.'

There he goes again, disarming me when my guard is down. Kane seems to know exactly what to say and when.

'It's okay, it's just... I've never told anyone.'

Kane nods thoughtfully, giving me the opening to proceed at my own pace.

'My nightmare is the same one, over and over. I don't know why, but I dream I was with my parents on Daxma-5 when the Wraith attacked. I know that's impossible. None of us were alive during the massacre. We weren't even born then – my parents never had children. I was cloned from their DNA samples here on Earth.

'But I'm right there with them, standing on the landing pad, waiting for an escape vessel to pick us up. I must be four or five, I'm not sure, but I'm old enough to walk. I have this huge knot of anxiety in my stomach. My mother grabs my hand and drags me through the crowd. Dad's ahead of her, pushing people aside, pulling us through. There's desperation in the air. People scream constantly. I hate the screaming. Explosions go off in the distance. Smoke rises over our heads. Glowing embers float down from the darkness. It feels like the end of the world.

'An escape vessel descends towards us. Its landing thrusters curl the smoke and embers into mesmerizing swirls. For a second, it looks magical. The crowd cheers. It feels like there's hope, like we're about to be saved. The vessel almost touches down when the Wraith attack. Six-armed creatures, twice the size of a human, swarm all over the vessel. They look like giant white monkeys. Their pale skin ripples with electricity. They're jumping off the platform all around us, ignoring us to attack the vessel. Their energy does something to the engines then it loses power and crashes onto the landing pad.

'That's when my world turns upside down. The landing pad slopes to one side. People slide off the edge and fall to their deaths. They try holding on to each other, but it's too steep. Then I see the huge hellish creatures waiting for us. They look like dragons, with glowing blue eyes. They're rippling with the same blue energy, inside and out. I can see all the way down their throats. It's like their insides are powered by nuclear reactors. We're all sliding straight into them. I watch bodies fall inside the glowing mouths and disintegrate into ashes. Mum covers my eyes. That's when I wake up.'

I take a deep breath and rest against the nest wall. I've lost all sense of time and have no idea how long I've been talking. I'm exhausted, but unburdened. It's taken a lot of emotional energy to relive the nightmare.

'Sounds horrific,' Kane says softly.

'It feels so real, like I was there. Every time I have the dream, I'm reliving the nightmare. It never changes. Every detail is burnt into my memory. I'll never escape it.'

I stop talking. If I say another word, I'll probably start crying. I've just told Kane my deepest and darkest secrets. My stomach churns again, nauseous. I can't believe I just opened myself up like that.

'The monsters in yours dreams sound like daxanoids and titanoids,' Kane says. 'It's no surprise you have nightmares about them. It was the beginning of the war. We've all had the Daxma-5 massacre drilled into us since we were old enough to read and write. You're not alone. I know lots of cadets share your trauma.'

'Really?'

'Plenty. Don't you?'

I wouldn't know. I keep to myself most of the time. Not that I'm about to tell Kane that. He's met a different side of me and I'd prefer to keep it that way. My reluctance to socialise means I've never been close enough to someone to talk about it. That's not to say I've never had a friend in the academy, I've had a couple over the last few years, but I wouldn't have called them close friends. I only knew them well enough to chat over dinner in the mess hall. They were more like casual acquaintances. We would occasionally clean out the dinosaur pens together, or team up for training drills, but nothing beyond that. They eventually moved to different dormitories and made real friends. It didn't take them long to forget about me.

But I've revealed enough about myself to last a lifetime. I need to divert Kane's attention away from my pitiful excuse for a life.

I answer his question with a lie. 'Of course I know a few.'

'And for every person who admits their fear, there's two more hiding it. The Wraith have proved our technology is powerless to fight them. They turn our robots against us and disable our weapons. Humanity has never been so vulnerable. That vulnerability is what keeps the trauma alive in all of us. It won't ease until we win this war. That's why our bonding is so important. What we achieve here, the relationships we forge, will determine the outcome of the war. We can't afford to fail.'

Kane's speech brings me back to the main thing I should be focusing on: bonding with a dinosaur.

'It's incredible to think how a species that went extinct 100 million years ago is now fighting for our future,' I say.

'The Wraith can override our tech, but they can't control a living creature as easily. That's why dinosaurs have become our weapons, and ultimately, our salvation.'

I speak the three-sentence oath that echoes through our dormitories every night before sleep. 'Learn from the past. Embrace the present. Fight for the future.'

Kane raises his hand and repeats the phrase.

We shake on it. Every cadet, regardless of barracks or birth number, shares the same undying loyalty to the cause.

'Would you mind looking out while I get some rest?' Kane asks.

'I'm not sleeping anymore tonight.'

Kane lays back and vanishes like an apparition in the inky-black shadows. I'm tempted to reach out and touch his boot, just to confirm he's really there and not some figment of my paranoid imagination. *Don't be stupid. Kane's no hallucination.* After a life of social isolation and anxiety, it's hard to believe such a genuinely nice person exists. He's unlike anyone I've met before. Like a brother I never had. Such a shame, I'm unlikely to see him again after tonight.

Kane's steady breathing fills the nest, reassuring me he is indeed a real person. It takes a minute for him to fall asleep, leaving me to guard our position for the remainder of the night. Good. I'm comfortable with my own company.

I hear little apart from the occasional crunch of twigs far below. Occasionally the stars vanish behind a passing pterosaur or quetzie soaring silently through the night sky, hunting for a late-night snack. I keep my head down, well below the edge of the nest, just in case.

The crescent moon eventually disappears behind the rim of the dome and the stars give way to a beautiful sunrise. Iridescent streaks of pink and orange spill into the enclosure and illuminate the prehistoric jungle, bringing with it the sounds of life.

Day two of the Bonding begins.

Something moves to the left of me. I turn around, half expecting to find nothing. A compy sits perched on the edge of the nest. It tilts its head like a bird and watches me with its beady black eyes. It's no bigger than a turkey, with a slim body, long neck, and skinny little arms and legs. Compsonathuses look like the least dangerous of all dinosaurs, but you can't let their diminutive size fool you, these lithe carnivores are savage pack hunters.

We're in trouble!

I refrain from making any sudden movement. Kane is still asleep. I cautiously edge my boot towards his and nudge him gently. He doesn't stir. Another compy leaps onto the opposite side of the nest, directly over Kane, and squawks at its companion.

Kane's eyelids flick open. He peers up and the compy looks down at him, hissing as it bares a mouthful of tiny, needlelike teeth.

A scratching noise emerges from the woven branches as the compys claw their way through. The overhead branch is now littered with them and several jump down to join the small army forming along the lip of the nest.

'What do we do?' I whisper.

'Get ready to climb,' Kane whispers back as he gently works a stick free from the wall of the nest.

A compy jumps down beside me and pecks at the bloodied bandage wrapped around my thigh. My heart sinks – they found us because of my wounded leg. I never should have stayed with Kane. I've put him in danger too. The compy nips and gnaws at my bandage and I gently brush it away, trying not to agitate it. The little creature squawks at me and two more jump down to join in.

'Don't excite them,' Kane says. 'I'm about to get us out of here. You ready?'

I answer with a sharp, desperate nod.

Kane stands and rips a long branch from the wall of the nest but the tip gets caught at the last second. His sudden movement startles the pack and they scurry about, squawking to each other as if hatching some master plan. Then, one by one, they spring off the nest and attack him. Kane keeps hold of the branch and shakes his head, keeping them from scratching his face.

I jump to my feet and swipe them off his shoulders.

They leap onto my leg, clawing and biting my bandage, attracted to the scent of my raw flesh. I kick them away, but they keep coming.

Kane finally wrenches the branch free.

'Get down!'

He swings it around in a 360-degree circle. I duck just in time. The branch swooshes over my head and compys go flying in all directions. Several land in the nest. I pick up one and hurl it as far as I can. I try it on another and it bites my wrist. I whack its leathery body onto the nest floor but it won't let go. Tough little bugger. I pound harder. One, two, three. The determined compy finally lets go, screeches at me, and scurries away.

Kane offers me a leg up. 'Come on!'

I step into his cupped hands and he boosts me out of the nest. The supporting branch is teaming with compys. I kick some off and trapeze-walk over the rest for the main tree trunk, squashing their tough little bodies under my boot. They squeal and squirm. A compy drops from above and lands on my chest, snapping at my face. All I can see is a mouth full of teeth. *It's going for my eyes!*

I panic and lose my footing.

Kane latches onto my collar, and we both fall onto the next branch. Compys rain down around us in a squirming swarm. I swing down onto a lower branch, then another.

CRACK!

The branch above me gives way. Kane plummets past me and crash-lands on a lower branch with a groan, regains his balance, and keeps descending. We work our way down, half climbing, half falling, and finally leap off the redwood trunk into a patch of ferns.

'Head for the ridge,' Kane says.

We break into a sprint for the boulders in the distance. Several compys keep pace with us, leaping over the logs and rocks with remarkable agility. After 20 metres or so, the persistent few give up and return to the pack.

I slow to a jog, limping heavily. Kane moves ahead and offers me his hand, keeping a brisk pace for the boulders. Further behind us, the compys swarm together, jumping and screeching excitedly.

'The compys won't give up that easily,' Kane says. 'They track prey for kilometres.'

'We should split up. They're attracted to my blood.'

'I'll get you started up the boulders first.'

'You don't have to help me. I can look after myself.'

'Of course – I didn't mean it like that.'

I push onwards, hoping I haven't offended Kane. Each step is more agonising than the last. Walking on this injury is exhausting.

We finally reach the boulders and I hunch over, lungs burning, straining to complete a sentence between gulps of air.

'Staying with me... puts you... in danger... you should leave.'

Kane doesn't respond. He doesn't need to - his disappointed gaze says it all. I get the impression he's a bit like me, a loner in his barracks. I don't understand how, though, as he's so nice and personable. Meeting Kane has given me hope that one day I'll meet people I can be close with. He offers me his hand and I shake it with a sting of remorse. *I wish we could stay together.*

'After you climb the lower boulders, keep to the right,' Kane says. 'There's a fissure that will take you to the top of the ridge. Watch out for quetzie nests - they're easy to spot from a distance but impossible to escape if you climb into one by accident. Stay off the outcroppings and away from the cliff faces. There's not many places to hide on the climb, so it makes you easy pickings for pterosaurs.'

I smile. Kane is overprotective, like a brother I never had. I can only guess that's how siblings behave. I've only known him for one night, but Kane's the closest I've had to a family in 18 years. I'd like to thank him with a kiss on the cheek, but manage the next best thing. 'Thanks. Good luck.'

Kane smiles. 'Take care, Zayla. This war needs people like you in command.'

SCREECH!

The persistent compys interrupt our farewell. Their skinny little bodies dart along the forest floor all around us, momentarily flashing in the pockets of sunlight.

Kane pushes me. 'Go!'

I stumble for the boulders, disappointed to be on my own again. *How will I even climb with this stupid leg?* The painkiller has worn off but I need to resist using my final shot until I enter the blue zone, as I'll need to be quick and nimble for my bonding. I reach the first waist-high granite boulder and scramble atop. My burnt thigh is stiff, cumbersome, and painful. I try not to bend it too much as I climb from one rock to the next. Minutes later, I'm several stories high, clutching my throbbing thigh.

I catch my breath and glance down, hoping to glimpse Kane one last time.

It's hard to see anything beyond the perimeter of redwood and pine trees. The forest floor is blanketed with ferns, hiding anything the size of a compy. The morning sun streams through gaps in the forest canopy, creating vibrant areas of green and yellow. Giant insects swarm into the pockets of warmth, where they swirl and dart about.

Nothing. No sign of Kane. *I hope he's okay.*

I grasp the next boulder and hoist myself upwards. Mid-climb, a moving shadow catches the corner of my eye.

Far below, a snout emerges from behind a redwood trunk, followed by a long neck adorned with a spiky mane. *The megaraptors are back!* A chill spirals down my spine. The creature moves stealthily through the ferns, stalking something in the forest ahead. It hasn't seen me up here on the rocks. Another raptor appears, then another, and the pack move in silent unison, heads extended forward, eyes unblinking.

I pin myself to the stone as the slightest movement is bound to draw their attention. I stare down into the forest like a statue, scanning the shadows for Kane. He must be somewhere close, unless he's up in the trees again.

A fourth megaraptor appears from behind a large fern and merges with the others.

I still can't see Kane. *Damnit, where is he?*

The raptors stand over two metres tall and share a unique mottled appearance. Blotches of grey-blue skin cover their bodies, deepening to black around their faces and down their backs while their gleaming black claws look as if they are carved from flawless obsidian.

Kane suddenly appears from between the boulders below me and steps towards the pack, both arms reaching for them. *He's trying to bond with the megaraptors!* The raptors aren't hunting Kane, they're being lured in by him.

My heart leaps with excitement as the lead raptor lowers its head to Kane. Less than a metre separates them as Kane raises a hand, fingers stretched open to greet the leathery grey snout.

I hold my breath, anxious for them to complete the bond.

The raptor inexplicably stops and Kane looks down, distracted by something at his feet. The raptor jerks its head backwards and their connection is severed. Kane shakes his leg and kicks at something beneath the ferns. The rest of the pack break from their hypnotic daze and suddenly look alert, claws outstretched to strike.

A pack of compys leap onto Kane, shattering his concentration. *NO!*

Kane stumbles backwards and vanishes between the boulders. The megaraptors screech and rush at him. Claws out. Teeth bared.

I should call out – draw their attention this way.

A bright pink light erupts from the boulders and illuminates the immediate area. Kane has used his flare in a last-ditch attempt to ward them off. I want to help, but I can't. I can only watch and hope he crawls to safety. All I hear is the savage scraping of claws across stone, barking, hissing, and a desperate shuffling of bodies in the dirt. The commotion lasts an eternity.

The glow gradually dies but Kane never appears.

I turn away and press my face into the stone, stifling a sob. *Kane didn't deserve to die like that. I should've done more to help him.* My moment of anguish passes and I come to my senses. I don't have time to feel guilty. This is exactly why the Union separated cadets and barracks for the Bonding. We can't afford to let our emotions get in the way.

I peer up at the imposing mountain of dark volcanic rock. The slope ahead leads to a rocky ridge that rises above the treeline and beyond that, it's a near vertical climb up a pterosaur-infested cliff to the caldera.

I'll never make it in my current state. I withdraw the final painkiller pen from my med-kit and stare at it with a sense of defeat. I was saving it for the blue zone, but it's no use if I don't make it in the first place. I flick the lid off and inject it directly into my burn. A cool, numbing sensation seeps through my thigh and I close my eyes, relishing the relief.

But I don't have time to stop. If I don't get climbing, I'll die like Kane.

5

I try to ignore the persistent throb of my burnt thigh and focus on reaching the ridge, one agonizing step at a time. *I wish the painkiller would hurry up and kick in.* The boulders gradually merge into a gravel incline and my boots crunch across it with every laboured stride, making me an easy target for a pterosaur. The ascent rises above the redwood canopy and delivers me to the base of the cliff where the air is a little cooler. It's been hard work to reach this point and sweat beads across my forehead. I wipe my brow and peer down upon the morning mists rising from the forest. Thankfully, there's no sign of the megaraptors. If they had tracked me, I wouldn't have made it this far.

There's a grim reason the pack didn't follow me. They were well fed this morning.

My thoughts drift back to Kane. Picturing his bare hands fending off those razor-sharp claws makes me shudder. I've seen the bloody aftermath of a carnivore attack. It's better if you don't survive. For his sake, I hope it was quick.

I unscrew the lid on my water bottle and take a long sip. The cool water lands on an empty stomach. I'm starving. I shake the bottle. Feels like there's less than a third left. I need to conserve some in case I'm out here another day.

I take a deep breath and face my next challenge. An imposing cliff looms over me, rising 100 metres to the ancient caldera. Deep crevices snake through the stone. The wider fissures resemble a beginner-level climbing course and could get me to the top nice and fast. On the downside, these open spaces expose me to quetzies and pterodactyls.

Kane's advice was spot on. He's directed me to a position where I can take my pick from multiple starting points, all with varying levels of difficulty.

I unclip a tube of rock-climbing chalk from my utility belt, shake some onto my hands, and rub them together. The white powder dries my sweaty palms and gives me some grip. I'm ready to climb.

Twenty metres to my right, a figure pounces from the mist and startles me. My first thought is *raptors!*

Nope, just a careless cadet stomping across the gravel. He hastily slaps some climbing chalk between his hands and drops the tube, then kicks it by accident as he attempts to pick it up. The chalk disintegrates in a cloud of white dust and covers his boots. He fumbles about, trying to pick up the pieces, oblivious to my presence. *What a mess. How the hell did he make it this far?* He leaves the chalk and begins climbing.

My heart sinks – *He took my route!*

I feel like running over there and shoving him back down the slope but there's no way I'm going anywhere near this guy. I could wait until he's picked off by a pterosaur (which won't be long), but I'm steering well clear of him. I won't be taking the straightforward route now, which leaves the most difficult crevice.

I'm up to the challenge. Aside from dinosaur studies, rock climbing is my favourite academy session. It's a solitary exercise, and because of that, I excel. It's the one lesson where I don't need to talk to anyone or be part of a team, I can just zone out.

But there's nothing peaceful about this climb.

The crevice starts off nice and gentle but the edges progressively close in and I find myself climbing a sharper, almost vertical angle. My hands have no trouble gripping the stone and I'm able to find enough nooks and ledges to secure the soles of my boots. The crevice tightens until I can't climb without bumping my head or scraping my back.

Damn! This way is harder than I thought.

The gaps looked big enough from below, but up here it's a different story. The rock closes in so tight above, I'll need to climb onto the open cliff for a section. I dig in my heels and jam my back against the stone, taking a moment to consider my two options: climb down and start again, or attempt the exposed cliff face.

I lean out of the crevice and assess the upwards route. The trickiest section I need to climb to is only three or four metres high, then I can take the fissure all the way to the top. There are plenty of indentations for my hands and feet on the open cliff face. I'm confident I can do it quickly.

Looking down, I'm 30 metres from the bottom, and almost halfway up the cliff. *There's no way I'm starting again.*

I chalk my hands, take a deep breath, and continue the ascent.

Inching forward, I reach the point where I can't follow the crack any further. I poke my head out, pick the nearest notch in the stone, and reach for it as the cliff suddenly plunges into shadow. From the corner of my eye, I see the sun momentarily dim behind a fleshy translucent wing. I promptly retreat, heart pounding, and jam myself into the crevice.

A gigantic quetzie, the largest pterosaur in the enclosure, circles the treetops. His enormous beak could skewer thirty cadets in a line and still have room for more. My legs turn to jelly. I'd fall if I wasn't jammed in so tight.

The quetzie flaps its wings and makes a sharp turn towards the wider crevices further along the cliff face, heading for my original route. Moments later, a blood-curdling scream echoes across the forest.

I peek out and find the quetzie clinging to the cliff face, body and neck arched back, probing the cracks with its beak. It stabs between the stone, kicking out plumes of dust and ripping vines. The beak finally hits its mark and pulls the hapless cadet from the crevice. He squirms like a worm plucked fresh from the soil as the quetzie tosses him up in the air and launches off the cliff to catch him mid-arc.

I wait for the quetzie to disappear, then tentatively poke my head out again. No pterosaurs in either direction. *Now's as good a time as any.*

I secure my feet, reach around for the ridge, and hoist myself out of the crack. I spread my arms and legs like a spider and climb. The disabling trembles I'd felt moments ago wash away with a surge of adrenaline. My senses heighten. Every indentation in the stone feels magnified under my fingertips. The breeze picks up and whips dust from the nooks and cracks, reminding me how precariously high I've climbed.

My bandaged thigh scrapes along the stone, leaving a smudge of blood. I'm too hyped to feel the pain, but I know I'll pay for it later. I reach the next fissure and haul myself inside, heart thumping like it wants to burst out of my chest.

I made it!

I don't look at my injured leg. I know it's bad. Above me, the fissure rises like a chimney to a protruding crag. Several metres above that, I can see the vegetation of the caldera draping over the edge. The remaining climb totals about 20 metres. No sign of any pterosaur nests.

I'm almost there!

I jam myself between the rock walls and inch my way up. It doesn't take long to reach the crag. Now that I'm here, I can see the protruding stone is actually the tip of a wide ledge set back into the cliff, hiding in a shadow of overhanging stone. I couldn't see the concealed ledge from the base of the cliff. I'll need to grip the crag with both hands and hang freely over the cliff before I can haul myself inside.

One slip and I'm dead.

I chalk my hands one last time. In the academy, we would never attempt a free-climbing manoeuvre as dangerous as this without ropes.

I swallow the lump in my throat and without looking down, I reach out and grip the ledge with one hand. With my heart in my mouth, I swing out and grab hold with my other hand to dangle 80 metres in the air with no support. The cool breeze whistles in my ears and makes me sway. I focus on the lift and give my arms everything I have.

As my chin nears the ledge, a pterodactyl beak protrudes from the space, mere centimetres above me. *Damnit!*

I lower myself to ease my arms and hang there, with nowhere to go. The beak hovers ominously. I've accidentally stumbled upon a pterodactyl nest. *What are the chances?*

But I'm not the only person here. Further up, a female cadet sits perched on a crag, staring at the pterodactyl, arms outstretched. The pterodactyl cranes its long neck towards her and raises its beak to her hands. They bond.

The cadet caresses the tip of the pterodactyl's beak and smiles at her new companion, then glances down at me and motions me to pass. The pterodactyl gives a compliant squawk and takes off, giving me access to the ledge.

Thank goodness! My arms are about to give up. I nod in thanks and haul myself up.

It doesn't take long to complete the rest of the climb and I crawl out of the fissure, using the vines and roots to pull myself onto the rim of the caldera. From here, I have a bird's-eye view of the redwood forest below, the perimeter fence separating the red and yellow zones, the rainforest beyond that, and all the way back to my starting point at the enclosure wall.

I take a moment to savour my achievement, proud to have made it this far. The Extinction Academy has lived up to its name over the last 24 hours. I've seen more cadets die in this brief time than I have during my entire life.

The ridge I'm standing on descends to the final perimeter fence that separates the yellow zone from the blue. Beyond the electrified fence lays the caldera of a dormant volcano. Now a swampy wetland, this enclosed habitat is dominated by a dense forest of soaring cypress trees. Hiding somewhere in that deathtrap is a carnivore meant just for me.

The thought of bonding with an allosaur or tyrannosaur fills my stomach with butterflies. I never expected the Union would select such a prime animal for me.

A gust of wind blows across the caldera. The lofty trees sway and a distant glint catches my eye, like sunlight reflecting off a body of water. It might be the central lake, or one of several hidden lagoons.

'HELP!'

The scream jolts me like a shock of electricity. I crouch behind a bush and peer over the top. Fifteen metres away, a female cadet hangs over the ridge, clinging to a vine. I can't see any dinosaurs – she's not being attacked. It's possible she reached the top and slipped. She glances in my direction, face wracked with fear and desperation.

Those piercing blue eyes make me shudder.

It's Reeva, from my barracks. Any impulse I had to race over there instantaneously vaporises.

'ZAYLA!' Reeva screams, scrambling to improve her grip. The roots of the vine half-rip from the soil and she drops further down the cliff.

This isn't me. I'm not about to let someone die – even Reeva.

I swallow every bad thing she has done to me like a bitter pill and run to help. I'm almost there when another cadet dives in front of me. He leans over the edge, takes hold of Reeva's forearm, and drags her to safety. They tumble backwards and sit there panting, leaving me standing there like an idiot.

'Are you all right?' the male cadet asks.

'Yeah, thanks to you,' Reeva says, glaring sideways at me. 'What took you so long, Zaz? Looked like you wanted me to fall.'

What can I say? Part of me wanted her to fall. Just being around her again makes me sick to the stomach.

'Sorry, I didn't mean to get in your way there,' the cadet says, turning his attention to me. He picks himself up and helps Reeva stand.

She flicks her dishevelled blond hair from her face with a self-important air and brushes off her fatigues. 'I'm Reeva.'

'I'm Avi.'

Avi offers his hand to me. 'Nice to meet you too, Zaz.'

I stare at his open palm for a beat too long and finally shake it with a heat of embarrassment rushing into my cheeks. 'Zayla,' I say, correcting him unnecessarily.

Avi gives me a questioning look. 'Zayla?'

I'm struck by Avi's handsome appearance. Jet-black hair frames his smooth olive skin. He sweeps a long fringe off his forehead, revealing deep-brown eyes that impart an immediate air of warmth and openness.

'Zaz is her nickname,' Reeva cuts in.

I hate being spoken for. *Obviously, I took too long to respond. Story of my life.* Social situations are hard enough, but with Reeva commenting on my every move, it's impossible to think clearly. I wish I could get out of my head sometimes and stop overthinking things but my thoughts always get in the way.

'I like Zaz,' Avi says, 'but what do you prefer?'

I'm too flustered to answer. Weirdly, I shrug my shoulders, even though I prefer Zaz. I just hate Reeva using my nickname.

Avi gives me a smile of acknowledgement.

That just makes me blush even more. I must look ridiculous with my pale skin, dark hair, and blaring-red cheeks.

'There's a drop pod nearby. I was about to open it when I heard the scream. We can all share it if you like.'

'Perfect, I haven't eaten in two days,' Reeva says.

Avi notices me limping as he leads us down from the ridge. 'You can get some healing gel for your burn from the pod. How did that happen?'

'My flare.'

'Zaz must be the only cadet in Beta barracks who could burn herself with her own flare,' Reeva scoffs.

Now I really wish Reeva had dropped off that cliff. She's so hurtful. She doesn't talk to me – she talks at me. Everything she says is a snide comment or a subtle dig to turn people against me. I wish I was quick enough to retort but I only think of witty comebacks hours later, when it's of no help.

I catch Avi surreptitiously watching me and he looks away. *What was that?* It didn't appear to be a derogative or condescending glance. He seemed more curious than anything. Still, I can't help feeling Reeva has planted seeds of doubt in Avi's mind about me, just like she does with everyone.

We trek single file through the trees separating the ridge and electrified mesh fence enclosing the blue zone. Avi leads the way, with Reeva in the middle, and me trailing at the back of the line.

'You can relax for a bit,' Avi says. 'I haven't seen any raptors or compys up here. We just need to keep an eye out for any pterosaurs. As long as we keep between the trees and the ridge, we should be okay.'

'What barracks are you from?' Reeva asks.

'Sigma. You're the first two I've met from Beta.'

'I bumped into a cadet from Omicron barracks. He didn't make it out of the red zone – got trampled by an anky.'

The casual way Reeva talks about the death of another cadet sounds cold and callous. Sometimes I wonder if she has feelings at all – she certainly doesn't have a conscience.

'What about you, Zaz? Have you met anyone before us?'

'I doubt it,' Reeva interjects. 'Zaz's too shy to meet new people. She prefers to work alone.'

'I met someone from Omega,' I blurt out over the top of her.

Reeva laughs. 'There's no such thing as an Omega barracks.'

'I've never heard of Omega,' Avi adds. At least he sounds willing to believe me. 'That means the Union followed the Greek alphabet all the way to the end, making twenty-four barracks in total. I always thought Upsilon barracks was the last, at number twenty.'

'There's a lot of things the Union doesn't tell us. But Zaz probably heard him wrong.'

'I didn't.'

'Where is he now, then?'

'His name was Kane. We stayed together until a pack of megaraptors killed him.'

'I hope you didn't hesitate to help him...like you did with me.'

That's it! I can't listen to this crap anymore. I slide my foot forward and catch Reeva's ankle, tripping her up. She falls and catches herself awkwardly on Avi's heel. Reeva leaps to her feet, red-faced. I've never seen her so embarrassed and angry. She raises her fist to me.

Avi grabs her wrist. 'All right, cool it. We're not here to fight one another.' Reeva tries to wrestle free, but he holds tight. 'We're at war with the Wraith, not each other. Agreed?'

'Fine,' Reeva hisses.

Avi tentatively releases her. I steel myself, convinced she's about to swing a sneaky punch. Reeva gives me a dirty look and storms past Avi. This isn't over. I've just stirred up the most fearsome predator in the entire enclosure.

6

Avi walks between us the rest of the way to the drop pod. That's a good thing. The separation gives Reeva a chance to cool down. Surprisingly, she hardly says a word the entire way – no doubt building up a barrage of insults for me. Reeva likes to put people down, especially those outside her friendship circle. But even her inner circle is not immune to her scathing remarks. I can tell Reeva likes Avi, and from her perspective, I did the worst thing imaginable. I embarrassed her.

The path between the trees opens into a clearing. The shiny metallic pod sits upright, half-buried in the ground like a giant dinosaur egg. Overhead, a swathe of broken branches shows where the pod crashed through the foliage.

We're lucky to find one. All drop pods are randomly jettisoned into the enclosure minutes before any cadets are released.

Avi runs his hand along the stainless-steel plating. His subcutaneous chip illuminates through the skin of his wrist. A sequence of three green lights illuminate on the reflective metal, and the pod opens with a hiss of pressurised air.

Reeva glowers at me: a clear warning not to approach the pod.

I'll let her gather what she needs before taking a turn.

Avi stands by, keeping watch on the ridge and treeline. I get the sense he's really watching us, making sure we don't go at each other again.

Reeva takes a couple of food containers, a new drink bottle, and a second flare, then sits on the far side of the clearing and starts eating.

Avi motions for me to go before him.

I'm more interested in medical supplies than food. I open the various compartments to see what's on offer and take what I need. Two tubes of medical gel – one of them is an antiseptic, the other a dermal sealant. Another pair of painkiller pens. I grab two flares and shove them under my arm. I'm too anxious and worked-up to think about eating, plus the hunger keeps me alert. My final selection is a new water bottle.

'I'm done.'

Avi assesses my haul. 'You didn't get any food.'

'I'll eat when all this is over.'

'Well, I'll leave some in case you change your mind.'

I give him an appreciative smile and find a spot to sit – as far from Reeva as possible. She watches me from the other side of the clearing. I try to ignore her, but I feel those blue eyes tracking me like targeting lasers. I'm regretting tripping her up. If we both get through this, I'm going to pay for it for weeks – if not years – to come.

Avi takes a seat midway between us and opens a food container.

I get to work on my leg. The makeshift bandage has stuck to the wound. I grit my teeth and peel it off. The material takes a layer of skin with it. My head spins. I feel like I'm about to pass out but I push through the wooziness and squeeze a healthy dollop of numbing antiseptic gel onto the burn. It works quick. The clear gel melts into the cracks of scorched skin, soothing my raw pink flesh.

I lather a coating of dermal gel over the top, which takes a minute to set, forming a protective rubbery barrier over my wound. With my leg fixed up, I realise I could do with a fresh pair of camouflage pants. The less exposed skin in the jungle, the better, particularly on the legs.

I return to the pod and shuffle through the remaining compartments. I find a pair of pants and change into them out of sight, behind the pod. I retie my shoes, slip on my utility belt, attach my items, and take a seat in the clearing feeling renewed and ready to go.

'So how are we going to do this?' Avi says.

'Do what?' I ask, thinking he's talking about resolving the spat between Reeva and me.

'I assume we're all heading into the blue zone.'

'I am,' Reeva says.

Avi looks at me.

'Me too.'

Avi nods. 'We can go in together or separate now.'

Reeva tosses her empty food container aside. 'I'm happy if we all go in together.' She jumps to her feet and strides over to me.

I'm not sure what to expect this time around. *Is she going to try and hit me again?* I stand to confront her, ready for anything. Avi rises, prepared to jump between us like a boxing referee.

Reeva puts her hand forward in a peace offering. 'I'm sorry. I deserved it after everything I said to you.'

I don't believe her for a second. Reeva doesn't apologise to anyone, least of all me. She's only doing it to look good in front of Avi. I suddenly realise I've been standing here too long, overthinking the situation. I reluctantly shake her hand. Reeva gives me a phony smile that only I can see and squeezes extra tight.

My stomach churns. If this is the calm before the storm, then I just stared into the eye of an incoming cyclone.

'So, we're sticking together then?' Avi asks.

I look between them, feeling the pressure to make a decision, and nod. *Why did I do that? I really want to go in by myself.*

'Great! We should get moving, then. We don't want to spend another night out here.'

A rustling sound carries across the clearing and all three of us spin around. A sinocalliopteryx stands across from us with its pointed snout buried in Reeva's discarded food container. The diminutive dinosaur resembles an oversized compy, except it's covered in vibrant feathers. The turquoise and dark-green plumage is the perfect camouflage against the surrounding foliage. The sino could have been standing a metre away, watching us, the entire time.

One thing is certain, it won't be alone.

I want to scold Reeva for being so careless. Food scraps should never be discarded near dinosaur habitats, and especially inside one! It's the first rule taught in the academy.

The foliage to our left and right comes alive. Two more sinos materialise from the leaves and creep towards us. They don't look that threatening in their pretty plumage, but these carnivores are vicious hunters. Their talons and teeth are flesh-stripping machines.

'Back up slowly,' Avi says.

He cautiously pulls the lid off his food container and tosses it onto the ground. The sinos rush at it and sniff the contents. Their heads dart up and down like birds, watching us and pecking at the container.

'When you're free of the clearing, run to the nearest hatch.'

I'm the first in line and inch backwards, keeping one eye on the shrubs, mindful not to step straight into the rest of the pack. This is an unfortunate turn of events. I hoped we could avoid rushing into the blue zone in a panicked and disorderly manner, the kind of commotion guaranteed to attract apex predators.

I reach the edge of the clearing and break into a sprint. My stomach is in my mouth as I barrel through the waist-high ferns. There could be a sino right beside me and I wouldn't see it for its perfect camouflage.

A ruckus follows close behind me. Breaking branches. Rustling. Panting. I don't dare turn around. One wrong step and I could trip. I burst free of the trees and veer towards the nearest access hatch in the electrified fence.

One hundred metres to go.

I have no idea who's behind me. I haven't heard a scream – a good sign Avi and Reeva are still alive.

I avoid the exposed rocks and sprint through a flat area of vegetation. Low-lying ferns and shrubs whip and scrape against my injured leg. I barely feel it, thanks to the dermal gel.

A blast of wind buffets me along, almost lifting me off the ground. I glance over my shoulder as a pterodactyl swoops in and hovers over the ridge. Each flap of its mighty wings propels me forward with a burst of air.

SCREECH!

The pterodactyl shifts its beady bird-like gaze between me, Reeva, and Avi. Any second now, it's going to pick one of us off.

I'm almost at the hatch. Thirty metres to go.

SCREEEEEECH!

A second pterodactyl swoops in, lands on the ridge, and shrieks at the first one . It waddles forward on its hind legs and wing elbows, stabbing its beak forward like a massive knife. It appears to be shielding us from the other one but I can't tell if it's trying to protect us or eat us. The hovering pterodactyl shrieks in protest and flies away, defeated.

Ten metres to the hatch. Five, four, three, two...

I leap inside the steel-plated entrance, slipping as I land. My knee hits the door and I spin about to land on my butt. I clutch my knee, unable to stand. *That hurt!*

Reeva and Avi's panic-stricken faces are seconds behind me. Trailing them is the pack of sinos: heads down, necks extended, all running full tilt.

'OPEN IT!' Reeva screams.

I drag my bottom across the entrance and lift my forearm up to the chip scanner. The magnetic lock *clunks* open, but I'm so sore I can't even stand to grasp the handle yet.

Reeva and Avi scramble past me. Avi grabs the handle and attempts to push the hatch open. 'It's jammed!'

In the heat of the moment, we all forget one crucial detail – the door can only be operated by the person who unlocked it. Problem is, there's no time left.

The sinos converge on the hatch. I'm the most exposed. Each pair of beady yellow eyes focuses on me. They crouch with their wiry arms open wide, claws extended, hissing at me through their bared teeth.

They're going to tear me to shreds.

Several sinos leap for me and I futilely raise my arms.

All three attackers are snagged mid-air by a pterodactyl beak. A blast of wind buffets us and a giant pterosaur swoops past, taking the writhing sinocalliopteryxes with it. The remaining sinos scatter, screeching and hissing, leaping back to the safety of the trees.

The pterosaur gulps down its catch and circles about to land in front of the hatch, kicking up a vortex of leaves and dust. I shield my eyes, convinced I'm next in line to be plucked from the entrance.

'It's okay!' calls a voice.

A cadet appears on the ridge, waving proudly. She walks up beside the pterodactyl, ducks under its wing, and pats it on the side. It's the cadet I encountered on the cliff.

'That was close,' she says.

The pterodactyl affectionately brushes her shoulder with its beak. She rubs her new bonding partner with equivalent affection and the pterodactyl waddles about to guard the area. I stand and finally get to read the cadet's name patch, TAYLOR-2548.

'Sorry I couldn't help sooner,' Taylor says. 'I had to scare off the other pterodactyl before I could get rid of the pack.'

'We appreciate it,' Avi replies, stepping from the hatch to shake Taylor's hand.

'The bonding is quick,' Reeva says, admiring the obedient pterodactyl. 'You're so connected already. It's like you reared the pterosaur since it was a flapling.'

'It's hard to explain, but hopefully you'll find out for yourself,' Taylor says, peering past us to the hatch. 'Good luck in there. They don't get any bigger and badder than in the blue zone.'

'Just the way we like it,' Avi says with a grin.

'Any tips on bonding?' asks Reeva.

'Yeah – find your dinosaur before it finds you. It's impossible to keep a mental connection if you're running for your life.'

In my mind, Taylor's comment validates one crucial point. I need to separate from Avi and Reeva. The three of us are a walking smorgasbord. If I'm on my own, I only need to worry about myself.

I'm confident I can track and find my dinosaur before it finds me. I struggle to interact with people, but I don't have the same problem with dinosaurs, even if they want to eat me. To them, it's nothing personal. Dinosaurs act purely on instinct. And that's what I like about them. Dinosaurs don't make fun of you. They're not interested in making you feel worthless or uncomfortable. To them, we fall into two categories: edible or inedible.

'We should go,' Avi says, checking his watch. 'Six hours before nightfall.'

Taylor salutes us. 'Hopefully I see one of you in training! Remember me if you end up being my squad leader.'

Avi nods. 'Will do.'

We bid our goodbyes with a salute, and Taylor leaves. I limp over to the hatch, turn the handle, and push the heavy metal door open.

Avi leans through the opening and checks in both directions, then steps through. I follow without hesitation, eager to go my own way. The hatch silently closes behind Reeva, sealing us to our fates.

My boots squish in the damp soil. The humid atmosphere is heavy and oppressive. A dense forest of cypress trees rises from the sodden landscape. This swampy wetland is the most biodiverse of the three zones and easily five or six degrees warmer. A thin film of sweat has already formed on my arms and forehead.

Reeva points out a trail of massive indentations where the reeds are flattened. 'Looks like an allosaur's been through here.'

Large puddles are still pooling in the footprints, seeping up from the deep mud.

'Those prints are minutes old,' Avi says in a hushed voice. 'We need to find some cover.'

Avi directs us towards a group of trees. I hesitate and glance in the opposite direction. *This is where I go my own way.*

Avi notices I'm not following and stops. 'What's wrong?'

'I'm going alone.'

His handsome brow furrows. 'You sure?'

Reeva rolls her eyes and sighs. 'If Zaz wants to go that way, let her. We're better off without her.'

Avi glares at Reeva. He seems ready to retort, but holds his tongue. Surely he can see through Reeva's self-obsessed persona. Her belligerent attitude should be a warning signal that she's dangerous to be around. Without me, I don't think he's game to be alone with her.

Reeva feigns an accused look. 'What? It's true.'

'Zaz is right,' Avi says, looking at me. 'We should separate. Just standing here talking jeopardises our chances.'

'Fine. I don't need either of you.'

Reeva strides off for the trees. Avi watches her pensively for a moment, then turns to me. 'Stay safe.'

'You too.'

Avi gives me a parting smile and darts off in a separate direction. Our positive departure leaves me confident and energised. It's rare for someone to take my side. Seems like everyone in my barracks is too afraid to speak up, or have an opinion. They usually pander to the popular people just to fit in. It's good to know that out here, we're back to a level playing field.

I survey the trees, looking for a place to start. I'm going to head left, as far from Avi and Reeva as possible. The ground shakes as I take my first step. *That's not good.* I freeze mid-stride, waiting for the next thump.

BOOM!

It feels like the volcano is waking up. This time, snapping branches accompany the shaking ground and I spin around, wondering if Avi and Reeva have heard it. Avi crouches in the grass about 30 metres away. Further on, Reeva hides behind a tree trunk.

CRUNCH!

A tyrannosaurus rex bursts through the line of trees right in front of Avi. The foremost tree topples over and smashes to the ground before him. The reddish-brown T-rex stands there and turns its head, sniffing the air with flared nostrils as it surveys the clearing. The T-rex's exceptional olfactory senses compensate for its mediocre eyesight. Saliva glistens across its yellow teeth. It grunts and lumbers forward. A thick drool of mucus hangs from its scarred mouth, just above Avi's head. This thing is ready to eat.

I'm torn between running and helping Avi. Unless he wants to bond with it. *Why isn't he moving? He could activate his neural implant.* He's probably too close. The T-rex could literally inhale Avi from that position.

Reeva and I have flares. We can distract the T-rex and give Avi time to escape. But Reeva needs to act first. She's hidden from the tyrannosaur's line of sight. I'm standing out in the open, the most exposed of all three of us.

Reeva slowly raises a flare. *Good, she's thinking the same thing as me.* I give her a subtle nod and her terrified eyes acknowledge me.

I hold my breath, waiting for her to make the first move. She's not doing anything with the flare. *This isn't the time to hold grudges. Why isn't she activating it?* I suddenly realise why. I'm now standing in shadow. The musty breeze blowing from behind me isn't the wind.

There's a second tyrannosaur looming over me, blasting me with its hot, putrid breath. I never even heard it coming.

I'm dead.

EXTINCTION ACADEMY

FLAME

BOOK I

ANDREW D. CONNELL

EREBUS BOOKS

1

The tyrannosaur looms over me, salivating, sniffing the air like a giant vacuum. Its dark mottled skin and stained yellow teeth fill my peripheral vision. Its breath stinks. I can't run. Any sudden moves and I'm dead. All I have to defend myself is a hunting knife and two flares, but the time to use a flare has passed and the voracious carnivore has me on its dinner plate. I peer over to Avi, crouched in the grass in the shadow of a second T-rex and facing a similar predicament to me. At least he has the trunk of a fallen tree between him and those monstrous bone-crushing jaws.

Our only hope is Reeva.

She stands 100 metres from my position, hidden in the treeline, able to distract the tyrannosaurs with one of her flares. It would buy precious seconds for Avi and me to sprint into the jungle. If she only had me to save, Reeva would be gone already. But she likes Avi. In the brief time we've known him, she's done everything to impress him, which includes insulting me at every turn.

That's nothing new. As cadets, we've lived together in Beta Barracks since we were kids, and Reeva has made my academy life a living hell.

I hate her. But right now, my life is in her hands.

Reeva detaches a flare from her belt and edges forward, keeping her fair skin and blond hair in the shadows. She has limited space to throw it. The boundary wall towers behind me, separating us from the dinosaurs in the previous zone. Both T-rexes will bump into the wall after a couple of strides if she throws it that way, so she needs to go long in the opposite direction, right over Avi and his T-rex, towards the lagoon.

Reeva ignites the flare and hurls it exactly where I hoped.

At last, she does something right.

ROAR!

The tyrannosaur standing over me bellows at the sizzling ball of light whizzing through the air. The roar is deafening. I want to cover my ears, but I can't move. The T-rex near Avi watches the flare with curiosity and chases after it, swooshing its massive tail. My T-rex joins in the chase and knocks me into the air.

I land on the grass and roll several times, rising in time to see Avi sprint for the jungle.

The pair of tyrannosaurs converges on the glowing stick, grunting and dipping their heads to sniff the smoke, neither willing to bite it. They're not fighting for dominance, which means they're a mated pair.

I peer in Reeva's direction and find she's gone. So is Avi.

It's each of us for ourselves now.

If there weren't two T-rexes, I'd attempt to bond with one of them. In this situation, I can't get close enough to one T-rex without the other eating me. If they split up, I might have a chance. Our neural implants can link and bond us with multiple dinosaurs, but only if they hunt in packs, and tyrannosaurs hunt alone.

Shame, I wanted a tyrannosaur.

I run towards the jungle, eager to escape before the flare dies and the tyrannosaurs follow our scent. The palm trees offer some shadowy protection as I plough headlong through the undergrowth. If there's an allosaurus or gigantosaurus lurking nearby, I'm going to run into them without warning.

I glimpse Avi in the dense foliage ahead, moving in the same direction as me, leaping logs and dodging branches with athletic agility. Like him, I need to get away from the zone wall and deeper into the jungle where there's better protection. A metal hatch in the wall swings open and I duck behind a tree to watch.

A cadet stumbles through the hatch, clutching her shoulder, hand glistening with crimson. She's injured. That's not good; her blood will attract the tyrannosaurs. These one-way doors between zones are situated every 500 metres apart, and once you come through, there's no going back.

The distant pound of footsteps resonates along the boundary. The tyrannosaurs have already picked up the scent and are on the move.

I want to scream and tell her to go back before the hatch closes, locking her in.

Too late. The pounding intensifies.

The cadet dives aside, narrowly avoiding a pterodactyl beak. A giant pterosaur is on the other side of the wall, stabbing at her through the hatch. It's too big to squeeze through and gives up. The hatch closes, but the girl has escaped one problem to face a bigger one.

A tyrannosaur bounds past me, head down, charging straight for her.

She's dead.

The Extinction Academy has lived up to its nickname in the last 48 hours. I've seen too many cadets die a gruesome death and I don't want to witness another. I'm about to avert my eyes from the carnage when something remarkable happens – the cadet attempts to bond with the T-rex. She calmly places one hand on the back of her head and activates the neural implant embedded in her brain.

The tyrannosaur bears down on her, jaws agape, ready to snatch her up with a single bone-shattering bite.

The cadet closes her eyes and reaches for the mighty beast with blood-soaked hands. Normally, the scent of blood would drive the carnivore into a frenzy, but it slows to a walking pace as she beckons the T-rex to lower its head.

I glance around, looking for the tyrannosaur's mate.

For now, it's nowhere to be seen and my chest flutters with excitement – she might succeed after all.

The tyrannosaurus's heaving ribcage eases and settles into a slower rhythmic breathing. It shakes its head, as if trying to fight off a hypnotic spell. The neural implant buried deep inside its brain is now linked to the cadet's, blocking its instincts to feast. If the cadet maintains focus until they touch, the Bonding will complete. The tyrannosaur obediently lowers its head and pushes its snout into the cadet's glistening hands.

I should keep running but I can't, now captivated by the moment. I've never seen anyone bond with an apex carnivore.

The T-rex jolts backwards as if electrocuted and the girl opens her eyes, smiling. The mighty carnivore manoeuvres over her into a protective stance and tilts its head to make eye contact with her. I want to cheer. *She did it!* Their tender moment represents the beginning of an unbreakable partnership. Months of training and further bonding will ensure they are in perfect sync before being sent to fight on Daxma-5.

I reach beneath my ponytail and caress my own neural implant, represented by a tiny bump in my scalp. It can only be activated by the subcutaneous chip in my index finger and must be pressed for five seconds. This safeguard ensures we can't trigger our implants by accident. The trick is, you need to time it perfectly – before you're in danger.

It won't be long before the long shadows consume the island and the carnivores begin their nightly hunt. I need to bond with a dinosaur before sunset and avoid spending another night out here.

I wait for a minute, hoping the second T-rex returns for its mate. That would make the tyrannosaur an easy target, but it seems they've separated.

I quietly move in the direction Avi was heading, towards the centre of the blue zone. This humid, swampy environment makes the previous two zones look easy.

I don't understand why the Union selectors want me to bond with an apex predator. Doing so leads to a command position, meaning I need to interact with people and give orders. My reserved nature is better suited to stealth and special ops, a specialised military division where you work alone or in small groups.

Thing is, I've always loved apex predators. Give me a tyrannosaurus, allosaurus, carcharodontosaurus, gigantosaurus, or spinosaurus any day of the week. Even the cannibal majungasaurus is fine with me. This zone contains all of them; the largest bipedal carnivores that ever stalked our planet. I couldn't tolerate bonding with something half my size, like a pack of compys or troodons. They're too small and irritating. The triceratops, stegosaurus, and dreadnoughtus are staple favourites and plenty of cadets from my barracks are keen to bond with any of them. But I'm not tempted, even by the majestic pterosaurs or elusive raptors. I'm drawn to the power and dominance of the largest carnivores. My instructors know this, and their reports may have influenced the Union division selectors. In hindsight, my designation to the apex carnivores shouldn't come as a surprise. These mighty dinosaurs might instil me with a trait I sorely lack – self-confidence.

'Zaz!' hisses a voice from the greenery.

I dip behind a log and hide. There's only two people I know of in the blue zone that know my nickname: Avi and Reeva.

'Hey, over here!'

I pinpoint the direction of the voice and find Avi crouched between a gnarly clump of cypress roots. He places a finger to his lips and motions me over. We only met for the first time a couple of hours ago, but I feel secure in his presence.

His deep-brown eyes greet me with a look of concern as I crawl over to join him. 'Are you okay?'

'I'm fine.'

'What about Reeva?'

I shrug my shoulders. *I'm not concerned about her. I hope I never see her again.*

'Would you prefer me to call you Zayla? Reeva said your nickname is Zaz, but she doesn't seem to like you, so I wasn't sure if it was something you liked –'

'You can call me Zaz,' I say. 'It's fine.'

Avi smiles. 'I know you wanted to go your own way in this zone, but there's a fresh kill ahead, half buried in the dirt. Looks like a cadet. I didn't want you stumbling across it by accident. Whatever dinosaur started its meal intends to come back and finish it.'

'Have you seen any tracks?'

'Majungasaurus, maybe allosaurus. It's hard to tell in the mud. There're footprints inside footprints. The carnivores are trampling all over the place.'

I shake my head and sigh.

'What's wrong?'

'I hate the way all these dinosaurs are jammed together. They never would have hunted this close to each other in the wild. They should be spread out over hundreds of kilometres. It makes their behaviour unpredictable.'

'Plus, they spend most of their lives being reared in cramped enclosures.'

I nod. *Finally, someone shares my concern for these animals.* 'They're confused. This enclosure looks natural, but there's nothing natural about it. The entire island is only ten kilometres wide and enclosed within a giant artificial dome. Unique biomes are crammed into three tiny zones, each one hardly big enough to sustain a single species, let alone the 25 they have packed in here. It's not about creating a natural habitat for these dinosaurs; it's about forcing us to bond.'

'You're right. Nothing about this is natural.'

My emotion gets the better of me. 'It's not!' I say, louder than is safe.

'It's refreshing to hear someone talk about dinosaur rights. The Union only sees them as weapons.'

'Like it or not, we're all weapons in this war.'

Avi acknowledges the truth with a pensive nod.

I've got to be careful about what I say. Any cadet that speaks out against the Union and their motivations is reprimanded, or worse. I don't want to be one of those cadets that suddenly goes missing from their dorm in the middle of the night, and I'd hate to bring that kind of suspicion upon Avi.

'Sorry, I get passionate about the plight of these animals,

sometimes more so than my own. Humanity brought them back from extinction to put in a zoo, then we adopted them to fight a war with no thought of their needs. We breed them, keep them locked up in pens, and study them. Not for their benefit, but for ours.'

'Don't apologise for having compassion.'

I smile. *I wish there were more cadets like Avi in Beta Barracks.*

Crack!

The noise of breaking branches interrupts us. Carefully we peer out from behind the roots and spy a mass of grey reptilian skin shift through the greenery. The obscured dinosaur sports a long neck with a cranium crowned in reddish-brown skin and a distinctive stubby horn.

It's a majungasaurus, or *junga*, as we call them.

Avi leans close and whispers in my ear. 'The junga's returned for its kill.'

The muscular theropod is similar in size and build to a T-rex but has a shorter, broader snout. It can take down a sauropod five times its height with a bite-and-hold technique, like the way lions strangle their prey. *Strange to think that lions are now unnumbered by the majungasaurus.* The junga's long muscular neck and stocky legs amplify its strangling power. You get caught in a junga bite, there's no escaping it. I've seen allosaurs and tyrannosaurs back away from a fight for fear of being pinned in their unbreakable bite.

'You wanna bond with a junga?' Avi whispers.

I shake my head.

'Me either. We'll have to go around.'

We creep through the undergrowth, away from the ripping and munching. The vile sounds make me feel like retching. I try not to picture the cadet being devoured.

Avi stops unexpectedly, and I bump into him.

'What is it?' I whisper.

He doesn't respond and remains crouched in the ferns, unmoving, as if turned to stone. A long translucent string of drool drapes from above and laces his brow.

My insides turn to ice.

Then I notice the textured, leathery skin under my hands. The root we're crawling over is no root – it's the muscular foot of an apex carnivore. A salivating allosaurus lowers its head through the trees to inspect us, snapping branches and blasting us with its fetid breath.

I watch Avi's hand slip onto to his belt. He unclips a flare and I dig my feet into the soil, ready to sprint.

SWISH!

A ball of bright pink light explodes in front of me. Avi rams the searing flare deep into the allosaur's eye and the beast reels away, shaking its head, its human-sized forearms futilely, grasping for the burning magnesium. Then comes the noise, like a thousand claps of thunder at once.

ROOOAAAR!

The allosaurus staggers about and bumps between trees, thrashing its tail. I careen through the jungle at breakneck speed, adrenalin raging through me, blind with desperation. Palm leaves whack my face. Branches scratch my exposed skin. *Where's Avi?* I lost him in the chaos, but I'm too terrified to stop. I'm on my own from here.

The ground vanishes beneath my feet and I'm suddenly airborne, somersaulting out of control.

I land with a heavy splat on my butt and sit there, stunned and spread-eagled on the muddy bank of a lake. I check my limbs, making sure I lost nothing essential. Arms, legs, and all fingers accounted for. Aside from a few bloody scratches, I escaped unscathed. *Unbelievable.*

I pick myself up and peer over the embankment towards the forest. It's difficult to see beyond the cone-shaped cypress trunks rising from the damp soil. Their unusual shape resembles a giant dinosaur leg. *No wonder we never saw the allosaurus.* I hope Avi made it to safety.

Splash!

I spin around in time to witness the settling spray of an enormous plume of water on the far side of the lake. A disturbance of bubbling water races across the surface. Something huge is lurking in the depths, and moving incredibly fast. *I've gotta get off this bank.* I leap up the shoulder-high slope, grasping at the slippery roots. I can't get a grip. The soles of my boots slip and sink into the mud. I glance over my shoulder as a spiny dinosaur sail emerges from the roiling bubbles, making a line towards me like a colossal shark fin.

My boots suction deeper into the mud. I feel like I'm moving in slow motion and can't escape, just like a nightmare.

The water swells as a broad glistening back breaks the surface to rise like an island from the deep water. Luminous green eyes emerge, followed by an elongated snout. The spinosaurus surfaces, water cascading off its humongous girth like a waterfall as it stands and blots out the sun. It's the largest carnivore I've ever seen, with a towering sail that makes it appear twice as tall. I stare, mouth agape, awed and terrified by the majestic predator.

The creature lunges for me.

This is it!

I close my eyes. Monstrous teeth clamp my lower leg like a vice and I hear my tibia and fibula crack. My broken leg bends like rubber and I flop backwards, draping from the almighty jaw, too petrified to feel pain. The upside-down world passes me by. I'm being taken across the lake. Water splashes in my face. *How am I still alive? Why hasn't he eaten me yet?* Next, I'm tossed high above the bank on the opposite side of the lake with a bird's-eye view of the jungle, then I'm falling.

Thud!

Darkness. An indefinite amount of time passes and I open my eyes. I'm lying on the muddy bank, numb all over. The spinosaurus stands over me, peering across the treetops. He's protecting his meal, checking for other predators before he eats me.

I try moving my arm. A hand appears in front of my face – my hand. *I'm not paralysed!* I reach for the back of my head and probe my matted, muddied hair. I locate the miniscule bump of my neural implant and press it with my index finger.

If I'm alive in five seconds, there's a chance I can bond with him.

The spinosaurus peers down at me and opens its jaws. *Not yet, not yet!* My implant is almost active.

Three... two... one...

A tingle of electricity shoots through me. Goosebumps ripple over my skin and culminate with an intense buzz in the back of my skull. My panic and chaotic thoughts subside, leaving me calm and composed. The spinosaurus angles his snout to one side and leans in for a closer look at his prospective meal. His reptilian eyes appear to recognise me, not as food, but something more. *It's working!*

I slow my breathing and focus on bonding with the prehistoric brain. His breathing slows and mimics mine as our bodies fall into sync. I raise my hands to his snout and feel the cool, textured skin. The physical connection seals our link.

I'm suddenly weightless, looking down upon my broken and twisted body through the eyes of the spinosaurus. His entire life flashes through my mind's eye. Cracking out of a birth egg... Living in a pen, being fed by cadets... Growing bigger, stronger... Being released into a new enclosure... Hunting and killing other dinosaurs... Swimming across the lake... and finally finding me.

In the same instant, I sense the spinosaurus experience my memories, like a snapshot of my life is being mentally transferred into his undersized brain.

We bond.

I return to my body and excruciating pain radiates up my leg. It's too much to handle. A dark veil shrouds my sight and I pass out.

My eyelids flutter open to a world of white and gleaming steel. The pain has gone. I'm lying on a gurney in an academy triage ward. I peer down at my broken leg, which is now straight and housed within a bone-regenerator capsule encompassing my knee to my ankle. I prop myself up to investigate. An ultraviolet light runs up and down within the translucent device, scanning and repairing my injuries. Sinister black and purple bruises run the length of my shin.

'How do you feel?' says a voice.

I lay back as a stern-faced nurse tends to me. She's older than I am, mid-thirties or forties. I'm not sure. I find it hard to tell people's ages, especially when every cadet in the academy is exactly 18 years old (give or take a few hours). Anyone over that and I'm guessing.

She assesses my vitals and types on the holographic chart beside my bed. 'You got off lightly compared to others in here.'

Lightly? I want to say. This woman has no idea what I've been through over the last couple of days.

The nurse raises my bed to a sitting position and I take in the rest of the ward. It's a high-tech, sterile environment. Walls of stainless steel are embedded with advanced medical devices and readouts. Nurses jostle about, all dressed in the same dark-grey suit and cap, moving from bed to bed, checking on cadets like me, and monitoring everyone's vitals on holographic displays.

'I'll get you something to eat,' <u>she</u> says. 'Don't worry, we'll have you up and walking by the end of the day.' The nurse leaves.

'Sleeping beauty's awoken!' booms a voice in my ear.

To my left, a cadet sits up in his bed. He's big, broad, and muscular, almost too big for the mattress. He watches me with his arms crossed, biceps bulging from his white hospital gown. A bone-regenerator covers his right foot like an oversized boot. He smirks at me, eyes beaming.

'Leave her alone, Tyson,' says someone from a bed on the opposite side of the ward.

I look over to find a cadet propped up on her elbows. Her legs are wrapped in silver foil. Nearby canisters feed a dark-red substance through translucent tubes into the foil, regenerating her skin. 'She's not interested in your mindless observations,' the girl says.

'Zayla can decide for herself,' Tyson says, looking at me. 'Isn't that right?'

I'm caught between them, unsure how to respond to their playful banter. Even on a good day, when I'm feeling socially confident, this kind of interaction is a stretch for me. I don't want to offend anyone, so I just shrug my shoulders, cheeks burning with self-conscious embarrassment.

'See! It's just you, Rosa,' Tyson exclaims.

'Zayla's being polite.'

How do they know my name? I glance at the hologram hovering over my bedhead in bold glowing text: [ZAYLA-8311] My name and birth number are emblazoned for all to see.

'What happened to your leg?' Tyson asks.

There's a sincerity in his voice now. I don't mind Tyson. I just wish his boisterous personality wasn't directed at me. As usual, I'm getting lost in my thoughts and over-analysing the situation. I should answer before...

'Obviously she doesn't want to talk to you,' Rosa says.

'It's okay,' I mumble. 'I was bitten by a spinosaurus.'

'Bitten?' Tyson blurt outs. 'You're damn lucky to be alive. How do you manage to get bitten without being swallowed?'

'I got caught between his teeth.'

Tyson laughs. 'Doesn't surprise me. Not much meat on ya. You're as skinny as a troodie. The spino probably wanted to use you as a toothpick.'

I hate it when people call me skinny. But coming from Tyson, it doesn't seem offensive. Anyone looks skinny next to him. Besides, his remarks come across as jovial and friendly rather than disparaging.

'Leave her alone,' Rosa says, flashing me a friendly look. 'Just ignore him. You were lucky to stay asleep for as long as you did. We've had to listen to Tyson's crap all day.'

'Oh, come on!' Tyson says. 'Deep down, you know you love the sound of my voice.'

Rosa groans and lays back, pulling her pillow up to block her ears.

'I'm only muckin' around,' Tyson says. 'So how did you escape?'

'Escape what?'

'The spinosaurus.'

'Oh... I bonded with it.'

Tyson jerks up with surprise and teeters unsteadily, staring at me with a look of bewilderment. For a second, I thought he might topple off the edge of his bed. Several cadets look my way. Their inquisitive gazes make me even more uncomfortable.

'Wow! You might be the meekest-looking cadet on this ward, but you got the most lethal pet out of everyone, including me.'

'What did you bond with?'

'Dreadnoughtus.'

I nod. *Am I meant to congratulate him? I suppose I should say something. Otherwise, he's going to keep asking me questions.* 'What happened to your foot?'

Tyson lifts his foot and brandishes the casing like it's a fancy boot. He's so strong. I barely have the strength to lift mine.

'Ah, I got a little close to –'

'He got trampled on by his own dreadnoughtus,' Rosa says, loud enough so everyone can hear. 'And that was after he bonded with it.'

Chuckles arise from the other cadets.

Tyson plonks his foot back on the bed, blushed in the face and a little crestfallen. 'Hey, it's early days. I haven't had a chance to train him yet.'

'Pity he didn't stomp on your throat. Then we wouldn't have to listen to you all day.'

A couple of chuckles turn into laughs.

'Hilarious!' Tyson retorts, slumping back into his pillow.

Rosa focuses on me. 'Hey, Zayla, what barracks are you from?'

'Beta.'

'I hear there're a lot of commanders coming out of Beta Barracks.'

'Really?' I ask, wondering who else I know might have survived. I don't recognise any of the faces in the ward. 'How do you know?'

'They're only rumours, a bit like the death count. Apparently the Extinction Academy notched up a record body count today.'

My stomach churns at the thought. *Do I really want to know how many cadets died trying to bond with a dinosaur?* Going in, we all knew it was going to be bad, but I can't resist not knowing. 'How many died?'

'Two-thirds.'

'Of which barracks?'

Rosa's expression goes cold. 'Of all barracks combined.'

I do the math in my head. *Twenty-five barracks, each with 100 cadets... That's over 1,600 cadets who lost their lives in the last 48 hours.*

'I don't get it. Why do we need so many casualties before we even get to fight?' Tyson says. 'Those cadets could have served the Union in other ways. They didn't need to die. Not every one of us is born to bond.'

Rosa urgently *shooshes* him and waits for a nurse to finish walking by. 'Watch what you say. Last thing we need is a reprimand thanks to you.'

The ward goes quiet for some time. No doubt everyone is reliving their experiences from the last two days. Sometimes I feel more like a prisoner than a cadet, and I know a lot of cadets feel the same. We've lived in the academy for 18 years – our entire lives – but we don't have the right or luxury to question our purpose here; humanity is counting on us to win this war.

The nurses wheel in two unconscious cadets. The first cadet has her arms encased in bone-regenerator units, while the seconds has his entire body is wrapped in silver foil, leaving only his neck and head exposed, showing a deathly pale face speckled with dried blood. *That doesn't look good.* Still no sign of Avi or Reeva. I hope Avi made it, but I can't say the same for Reeva. Hopefully, I've seen the last of her.

Rosa shifts with a grimace and gingerly adjusts her legs.

'What happened to you?' I ask.

'I accidentally fell into a pterodactyl nest. The newly hatched flaplings shredded my legs. I was lucky to bond with their mother before they ate me.'

My heart rate picks up. 'You were in the yellow zone!?'

'Yeah, it was brutal. You did well to make it through that raptor-infested redwood forest and climb the cliff into the blue zone.'

'Did you see anyone else?'

'Not many. Why, who are you looking for?'

'A friend.'

I doubt she saw Kane, the mysterious cadet from Epsilon Barracks who saved me. Last time I saw him, he was being attacked by a pack of megaraptors. If not for him, I never would have made it through the first night. I owe him my life.

'Does your friend have a name?' Rosa asks.

'Kane.'

'No, sorry. If you know what barracks he's from, I might be able to help.'

I pause, not sure how to respond. I had never heard of Epsilon Barracks before I met Kane, and he's the only cadet I've ever met that didn't have a birth number. I always believed there were only 20 barracks, all named after letters from the Greek alphabet. If Epsilon existed, that would make 24 barracks, adding the letters phi, chi, and psi to the list. Maybe these extra cadets are part of a covert, top-secret program we don't know about. Why would Kane even make up such a story? In the end, I figure it's easier to lie.

'I don't know where he was from, but he helped me.'

'Well, hopefully he made it,' Tyson cuts in.

I give a thoughtful nod. I hope Tyson's right.

Rosa waits for a nurse to walk by and speaks in a hushed tone. 'The nurses on this ward rank higher than the ones from our barracks.'

A nurse checks on the cadet in the bed next to me and we all go quiet. I observe the insignia on her uniform, trying not to look conspicuous. I didn't notice it before, but Rosa's right: the triceratops insignia pin on her lapel has three wings, instead of the standard two we see on the nurses in the barracks infirmary.

I look at Tyson as the nurse walks off. 'What does that insignia mean?'

He shrugs. 'I dunno.'

'They're sorting us into potential divisions, maybe platoons,' Rosa says. 'We have command, special ops, and infantry classes all in the one ward. None of us are from the same barracks, and we've all been assigned new codes.'

I check my hologram. Beneath my name and birth number is a new barcode and ten-digit numerical code. Tyson and Rosa share the same barcode. Looking around, I see every cadet on the ward has been assigned the same code.

'I overheard one of the nurses talking,' Rosa continues. 'Apparently we're being moved out to our new barracks tonight.'

'Does that mean I'm stuck with you?' Tyson says.

'Don't worry – special ops don't mix it with the grunts.'

Tyson feigns a disappointed face. 'Oh, too good for us in infantry? Is that how it goes now you're special ops?'

'Depends,' Rosa responds, looking at me. 'What does our commander say?'

Tyson's gaze joins hers. 'What do you say, Commander?'

Now I'm really being put on the spot.

It feels like everyone on the ward is watching me, even the nurses. *Am I supposed to say something witty or serious here?* I wish I knew. An uncomfortable heat rises to my face. I'm embarrassed, yet again. This is not how a potential commanding officer in meant to act. They're still looking at me, waiting for me to respond.

'I don't know,' slips from my lips.

Rosa and Tyson overlook my remark and continue bickering, ignoring me for the most part. Their personalities match their divisions. Tyson has bonded with a dreadnoughtus, a huge sauropod species that makes up part of the infantry division. His confidence, bravado, and brute strength will fit right in with the frontline fighters.

Rosa bonded with a pterodactyl, which places her in special ops and stealth. Her astute observations and skills of deduction are already at work. She's noticed minor details that Tyson and I overlooked, like the codes beneath our names, the insignias on the uniforms, the fact we're all from different barracks. It makes perfect sense for her to work in special ops.

But me, I'm an anomaly. Why did the Union designate me to bond with an apex predator like a spinosaurus, a dinosaur with the potential to lead into a command position? I'm way too shy and introverted. It must be a mistake.

I spend the remainder of the afternoon keeping to myself as much as I can. We are fed a standard ration meal on a plastic tray. Basic vegetables and a chunk of brown protein that is supposed to mimic meat. I doubt real meat tastes this plain. I'm no expert, though – I've never eaten the flesh of a real animal.

I pick at my food. My nerves have unsettled my stomach.

Fewer cadets are wheeled in as the day draws to a close and the new arrivals have less severe injuries and only require simple attention. I wonder how many cadets came through the Bonding unscathed.

The setting sun casts a warm glow through the windows. It's the only way I can tell how much time has passed. A nurse approaches, pushing a trolley. She examines the bone-regenerator on my lower right leg and activates the built-in control panel. A hologram of my tibia and fibula project above the unit. The bones appear straight and normal.

'Looking good,' she says, typing across the panel. 'You're all done.'

The casing opens, exposing my leg to the open air, like someone just opened a fridge door on my skin.

The nurse taps my knee. 'Lift up.'

I raise my leg and she removes the unit, places it on the trolley, and moves on to Tyson. I sit forward and massage my lower leg. The bruises have faded to a faint blemish, but my skin feels hot, like it's been baked in an oven. I hop off the bed. A tingling sensation races up my leg as I stand on the steel floor and wriggle my toes. Weird sensations aside, my leg feels strong.

'You're good to leave,' the nurse says, looking my way. 'Report to the far end of the ward.'

I follow the other cadets and we assemble at the end of the ward in two lines, all dressed in the same white hospital gowns.

The door slides open and two hard-faced corporals enter, followed by a tall, well-presented brigadier. The three of them wear the same black military uniform with the pins on their lapels and berets denoting rank. The brigadier assesses us with a cool, steely gaze. His tough, chiselled features, perfect buzz cut, and clean-shaven appearance is immaculate, even by Union standards.

'Attention, cadets.'

We straighten our lines and stand to attention. Every cadet knows the punishment for being sloppy or tardy is a shift cleaning out the dinosaur pens.

'I'm Division Brigadier Ramsey. I've been tasked with escorting you to your new barracks. Scan your ID chip on the way out and collect a fresh uniform. You have two minutes to dress and assemble in the outside corridor.'

I shuffle into place behind Tyson. Our line moves fast. Tyson steps forward and holds out his forearm. The corporal scans it with a handheld scanner and waves him on.

I step up.

The corporal scans the chip in my forearm and gives me a double look.

I hold my breath. *What? Is something wrong?* I notice the glowing readout beneath my skin: [ZAYLA-8311/SPINOSAURUS] My name and birth code have always been there, but the dinosaur genus is a fresh addition. The glowing text disappears.

The corporal barks at me, 'Keep moving.'

Outside, another corporal hands me a correct-sized uniform. Arms laden with fresh new clothes, boots, and beret, I join the female cadets in the adjacent change rooms. White hospital gowns are hastily discarded across the floor and everyone dresses like their lives depend on it. There's no time for modesty. One of the girls falls over, legs half in her pants.

It looked funny, but we don't have time to laugh.

I slip on my grey-green camo pants on, then a black singlet, followed by a dark-grey t-shirt over the top. I gather my hair back, tie it in a knot, and pull on my beret. Lacing up my chunky black boots takes the longest, but I speed through and chase the last few girls into the corridor.

Brigadier Ramsey stands between the change room exits, eyes on his watch.

'Ten seconds!' he bellows.

We march through the facility at a brisk pace. The long glass corridor overlooks multiple levels within the complex. Other glass corridors crisscross through the facility like tunnels in an ant nest, with hundreds of cadets heading off in different directions.

The corridor leads to a long platform, part of the tube and monorail system that connects the surrounding islands and facilities. A mag-lev train waits for us, doors open. We merge with another two groups of cadets and file onto the train in an orderly manner.

After 18 years in the academy, we all know how to assemble and move silently with minimal direction. Assembly after assembly, this regimented behaviour has been drilled into us since we were kids.

I end up beside the carriage-long window. The doors close and the train departs, slow at first, but within seconds we are travelling at a dizzying speed. I've lost sight of Tyson and Rosa and now surrounded by strangers. The tube goes dark for a moment, then natural light spills in through the windows.

Our train shoots out of the facility like a bullet and hurtles across the ocean towards the setting sun. The island shrinks behind us, if you could call it that. It's more building than island. The entire land mass is enclosed within a megalithic steel wall. A rocky coastline juts out from the base of the structure, the only clue there's a volcanic island hidden within. The impenetrable fortress keeps the dinosaurs safely locked away. Multiple mag-lev monorails run parallel to ours for a short distance, then fan out across the glistening water, heading for separate islands and barracks. The Union's network of monorails, dinosaur enclosures, training facilities, barracks, and buildings are constructed upon the *Ring of Fire*, an archipelago somewhere in Indonesia. As cadets in training, that's all we're told.

Those around me jostle for a peek out the window.

This is the only time we get to see the outside world, through the carriage windows. It's a precious glimpse of what we're fighting for – a world we've never experienced.

Another train momentarily catches up to ours and a carriage-load of cadets stare back at us. Some wave while others make humorous faces on the glass. I chuckle to myself. I don't have the confidence to be that silly, but I'm glad others do.

Our train veers left and zooms towards a shadowy island of towering peaks and sheer cliffs. Multi-layered barracks bloom from the steep verdant slopes, glistening like massive metallic mushrooms in the pink-peach sunset. This is our new home until we are sent off-world to fight.

Moments later, the train pulls into a station built deep within a cliff and we file outside to assemble on the platform in stifling humidity. A series of numbered gates lead to well-lit tunnels that burrow up into the island's interior.

The microchip in my forearm vibrates with an illuminated message beneath my skin: [ZAYLA-8311/SPINOSAURIDAE: REPORT TO GATE 1-A]

Everybody gets their message at the same time.

Most cadets are close to their designated gates. Brigadier Ramsey stands at gate 1-A with his data pad in hand, observing us with a discerning gaze. Once assembled, he leads our group of 50 or more cadets through the tunnel, beyond which, a combination of escalators, travelators, and bridges weave through the island's natural environment. We cross a deep ravine, walk behind a waterfall, and up through a lush jungle to emerge on the island's highest peak. The sun has now dipped below the horizon, leaving a violet sky blanketed with stars. At the end of the walkway stands our new barracks, lit up like a mini-city among the palm trees.

Ramsey marches towards the main doors. 'Move inside. Locate your dormitory and prepare your beds. Dinner in 30 minutes. Lights out at 21:30.'

Everyone hustles inside. Our forearm chips guide us to our correct dormitory and right up to our designated bed. A pile of neatly folded linen, one pillow, and bare mattress is all that awaits us. My name, birth number, and bonded dinosaur genus are displayed at the foot of my bed for all to see. I wish it wasn't.

I make my bed and inconspicuously glance about, searching for familiar faces. A few beds away, Tyson flaps his sheet in the air and it sails sideways, completely missing his mattress. I smile to myself and peer in the opposite direction to find Rosa, puffing up her pillow and placing it on a perfectly made bed. She was right all along – we ended up in the same group.

Avi enters the door at the far end of the dorm. *He made it!*

The tense knot in my chest loosens a little. Three people I like in the same dormitory as me, it's a miracle!

A voice hollers through my ears. 'I can't believe it!'

I spin around to find Reeva standing behind me, hands on her hips, face brimming with a dangerous smugness. My stomach does a somersault. I feel sick. Reeva reads the ID on the end of my bed and raises one eyebrow.

'I think they got your details wrong Zaz,' Reeva says loudly, looking about to make sure everyone's listening.

I dare not look, I feel everyone staring already.

Reeva pauses for maximum effect and continues. 'Shouldn't your ID read *spinelessaurus?*'

Laughs echo through the dorm. I'm too humiliated to move. My cheeks are burning with embarrassment, but there's something more fuelling my bright-red face...anger. I feel like punching

Reeva's perfect little nose. *If my spinosaurus were here, I'd show you who's spineless.* But no matter what I do now, the damage is done. Within the first minute of being here, I'm the laughingstock of my dormitory. Once that role is filled, it's impossible to shake. From now on, I'll be known as *spinelessaurus.*

Reeva strides off with a taunting wink. I want to grab her blond ponytail and wrestle her to the floor, but I can't. I'm not that brave. Maybe she is right, maybe I am spineless.

I spend the first dinner in my new barracks sitting by myself at the back of the mess hall. I'm not in the mood to talk to people and would rather be alone to avoid attention. From my seat, I can see where everyone is sitting. Despite their incessant banter, Tyson and Rosa join one another at the same table. I don't think they've seen me, otherwise they might have come over. I'm surprised to see Avi join Reeva's rowdy table. Deep down, I hoped he might sit with me.

After dinner, I strategically avoid bumping into anyone I know as we return to our dormitories. I just want to go to bed and process everything. I'm emotionally exhausted, and in desperate need of some personal downtime.

The lights turn off right on time at 21:30. Some cadets are asleep and snoring within minutes. *Lucky them.* Others chat across the beds in hushed voices, budding new relationships forming within the whispers and giggles. I insert my Union issued noise-cancelling earbuds and block out the sounds – one of the few personal perks we can receive upon request.

I wish I could fall asleep, but my mind is racing.

Tomorrow's schedule is split in two. For the first half of the day, I have theory and history classes on this island, then in the afternoon, we will all be transported back to the enclosures and reunited with our dinosaurs. My heart palpitates just thinking about it. What will our first session entail? I close my eyes and try envisioning us training together. All I see is that huge spine sailing across the lake, his gargantuan body, those cunning, luminous green eyes, and that long crocodilian snout filled with teeth.

My bed feels like its vibrating. I open my eyes and realise it's my pounding heart, thumping through my body like a tribal drum. I'm having a panic attack!

I close my eyes and force my thoughts to slow down, keen to get a grip before I embarrass myself. I slow my breathing and my pulse stubbornly follows.

A familiar, comforting light spills in from the doorway at the end of the dormitory. A corporal stands guard, watching over us like well cared-for children. His presence settles my anxiety, and slowly, my mind wanders off to sleep.

I awake the next morning after a deep, sound sleep, and enjoy a rare moment of silence. By some miracle, I was spared my persistent nightmare. For as long as I can remember, my dreams have been haunted by the death of my parents on Daxma-5. I'm right there with them as the Wraith attack, swarming over the base, taking down our escape shuttle, holding my mother's hand right up until the moment we slide off a collapsing landing pad into the glowing jaws of a Wraith-possessed titanoid. The images usually have me waking in a sweat and gasping for air; the last thing I need in my new dormitory.

Just laying here thinking about it makes me anxious.

I know it's only a dream, but it feels so real, as if I'm reliving our final, tragic moments as a family. Thing is, it's impossible. I was cloned from my parent's DNA backups long after they left Earth to terraform Daxma-5, just like every other cadet in the academy. There's no way I was with my parents when they died, which makes my dream so unusual.

I've only told one person about my nightmare, but he's dead.

After breakfast, we gather in the outside quadrangle with cadets from all over the island for our first assembly. We dutifully line up in straight rows and face the podium. A lush jungle embraces the spacious area, with the island's main peak looming in the background. The morning air is alive with a buzz of insects and exotic bird calls.

I stand to attention, chin up, head facing straight ahead. But my eyes wander.

Brigadier Ramsey watches us from the sidelines and chats with Union officials. They walk together in a group and occasionally stop to observe cadets in the lineups, typing into their handheld data pads.

I'm curious. *What are they talking about?*

Earth's international anthem blares through the quadrangle. To me, the Union-commissioned piece of music sounds more akin to a self-indulgent fanfare than an anthem for humanity. The bombastic horns and drums come to a finish and a life-sized hologram of Galen Thoms, the leader of the Union, materialises centre stage. From my distance, he looks real, except for the odd digital glitch. His grey hair and wrinkled features are a rare sight in the academy, as we hardly ever see anyone over the age of 50.

'Good morning, cadets,' Galen says brightly. 'I wish I could greet you in person, but with thousands of you spread across an entire archipelago, I cannot be everywhere at once.'

Galen sounds sincere. As a leader, we all believe in him, even though he never visits us in person. There is always an excuse, which makes me think he might be an AI simulation, programmed to say whatever the Union wants us to hear.

'I hope you're all settling well into your new barracks. Congratulations on graduating to the academy's highest level. Every one of you has been here since birth. Your first lessons started at three years old, and now, 15 years on, you're ready for the tests ahead. I know you will approach these new challenges with the same vigour and enthusiasm you've shown so far.

'I understand many of you lost friends yesterday. But take comfort in knowing their sacrifices were not in vain. Like you, they swore to protect the future of humanity, whatever the cost. Our enemy, the Wraith, hides in plain sight, ready to strike at any time. We are better prepared than ever before, and with your service, we will retaliate for the first time. This offensive will ensure the safety of the generations to come. Your children will be the first to live freely among the universe, without the Wraith threat.

'Like you, I share the pain of losing those close to you. My family perished on Daxma-5 alongside thousands of colonists, all of whom were your biological parents. But since then, I have built a new circle of friends. And family. I count each of you among them. Going forward, you will do the same. Create new friendships, rise to your challenges, and grow from your losses. This war cannot be fought alone. We will stand together and face our enemy with unwavering courage and resolve.'

The quadrangle vibrates with furious applause.

I join in, a little less fervently than everyone else. I believe in the Union, but I'm not a die-hard fanatic. Most cadets are. But true to form, I'm the odd one out.

'But don't just take it from me,' Galen says. 'Here are some messages from the families and people you're training to protect.'

A massive screen projects onto the open space behind Galen. A youthful family of four appears: a mother, father and two infants. 'Thank you, cadets,' the mother says in a sweet, endearing tone. 'Without you, we wouldn't feel safe. Your efforts have given us hope for the future.'

The image cuts to a male construction engineer on an off-world base. He lifts the welding visor off his face and looks at us, eyes alight with hope. 'We've started rebuilding, confident you will protect us when the time comes.'

Next up, a lady farmer walks through a field filled with wheat. 'Years ago, we saved our planet from a climate catastrophe. Since then, Earth's resources have never been healthier. But the Wraith place all this in jeopardy. Earth will never be safe. Not without your protection.'

The screen then fills with a chequerboard of compassionate and encouraging faces. The overlapping voices acknowledge and thank us for our service. New faces replace the old, adding to the chorus of gratitude.

My chest swells with warmth. These strangers are the reason we fight, and when this war is over, every cadet can be a part of that world and have a real family one day.

The collage of faces fades, leaving Galen's hologram in the centre of the stage. He gazes upon us as a father would his children, and salutes us.

Several hundred cadets snap their boot heels together in unison. The harsh noise reverberates through the quadrangle as we salute him back.

Galen holds his salute as his hologram dematerialises. His proud face breaks down into a million bits of data and floats away like grains of sand in a breeze.

Brigadier Ramsey takes to the stage, surrounded by a throng of corporals and officials. A microphone ball ejects from the stage floor and hovers in front of him.

'Good morning, cadets.' Ramsey's stern booming voice is a stark contrast to Galen's paternal tone. 'New classes begin today. Weekly timetables, directions to classrooms, and all necessary information is available at the data hubs, accessible via your subcutaneous ID implants. Only contact an official if your problem can't be resolved via the hub. Before we move onto today's curriculum, I would like to bring attention to two cadets who stood out during the Bonding. If your ID chip flashes, please join me on the stage.'

Everybody checks their forearm and looks around. I peer over the sea of heads, anxious to see who's been summoned. Somebody to my right, a couple of rows ahead, walks towards the stage. I can't see his face, just the blond hair beneath his grey cap. The cadet next to me gives me an odd look. *What's wrong with her?*

'You need to go up to the stage,' the girl whispers.

'Huh?'

She eyeballs my forearm. 'Your ID chip is flashing.'

At first, I think she's joking and glance over my shoulder to find Reeva, convinced she put the girl up to it. Reeva would do anything to make a fool of me, but she's nowhere to be seen. I check my forearm and do a double-take. It's flashing!

I feel the blood drain from my face. I must look as pale as a sheet. My heart stops for an extended pause, then hammers into action as a tsunami of adrenalin rages through my body. I'm suddenly light-headed and nauseas. *Don't pass out in front of the assembly!*

The girl reaches towards me. 'Are you okay?'

'I'm fine,' I say sharply.

Standing on stage in front of everyone represents one of my worst fears, but fainting into the arms of a cadet in front of the entire assembly is far worse. That kind of humiliation would never be forgotten.

I head for the stage as if I'm walking on air. Staring blindly across the sea of curious faces, I see none in particular. As I approach the left side of the stage the other cadet reaches the right. He ascends the steps with a limp, face down, as I hustle up and stand beside Brigadier Ramsey, anxious to get this over with. The mysterious cadet reaches the top step and looks up.

Goosebumps race up my arms. I never thought I'd see that face again.

It's Kane from Epsilon Barracks, the cadet I met on the first day of the Bonding. He saved me from a pack of megaraptors and showed me a safe path to the final zone where I bonded with my spinosaurus. He should be dead. His face bears three purple scars that stretch diagonally across his forehead, over the bridge of his nose, cheeks, and chin, to finally wrap around his neck. They are partially healed and most likely midway through a treatment of dermal rejuvenation.

Kane winks at me as if to say, *I'm all right*.

The pressure of standing in front of all these people instantly vanishes. I'm so relieved to see him alive and on the mend. It makes everything else seem less important, even standing up here. *Well, almost*.

Kane hobbles over and stands on the other side of the Brigadier.

Ramsey addresses the assembly. 'These two cadets have shown extreme courage in the face of adversity. Both stared into the cold face of death and live to fight another day. Their bravery has been awarded with the most lethal dinosaurs in the academy. Kane bonded with a pack of megaraptors, and Zayla with a spinosaurus. The very creatures that tried to kill them now work alongside them, and they are stronger for the experience. I know all of you shared similar experiences, some easier than others. But I want you to remember, even when things seem like they can't get worse, there is hope. Kane and Zayla stand before you, proof you can achieve anything.'

The cadets shower us with applause, not as enthusiastically as they did for Galen, but enough to bring my goosebumps back. This is the first time I have been called out for an achievement in academy assembly. It feels good, in a nerve-wracking way. I take in the admiring faces and relax a little. Eventually, my eyes are drawn to the only cadet not applauding – Reeva.

My stomach twists into a knot. *Trust her to spoil the moment.*

The applause subsides and Ramsey continues his speech. I'm too preoccupied to listen as I try avoiding looking in Reeva's direction. Now all I want to do is get off the stage. Ramsey finally finishes and I return to my line. I look for Kane, but he's lost in the rows of grey uniforms and berets. The assembly ends and everyone heads to the circular data hubs for their timetables.

I push through the crowd, keen to avoid any attention. Part of me wants to find Kane, but I'm actively trying to dodge Reeva. Cadets pull me up to congratulate me but I nod and hurry off without saying anything, shoulders stooped as if I might shrink out of sight.

I find one of the quieter data hubs and access my lessons for the day.

I spend the next half hour familiarising myself with the island's complex of classrooms, tutorial halls, and general facilities, trying not to get lost. Everyone seems to know where they're going except me. We all hustle along a never-ending maze of glass corridors, sky-high escalators, and elevated walkways that dissect the lush, picturesque island.

A last-minute dash delivers me to my first classroom on time and I join the line of cadets shuffling inside. The left side of the room is dominated by a wall of floor-to-ceiling windows overlooking the ocean. Natural light bounces off the shiny steel architecture, creating a bright, airy space filled with rows of cadet workstations. The back few rows are already taken, forcing me to move midway into the room to find an empty desk. I prefer the back row – it draws the least attention.

I take a seat and rest my forearm on the desktop, allowing the scanner to read my ID chip. It beeps, and a holographic workspace appears in front of me. I'm ready for my first lesson.

A stern-looking Japanese man in a grey uniform enters the classroom from a side door as the last few students scurry to their desks. He places his data tablet on the lectern and stands before us, arms behind his back, rigid as stone. Once there is silence, he strides down the centre of the classroom.

'Welcome, cadets,' he says in a commanding voice. 'My name is Suda Satoshi. I am your lecturer for this semester. Let's begin with a recap. I want to see how well you know your history. Who can tell me about the origins of the Union?'

An eager cadet to my right presses the answer button on her workspace. Her name appears in bright green holographic text and slides up to hover over her display.

Suda raises a hand to acknowledge her.

'The Union was founded 200 years ago by the U-Genix Corporation.'

Suda gives a firm nod. 'Yes, and what made U-Genix so unique?'

'The U-Genix Corporation became a global phenomenon after resurrecting extinct animals. They started with the western black rhino in Africa in 2031, then resurrected lions, gorillas, and other modern-day species. They built protected habitats for the animals, then moved onto older species, like the woolly mammoth and saber-toothed tiger. Theme parks were built to observe the animals in their natural environment. U-Genix invested the money made from their attractions into a global wildlife program.'

'Correct. And where were the first complete dinosaur DNA strands found?' Suda asks, looking about the room. 'Someone else?'

Several answer holograms flash.

Suda picks a male cadet near the front of the class to answer.

'Antarctica. The ice was melting at an unprecedented rate. Hundreds of dinosaur species were found in the melt. They were the best-preserved specimens ever discovered. U-Genix resurrected two dinosaurs, a male and female coelophysis, nicknamed Adam and Eve.'

'That's right, and how did Adam and Eve change the world?' Suda says, motioning to another male cadet for the answer.

'They inspired U-Genix to build the first dinosaur theme park. It made them trillions of dollars. They built parks on every continent, resurrecting and adding more species every year.'

'And how did U-Genix invest that wealth?'

'They enforced a worldwide program to eliminate pollution, waste, and avoid a total climate collapse. They replanted forests, cleaned up the oceans, and designed a plastic-eating algae that rescued us from drowning in our waste. Within ten years, the global temperature had reduced by several degrees. The oceans receded and the glaciers returned. U-Genix succeeded where governments had failed.'

Suda walks between the desks, listening and nodding. He walks straight up to my desk and locks his gaze on me. 'How did the world respond?'

Butterflies flutter through my chest. *Is he asking me the question?* I didn't press my answer button but others around me did.

Suda motions to the auburn-haired cadet sitting next to me for the answer. I sigh with relief and read her name before it disappears: [ABBY-2758/STEGOSAURUS].

She gives me a friendly, sidelong smile that breaks up the light-brown freckles sprinkled across her face. Abby gives Suda her full attention and answers. 'People had more faith in U-Genix than their own governments. Many of the once-great nations were overridden by poverty and crime. U-Genix introduced housing and community plans to take people off the streets. They gave them jobs, working for the betterment of the world around them rather than for themselves.'

'Correct, and when did the last independent government cede?

'China, in the year 2115.'

'That's right. And in the 200 years since then, U-Genix has reversed what international leaders claimed was irreversible. Climate change. By that point in history, independent governments and states had become relics of an old, outdated model. U-Genix dismantled all weapons of war and recycled those resources into the future of humanity. Someone give me examples of how.'

'We used the steel and technology to build our first base on the Moon,' answers a female cadet from somewhere behind me. 'It became a manufacturing facility for our interstellar fleet.'

'What else?'

'U-Genix built the first warp drive and sent a team of deep space colonists on a one-way mission to find habitable new worlds. One hundred years later, we colonised our first Earth-like planet.'

'And how many worlds beyond our solar system have we colonised since then?'

Multiple holograms light up around me and bathe my desk in green light. Now I feel like the only cadet who hasn't answered a question.

'Fifty-six habitable worlds,' the cadet in front of me responds. 'Four contain atmosphere and gravity equivalent to Earth.'

His answer brings Suda close to my desk. *Oh great!* I think, subtly shaking my head. *Don't bring him back over here.*

'That's right. But everything the Union has achieved is under threat from the Wraith, an energy-based species indigenous to Daxma-5. Our advanced technology is useless against them. That is why we have turned to creatures from our past to save our future.' Without warning, Suda turns his attention to me. 'Zayla, tell me about your dinosaur.'

What? I didn't even press my answer button. I swallow the dry lump in my throat, mortified. If I don't respond, I'm going to be even more humiliated.

'My spinosaurus is a theropod from the spinosauridae family of dinosaurs. The first known remains were found in Egypt in 1912, over 400 years ago. A complete DNA sample was first discovered in the Antarctica melt of 2047. Successful resurrection took place 15 years later –'

'That's correct, Zayla, but I don't want a fact check. Tell me about your dinosaur. What makes your spinosaurus so unique?'

'It's the largest carnivore that ever lived. It can hunt in water just as well as it does on land.'

'No, you're telling me facts we all know. I want you to tell me what sets your dinosaur apart from every other prehistoric animal roaming these islands.'

I stare blankly at him, unable to think of another thing to add. I'm getting hot and uncomfortable.

'You!' Suda exclaims, pointing his finger at me. 'You are what makes your dinosaur unique. Your neural implants enable you to telepathically bond, elevating that primal dinosaur brain to give it purpose.' Suda leaves returns to the front of the classroom. 'The same applies to every cadet in this room. Your dinosaurs are your weapons. They are your lifeline, and humanity's salvation.'

I stare straight ahead, but I can feel a lot of cadets watching me, assessing me. That's twice I've been singled out this morning. I'm a magnet for attention.

One cadet won't stop staring – the girl to my immediate right, Abby. Her blatant gaze is difficult to ignore, so I glance over and she gives me a broad, toothy smile. *What the hell does she want?* I'm not sure how to respond. Is she being genuinely friendly or smarmy? I wouldn't know, since making friends has never been my strong suit. Maybe I should smile back. I take too long to respond and Abby faces the front of the class, no doubt perplexed by my stonewall expression. *Great! I can make someone feel as uncomfortable as me.*

I spend the rest of the lesson wondering if I missed an opportunity to make a friend. It would be nice to have one person in class to talk to.

4

There is a palpable air of excitement in the mess hall at lunch. Everyone is talking about our upcoming dinosaur sessions this afternoon. Reeva and Avi's friendship groups have congregated to create the largest, noisiest table. I'm not surprised. Being some of the most popular cadets in the barracks, their friends were destined to gravitate towards one another. Avi glances my way several times, but I look away and pretend not to notice. If not for the influence of his friends, I get the feeling he might sit with me instead. Smaller friendship groups are scattered across the remaining tables, leaving gaps here and there.

I'm the only one sitting alone. *No surprise there.* But that's more by choice than circumstance. Any normal cadet would attempt to make new friends in a new barracks. Unfortunately, I'm not a normal cadet.

I toy with my food, too nervous to eat. Eighteen years in the academy has been building to this day–the first one-on-one session with our dinosaurs. It's a chance to enhance the telepathic link we established in the Bonding and forge permanent neural pathways – or, in simpler terms, build trust with our prehistoric partners. They are our weapons in this war. At least that's how the Union perceives them.

But for me, they represent much more than that, I consider them our pets. My pet just happens to be the most lethal carnivore in the academy. I still can't believe I'm the only cadet to bond with a spinosaurus.

I look about, hoping to find Kane. I haven't had a chance to talk with him since the assembly. It's my fault the megaraptors tore him to shreds him during the Bonding. At the very least, I owe him an apology.

Abby, the girl who sat next to me in class, takes a seat at on the opposite side of the hall, alone. She hasn't seen me. Her lonesome figure is a mirror image of my solitary self. Part of me wants to walk over there, sit next to her, and apologise for ignoring her in class. I wish I was confident enough to enact my good intentions. I'm not looking for a best friend, but I don't want to be a loner forever. I sigh. It makes me tired just thinking about it. *Socialising shouldn't be this complicated.*

Brigadier Ramsey strides into the mess hall, a trail of corporals and officers close behind. 'Trains leave in 30 minutes. Check your implants for your departure platform.'

Seconds later, my forearm vibrates with the message: [PLATFORM 1]

Too soon it's time to go. I force down a couple of mouthfuls, certain I'll need the energy later. At times like this, it feels as though the Union are herding us around like livestock. The lively chatter recedes as people shovel down their last few mouthfuls and hand in their trays, cheeks bulging with food as they scramble for the exit.

My stomach churns just thinking about the day ahead. *What am I supposed to do with a fully-grown spinosaurus? How do I build a relationship with a 20-tonne killing machine?* It's not like we can just sit down, talk, and get to know each other. I'm so preoccupied with concern, I don't recall walking from the mess hall to the mag-lev station. I push through the crowds and take the escalator down to my platform. It's a lot quieter on the lower platforms, with only a handful of cadets waiting to board the train. I don't recognise any of them.

'I'm shocked!' The voice makes me spin around to find Reeva coming up behind me, smirking. 'You didn't get a special departure platform all to yourself?'

Her comments draw the attention of the surrounding cadets. I bottle up. No witty comebacks from me. Reeva has caught me off-guard yet again.

'Just kidding, Zaz. You know, the only reason they chose you to go on stage was because of your spinosaurus. How did you bond with it anyway? Must've been by accident.'

I'm about to return the insult when Avi jogs up behind her, bristling with enthusiasm. 'How exciting is this? First session with our dinos. Hey, Zaz, incredible job on the spino.'

'Thanks' I say, relieved.

'I was going after a spinosaurus too. Apparently, there weren't many ready for the Bonding, so you got one of the rare predators.'

I nod, feeling the heat of embarrassment rush into my face. I don't deserve the praise. Skill had nothing to do with my bonding, which was random and unplanned, but I'm not about to tell Avi that. I should draw his attention off me before my face turns bright-red. 'What did you bond with?'

'An allosaurus. He wasn't my first pick, but I got caught in a bond-or-die situation. He's nowhere near as big as yours, but he's smart and fast.'

'I look forward to seeing him.'

'How do you feel about your first session?'

'Nervous.'

'Nervous!' Reeva repeats so everyone can hear. 'The hardest part's over. You survived the Bonding. What's there to be nervous about?'

'Everything. We've never done anything like this before. I just hope he likes me.'

'That's irrelevant. You don't need to be best friends with it. Just tell it what to do and it will obey your orders. It's a weapon, not a pet.'

Funny, I was just thinking the opposite. That's why Reeva and I will never get along. We see the treatment of these animals from different perspectives.

'Our dinos might never be as loyal as a dog,' Avi says. 'Their minds are too basic for that.'

'Exactly,' Reeva adds.

'But I see Zaz's point. We should be kind and treat them with respect. Our neural implants are more than just a tool to give orders – the way we interact with our dinosaurs is what will imprint most on their memories. That's the best way to train them.'

Reeva dismisses Avi with a disinterested shrug and returns to her group, where she can dominate the conversation. Having Avi agree with me represents a minor victory.

A driverless mag-lev train glides to a stop alongside our platform. It's only two carriages long compared to the 20-carriage train that brought us here yesterday. I count roughly 30 cadets on our platform, all of whom represent the commanders in a training division. It's a small number compared to the infantry divisions that comprise the bulk of our forces. They must be spread across multiple platforms, heading to different destinations. I don't see any stealth cadets either, who account for low numbers, like the command division.

We board the train. Seconds later, we hurtle away from the island across a vibrant cerulean ocean. The white sandy beaches, coral atolls, and crystal-clear waters of the archipelago look so inviting. It's unfair. Why can't the Union give us one day of freedom in the outside world before we deploy for war?

Considering our sacrifices, we should be allowed that one privilege.

Our train passes through a cluster of smaller islands. Towering steel walls overshadow their coastlines to keep the dinosaurs locked inside. Several monorails divert to these islands, but my train travels further out to sea. Soon after, our carriage falls into the shadow of the largest island in the archipelago, the volcanic island I was on yesterday for the Bonding.

I secretly rub my clammy hands on my pants. Strange. I feel more nervous now than I did before bonding with my spinosaurus.

Our train rockets towards the island shore at breakneck speed. To the uninitiated, it looks like we're about to plough straight into the rugged cliffs. I remember the first time I visited this island. I closed my eyes in terror, convinced we were going to crash.

We pull into the subterranean station and come to a gentle stop. Five stern-faced Union officers wait for us on the platform, data pads in hand. Their storm-grey uniforms impart an ominous feeling today. As we exit the train, they call our names and divide us into groups of six, with Avi and Reeva both separating from me.

My instructor introduces herself. 'I'm Officer Nadja Schulze. I've been personally assigned to each of you as your instructor, guide, and assessor. Every time you arrive on this island, you report to me. Understood, cadets?'

We all salute and respond in unison. 'Yes, ma'am.'

I recognise Nadja's subtle German accent. Union officers are represented by all races and nationalities. Independent countries and governments were dissolved and merged into the Union years ago, but cultural differences from their home countries persist.

Nadja leads my group through a labyrinth of gleaming metal corridors and escalators.

'Your first session establishes a behavioural baseline with your dinosaur,' Nadja says. 'This test measures the strength of your neural connection and scales it accordingly.'

The male cadet ahead of me speaks up. 'How do we do that?'

'Each of you is zoned into small, isolated areas of the island. We have not fed your dinosaurs for the last 24 hours. They are hungry and irritated. Live prey will be introduced into your zone and it's up to you to manage your weapon: tell it when to feed and when to wait. You will receive feeding instructions via a communication bracelet.'

I wish they wouldn't call them weapons. Even though dinosaurs are genetically bred, they are living creatures. We should treat them with same respect and compassion as a nonextinct species. The fact they died out shouldn't make them less worthy.

We walk along a long, gently curving passage. Long windows on the left side offer a view into the island's jungle habitat. Nadja stops in front of a steel door reinforced with chunky magnetic locks. 'Does anyone have any questions?'

Yeah, about a million! I feel like replying. But I don't want to be the only one asking questions, so I keep my mouth shut. My companions look anxious, probably thinking the same as me.

'Good,' Nadja says. 'You have spent your academy lives preparing for this moment. You know how the neural implants work. Just remember, even at this tenuous beginning, you are in control of your weapon. It will only attack to feed if you command it to do so. Control your thoughts. Don't let them control you.'

Oh great! I wish she hadn't told us that. I have enough problems controlling my anxieties.

Nadja checks her data pad. 'First up, I have Zayla-8311, assigned to a level one apex predator, spinosaurus. This is your enclosure. You've been allocated a one square kilometre pen, the largest of your group.'

A small compartment beside the door slides open and an electronic wrist bracer ejects from the hole. Nadja locks it around my left wrist and the tiny screen illuminates with my personal details. 'Further instructions will appear on the bracer.'

The door's magnetic locks release with a loud *clunk*, making me jump. The metre-thick steel door opens inwards, unleashing a gust of humid air into our air-conditioned passage. A lush green rainforest awaits me on the other side; beyond that, the caldera of an extinct volcano rises into the hazy atmosphere, encircled by immense metal walls and dome. My insides run cold, like someone spilt a tub of ice down my top. *I'm not ready for this.*

Nadja watches me with an expectant gaze, eager to move on.

I swallow the lump in my throat and step over the threshold.

The door seals shut behind me, isolating me from the high-tech structure within the prehistoric biome. My heart hammers. This area looks bigger than one square kilometre. I can't see any perimeter walls or fences through the trees, and check my bracer for instructions. Nothing. The screen is blank.

What do I do now?

Distant roars resonate along the enclosure walls. Birds scatter overhead, nothing prehistoric. I edge towards some waist-high ferns and peer into the misty rainforest. The trickle of running water leads me to a stream, snaking down through the landscape from the volcano. I follow the water upstream. It's tough going. I jump from one side of the stream to the other, avoiding the massive roots strangling the bank.

I don't know where I'm going, but feel safer on the move. I clamber over a clump of roots and jump to the opposite bank. The ground rumbles as I land, as if my feet bore the weight of a dreadnoughtus. *That wasn't me.*

I freeze in position, poised, ready to run. The treetops upstream swish and thrash about. *That's not the wind.* Leaves fall around me like confetti.

CRUNCH... CRACK... THUMP... THUMP...

A massive webbed foot emerges from the mist and stomps on the stream.

THUMP!

The foot blocks the water flow as four gleaming black claws pierce the hard stony riverbank like it was soft sand. A second foot appears from the shadows, uprooting a small tree as it rises and then stomps down in the area beside the stream.

THUMP!

Every muscle in my body tenses, immobilising me with fear. I couldn't run if I wanted to. I can't even breathe.

An impossibly long snout breaks through the treetops and descends towards me. Large conical teeth protrude from the tip of the snout, followed by smaller teeth, leading back along its jaws like a gigantic crocodile.

My petrified stare meets a pair of luminous jade eyes with narrow black pupils. It's my spinosaurus.

We gaze at each other in silence, tenuously linked by our neural implants. Time draws to a stop as I behold the mountain of muscle and teeth, awed by his gargantuan physique. His leathery underbelly bears a shade of light-grey, changing to blue-grey up his sides. His snout bears a darker navy stripe that emphasises his piercing eyes. The navy stripe continues down his neck and along his length, all the way to the end of his tail. A majestic sail covers the rigid dorsal spines rising from his back. The vertical sail is striped with shades of blue and grey that taper off to a bluish purple near the top. *He's beautiful!*

My lungs finally protest and inhale a huge gulp of air.

The spinosaurus does the same. His cavernous throat opens like a wind tunnel and sucks my hair forward.

I teeter in place, convinced I'm about to be sucked inside. The diverted stream is now rushing over my ankles, getting stronger by the second as my boots fill with water. I slowly rise, so as not to alarm my spinosaurus, and step out of the torrent.

The spinosaurus observes me with curiosity, then removes his foot from the stream and places it on the opposite bank. The stream resumes its normal course as he stands astride, watching me, one foot on each bank.

My lips curl up in a smile. *Are you copying me, Spino? Spino... I like that.* His nickname just popped into my head, makes him feel less imposing.

I dip my right boot into the water and look up. *Okay, can you do that?*

Spino places his right foot in the stream, holds for a second, then returns to his original stance.

I nod. *So far, so good.*

'Let's try that again, but faster.'

This time, I stomp my boot in the water and create a small splash.

Spino raises his foot and stomps down in the middle of the stream. *Bad idea!* A wall of water drenches me from head to toe and knocks me back a few steps. I laugh, more out of relief than amusement.

Spino assesses me with bright, intelligent eyes, cocks his head, and makes an odd barking noise. *Is that a laugh?*

Surely not. Dinosaurs don't laugh. He must be mimicking me. I wipe the water off my face and pick up a nearby branch. 'All right, let's see if you can fetch this.'

I hurl the branch onto the bank beside him.

Spino tilts his head towards the stick, scrutinises it, and hesitantly sniffs the air.

'That's it. Pick it up and throw it back.'

Spino looks at me, then back to the stick. He seems confused.

'Go on!'

He suddenly lunges forward and scoops up a toppled tree. *Oh no! I didn't think this through.* The stick was too small for him to pick up. Spino rises to full height with the tree between his jaws, ripping through the rainforest. He swings his head and releases the tree in my direction. I dive to the bank as the tree lands beside me in an explosion of leaves and branches.

The debris settle and I gingerly pick myself up.

Spino looks down at me, eyes twinkling. I think he enjoyed that. He appears to have a playful nature. His size and markings are equivalent to an adolescent spinosaurus, which means he's a teenager, possibly the same age as me.

Spino's attention is suddenly drawn to the tree trunk he just threw.

A tiny compsognathus stands on the trunk, head raised, tail down. The scrawny theropod screeches at Spino. It sounds agitated. I'm not surprised – the flying tree must have obliterated its habitat.

Spino sucks in a lungful of air, leans forward, and roars back.

I cover my ears. The thunderous roar vibrates through my body like an explosion, minus the heat and destruction, and creates ripples in the stream. The compy digs its claws into the bark and rides out the hurricane-strength roar.

After what seems like an eternity, Spino finishes and raises his head with pride.

The determined compy raises its head and screeches back.

What's he trying to prove? I wonder. There is no competition between these two dinosaurs.

Another compy jumps onto the trunk and they screech in unison. Several more follow and join in the shrill chorus. They're not interested in me yet, but remain defiant in the face of such an overwhelming foe. I've never seen anything like it. The compys suddenly leap over one another towards Spino. His eyes widen and he steps backwards, stumbling through the undergrowth.

What's going on? Is he scared?

The diminutive theropods, no more than a foot tall, continue their march forward, screeching and squawking like hatchlings. Spino takes another frightened step back.

I can't believe it. He's terrified of compys!

Of all the dinosaurs to bond with, I end up with the neurotic one.

My chest suddenly tightens and my heart rate increases. I can barely breathe. I'm not scared, but have all the symptoms of a panic attack. Then it hits me – I'm experiencing what Spino's feeling. I'm not scared of the critters in the slightest. The pesky scavengers are just plain annoying. I pick up a stick and charge the pack. 'Argh!'

I knock three off the trunk with a single swing and they go flying into the jungle, writhing about like snakes. 'Hah! Didn't expect that, did you?'

Whoop! I swing again and two more go flying.

The remaining compys scatter and leap about, screeching at me. Now I'm the threat. One leaps onto my chest but I swipe it off and stomp on its tail. The creature shrieks and scurries into the ferns, taking its friends with it.

I face my cowering carnivore. Spino stands with one leg askew, ready to sprint away from danger. I gingerly approach, hands raised to settle him. 'It's all right, they're gone.'

Spino makes a whimpering sound. Those big green eyes look afraid.

A horrible thought enters my mind. Reeva might have been right after all! Did I bond with the world's first *spinelessaurus*? That's impossible. The spinosaurus is the most fearsome carnivore that ever lived.

Or so I thought.

My wrist bracer vibrates and a message scrolls across the screen:
[FEEDING EXERCISE INITIATED: DESIGNATED MEAL-SAUROPOD/STATUS LIVE]
Great. Our first session is a simple feeding exercise. I've fed
hundreds of dinosaurs in the academy, from carnivores to
herbivores. The big difference now is the live prey. Carnivore
feeding sessions always took place with prepared meat. I've never
killed anything in my life, let alone instructed another living thing
to kill. I'm not sure how this is going to go down.

I look up at my skittish spinosaurus. 'You hungry?'

Spino grunts and shuffles his legs into a balanced, less awkward
stance. His greatest fear, the shrieking compys, have fled into the
jungle. At least I hope that's the only thing he's afraid of. I can't go
to war with a nervous dinosaur.

Somehow, I need to make him feel safe in my presence. If I can
get close enough to touch him, it might help strengthen our bond
and give him some comfort. I tread lightly, mindful not to spook
him as I draw near. My head is almost level with the knee of his
hind leg as I reach up and gently place my hand on his rock-hard
quadriceps. His warm, leathery skin is softer than I thought. Spino
swings his head about and positions his nostrils level with my face.
Six feet behind the tip of his snout, those jittery green eyes observe
me as I rub his leg, nostrils twitching as he sniffs me.

'What should I call you?'

Spino sniffs me again. His narrowed eyelids relax and open wider. I think he likes the sound of my voice.

'It's time we gave you a name. I've been calling you *Spino* in my head. I know it's not that inventive, but it feels right. What do you think?'

Spino parts his toothy snout and makes a deep rattling sound, similar to the way cat purrs.

I rub his snout. 'Oh, okay, sounds like you agree.'

He widens his jaws and bellows, rolling his pink tongue along the roof of his mouth. His tongue is twice the length of my bed and just as wide. The corners of his mouth glisten with saliva.

'Hungry, huh? Let's go sauropod hunting. You lead the way.'

I follow the path of flattened ferns and bushes left in his wake. For such large feet, Spino navigates the undergrowth with surprising agility. He reaches a tight clump of trees and somehow squeezes his girth between the trunks. He stops, raises his head over the leafy canopy, and sniffs the air. Strange. He hasn't seen a brontosaurus or dreadnoughtus yet, their necks should be easily visible in our one-kilometre zone. Spino cranes his head around, nostrils chasing a scent, then suddenly stomps off.

I race after him. Spino cuts a V-shaped swathe through the foliage as he powers ahead, stomping on small shrubs and saplings, creating a path for me to follow.

We come to a glade and find a juvenile diplodocus, no more than a couple of months old, writhing on the ground like it fell over and can't get up. The poor defenceless creature has its rear legs chained to a metal stake. *What the hell?* It squeals at Spino like a terrified infant, those big brown baby eyes filled with dread.

My wrist bracer lights up with a message: [INSTRUCT WEAPON TO KILL TARGET]

Spino opens his deadly maw and lowers his head, salivating over the easy prey.

'No, Spino!' I yell without thinking.

Spino stops, swings his head around to face me, and gives me a warning growl.

What am I doing? I shouldn't be stopping him. My objective is simple:

lead Spino to his meal and tell him to eat. I didn't realise killing a defenceless diplodocus was part of the plan. Spino wouldn't hesitate in the wild, but he also wouldn't hunt a juvenile. He'd be chasing bigger game. There's not even enough meat on this baby diplo for one meal. There must be a larger diplodocus nearby and this juvenile is the bait.

[INSTRUCT WEAPON TO KILL TARGET] flashes again.

No way! This isn't right. Spino snorts and sniff the infant, struggling to suppress his carnivore instincts as he waits for my permission.

I glance up at the enclosure walls. *Where are those faceless Union workers watching us from?* This is wrong. It's not a proper test. If we were facing a fully-grown diplo or any other mature-age dinosaur, I could accept that. But this goes against every fibre of my being.

'It's just a baby,' I cry out, not expecting a reply.

Spino roars at me. *Are you protesting my hesitation or copying me?*

I check my bracer, hoping, wishing, for a revised instruction. Am I really going to deny Spino his meal? Doing so could negatively affect our relationship and he might not trust me next time. My bracer vibrates. [INSTRUCT WEAPON TO KILL TARGET]

The baby diplo looks at me with those pleading eyes. I'm torn. *I can't do it.*

My bracer emits a high-pitched tone and a new message: [LESSON FAILED – RETURN TO EXIT]

'Wait!' I yell at the walls. 'Send us something bigger. Spino hasn't eaten yet.'

Too late. A swarm of herding drones swoop in through the treetops and surround Spino. They mercilessly zap him with electric shocks and force him away, denying me the chance to connect with him one last time.

I reluctantly leave the whining diplo and follow the stream back to the boundary wall. The exit hatch swings open and Brigadier Ramsey stands waiting on the other side. He barely acknowledges me as he waves me inside, head buried in his data pad.

This isn't good.

I enter the passage and stand to attention. The door seals shut behind me, muting the rainforest. It's dead quiet. Too quiet.

Ramsey speaks without looking up. 'Zayla–8311, you disobeyed a direct order to feed your spinosaurus. Explain.'

'I don't see how it was fair, sir?'

'Fair? Why should it be fair? There's no such thing as fair in war.'

I'm about to fire back in frustration, but common sense prevails, and I bite my tongue. I must remember my place. I'm speaking to a Union Brigadier.

'What?' Ramsey says, finally shifting his eyes to me. 'You were about to say something.'

'I'd rather not, sir.'

'You have permission to speak freely.'

His offer takes me by surprise. Union personnel are not usually this open, especially commanding officers. 'What does spoon-feeding my spinosaurus a baby diplo have to do with war? There was no fight. No competition. There was barely enough meat on the infant to whet Spino's appetite. There must have been a mistake.'

'There was no mistake, cadet.'

'Then I don't see the point, sir. I thought this lesson established a bonding baseline, to measure my relationship with Spino.'

'And it has. Your performance in the Bonding proved you have the skills and survival instincts for war. Pair those strengths with the largest carnivore in our inventory, and you possess everything needed to reach the highest levels of command. Cadets like you can turn this war around. I don't want to see that opportunity squandered by emotional weaknesses. There is no time for sympathy or reflection when you are given an order. You allowed your emotions to get the better of you in there. This was never a test to see if you could feed your dinosaur – that's a given. It was designed to put your empathy to the test, to see how it affected your decision-making and ability to follow orders. Do you understand?'

'Yes, sir.'

'Good. If you're so keen for a fight, next time I'll ensure you get one. Until then, think about what I've said.'

'I will, sir.'

'One more thing. I recommend you not confuse your asset like that again. It's a lethal 20-metre-long slaughtering machine, not a pet. Your neural links are still forming, meaning it can turn on you in a second if you deny its primal instincts. Never forget that.'

'I won't, sir.'

'You're dismissed. Return to your departure platform and wait for a train.'

I salute Ramsey and leave, not sure if I was told off or given an indirect pep talk.

'Oh, and cadet!' Ramsey calls after me. His stern brow softens. 'Your spinosaurus will be fed tonight...in case you were wondering.'

'Thank you, sir.'

My spirits lift a little. At least this disaster ended on a better note for Spino. It's a long, lonely walk through the facility, not a cadet to be seen anywhere. This walk of shame makes my failure feel worse. I was the only cadet pulled out of their session prematurely.

I enter a long passage set inside the island's main wall, with expansive windows overlooking the coastline and ocean. The low sun shimmers across the water, casting a kaleidoscope of warm hues up the wall's steel plates. But the picturesque view is lost on me. I'm so confused. *How do I move forward with Spino?* Sure, he's a killing machine. I know that. He almost ate me the first time we met. But I felt a connection during our session today, something beyond our neural link. Could we become friends? The Union don't promote that side of the Bonding. But I don't see how I can enhance our bond and create a working relationship without getting emotionally close. I need that connection to make this work, and I have a feeling Spino needs it also.

The sun has set by the time the cadets join me on the mag-lev platform. I keep to myself and avoid being drawn into their conversations. I don't want to hear how well everyone else did, especially when I failed so miserably.

Upon our return, I head straight to my dormitory, head down. I shower, dress in a fresh set of casual fatigues, and join the dinner queue in the mess hall. Our vegetables, protein steaks, and beverages are served on trays, one after another, in identical, perfectly sized portions. The Union cooks restock the queue like automatons, replacing a meal tray as soon as one is taken. There's a lot of hungry mouths to feed tonight.

I take a meal and find a quiet position along the edge of the hall, close to the exit. It's easier to find a vacant table tonight, as most cadets have converged into rowdy cohorts.

A soft-spoken voice interrupts my first mouthful. 'Do you mind if I sit at your table?'

It's Abby, the girl from my class who was sitting alone at lunch. She stands before me, meal tray in hand, poised to hightail it out of here if I say no.

'Sure.' I swallow with a gulp. 'That's fine.'

Abby sits at the far end of the table on the opposite side. I wasn't expecting that. I thought she wanted to sit opposite me. We eat our meals in silence, pretending to ignore one another. *Great, two introverts who can't start a conversation.*

Abby finally breaks the deadlock. 'How'd you go today?'

Of all the questions she had to ask! In retrospect, I should have expected it. I don't want to explain everything to a girl I don't know. I'm not sure how to respond, so I just shrug my shoulders.

Abby looks down at her plate and despondently toys with her food. 'Don't worry. You couldn't have done worse than me.'

'Really?'

'Yeah, it was so embarrassing. I'm sick of hearing everyone else brag about how well their first dinosaur session went. Aren't you?'

My mouth curls into a subtle smile. 'Yeah, I suppose.'

Abby suddenly slides her tray along the table and shuffles over to sit opposite me. She leans closer and speaks to me as if she's known me forever, her reserved demeanour now transformed into eager enthusiasm. 'Tell me about your spinosaurus. I've always loved them. Is that what you wanted?'

Her sudden intensity makes me draw back. I'm not used to talking so close to people. I prefer more personal space. 'No, I wanted a tyrannosaur.'

'I love them too. Well, anything bigger than me, really. I'm not a fan of small dinosaurs.'

I chuckle. 'Me too.'

'What's it like to control the biggest carnivore in the academy?'

Abby's interest forces me to reflect on my session with Spino in a different light. Since then, I'd only focused on the negative aspects, but putting those aside, I can see how incredible it was, tapping into that raw, primitive power. Thinking about it gives me goosebumps.

'Well?' Abby insists, almost climbing over the table for an answer. 'How was it?'

'It was exhilarating.'

Abby whacks the table with her palm. 'I knew it!'

My fork bounces off the table and clangs across the floor.

'Sorry 'bout that,' Abby says, promptly picking it up for me. She wipes it with a napkin and hands it back. 'I get excited easily. So, tell me more.'

I observe my fork, not convinced it's entirely clean. 'What do you want to know?'

'Did you connect straight away? Did he remember who you were?'

'Yes, to both questions... I think.'

'Did he obey your instructions?'

'He did.'

'Oh, you're so lucky. What was your objective?'

I pause, my next mouthful halfway to my mouth. I should have known that question was coming. Best to divert this line of enquiry before it gets more uncomfortable. 'We had to hunt for a meal. What about you? How did you go with yours... It's a stegosaurus, right?'

Abby rolls her eyes. 'It was a total disaster. She wouldn't stay focused. I had to really concentrate to get her to complete the simplest things. Then I'd get her to do one thing, but the moment I lost focus, she'd wander off and eat leaves.'

I stifle a giggle. 'What was your objective?'

'All I needed her to do was move a bunch of boulders out of the way, then toss a log across a ravine so I could get to the other side.'

'Did you complete it?'

'No,' Abby says, stabbing her next portion of food. 'It took so long to move the boulders, by the time we got to shifting the log, I was exhausted. I don't whether to blame me or her. It's hard to stay focused when she won't obey.'

'Did you get close enough to touch her?'

'Not yet. She's wary of me. It makes me nervous. I don't want to end up on the end of her spiked tail.'

'Next time you're with her, spend some time to get close. Take it slow. Try to make a physical connection. It helps a lot.'

Abby nods, as if some great secret has been revealed. 'See, that's why you have an apex carnivore. You're all over it on your first day. I bet you sailed through your objective with time to kill.'

I smile at the irony. I like Abby – she helps put things into perspective and makes me feel a little better about my day. The least I can do is reciprocate the good will, make her feel better too. 'I didn't sail through. To be honest, I failed miserably.'

Abby's eyes widen with shock. 'I don't believe it.'

'It's true. I even got reprimanded afterwards, it was that bad.'

Abby stares at me in disbelief. 'Are you serious?'

I nod, feeling a huge weight lift off my shoulders. We continue our meals in a happier, more relaxed atmosphere, as if we've known each other longer than a few minutes.

Abby nods at someone over my shoulder. 'That's the guy who was on stage with you at assembly this morning. What's his name?'

'Kane?' I whisper.

I want to turn around, but he might see me and I'd have to acknowledge him and start a conversation. It would be weird if I didn't. Now it's all getting too hard and awkward, and I just exerted all my social energy with Abby. I'd rather catch up with Kane when there's nobody around. Regardless, I can't resist the tiniest of details. 'Is he looking?'

Abby covertly watches him while she eats. 'Not at the moment, but he has been.'

'Have you ever seen him before today?'

'No. Have you?'

'I met him during the Bonding.'

'He's cute. Looks like he got messed up bad, though. Those raptors are vicious.' Abby suddenly looks down and toys with her food. 'I think he's coming over.'

My heart starts hammering, like I'm running. *Should I turn around or pretend we haven't noticed him?*

Abby breathes easy. 'False alarm. He's walking back to the counter, putting his dinner tray away. Now he's walking out. On his own.'

'Thanks for the commentary.'

'Are you avoiding him?'

'No, why?'

'I don't know. You said you knew him – I thought you might want to talk. Doesn't look like he knows many other cadets.'

'I'll catch up with him.' I tidy up my tray and stand. That's as much social interaction as I can handle for one night. 'It was nice talking to you, Abby.'

'Sure,' Abby says, looking vexed by my sudden departure. 'I'll see you tomorrow – we can sit together if you want. I don't know anyone else in our class. All my friends ended up in different barracks after the Bonding.'

I hesitate, anxious to leave without appearing rude.

'Sorry, I talk too much,' she says.

'It's fine. Nice talking to you.'

Abby smiles. 'See you tomorrow.'

I make my escape, smiling to myself. Meeting Abby has lightened my mood and taken some of the pressure off my classes tomorrow. I'm glad we talked. It's a relief to know I wasn't the only one who failed the first session with their dinosaur. It's clear to me now, our assessors created situations to exploit our weaknesses. Sounds like they tested Abby's ability to maintain focus. She talks so fast; I can only imagine how much her mind flips from one thought to the next, leaving her poor stegosaurus bombarded with instructions. No wonder it wandered off to feed midsession.

Me, I'm a different story. I've always been sympathetic to animals, regardless of whether they were born naturally or in a lab. They're all living creatures, with thoughts and emotions. Every cadet in this academy was born in a lab, including me, so it's no wonder I'm passionate about it. But I like to think my empathy comes from my parents, that it was passed down through their DNA. The Union assessors see my empathy as a weakness, and that's why they placed a helpless baby diplo in my enclosure – to see how I reacted. I have to remember we're at war. There may come a day when I need to put my emotions aside and do what's necessary, despite the consequences. A decision that could mean the difference between life and death.

Night has come by the time I walk outdoors towards my barracks. The leafy jungle setting is now illuminated by spotlights and cadets stroll past me, chatting, enjoying the warm night before the lights are turned off. I sit down on a bench seat, content to enjoy the relaxed atmosphere and decompress.

'Zayla?'

My quiet moment is over before it began. Kane jogs up the nearby steps and approaches. His limp is gone and the scars across his face have faded to the point where I have to search hard to see them. 'I'm not interrupting, am I?'

My desire to be alone evaporates in one excited heartbeat. 'No. No, that's fine.'

'Can I sit?'

I shift along and give him space. What I really want to do is give him a crushing hug. *I wish I had the confidence to express myself.*

'I'm so glad you're alive,' I say. 'I wasn't sure I'd get a chance to thank you.'

Kane smiles warmly. 'Likewise.'

'Huh? You're the one who saved me from the pack of megaraptors. What do you need to thank me for?'

'For luring the gnarliest pack of megaraptors right to me.'

'But they almost killed you!'

'Sure, but I wouldn't have bonded with them otherwise.'

'I suppose you could look at it that way.'

'You did really yourself. A spinosaurus! They don't get any bigger and stronger than that.'

'It wasn't my first species of choice. I was going for a T-rex.'

'You got a lucky upgrade then.'

'Lucky sums it up. I was hanging upside-down from his jaws, my leg crushed between his teeth. I was so close to being eaten, it wasn't funny.'

'Join the club. My raptors tore me inside out. I saw parts of my body I've never seen and never want to see again. I'm not sure how I bonded with them in such a state, but I'm glad I did.'

'Sounds excruciating.'

'You have no idea. We're fortunate the academy has state-of-the-art medical facilities. Better than the outside world, apparently.'

'Yeah,' I say, distracted by Kane's disarming nature.

It's like I've known him for years, but I can't figure out why. I've never had this feeling with anyone. He's familiar, like a long-lost friend or relative, and maybe that's why I opened up so quickly the first time we met. We spent the first night of the Bonding hiding in an abandoned pterosaur nest. Kane watched over me as I slept and was inadvertently given a front-row seat to my disturbed sleeping habits. Of all the times to dream about dying with my parents on Daxma-5. He saw me at my most vulnerable and is the only one who knows my nightmares.

'Have you settled into your new barracks?' Kane asks.

'Yeah, I suppose.' I don't sound that convincing, even to myself.

'And everything else all right?'

Kane maintains eye contact with me, giving the impression he wants more. *Is he really asking if my nightmares have returned?* Part of me wishes I'd never told him. I don't want him to tell anyone else. He finally nods. 'That's good.'

'What about you?'

'Yeah, it's been okay. My dorm's on the lower section of the island. I've overheard a few people talking about you in my barracks.'

I sit a little straighter. 'Me?'

'Yeah, don't worry, it's nothing bad. In fact, it's the opposite.

They're all hoping to team up with you when we start the joint training exercises.'

'But they don't even know me. They're probably just saying that because of my spinosaurus.'

'Don't be so hard on yourself. You should be proud of your dinosaur and what you've achieved. Very few cadets can wrangle in an apex predator like you did.'

'It was just dumb luck. I didn't really earn my spinosaurus.'

'That's not true.'

'How so?'

'You made it through all three zones. You evaded dozens of lethal species to make it to the inner blue zone. Luck will only get you so far, and certainly not as far as you did. So many cadets never made it half as far as you. And those who did, I'll bet only a small percentage bonded with the dinosaur they intended.'

Kane may be right, but I still feel like an imposter.

'Have you thought about who you'll team up with for the joint exercises?' Kane asks.

'Not really. What about you?'

'I was thinking we should team up.'

I want to say yes, but I sense there's something more going on with Kane. He looks at me differently than every other male cadet. His gaze lingers on me longer than necessary when I'm not looking at him. It's not unsettling or creepy. I like it, but he feels like a brother instead of someone I could be attracted to. Maybe we were friends as children and separated into different barracks at some point. I can't remember. Everything before my teenage years is a bit of a blur. I'm not sure why. Plus, the Union forbids relationships in the academy, so any chance of something romantic happening is virtually nonexistent. At least from my side.

Kane gives me a puzzled look. 'You don't think it's a good idea?'

I snap back into the moment and bumble my words. 'Sorry. Yeah, of course, um... It could work.'

'O-kay.' Kane sounds less than certain with my response.

I didn't mean to sound unenthusiastic, it just came out that way.

I try making up for it with the first thing that pops into my head. 'Next time you're at dinner, you should join me and Abby. Only if you want to, of course.'

Kane smiles. 'I will.'

His beaming expression looks like I just made his day. *I like his smile.* A bell sounds through the facility, indicating it's time to return to our dormitories. We say goodnight and head off in opposite directions. For the second time tonight, I walk away from someone with a smile on my face. My life in the academy has improved.

I jolt upright in bed at 5 a.m. the next morning as the stark dormitory lights flicker to life. Two Union trainers dressed in dark-grey t-shirts, camo pants, and black boots march inside and kick the feet of our beds, screaming at us to get up. Their slicked-back hair, muscular arms, tanned complexions, and booming voices are too much to handle this early in the morning. Everyone reluctantly crawls out of bed and scurries about for their clothes, bleary-eyed and groggy.

'Hurry up, cadets!' bellows a scary, super-fit female trainer. 'You're doing a 10-kilometre run before breakfast.'

The male trainer storms past, glaring at me. 'What are you waiting for? Breakfast in bed?'

'Yes, sir, that'd be nice,' says a brazen cadet.

I look over to see who it is, struggling to drag my pants on. It's Tyson, boldly standing there in his underwear, camo pants in hand.

The female trainer storms over. 'You think you're funny, cadet? Drop and give me 50 push-ups.'

Tyson flings his pants aside and gets down on the floor with a groan.

I reach under my bed, grab my boots, and yank them on while I watch Tyson power through his punishment. He does the push-ups like they're nothing.

The male trainer passes me again, eyeing my progress. 'Get those boots laced up, cadet. You're no good without them.'

Tyson is the last cadet to pull on his boots. Everyone stands to attention at the end of their beds, watching Tyson from the corner of their eyes, waiting for him to finish. Once ready, the trainers chase us out of the dormitory, clapping and screaming.

I hate unannounced fitness sessions.

The trainers set a brisk pace through the complex of tunnels, walkways, and bridges that weave through the island's rugged slopes. I can handle the distance, but the steep inclines destroy my legs. Several cadets struggle to keep up and drop to the rear of the pack, but I manage a steady pace behind the leaders. A complete lap of the island brings us back to the dormitory as dawn breaks. There's barely time to recover as it's straight into the showers. I dress in fresh fatigues and head off to breakfast, invigorated, alert, and ready to take on the day.

Something feels different about today. I don't recall dreaming last night, yet strange visions fill my mind over breakfast. A clear night sky filled with stars...treetops swaying in a breeze...reflections of a full moon across dark water. They feel more like memories than visions. I'm certain my connection with Spino is the reason, as though I saw through his eyes last night.

I finish breakfast, return the tray, and head off for my first class. It's a welcome surprise to find Abby waiting for me outside our classroom.

Reeva brushes past me, closer than necessary, and eyeballs Abby with an air of condescension. 'Finally made a friend, Zaz?'

I'm caught on the back foot again. No witty comebacks. A flush of embarrassment rises to my face and I choke up, cheeks glowing like emergency lights.

The girl accompanying Reeva cackles like a hyena. It's Lani from my old Beta Barracks, and one of Reeva's long-time friends. She reminds me of a doll with her black ringlet hair and blemish-free brown skin. The pair have been partners in crime for as long as I can remember.

Abby glares at them. *That's not a good idea.*

'What are you looking at?' Reeva says.

'I'm confused. I thought T-rexes hunted alone.'

Inflammatory *oohs* sound from the onlookers. Several cadets chuckle as they pass. Reeva's face goes a shade of pink. *I can't believe it. Is she embarrassed?* Reeva turns up her nose and keeps walking. The second she is out of sight, I burst out laughing. I quickly stifle my reaction and look around, wary of Reeva's web of spies.

'You like that?' Abby says.

'How did you come up with a comeback so quick?'

'I'm a fast talker, in case you hadn't noticed. Stupid dino puns just pop into my head.'

'You're lucky.'

'Keep me around. I'll have 'em lined up like a pack of compys ready to pounce.'

'You should be careful. Reeva's training for command with a tyrannosaur. If you end up in her platoon, she'll make your life a misery.'

'I don't care. I stick up for my friends. Anyway, I won't need to worry about that.'

'Why not?'

'Because you'll choose me for your platoon. By the way, why did Reeva call you *Zaz*?'

'Zaz is my nickname from my old barracks.'

'It's the only nice thing that's come out of Reeva's mouth. I like it. It suits you.'

I notice Avi down the hall, standing with a group of friends, more interested in me than joining their conversation. He smiles and my heart skips a beat. *Is he smiling at me?* I turn around, but there's nobody behind me. Abby has walked into the classroom and left me standing on my own. This has suddenly become awkward. I flash Avi a smile and dart off before my face turns red. *Being shy is such a curse.*

Abby has saved me a desk at the back of the room next to hers. I take a seat, activate my holographic workspace, and check my timetable. I'm feeling hot and flustered and it takes me a moment to focus. We have theory this morning, a break for lunch, then another session with our dinosaurs in the afternoon titled [PHASE 1: COMBAT SIMULATION].

'We have combat sims this afternoon. The Union isn't wasting any time.'

'Oh, great!' sighs Abby. 'My stegosaurus will be off eating berries while my arse gets tasered into oblivion.'

I chuckle. 'You should give her a name.'

'Like what?'

'Whatever comes to mind. What was your first impression of her?'

'Lazy.'

I laugh harder this time. 'I'm sure she's not. You should think of a name. It might improve your bond.'

'I suppose,' Abby says, sounding less than convinced.

Rosa and Tyson take a seat a couple of rows ahead of me. Tyson notices me. 'Hey, Zaz, how's your spinosaurus going?'

Several cadets turn and look at me, waiting for my response.

'Good,' I say, bottling up. I loathe being put on the spot in front of everyone.

Rosa elbows him in the side. 'Leave her alone. Can't you see she doesn't want to talk to you?'

That's not true, I think. *Pity I can't say it out loud.*

Avi and his friends enter the classroom, stealing everyone's attention. All four of them are handsome, confident, and from what I've heard, have some of the best apex predators in the academy and are tipped to make command positions. His group is popular with all the girls, but Reeva and Lani are first in line to flirt with them. Reeva is so obvious, it's clear she wants Avi to sit beside her. His friends take up the seats beside Reeva and Lani, but Avi leaves them and walks towards us. There's only one spare desk over here, and it's next to me. *What the hell is he doing?*

'Hey, Zaz, is anyone sitting there?' Avi asks in a casual, confident voice.

I shake my head.

'Do you mind if I sit next to you?'

'That's fine,' I say softly, keeping an eye on Reeva. *She won't appreciate this.*

Avi leans across my desk to shake hands with Abby. 'Hey, I'm Avi. I've seen you and Zaz hanging out together. Nice to meet you.'

Abby reaches over me to shake his hand. 'You too. I'm Abby.'

'Sorry, I should've introduced you,' I say.

'Yeah, Zaz,' Abby says, raising her eyebrow at me. 'Where's your head at?'

Avi activates his holographic workstation and acts as though it's situation normal. It's so strange. I met him a couple of days ago and spoke to him without a problem, but now that he's paying me extra attention, I'm uncomfortable.

A private message from Abby appears on the lower right corner of my holographic workspace. 'You have a not-so-secret admirer!'

I promptly terminate the message before Avi has a chance to read it. Abby gives me a mischievous grin, to which I reply with a friendly glare. *She'd better not do anything else to embarrass me.* I go bright-red at the slightest thing. Just when I think it's all over, I notice Reeva sending me dagger-eyes across the room.

Our lecturer, Suda Satoshi, enters. He stands at the front of the room and waits for quiet before talking. 'The path to knowledge can only be walked humbly.'

Suda lets his statement resonate with us before continuing.

'Today, you will take your first steps along that path. We will examine the Daxma-5 massacre in detail and reveal why the indigenous species went from docile creatures to a rampaging force that killed over 30,000 colonists. We will explore why this threat extends beyond Daxma-5 to endanger all life in the galaxy. This information is classified to those serving directly in Union. The general populations, including all local and off-world colonies, have only been told a partial truth. Now that you've bonded with your dinosaurs and are training for war, you have gained the security clearance to everything we have learned about the Wraith. Your permissions should appear on your workspace now.'

A message in glowing green scrolls through the middle of my

hologram, [SECURITY ACCESS GRANTED ZAYLA-8311/SPINOSAURUS: CODENAME: FLAME]

Everyone in the room receives a personalised version of the same message.

'Why was this information restricted?' asks a cadet.

'If the public were to learn the truth about the Wraith, there would be unbridled panic, which would quickly lead to chaos. Society would break down.'

'What truth?'

'That is what you will learn today. This knowledge forms the foundation of your training and will prepare you for the battles on Daxma-5. We are fighting a foe that is seen, and unseen.'

My hologram changes into a detailed star chart. It zooms through the cosmos to demonstrate what Suda explains.

'Daxma-5 is located in the Constellation of Nyra, approximately 1,356 light years from our solar system. It's twice the mass of Earth and orbits an orange dwarf star. The first colony was constructed there 53 years ago on the northern continent. Air and gravity are equivalent to Earth, allowing a host of carbon-based life forms to evolve in a similar way to lifeforms on our planet.

'Xenobiologists have broken the species down into four main categories. Daxanoids, a land-based bipedal species they believe to be an evolving species akin to humans. Caves and subterranean spaces are infested with arachnoids. These giant arthropods resemble spider-like carnivores that weave kilometres of underground webs beneath trap doors. The plains, jungles, and forests are home to the titanoids. Much like our dinosaurs, they are a mix of bipeds, quadrupeds, and hexapods, ranging in height from a metre to a couple of hundred. The skies are dominated by darasaurs, aerial predators equivalent to our pterosaurs. Daxma-5's oceans were being studied at the time of the massacre, so our data on the aquatic life forms is incomplete. But the information gathered so far reveals an abundance of life.'

Images and descriptions of the species appear on my hologram in columns. There's so many shapes and sizes, it's overwhelming. The varieties bear an uncanny resemblance to life on Earth, as if they could have evolved here on an alternate timeline. But the extra eyes, limbs, and bold colours are unlike anything in Earth's biological record.

'Study and memorise every one of these creatures,' Suda says. 'They comprise two-thirds of your end-of-term exams. But more importantly, a sound knowledge of these creatures may save your life one day.'

Suda gives us a moment to assess the encyclopaedia.

Scrolling the list sends a chill down my spine. These creatures haunt my dreams, and now I have more to add to the nightmares. I'm torn between horror and fascination, but if I learn enough about the species, it might help demystify them and end my night terrors.

Suda wanders between our desks. 'Our colonies on Daxma-5 lived alongside these life forms for 35 years. From the first landing, our colonists were careful not to encroach upon their habitats. They remained respectful and studied them from a distance before expanding their bases, but despite their efforts, it was not without loss of life. The colonists learned from their mistakes. They avoided deep ravines and rocky mountains to reduce the arachnoid threat and expanded onto the open plains, low-lying rainforests, and jungles. For a time, the colonists believed they had cultivated a harmony between themselves, and life on Daxma-5. What changed?'

Suda surveys the room, waiting for someone to answer. Abby's hologram illuminates green and Suda nods for her to continue.

'Every life-form on Daxma-5 lives in symbiosis with the planet's electromagnetic field, but the colonists didn't know that. Once their nuclear batteries depleted, and the solar panels couldn't generate enough power for the growing population, they switched over to electrical generators that drew energy from the planet's electromagnetic field. That's when the indigenous life forms turned on us.'

'Correct. But as we all know, the truth is far more dire and complicated.'

Our holograms change to high-resolution video footage. A platoon of dropships land around the smouldering ruins of the Daxma-5 colony after the massacre. Casualties lay strewn about, not a single body in one piece.

The classroom is dead quiet.

I want to look away, but can't. My heart pounds. The Union has shown us footage like this since we were old enough to comprehend death, conditioning us to accept gore and the brutality of nature. We see it in the dinosaur enclosures. Creatures kill one another. It's a part of life. Every cadet is expected to have grown immune to the sight of blood and dismembered bodies, animal, or human. I never have.

'You are now watching the Union's counterstrike,' Suda says. 'We have not released this footage to the public.'

The dropship gangways open and squads of hulking robots march across the scorched landscape, brandishing heavy-assault plasma rifles. Standing twice as tall as a human, with tiny heads buried between broad armoured shoulders, the robots resemble an army of ogre-like giants with yellow glowing eyes.

'After the formation of the Union, there was no need for human armies or weapons of mass destruction. However, a top-secret army of robot marines were hidden on moons throughout colonised solar systems, devised as an emergency backup force and created specifically for situations such as this. These automatons were brought in to secure the Daxma-5 colony and search for survivors.'

My hologram shows lightning bolts striking the colony from multiple angles. Highly charged energy waves ripple across the landscape, electrifying everything in their path. The robots freeze mid-stride as if someone hit a giant *off* button.

'Our marines lasted minutes before being immobilised by an electromagnetic pulse. As a last resort, we sent in Union security squads to secure the colony.'

The image cuts to footage of more dropships arriving. Human squads spread through the abandoned colony, searching the streets, buildings, and vehicles for survivors. They form a perimeter around the base, set up long-range communication transmitters, and hunker down for the next fight.

'Little did we know, the electromagnetic pulse was our first encounter with the Wraith, a sentient life form that exists as pure energy. They live throughout Daxma-5, riding the electromagnetic waves that permeate the planet. This unseen force took control of our robot marines and turned them against us.'

The dormant robots spring to life and massacre the Union forces, slicing them to pieces with their plasma weapons. Multiple angles depict the carnage in glistening high resolution as the bodies pile up.

'Five thousand Union members died in that attack.'

I struggle to watch. There's only so much death I can handle in one lesson. I avert my eyes from the footage to find I'm the only one not watching their hologram. I've failed one test due to my empathetic nature and I can't afford another failure, so I force myself to watch.

'But that was only the beginning,' Suda says, eyeing me as he walks by. 'The Wraith are a highly intelligent and aggressive species. In the first instance, they took control of Daxma-5's indigenous species and used them to massacre the colony. When we returned, they took control of our technology and turned it against us. We inadvertently gave the Wraith the ability to leave the planet and strike us anywhere.'

[ZAYLA-8311 ACCESS GRANTED: WRAITH INFESTATION] appears on my workspace. A series of interstellar maps fill my screen with deep space Union fleets highlighted in glowing yellow markers.

'Our situation is more dire than the general population have been told. The Wraith control 100 per-cent of our forces around Daxma-5, including all robot marine squads, military dropships, and tactical interstellar vehicles.'

'How did they manage that?' a cadet asks.

'The Wraith used our long-range transmitters on Daxma-5's surface to hijack our orbiting armada. They disabled all life-support systems, murdering everyone aboard. A further 10,000 Union lives were lost in the blink of an eye. To this day, those victims endlessly orbit Daxma-5 in giant metal tombs. For the last 18 years, the Union has used a deep space electromagnetic storm as a cover story to explain why we haven't returned to Daxma-5. But we're living on borrowed time. The Wraith could launch a pre-emptive attack and wipe out humanity with the flick of a switch. If the general population uncovered the truth, there would be panic throughout the colonies. Nobody would feel safe. It would undermine faith in the Union.'

Footage of the deceased crew members fill my screen. Their lifeless, decaying bodies float about in zero gravity. Each haunted expression stares straight through me, pleading from beyond death for justice. Anger replaces my fear, reminding me how the Wraith killed my parents. But they were just two out of thousands who perished. And for what? Because we started using the natural electromagnetic power on Daxma-5? The Wraith must pay for what they've done.

Rosa's hologram lights up and she asks a question. 'It's been 18 years since the massacre. Why haven't the Wraith attacked us in that time?'

'Because we severed the link before they could inflict more damage,' Suda replies. 'We destroyed all deep space relays in the Nyra Constellation. The Wraith are not made of physical matter and therefore perceive time differently to us. A decade in human years might be ten seconds in Wraith time – we just don't know. But their threat is ever-present.'

'Why don't you just fire a nuclear weapon into the planet?' Tyson asks.

'Because they can turn any form of electronic technology against us. We can only fight the Wraith with biological entities.'

'What if they turn our dinosaurs against us?'

'They can't. The Wraith can only control biological species indigenous to Daxma-5. That's why the colonists and their pets were never affected.'

'What about our neural implants?' Reeva asks. 'What's stopping the Wraith from overriding them and taking control of our dinosaurs that way?'

'Or us,' Lani adds.

Suda shakes his head. 'Your neural implants are constructed from organic components and powered by your body's own electrical signals. The Wraith won't be able to see your neural implants, as your biological physiology masks them. Your assets implants work the same way. That's why we chose dinosaurs as our weapons in this war. They possess the strength and agility to defeat our robot marines and counter Daxma-5's indigenous species.'

'I don't like the idea of waiting around for them to attack,' Tyson says. 'What's our mission?'

'Your mission has been 18 years in the making. The Union artificially grew every one of you from your parents' DNA, parents you never had the privilege to meet. The Wraith stole your chance to live a normal life. To have a family. But the Union has given you a chance to avenge what you lost. We are going to strike the Wraith on Daxma-5 and end their threat once and for all.'

As scared as I am, Suda's words fill me with hope.

Lunch in the mess hall is a lot quieter than yesterday. Even Abby, who is usually bursting with conversation, eats in silence. The Wraith threat feels closer than ever. We feel vulnerable, and as Suda said, *living on borrowed time*. The Wraith are a nonbiological, invisible enemy, and can't be suppressed like other biological life in the universe. We can't rely on Union weapons or technology to fight them, which means no military support, making us the first and last line of defence. We fight to win, or die 1,300 light years from Earth beside the graves of our parents.

After lunch we assemble on our designated mag-lev platforms for transport to our dinosaur's island. My train arrives, and everyone boards in silence. Seconds later, we hurtle from the protected cavern into a maelstrom of storm clouds.

A tropical cyclone rages across the archipelago. Sheets of rain pelt the windows, and gale-force squalls buffet the train. Our carriage rattles and shudders. Several cadets gasp and some cling to each other for support. It feels like we're about to shoot off the monorail and plummet into the tumultuous sea, but our driverless train ploughs on, straight into the eye of the storm. The howling gale sounds like an angry god, warning us to turn back.

I wish we could turn back. The oppressive weather weighs on my grim mood. I don't feel confident about the combat simulation with Spino today.

Our train pulls into the same volcanic island as yesterday. Officer Nadja Schulze is there to greet us again. She checks in our group in and we negotiate the escalators and travelators burrowing through the monolithic wall enclosing the island. One by one, each cadet is dropped off at their entrance hatch. Today, I'm lucky last.

Nadja leads me all the way up to Level 102. I peer through the window beside the hatch, guessing we're level with the top of the volcano, but all I can see is torrential rain.

'Zayla–8311, this is your entry hatch. We've assigned you a section of swamp backing onto a ridge on the edge of the caldera. Your combat scenario includes four robot marines and six velociraptors, replicating a Wraith response to an incursion on the Daxma-5 colony. We suspect the Wraith would activate our robot marines, followed by the indigenous species, hence their inclusion. Your enemy will attack in three waves. Robots first, velociraptors second, followed by a final wave of robots. Use any means necessary to disable them. Do you have any questions?'

Yeah, I do! I think. *Why such an advanced first session?* My stomach churns as I glance out the window. I'm not ready for this. 'Do I have time to study the terrain and prepare?'

'Preparation is not important at this stage of your training as you're still in the assessment phase. We're measuring the strength of your bond, or to be more precise, your stem power.'

'What's my stem power?'

'Your most primal survival instincts. Under moments of extreme pressure, there's no time for rational thought. We're measuring how your primal instincts align with your spinosaurus.'

'You want me to think like a dinosaur?'

'As your bond develops, your minds should begin to think as one. You provide the higher reasoning and problem-solving, while your spinosaurus enhances your physical senses and basic instincts. It's up to you to find a balance between the two.'

Nadja opens the hatch.

Wind howls inside, inviting a barrage of heavy rain drops into the passage. I shield my eyes and peer through the opening. A metal gantry extends out to the caldera ridge 50 metres away. High overhead, the island's dome is half closed over the wire netting, semi-protecting the island from the full force of the cyclone.

Nadja holds her beret from blowing off and yells above the gale. 'Something wrong, cadet?'

'No, ma'am,' I shout back.

I step outside and grip the railing to pull myself onto the gantry, feeling like a wall of invisible hands are forcing me back. The metal door slams shut behind me. *No going back now.* A powerful squall lashes my face with rain and tosses me against the railing. I peer over the side at the sheer cliffs of black volcanic rock. Torrents of water cascade down the face and transform into mini-tornadoes that swirl across the jungle canopy far below.

This is ridiculous! I need to get off this gantry.

I grasp the railing and drag myself to the far side. One slip, and I'll blow away. I push off the end and crawl into a protected alcove. A rocky path leads me down off the ridge into the caldera's swampy basin, where I slip down a muddy bank into knee-deep water.

The unforgiving wind whips up the surface of the water, turns it into upward rain, and blasts my face. *Can this get any harder?*

Directly ahead, the enormous shadow of a dinosaur materialises amidst turmoil, immovable and dead-still against the backdrop of thrashing trees. The hulking silhouette watches me, obscured by the impermeable downpour. *That better be Spino.*

'Spino! Is that you?' I scream into the wind.

Lightning flashes overhead. It strikes the rim of the dome and creates a shower of sparks illuminating Spino. His bright green eyes find mine in the burst of light and he bellows, then stomps through the shallow water towards me.

I stand my ground, legs trembling, unable to tell if I'm cold or petrified. Probably both.

'It's okay,' I cry. 'It's just a storm. I'm here.'

Spino stops just metres ahead of me and lowers his head.

Waves of water created by his footsteps crash over my legs. I reach up to console him as the rainwater rushes off his snout and soaks me. His leathery skin feels warm and comforting in the cold. I close my eyes and send him calming thoughts. *Good boy. Don't worry. The storm will pass. We're safe with each other.*

Spino grunts and nudges me.

'That's right. You remember me, don't you?'

Spino nudges me harder and I fall back into the water, laughing. His budding affection is a welcome relief.

Spino suddenly stands upright and pivots. His tail swooshes over me as he steps back to shield me beneath his underbelly. I'm protected from the rain between his two hind legs, like standing under a shelter.

'What's the matter?' I say, rubbing his leg.

Peering out, I can't see much through the storm. I wonder what he's looking at. *He senses something I can't. Why can't I feel it?*

Nadja's comment springs to mind: *Your spinosaurus enhances your physical senses and basic instincts.* I close my eyes and focus on enhancing my neural link with Spino. Nothing. It might be easier if I could hear his breathing over the howling wind and driving rain. I place my hand on his underbelly and feel Spino's ribcage move with each cavernous breath. The storm gradually becomes white noise until all I can hear is Spino inhaling and exhaling huge volumes of air. My breathing slows and falls in sync with his.

An unpleasant smell arouses my senses, a harsh mix of sulphur and burnt paper. I'm tempted to open my eyes, but I concentrate on the smell. A subtle vibration hums through my body, precise, like a motor, growing stronger by the second. I'm sharing Spino's senses, feeling the mechanical motors approaching us.

The robot marines are close!

I open my eyes. No sign of any robots – just rain and more rain. I can barely make out the trees bordering the swamp. *How does Spino sense anything in these conditions?* Regardless, his highly attuned senses are a distinct advantage.

It's up to me to make use of them.

We need to destroy the robots before the velociraptors attack. Spino has incredible size and power, but his jaws and tail will only get us so far. We need a weapon, something large enough to keep our adversaries at a distance. The cypress trees on the far side of the swamp offer just that.

'Go!' I scream, pointing to the trees.

Spino doesn't move. *Does he understand me?* I close my eyes, put my hand on his leg, and call again. 'Go to the trees!'

Nothing. Spino is dug in like a stubborn stegosaurus. I don't blame him. It's my fault. I'm unfocused and fuelled by panic. A million thoughts are racing through my mind, clouding my intentions. I need to lead Spino across the swamp and show him what I want. I dart between his legs, back under his tail, and return to the embankment. My boots slosh and stick in the mud, leaving me stuck on the bank. I'm getting nowhere fast. Turning around, I find Spino watching me, head tilted with a look of curiosity.

'Wanna give me a hand?'

Spino nudges me up and over the embankment with his snout, sending me somersaulting through the sodden grass. I jump to my feet. From this elevated position, I stand level with his head. *Perfect!* I run for the trees and wave him along. 'Come on, follow me.'

My stubborn spinosaurus finally trudges after me, creating huge umbrella-shaped splashes with each step. I work hard to stay ahead, but my legs are tired from the 10-kilometre run this morning. *Couldn't our fitness instructors have picked a better day?* Maybe it's part of their plan, to push us to our physical and mental limits. I scramble over to the nearest tree trunk and hug it.

'Grab this,' I scream.

Spino looks at me and retracts his head as if to say, *What are you doing?*

I demonstrate, lifting the trunk. 'Rip it out!'

He watches me but doesn't react. *That's confusion clouding his eyes.* I'm not getting through to him. I suddenly remember, we've done this exact thing before when he almost flattened me with a freshly plucked tree during our first session. Maybe I just need to lead by example. Looking about, I'm surrounded by waist-high saplings. I grab the nearest sapling and pull. The waterlogged soil releases the roots with a *slop,* and I jump up, waving it in Spino's face.

'Do it! Copy me.'

Spino arcs his head back and watches me, seemingly amused by this tiny human behaving in such a crazy manner. *Come on, copy me.* Spino makes a *humph* sound and suddenly steps forward. His webbed foot sinks into the muddy bank as he cranes and rotates his head to bite the tree trunk I hugged moments ago.

Crunch!

Spino locks the cypress tree in his jaws and rips it free. I dive aside to avoid the roots and falling clumps of mud. Spino steps returns to the swamp with the tree protruding from his jaws, looking back at me with an air of accomplishment.

I leap to my feet. 'That's it! Well done.'

Spino snorts and whips about to face the opposite side of the swamp. I duck as the tree whooshes over me, scraping my back with branches.

'Whoa! Watch it with that thing!'

A pair of glowing yellow eyes emerge from the trees across the water. A 12-foot Union robot marine marches through the foliage, steady and precise, unaffected by the gale-force wind and rain. Its metal skeleton is protected by armour plates across the chest, shoulders, and head. The robot withdraws a massive restraining pole tipped with a high-voltage taser.

Nearby, a second robot stomps into view brandishing a heavy-duty metal grasper, big enough to clamp Spino's head in its grip. I've seen this classic subdue and restrain procedure used by pairs of Union dinosaur wranglers before. If they capture Spino, it's an instant fail, for both of us.

Crack! The first robot activates the restraining pole and bright blue energy crackles along its length. One strike will be enough to immobilise Spino and kill me.

I rush at the first robot and throw my sapling as an example for Spino. It gets picked up by the wind, changes direction, and whacks Spino on the side of the head. He gives me a disapproving blink as it slips off his head.

I raise my hands and shrug my shoulders. 'Sorry. You know what I meant.'

Spino pivots to the side, turns his head to gather more power, then swings around, unleashing the trunk with all his might. It cuts through the gale, leaving a vortex of rain and mud in its wake. The robot raises its arms in defence, but is no match for the incoming cypress tree. *THUMP!* The robot tumbles backwards under the tree, dropping its restraining pole, as the storm consumes the ensuing sparks and explosions. Pinned under the trunk, the mangled machine writhes about like a raptor stomped on by a brachiosaurus.

The second robot breaks into a perfect sprint across the swamp and snaps open the metal grasper, aiming for Spino's neck.

'Look out!' I shriek.

Spino flinches, as if speared by my voice, and roars at me. I see the fire in his eyes now. He's in fight-or-flight mode, adrenalin levels spiking. Spino faces the robot and stomps through the swamp towards it.

'Hit it with your tail!'

Spino changes direction a second before flesh and metal collide. The grasper snaps closed on empty air, missing its target. His tail impacts the robot flat across its chest armour.

Wham!

The marine becomes airborne as shattered armour flies off in all directions. The robot lands with a heavy plop in the swamp, sparking and smoking. Spino rushes over and stomps on it, forcing the machine beneath the muddy water. It's gone in seconds, leaving just the grasper poking from the water like a grave marker.

I sprint around the edge of the swamp and retrieve the restraining pole which is still crackling with electricity. I deactivate the taser, flick the control switch, and the telescoping pole retracts to half its length, allowing me to handle it. Holding it away from my body, I reactivate the taser and wield it like a sword, confident I can bring a dreadnoughtus to its knees.

Arrk! Arrk!

The guttural bark raises goosebumps down my back. *I know that noise all too well.* I spin around to find five velociraptors creeping from the foliage, heads forward, nostrils flared, the black vertical pupils of their reptilian eyes fixed on me. Lightning strikes, highlighting their sickle-shaped hind claws stepping through the grass.

I wave my taser but their stride doesn't falter.

At best, I can ward off one or two with my pole, but not six at once. I edge backwards for the swamp as the raptors spread out and encircle me. *Where the hell is Spino?* The raptor to my left launches into the air. I trip backwards in fright and awkwardly wave the taser pole at those razor-sharp claws, a second from being sliced and diced.

Spino catches the raptor mid-flight in his mouth and bites down, crushing the predator with a bone-crushing crunch. It screeches and goes limp.

One by one, the raptors launch over me, stabbing and slashing at Spino. By the time I stand, he's covered in them. His sail bends sideways, bearing the weight of a raptor as it rips a hole through the thin layer of flesh with its claws. Another hangs off his neck, one his torso, and another from his tail. Spino thrashes about in a futile attempt to throw them off, but the more he moves, the harder they dig in, carving deep crimson divots into his flesh. Fresh blood streams down his flank.

I sprint along the elevated embankment alongside him, my taser pole crackling like mini bolts of lightning in the rain. It's dangerous and unwieldy in the wind, but still my best chance at removing the raptors.

Spino spins in circles, snapping at the raptors, stumbling unwittingly for the cliff at the edge of the caldera. If he's not careful, he'll topple over the ridge.

'Slow down!' I scream. 'I can help.'

Mid-spin, Spino's terrified gaze finds mine. In that fleeting instant, he understands my intentions as if we were one mind. *This is what full stem power feels like.* He lowers his head towards the embankment, bringing the raptor clinging to his neck within reach. I jab the taser into the raptor's spine.

CRACK!

Sparks fly, followed by an intense burst of light. The raptor's jerks its head back with a distressed shriek, then drops off. Spino recoils, partially stunned by the taser. He shakes his head, regains composure, then stomps on the stunned raptor, driving it down into a muddy grave. He cranes his head around and snaps at the raptor hanging from his sail. The brazen raptor hisses back. Spino strikes again and catches the raptor's head in his mouth. He drags the writhing creature off his lacerated sail, lifts it high into the air, and bites, decapitating it.

The headless raptor splashes down metres in front of me.

Spino spits the severed head at the remaining raptors. The pair screech in defeat, leap off, and dart for the protection of the jungle.

'Yeah! We did it.'

Spino growls and sniffs his wounds.

I jump down the embankment and approach him with caution, deactivating the taser pole so as not to startle him. He whines and winces as he inspects his wounds. It's easy to forget he's only a juvenile and a similar age to me in dinosaur years, and like myself, never had a fight as brutal as this. I stroke his hind leg and his muscles twinge.

'It's okay. You're safe now.'

Spino lowers his head and flashes me a sad look. I'm convinced those are tears streaming from his eyes, but it's impossible to be sure in the incessant rain.

Whoosh!

A pair of fiery streaks rise above the ridge. The wind sucks away the trails of smoke, revealing a pair robot marines equipped with jetpacks. They swerve and fight the gale to land on the rocky ridge, one carrying a gun loaded with a wire net, the other, a pulse rifle.

Geez, when do we get a break?

Spino roars at them.

The robots aim their laser sights, but have trouble locking on us in the storm, and continuously readjust. I look around in desperation. Our best cover is the rocky alcoves of the caldera rim, right below them. It seems insane, but I run straight for it.

'Follow me!' I scream, waving Spino onwards.

He looks at me, the robots, then stomps off in another direction.

Oh no! What's he doing? I can't stop to find out. From the corner of my eye, I glimpse something in the jungle keeping pace with me, getting closer, heading in a direction to cut me off. A flash of lightning illuminates the grey mottled skin of a raptor. *They're not finished with me yet!*

But it's the raptor I can't see that terrifies me more. It could be racing up behind me, claws spread to eviscerate me.

I suddenly realise my hands are empty. *Damn it! I'm an idiot.* I'm on an intercept course with the raptors and robots and left my taser pole behind. *Where's Spino?* I don't have time to turn around. I can't stop running. I'm almost at the ridge.

The raptor bursts through the scrub ahead and makes a sharp turn that cuts me off. I'm about to run straight into those razor-sharp claws.

PLONK!

Spino's massive, webbed foot stomps down between me and the raptor. I crash into his rock-hard calf muscle and bounce off. The raptor shrieks and scurries off, tail in the air. That's when I see the second raptor coming up behind me, moments away from ambushing me, but it retreats, like its companion.

Spino looms over me, flaunting a large log in his mouth. He checks on me, then charges the caldera ridge as the robots land on the rocks. Their laser sights track along the log and converge on his head, about to shoot. Spino uses his forward momentum to hurl the log. It whistles through the air like a missile and takes out the robot with the pulse rifle.

BOOM!

The robot explodes and the log obliterates into a million splinters.

Spino crouches in front of me, taking the brunt of the explosion across his side. He howls as a dozen spear-sized splinters impale his sail.

A sharp pain seizes my upper body. I wince and grab my shoulder. I'm not injured, but I feel every one of those bloody spikes piercing Spino's flesh. *Our stem power works too well.*

Spino rises and soldiers on, limping towards the last robot. The marine tracks him with his laser sight and net gun. Spino picks up a mossy boulder in his jaws, with just metres separating him and the robot. It's going to be close.

BANG!

A steel net unfurls from the gun and harpoons Spino's hindquarter against the ridge. Pinned in place, Spino still manages to hurl the boulder. The robot's armour is no contest for the giant rock. The marine explodes and blazes over the island like a meteor, swiftly extinguished by the storm.

I stagger over to my war-torn companion.

Spino squirms to break free from the metal net. The high-tensile, unbreakable wire slices a bloody latticework into his skin. He looks at me and whimpers. I try pulling the net from the rocks, but it won't budge. The pegs are driven into solid stone.

'Don't worry, I'm here.' Spino hears my voice and fights harder. 'Stop. Don't fight it. You'll make it worse.'

I don't get it. My voice usually settles him.

CRACK!

Lightning strikes overhead. The forks reflect in Spino's eye, revealing the silhouette of a raptor poised on the rocks behind me.

My heart stops. A wave of dread washes over me. Spino was trying to warn me this entire time, but I wasn't listening. The raptor crouches and hisses, preparing to pounce. My heart hammers back to life, alerting me to an even worse danger.

Where's the other raptor?

A blur of grey skin, claws, and teeth launches from the swamp.

Spino bumps me backwards with his snout and snaps at the raptor, saving me from the deadly attack. I tumble into a rocky crevice with the sounds of a savage fight trailing me. Desperate shrieks, hisses, and claws scraping across stone echo through the tight space. My heart sinks. I can't run back to get the taser pole in time. There's nothing I can do to help Spino. Unless...

The gantry! I just have to get them on there.

I crawl up through a crevice against a torrent of rainwater and emerge on a windswept ridge, the cliff on one side, the swamp the other. The gantry is a quick sprint from here. Looking back, I can see Spino's torn sail and the top of his head moving behind the rocks. He's still incapacitated and fending off the raptors.

I jump up and wave my arms, screaming into the wind. 'Hey! Over here!'

For a moment, there's nothing. No response. Just the howling gale. Then a raptor leaps onto a nearby crag, followed by its mate a second later. They look at me, then at each other. *ARRK! ARRK! ARRK!*

Suddenly they're bounding over the rocks for me.

I about-face and sprint for the gantry. The raptor claws clack across the rocks behind me, getting louder as they gain ground. I leap onto the gantry and slip on the metal plating, winding myself against the railing. Doubled over and gasping for breath, I fight against the wind and stumble up the incline towards the sealed hatch.

I don't expect the Union assessors to open it for me.

The raptors reach the narrow gantry at the same time and collide. There's only room for one at a time. They bark and snap at each other, quarrelling over who goes first. The larger raptor forces the other back and takes the lead.

I reach the far side of the gantry locate the control panel beside the door, open the hatch, and hold my trembling hand over the button to retract the gantry. Peering over my shoulder, can barely see through the rain pelting my face. I have to wait until both raptors are aboard, or this won't work.

'Come on. What are you waiting for?' I yell. 'Come and get me.'

The raptors jostle up the gantry, bumping awkwardly off the balustrade, unsure how to navigate the unnatural space.

I slam the button with the palm of my hand.

The gantry retracts from the ridge and telescopes inwards towards me. The raptor coming up the rear is caught unaware. Its back foot suddenly has nothing to stand on and it plunges into the void below. The lead raptor senses the danger and scrambles towards me, struggling to grip the slippery metal panels. I almost feel sorry for it. *Almost.*

The raptor runs out of gantry and topples off the end.

I hit the button to stop the gantry and slump against the door. I'm drenched and exhausted, but alive, and so is Spino. I should be relieved, but it was a messy victory, and I can't shake the feeling I failed the session.

Either way, I'm about to find out.

My suspicions were correct – I'm in trouble. Instead of catching the train back to the barracks with the other cadets, an armed Union guard marches me through the island facility to an undisclosed location. I'm soaked through and the air-conditioned passage makes me shiver. There was no opportunity or offer to change into dry clothes, just a quick march in my sodden, squelchy boots. I leave a trail of glistening shoeprints on the pristine white floor.

We traverse an endless maze of escalators, walkways, and bridges to arrive the highest level in the enclosure walls. From this vantage point, I can see the full breadth of the volcanic island within the superstructure. I peer through the window onto the sweeping caldera, hoping to glimpse Spino on the ridge. The rain appears to be easing, but I can't see anything from this distance. I just hope the Union handlers have released him from the net.

The guard glares at me over his shoulder and I hustle into line behind him. His stubborn silence makes me anxious.

I go over the combat session in my head. There are so many things I could have done differently, more efficiently.

The guard directs me into a dimly lit meeting room. A long boardroom table runs alongside a wall of floor-to-ceiling windows. Outside the island walls, the cyclone is clearing. The archipelago emerges from the haze and the first rays of sunlight poke through the grey clouds, casting a spotlight of blue water upon the ocean.

Three familiar figures sit at the end of the table: Brigadier Ramsey, Suda Satoshi, and Nadja Schulze. None look up. They silently scroll through their holographic data screens. I see my details [ZAYLA-8311/ SPINOSAURUS] on the bottom corner of all three holograms. *This isn't good.* Butterflies race through my stomach. The guard leaves the room and I stand with my hands behind my back, trying not to shiver.

Ramsey finally looks up. 'Zayla-8311, how do you think your session went?'

I don't immediately respond. I'm not sure what to say. What do they want to hear? Their steely expressions infer I should choose my words carefully. On the surface, my survival feels like a victory. I avoided injury and kept Spino alive, but deep inside, I know I failed. It's difficult to admit to myself, let alone to my superiors.

'I think I failed.'

'What makes you think that?'

'I escaped with my life, but was stranded on the gantry. I saved my spinosaurus, but he was incapacitated. We were easy targets. I didn't have many options left.'

'Your brief assessment mirrors ours. I'll list the problems in more detail. You took approximately 97 seconds to reconnect with your asset. That's too long. You need to get that down to single digits, and ultimately aim for an instantaneous connection. Once you were in telepathic sync, you wasted another minute and 22 seconds demonstrating your intentions to your asset. You successfully eliminated the first two robots and secured the taser pole. That weapon should have been enough to keep the raptors at bay, yet you faltered, allowing the pack to attack your asset. That failure triggered a downward spiral, where you were no longer on top of the situation. Luck and circumstance ensued. You survived the raptor attack and subsequent robot assault, but the cost was too high. You wasted 2 minutes and 45 seconds in a futile attempt to release your asset from the net. You should've used that time to prepare for the raptors. And as you observed, your escape onto the gantry was a dead end.'

'Yes, sir.'

Nadja scrolls through her hologram. 'You reached 100% stem power with your asset for approximately 47 seconds out of 15 minutes together. That equates to 5.22%. For an apex predator and a cadet in line for a command position, we expect that to be no lower than 78%.'

The three of them stare at me, unblinking.

I shift nervously on the spot, wondering if I'm meant to respond to the intimidating statistic. I'm well below the standard.

'Enhancing your stem power is just one part of the problem,' Suda adds. 'You need to improve your problem-solving. Never aim for a 100% solution to any problem. If you spend too long devising the perfect solution, you will end up behind. That split second or two is enough to give your enemy the edge. Aim for 80%. This allows for flexibility.'

'Yes, sir. I will.'

Suda's stern expression softens. 'I'll give you credit for using the gantry. It's a good example of thinking outside the box. Normally, that gantry would be retracted the moment you entered the enclosure. You were lucky – a lightning strike short-circuited the electronics and locked it in the extended position. Fortunately, power to the controls was rerouted moments before you activated it. Don't expect such advantages on the battlefield.'

'I won't, sir. I'll remember that for my next session.'

Ramsey deactivates his hologram and leans forward. 'Do you have any questions before we pass our academy recommendations to the Union?'

'Yes, sir. Can I ask what role I am being recommended for?'

Ramsey regards Suda and Nadja, who both nod in agreement.

'First Lieutenant.'

My stomach does a nervous flip and suddenly, my shivering is harder to control. I wasn't expecting to be nominated for such a senior role so early in my training.

'Is there something wrong, cadet?'

'I've failed twice. Why am –'

'Because we see potential. You and your asset represent a significant investment to this academy and the Union. On the battlefield you will lead specialised platoons, and provide discipline and counselling to the ranks beneath you. We envision you taking part in Operation Flame, the second planned offensive on Daxma-5.'

I stare blankly at them, contemplating all the reasons this role is wrong for me. It feels like the room is being sucked into a vacuum. I lose all sense of time.

'Do you agree with our decision?' Ramsey's voice pulls me back to reality.

Now I feel nauseas. I should explain my case, it's now or never. I can't believe they overlooked my one glaring weakness. I swallow the lump in my throat and muster up a modicum of confidence. 'I don't believe I'm right for the position.'

Ramsey's brow furrows. 'Why is that?'

'I lack the social skills to lead a platoon. I believe I'm better suited to second lieutenant.'

'Your opinion is noted, but we stand by our decision.'

I straighten and raise my chin. 'Yes, sir.'

'Keep working hard,' Suda says. 'Your social skills will improve when you become more confident. Believe in yourself. Learn from your mistakes.'

'Push yourself and trust your asset,' Nadja says. 'He will rise to any challenge.'

Ramsey sits back in his chair, reactivates his hologram feed, and focuses on his next task. 'That's all, cadet. You're dismissed.'

I salute them and leave the room. The guard waiting for me outside leads me to the mag-lev platform. Should I feel thrilled or terrified? My instructors were harsh, but honest. I don't share their faith in me. It's a weird situation, like they know more about me than they let on. All I can do is trust their opinions and focus on improving.

I arrive at the deserted platform and board an empty train. My solitary journey back to the barracks mirrors my life – as if I'm blindly hurtling forward on an express train, destination unknown.

There are no stops. No places to jump off. And if I fail to heed the wisdom of my instructors, I'll end up a casualty of war on a distant world.

By the time the mag-lev train delivers me home, most cadets are showered, dressed, and on their way to the mess hall for dinner. I keep my arms crossed in a futile attempt to keep warm, feeling like I've been shivering for days. I spend extra time in the shower, head under the faucet, enjoying the heat as my core warms. *This is the best shower ever.*

Afterwards, I find Abby in the mess hall, sitting at the same table as last night. She eagerly waves me over.

'I thought you weren't coming,' Abby says as I place my tray down opposite her. 'I heard a rumour you didn't come back on the train with the other cadets. I was worried something happened to you.'

'Just enjoying a hot shower. I could have stayed in there all night.'

'I know. It was freezing out there today. You think the academy could have postponed our session because of the cyclone.'

I eat, content to listen to Abby as she gives me a detailed breakdown on the combat simulation with her stegosaurus. I'm glad she didn't ask why I was late. I don't have the energy to explain myself.

Kane approaches our table, tray in hand. 'Hey, Zayla, do you mind if I sit with you guys?'

I gulp my mouthful with surprise and make the obligatory introductions. 'Abby, this is Kane. Kane, Abby.'

'Hi, Kane, nice to meet you. Zaz has told me all about you.'

'Is that right, Zaz?' Kane says with a playful grin, taking a seat next to me.

What the hell is Abby doing? It sounds like I've been droning on nonstop about him. I should be careful what I say around her.

'I like your nickname,' Kane says offhandedly, eating his first mouthful.

Abby gives me a subtle look and raises an eyebrow. I know what she's thinking: *Another boy is interested in you.* I hate the attention. I don't want anyone interested in me, and would prefer to go unnoticed in the academy.

'Hey, sleeping beauty!' booms a voice from behind. A heavy hand lands on my shoulder. 'I swear you've been avoiding us since the med-bay.'

I turn around and find a mountain of muscle standing over me. 'Tyson!'

Rosa peers over his shoulder and rolls her eyes at me. 'I don't blame you, Zayla. You're lucky. I've been trying to ditch this buffoon ever since. I can't believe we ended up in the same dorm as him.'

Tyson chucks his tray down and plonks himself by my side. 'I'm Tyson,' he announces to everyone at the table. 'But most people call me *Bison*.'

Abby stifles a laugh.

'I hope you don't mind us joining you,' Rosa says, sitting beside Abby. 'Tyson shares more than just a physical semblance to his nickname – he has the manners to match.'

'Don't be cruel,' Tyson mumbles through a mouthful of food. 'That's insulting to bisons.'

'There's no such word as *bisons*.'

'What do you call a herd of bison, then?'

'A herd of bison,' Rosa says bluntly.

Tyson brushes her off and shovels in another mouthful of food.

I watch them with a smile on my face. Rosa loves complaining about Tyson, but she clearly enjoys being around him. They're an odd couple, but I like their playful banter.

'This is Abby and Kane,' I say, finishing the introductions.

'Oh, yeah. You were called up to the stage with Zaz,' Rosa says, recognising Kane. 'You bonded with megaraptors, right?'

'Yeah, a pack of six.'

'You're in the stealth and special ops division with me. I bonded with a pterodactyl.'

'Impressive. I've heard a lot of cadets died trying to bond with pterosaurs.'

'What about you, Abby?' Rosa asks.

Abby sighs. 'Oh, only the most stubborn stegosaurus in the academy.'

Tyson perks up. 'You're in the infantry, then. Nice to meet another grunt. It's exhausting keeping up with all these budding commanders, feels like I'm constantly being assessed.'

Abby laughs.

'Nobody's forcing you to hang with us,' Rosa says.

Tyson lines up a pea on the edge of his plate and flicks it at Rosa. She deflects it with her spoon and it lands on Abby's plate.

'Don't be so disgusting,' Rosa says.

Abby observes the pea sitting in her mash. 'Nice reflexes.'

'Hey, Bison,' Kane says. 'Just remember, commanders are only as good as their soldiers.'

Tyson slams the table with an excited fist. 'Damn straight!'

Abby picks out the rogue pea, places it on a spoon, and prepares to flick it back. 'Bison, I believe this belongs to you.'

'Fire away,' Tyson says, opening his mouth to receive the green projectile.

Abby flicks it across the table. Tyson shifts to the right, lowers his head, and catches the pea on his tongue, but he overbalances on his chair and crashes to the floor. The noise reverberates through the mess hall. Hoots and laughter erupt through the hall as everyone turns to see what the ruckus is all about. Tyson jumps to his feet, raises his arms in the air to the cheers, then takes a bow. Everyone at our table bursts out laughing. Tyson rights his chair and sits beside me, not looking embarrassed in the slightest. He doesn't need to feel humiliated, not when I can shoulder the burden for him. Just having everyone peer in our direction makes me go red. I don't know where to look.

My eyes find the one face that isn't smiling: Reeva's. She glares at me across the hall, unimpressed. I look away, mindful not to stir her up.

Reeva is probably still annoyed that Avi sat next to me in class instead of her, and now to rub salt into the wound, my friends are attracting all the attention. She's used to being the centre of the universe, with everyone orbiting her.

After dinner, everyone from our table leaves as a group to walk back to the dormitories. The tail end of the cyclone creates a cool evening breeze. The paths are littered with palm leaves and puddles of water. I'm content to listen to my ever-growing group of friends chat among themselves. Just being around them helps me blend into the academy and feel like a normal cadet for a change.

Kane abruptly departs the group. 'I'll see you guys tomorrow.' He smiles and makes lingering eye contact with me.

'See you,' I say.

Kane rushes down a set of stairs and disappears along a path leading to a lower section of the island.

Abby jabs my side. 'What is it with you and the handsome male cadets?'

I feign ignorance. 'What do you mean?'

'That's the second guy who's gone out of his way to sit next to you today.'

'So?'

'He obviously likes you.'

'Hey, I just wanted to sit with you guys,' Tyson butts in. 'No ulterior motives on my part.'

Abby gives Tyson a friendly punch on the arm. 'I didn't mean you, Bison. Not saying I don't think you're handsome.'

Rosa laughs. 'For a bison, that is.'

We all laugh, including Tyson. He might be boisterous, but it's good to see he can take a joke at his own expense.

'Stop holding out on me,' Rosa says. 'Who was the other guy who sat next to you today?'

'Avi,' Abby announces before I can respond.

'The same Avi from our dorm – the one who's in the apex predator command program?'

'That's the one,' Abby cuts in again.

'Oh, yeah, every girl in the academy is talking about him. He likes you, Zaz?' Rosa says, a glimmer of delight lighting up her eyes.

'He just sat next to me in class, that's all.'

'That's only half of it,' Abby says. 'Avi left his friends with Reeva and Lani to sit next to Zaz. Reeva gave Zaz the stink eye for the rest of class.'

'Hey, Zaz,' calls a shrill voice from behind. I spin about. Reeva, Lani, and their gang of followers come up fast. 'Are you too good to come back on the train with the rest of us today?'

'Speak of the devil,' Abby says under her breath.

I turn my back to them and keep walking. 'Just ignore her.'

Reeva's persistent voice follows me. 'Seriously, where were you?'

I continue walking, hoping – wishing – she would just leave me alone. She won't stop until she's found out where I was this afternoon because she needs to know everything about everyone, especially me.

'Seriously. What are you hiding?' Reeva says.

'Nothing,' I call over my shoulder.

Tyson stops and confronts them. 'You got a problem?'

We all turn around.

Reeva pulls up, a little intimidated by Tyson's rebuke, and lowers her voice. 'Be careful. If Zaz asks you to join her division for the group exercises, I'd think twice before committing if I was you.'

'Nobody asked for your opinion,' Abby says.

'Just a friendly warning, that's all.'

Rosa butts in. 'Why should we listen to you?'

'Because I know Zaz better than any of you.'

'What's that supposed to mean?'

'Have you ever wondered why Zaz doesn't have any friends from her old Beta Barracks?'

'No, but I'm wondering why you do,' Abby says.

Tyson bursts out laughing.

Reeva shoots Abby a condescending look. 'Hilarious, Steggo!'

'Steggo!' Lani squeals in laughter. Reeva's group cackle like a pack of squawking troodons.

Abby's cheeks go red. I've never seen her humiliated. Her lips pinch tight, and she narrows her furious gaze on Reeva. I ready myself to step between them.

Reeva isn't bothered and continues to goad her. 'Isn't that what you bonded with? A stegosaurus?'

'So? What's wrong with that?'

'Nothing. I suppose it's the best a grunt can expect.'

Abby clenches her fists. Punches are about to fly. I hold Abby's arm back.

'Hey!' Tyson says, stepping forward. 'Watch what you say. Us grunts look out for each other.'

Reeva glances sideways at him. 'Back off, muscles. Better watch what you say. I might be your superior officer one day.'

'Not if I have anything to say about it.'

I finally step forward, heart racing. 'It's all right, Tyson. You don't have to jeopardise your position. I can look after myself.'

Reeva scoffs. 'Yeah, that's what you're best at.'

'We don't care what you say,' Abby says.

'Fine, don't take it from me then. Just ask Kane. I'm surprised he's even talking to you, Zaz, after you left him to be killed by a pack of megaraptors. Why didn't you stop to help him? That's the least you could do after he saved you from the same pack the day before.'

'You don't know what happened,' I say. My words come out soft and fragile, but inside, my emotions are raging. I can't tell if I'm about to burst out crying or strike Reeva's lying little mouth.

'Have you told your friends how you left me hanging off a cliff to die during the Bonding?' Reeva plays up to the growing crowd of onlookers with a fake display of emotion. 'I know you hate me, but you didn't have to leave me to die.'

An uncomfortable silence follows.

Whispers of doubt filter through the crowd of cadets. Some frown, others shake their heads. I can't say anything to salvage my reputation, not when I've already been judged.

'Why should we believe you?' Rosa says.

'If you don't believe me, just ask Avi next time you see him. He had to save me, even though Zaz was right beside me. She could have helped me with no danger to herself.'

Reeva waves her friends away and addresses the crowd. 'Keep it in mind when you sign up for the group exercises tomorrow. You need a leader you can trust with your life.'

I watch Reeva leave, feeling like I've been gutted by a raptor. The crowd disperses and several cadets give me a dirty look as they pass.

'Don't worry,' Abby says softly. 'I'll be signing up for your squad.'

Tyson gives me a friendly pat on the back. 'Me too. You should've let Reeva fall off that cliff.'

'She's got it in for you bad,' Rosa says. 'What happened between you two?'

I stare at her blankly, wondering what to say. I've never told anyone why Reeva hates me, but I'm too angry and upset to talk about it now.

Abby takes me by the arm and drags me away. 'Doesn't matter. Whatever happened, I'm sure it's not your fault.'

My body involuntarily quivers in response to her comment. Abby couldn't be more wrong. Reeva has every right to make my life a living hell after what I did all those years ago.

9

Desperate screams fill me with dread. The surrounding wall of human bodies shifts and heaves with a life of its own, threatening to crush me. I struggle to breathe. The little amount of air I get down here is tainted with smoke. Overhead, the small pocket of scarlet sky visible through the crowd is littered with rocket exhaust trails. My mother drags me through the mob, clutching my hand so tight it hurts. I'm young, and barely up to her waist.

I've lived this nightmare countless times, trapped in my five-year-old self. I know it's a dream, but I still can't wake myself from the Daxma-5 massacre.

Mother trips and drags me down. A man grabs her arm and yanks her back up before the mob tramples us. It's my father. His warm hazel-coloured eyes, dark-red hair, and trimmed beard is familiar and comforting. He pulls us through the packed bodies, picks me up, and shields us as best he can from the chaos.

Now I see everything from my father's arms. We're running away from the colony buildings across a crowded platform that overlooks the purple landscape of Daxma-5. Several launch pads lay ahead. The last escape shuttles lifts off, sending a billowing cloud of white exhaust towards us. I hug Dad tight and look to my mother for reassurance. She smiles, but her sweet face carries a haunted expression. Her pale skin, blue eyes, and dark hair are just like mine – like I'm looking upon an older version of myself.

Dad peers skyward and hands me to Mum. 'There's another escape shuttle coming in. It's adjusting its descent towards the other launch pad.'

He takes Mum by the arm and forges against the crowd in the opposite direction.

Mum fights the surge of bodies like a fast-moving tide and fends off the colonists with her elbows. 'Hold on tight, Zaz.'

BOOM!

A colossal explosion erupts from the colony buildings, and our platform shudders. A roiling plume of fire and smoke unfurls into the sky, showering us with glowing embers. They look pretty, like a native swarm of Daxma-5 fireflies. The incoming shuttle ignites its descent thrusters, churning the embers and smoke into a fiery maelstrom.

I shield my eyes as the burning specks land on my forehead, stinging my skin. The terrified screams suddenly turn into cheers.

'We're saved!' someone screams.

The tide shifts and the three of us are dragged along with the crowd in a frenzied scramble for the final escape shuttle. The exhaust fumes clear, revealing a towering silver vessel as it touches down on the landing pad. It stands before us like a building, ten or more stories high. I burst with excitement, even though I know our victory is short-lived.

We surge forward with the crowd, shoulder-to-shoulder, fighting to stay above the bodies. One slip and there's a mass of colonists behind us, unintentionally set to trample us to death.

BOOM!

A second blast detonates nearby, catapulting several colonists into the air. Their floppy bodies plummet into the crowd on our right. Our entire platform shudders and tilts diagonally, causing everyone to fall over and slide towards the edge.

I peer over the sprawl of bodies and see the daxanoids swarm over our escape vessel. Their six lanky arms and two short legs allow them to swing across the hull like giant white monkeys. Strange blue energy ripples over their pale, hairless skin, which transfers through the hull of the ship, triggering a series of interior explosions.

Mum fights to keep me above the crowd as Dad loses his grip and slides towards the edge of the platform.

The angle rises sharply, increasing our rate of slide. Everyone screams. Some colonists topple over the edge and plummet to their deaths hundreds of metres below, while a lucky few cling to the railing.

A titanoid rises from the plum-coloured jungle to attack our platform. The demonic beast is twice the size of a tyrannosaur and similar in shape, bearing glowing white eyes, with the same blue energy arcing over its leathery skin as the daxanoids. Bolts of electricity dance within its gaping maw like a power generator. Several colonists fall inside and are instantly vaporised by the raw energy.

These docile, indigenous lifeforms have been possessed by the Wraith to kill us.

Two more titanoids converge on the platform, mouths open, intent on devouring the unfortunate souls that topple over the side.

Dad tumbles over the railing and dangles over the mouth of a titanoid. He hooks one arm around the steel balustrade and holds out the other to catch us. His body is silhouetted against the waiting mouth, so bright it's like the sun rising to consume him.

Mum places one hand over my eyes and whispers calmly in my ear. 'I love you, baby girl.'

I awake with a jolt and sit upright in bed. My singlet is drenched in sweat and my heart is pounding. A blinding light flashes at the foot of my bed, startling me. For a second, I think I'm back on Daxma-5, about to fall into a titanoid mouth. I shield my eyes and gather my senses. The damp sticky bedsheets draw me back to the harsh reality of my dormitory.

I hear giggling, then observe a shadowy figure scurry off in the darkness. I glimpse Reeva's blond hair as she climbs back into bed. Not that I needed confirmation – there's only one cadet shameless enough to photograph me in such an exposed state.

A Union guard enters the dormitory and marches between the beds, shining his flashlight across the sleeping (and pretending to sleep) cadets. For anyone caught out of bed, it's a guaranteed detention cleaning out the dinosaur pens.

Compared to how I feel right now, shovelling stinky dinosaur crap seems like the best job in the world.

I lay down on my soggy mattress. *Yuck!* My moist pyjamas have cooled and cling to my skin like a wet towel. I pull the blanket up to my chin, trying not to shiver as the guard's torchlight passes over my bed.

I feel like running over to Reeva's bed, grabbing her data recorder, and smashing it in half. How dare she take a holographic image of me at my most vulnerable! I'll be the laughingstock of the academy if that image circulates. Add the doubt and rumours she's spreading about me, Reeva has enough to make me look deranged and unstable in front of everyone, including my friends. The humiliation would be unconscionable. I'd never recover. Nobody would talk to me again.

A grinding noise distracts me from the spiral of negative thoughts. *What is that?*

It's me! I'm grinding my teeth so hard my ears are buzzing. I hold the blanket over my shoulder in a clenched fist, my entire body rigid with stress. I feel like vomiting straight over the edge of my bed.

With selections for group exercises tomorrow, this could be part of Reeva's plan to undermine me. How do I deal with her without making a fool of myself? My emotions surge through me like a tsunami and I can't hold back the tears any longer. I bury my face in the pillow and cry.

The next morning, I awake exhausted.

Our fitness instructors rally us out of bed and lead us on another run around the island. But I feel like I've run a marathon through the night and struggle to keep up. I fall to the back of the pack and stay there for the duration. I'm the last into the showers and skip breakfast in the mess hall, avoiding any chance of running into Reeva. I'm too stressed to stomach food.

I arrive at the morning class. Abby has already taken a seat without me a few rows from the back of the room. My suspicions immediately kick into overdrive. *Why didn't she wait for me in the hall like usual? Am I being paranoid, or is she avoiding me? What does she know? What if she's seen the image of me from last night? She might be too embarrassed to be around me.*

I walk towards her, heart banging against my ribs like a wild, caged animal. She hasn't seen me yet. I could make a quick detour and take a seat close by, pretending I haven't seen her, just in case she doesn't want to sit next to me. I know I'm being stupid, but I can't help it.

Abby glances up, smiles, then furrows her brow with concern. 'Are you all right?'

I take a seat next to her as if nothing's wrong. 'Why?'

'You look pale.'

'I'm always pale,' I say, avoiding too much eye contact. I feel like she'll be able to read the sadness behind my eyes. The truth is impossible to hide. I've been crying all night.

'You don't look yourself.'

I activate my holographic workspace and look busy. 'I'm fine, just tired. That's all.'

Abby nods and returns to her hologram, but I feel her glancing sidelong at me.

I feel guilty for lying. I'm anything but fine. My cool exterior masks a fragile version of myself. I thought bonding with a spinosaurus would make me stronger, more resilient. I could do with a little of his fearless instincts now.

Reeva enters the classroom with Lani and, surprisingly, doesn't pay me any attention. I timidly watch her through my hologram, expecting her to look my way. I strain to hear her conversation above the chatter, wondering if my name is being thrown around.

Avi and his friends enter and sit midway between Reeva and me, a couple of rows ahead. Avi doesn't turn around to acknowledge me. That's strange, he knows where I sit. *Why isn't he turning around?*

'Are you sure you're okay?' Abby asks.

I recoil from my hologram, suddenly realising how obvious I must look. I gaze at Abby, wishing I could tell her what's on my mind. But that's not me. I don't burden people with my problems. I never have, never will. I don't want sympathy.

'If it's about last night, don't worry,' Abby says. 'Reeva's a total bitch.'

'You mean about what she said?'

'Yeah, of course. What else could it be?'

Little does she know. I smile, relieved to have someone on my side. Abby doesn't seem to know about the photo – surely she would have said something if she did. Reeva must be keeping that embarrassment up her sleeve for the right moment. Our teacher, Suda, enters and takes his place at the front of the class.

I prepare my hologram for the class and look up to find Avi peering over his shoulder at me. Butterflies flutter through my chest. *How long has he been watching me?* He gives me a warm smile and faces the front.

His gesture of friendship lifts my spirits and my day doesn't seem so bad now.

'Good morning, cadets,' Suda says. 'In light of the upcoming selections for your group exercises, today we will break down the three divisions and their roles in battle. By now, all of you know that each dinosaur species is assigned a specific role. On the battlefield, you should be able to distinguish between infantry, special ops, and command simply by identifying the species. The Union has not had an operational military force for 300 years, so the hierarchy is based on military regimes from the twentieth century.'

Lani's hologram lights up green.

Suda motions for her to continue.

'If our divisions are based on historic military hierarchies, why isn't there an option for promotion? Why are we designated a rank for life?'

'The Union has carefully assigned each dinosaur to their division based on centuries of observation and study. Your assets possess vastly different brains, making them suited to specific tasks. The special ops assets have larger occipital and parietal lobes, giving them enhanced eyesight, depth perception, and problem-solving. Those with a dominant cerebellum are good at learning, have an increased attention span, and are better at controlling their primal instincts. Command assets fall into this category. The infantry division assets share a more balanced brain anatomy. Their frontal and temporal lobes, thalamus, and basal ganglia operate at the same level of complexity as their occipital and parietal lobes, making them reliable, all-round fighters that are good at following orders.'

'But our assets only represent half of a partnership. What about us?' Lani says, looking around the room. 'Like me, I'm sure there're plenty of cadets in the academy who have the ability and motivation to rise through the ranks. Why are we denied that opportunity?'

I smile to myself. It's obvious Lani isn't happy with her sauropelta being locked in the infantry division. She couldn't be more obvious.

'You can be assigned to a lieutenant position temporarily,' Suda says. 'If your lieutenant dies during battle, then the highest ranked special ops officer assumes the position until another lieutenant takes over. If there are no special ops officers available, which is highly unlikely, then the highest ranked infantry officer takes over.'

'I don't think it's fair we're locked into divisions for life.'

'Lani-5946, you're focused on the wrong thing.'

'But –'

Suda raises his hand, cutting her off.

'This war won't be won with a fleet of commanders alone. You all have very important parts to play. No division will succeed without the other. Remember, study each species in depth, not just your own. Familiarise yourself with their traits. Talk to your comrades; ask them about their assets. Nothing beats first hand knowledge.'

My hologram illuminates with a list of dinosaurs and their relevant divisions. A small three-dimensional image of each dinosaur rotates next to the name:

INFANTRY	SPECIAL OPS	COMMAND
Ankylosaurus	Coelophysis	Allosaurus
Dacentrurus	Mapusaurus	Carcharodontosaurus
Deinosuchus	Megaraptor	Giganotosaurus
Dreadnoughtus	Pterodactyl	Majungasaurus
Pachycephalosaurus	Quetzalcoatlus	Spinosaurus
Saichania	Sinocalliopteryx	Tyrannosaurus Rex
Sauropelta	Troodon	
Stegosaurus	Velociraptor	
Triceratops	Compsognathus	
Utahraptor		

I touch the spinosaurus and enlarge the image, half expecting to see Spino. I'm disappointed to find the dinosaur on display is an older specimen with grey-green skin and a scarred snout.

'Don't just focus on your asset during your group exercises,' Suda says, deliberately eyeing my hologram as he walks by my desk.

I minimise the image of the spinosaurus, feeling Suda's comment was directed at me.

'This is the perfect opportunity to learn each other's strengths and weaknesses.'

Avi's hologram lights up and Suda nods at him. 'What are we doing in our group exercises?'

'Each unit will be assigned a unique incursion mission with a set of objectives. These objectives encompass combat, surveillance, and infiltration. You will need to complete each stage to achieve the end goal. Success requires coordination and cooperation. The missions are spread across every dinosaur enclosure in the archipelago. Your exact objectives will be revealed the night before, so you'll have time to strategise. There will be two weeks of group training and then all units will enter a leader board. Rankings are rated on speed, and only completed missions count. There will be special rewards for the top five teams.'

The classroom livens up with excited chatter.

Abby leans closer and whispers, 'I wonder what the reward is?'

'Isn't that unfair for the cadets that don't finish on top?' a cadet says from the back of the classroom.

'Then finish on top,' Suda says sharply. 'There's nothing fair about war. That's why your unit selection this morning is crucial. Don't make choices based on friendships. This is not a game, nor a popularity contest. Your lives may one day depend upon the choices you make today.'

'Will our group exercise units be the same as the ones we go to war with?'

'No, but your group exercises help inform our war selections. Final lieutenants, units, and divisions will be decided well before it comes time for deployment.'

'When will you select the final positions?' Reeva asks.

'Based on your current progress, we have recommended a handful of cadets for First Lieutenant positions. We are just waiting to see how they perform in the group exercises.'

I sneak a look at the cadets sitting around me, wondering if anyone else is nominated besides me. I might be the only cadet in the academy who has been told about their nomination. Reeva obviously hasn't, or she wouldn't have asked the question. That gives me a boost of confidence. I watch Avi, hoping he might throw me a look or give away a clue that he's been nominated. I'd love to work with him.

'How are lieutenants chosen for the group exercises?' Reeva asks. 'Are they chosen by the Union based on our current performance?'

I detect a waver of concern in her voice. She's fishing for information, trying to determine if she might be nominated.

'The Union is not involved in the selections at this stage,' Suda replies. 'Command positions for your group exercises are determined by the votes you cast today.' He returns to the front of the classroom and stands behind his lectern as a hologram illuminates beside him, showing a graphical tree of command, special ops, and infantry positions.

'Every cadet in infantry and special ops divisions enter two votes for their preferred commanders. The cadets with the most votes are assigned a temporary First Lieutenant status to their unit, with six positions available for each barracks. Successful lieutenants choose another lieutenant to work alongside during the group exercises as they work in pairs. Remaining cadets in the command pool who did not receive enough votes operate as Second and Third Lieutenants, complete with their own unit selections and missions.'

Suda spends the remaining part of the lesson breaking down procedure and protocol. It's all very dry stuff. I'm so tired. It's hard to focus, so I spend most of the time staring into my hologram, skimming mindlessly through dinosaur species, military ranks, and unit structures. In the back of my mind, I'm fretting about the selections, doubting anyone will vote to be in my unit. I'll end up being a Third Lieutenant if I'm lucky.

The only thing I have in my favour is Spino. I'm the only cadet in the entire academy with a spinosaurus, and even that could end up working against me. Cadets won't choose me because they think I'm worthy of command, they'll be signing up to my unit because of Spino.

'What's going on with them?' Abby whispers, nodding towards Reeva.

Reeva and Lani peer over their shoulders towards me, laughing quietly and whispering to each other.

My insides turn to ice. *What are they up to?*

Cadets around the classroom glance my way, giggling and sneering. I shrink into my seat and hide behind my hologram, certain everyone has seen the photo Reeva took last night.

Suda rises from his desk, disturbed by the commotion. The laughter swiftly recedes. Reeva and Lani suddenly look busy and pretend to study their holograms. Suda surveys the room with a formidable gaze, eager to punish those responsible for disrupting the peace.

Abby is oblivious to the in-joke circulating the room. Whatever had the cadets so entertained, she wasn't included. It seemed to be Reeva's close friends and the select few she deems worthy of her inner circle. That's how Reeva operates. She starts with a few loyal friends, then slowly casts her net out to those inclined to follow her lead, usually the popular cadets. Being attractive helps. I've never seen Reeva befriend the odd or quirky cadets – it's always those with lots of friends. Eventually they all fall into line, blind to her discriminatory ways.

As soon as the class finishes, I rush outside.

Abby races to keep up with me, probably thinking I'm excited about the selections, but I'm trying to keep my distance from Reeva. We follow the crowd outside to the main quadrangle, where multiple voting stations are set up. Every cadet in the command program, across all barracks and islands, is listed across the selection touchscreens. A running tally of votes hovers above each station in vibrant holographic banners. Cadets from all over the island huddle around and cast their votes, chatting fervently as new names and votes appear.

My stomach twists into a knot. This is more stressful than I imagined. There are so many unfamiliar faces, it's overwhelming.

Cadets with votes begin appearing on the banners, faces emblazoned several stories high for all to see, complete with name, birth number, barracks, and the most important information of all, their dinosaur.

[MAIA-4756/MAJUNGASAURUS-B023]
[WYNNE-8219/GIGANTOSAURUS-B013]
[NOAH-1685/ALLOSAURUS-B034]
[REEVA-6333/TYRANNOSAURUS-B010]

'Urgh! No surprise there,' Abby groans. 'I'm going to vote. Hopefully it will knock Reeva down a space or two.'

Abby pushes through the crowd. I stick close and glance up at the banners. My mouth is dry with anticipation. Now I'm not sure what's worse, my name and face appearing, or not. I peer over Abby's shoulder as she scrolls through the alphabetical list of cadets. My name is guaranteed to be the last on the list. Just another detail that will work against people voting for me.

Abby finds [ZAYLA-8311/SPINOSAURUS-B010] and selects it. The cadet beside her sees Abby's selection, then scrolls down to the bottom of the list and chooses me. *Oh great!* I want to get out of here before I'm recognised. I grab Abby and lead her away.

Tyson spots us across the sea of heads and directs Rosa towards us. His booming voice reaches us first. 'I hope you're not voting for yourself.'

'Don't be stupid,' Rosa says, grabbing him. 'Come on, let's vote before it gets too busy.'

Abby and I retreat to the edge of the quadrangle and watch from a quieter position as more cadets file into the quadrangle. They form noisy crowds around the voting stations as new names populate the results. Cadets with more votes rise to the top, pushing others lower.

[MATEO-4158/TYRANNOSAURUS-B006]
[RADINKA-2028/MAJUNGASAURUS-B008]
[SEONG-6914/CARCHARODONTOSAURUS-B032]
[AVI-0995/ALLOSAURUS-B010]

Cheers arise from somewhere in the crowd. Abby and I peer over the crowd, attempting to locate Avi's fans.

Abby nudges me and points to the banner. 'Look!'

I can't believe my eyes, but it's there for all to see:

[ZAYLA-8311/SPINOSAURUS-B010]

Beneath my name is my ranking, position 32 of 50. It changes before my eyes, rising steadily through the twenties and into the teens.

'Wow! You're catching up to Reeva.'

I was so shocked I didn't take note of her position at number 5. Avi sits at number 11. The votes are coming in so fast, the top 20 cadets are going up and down like yo-yos. Next thing, I've overtaken Avi and climbed into single digits. Reeva holds on to the top 10. There aren't many cadets with a tyrannosaur, but those with one stick near the top.

My name progressively climbs to the top spot.

I shake my head in disbelief. 'I don't understand what's happening.' My stomach is doing flips. I don't want the top spot. It's only going to draw more attention from the one person I want to avoid: Reeva.

Abby laughs, 'That's so cool, you might beat Reeva.'

Now I feel nauseated. *I don't want to beat Reeva.*

Tyson rushes over. 'Look at you go, Zaz!'

'We just voted,' Rosa says, joining us. 'It looked like everyone at the voting station was scrolling down the list, looking for your name.'

'It's only because of my spinosaurus,' I say.

'Nah, don't be so modest. They like you.'

'What? Nobody knows me. I've barely met anyone in our dorm except for you guys.'

'Trust me, they know you.'

'How?'

'Don't forget, you were called up in front of the assembly after the Bonding. Everyone knows you.'

I hadn't thought of that. Kane was called onto the stage as well, but he's not being voted on because he's in the special ops division, not command. My recognition at the first academy assembly is now fuelling my popularity. I wish I'd never been singled out like that.

My name climbs the list, causing others to drop. Reeva sticks in the top five while Avi climbs the ranks like me. A beeping tone rings through the quadrangle and the final votes are locked in. The list of names is replaced by the message [CONFIRMING RESULTS]

'I can't watch,' I say, making for a quick exit. 'I'm going back to my dorm.'

Tyson grabs my arm. 'Don't be stupid.'

The results appear one by one, starting with the bottom position.

6. [MAIA-4756/MAJUNGASAURUS-B0235]
5. [WYNNE-8219/GIGANTOSAURUS-B013]

I'm tempted to slip away, but my anticipation and curiosity is slowly getting the better of me. The top six cadets will divide into three groups of two, with the pair sharing First Lieutenant duties for the first exercise. *I'd hate to be paired with Reeva.* My stomach drops at the thought.

4. [SEONG-6914/CARCHARODONTOSAURUS-B032]
3. [ZAYLA-8311/SPINOSAURUS-B010]
2. [REEVA-6333/TYRANNOSAURUS-B010]
1. [AVI-0995/ALLOSAURUS-B010]

My friends cheer and pat me on the back, almost knocking me over. It takes a moment for reality to sink in and find my feet.

I finished in third position!

I can't believe it. The situation feels surreal, like some crazy fever dream. I'm light-headed and giddy with surprise, and clutch Tyson's shirt for support. Cadets I've never met approach me, arms open like old friends, eager to introduce themselves and congratulate me. Their cheerful faces merge into a blur of smiles, and their well-wishes an endless drone of praise.

This could be the best thing that ever happened to me... Or the worst.

10

I'm in a daze, still trying to wrap my head around finishing third on the voting ladder. I stay outside in the quadrangle and force myself to mingle with the steady stream of enthusiastic, unfamiliar well-wishers. It's one of those rare moments in academy life when we are allowed time to socialise. But it's not without a purpose. I should use this time to figure out who I want for my unit. The intense social interaction is overwhelming at first, but having Abby, Tyson, and Rosa by my side makes talking to strangers a little easier. Tyson's jovial personality is a great ice-breaker and takes the pressure off meeting people. In the end, I lose track of how many cadets introduce themselves, keen to team up with me.

It appears Reeva's attempts to bad-mouth and undermine trust in me didn't work.

Seong and Wynne are the only two cadets in the top six I don't recognise. Maia isn't in my dormitory, but she's stationed on our island. I've seen her around. She catches the same train as Avi, Reeva, and me out to the training enclosure, and occasionally talks to Avi, but I haven't seen her associate with Reeva. That's good for me.

The command selections have already created a divide among the cadets. Those loyal to Reeva hang together in a boisterous group, snubbing their noses at anyone they don't like, talking and laughing like they run the academy.

The remaining cadets are a mix of friendship groups. Most wander the quadrangle, moving from one group to another, sizing Avi, Maia, and myself as potential comrades. We may not have been their first choices, so they're probably figuring out who they prefer.

It's clear I attract a certain type of cadet. Most come from smaller friendship groups – what you would generally consider 'the quirky ones.' If I were in their position, I'd choose someone like me. I've never been drawn to the popular cadets or aspired to be liked by everyone, and if I had a choice, I wouldn't choose to serve in a command position. But it seems my days of flying under the radar have ended. Finally, a familiar face emerges from the crowd.

Kane greets me with a proud smile. 'Well done.'

'I didn't do anything.'

'Are you sure about that?'

I shrug my shoulders.

Kane leans close and lowers his voice. 'A lot of cadets like you. They feel like they can relate to you.' He casts an eye over to Reeva. 'Unlike others.'

I grin. *Now that's something I can relate to.* 'So that's why you voted for me instead of Reeva,' I tease, not expecting a serious reply.

'Among other reasons.'

I'm about to ask his reasoning, but Kane's intense gaze just answered the question in more ways than words could ever describe. *His feelings for me run deep.*

He stares into my eyes and the world fades away, leaving just the two of us. A warm tingling ripples through my chest as my mind races to catch up. I sense his attraction to me – it's elusive, yet powerful, and draws me to him like a magnet. His feelings for me have been there all along, I just haven't paid enough attention to acknowledge them.

But I'm not sure I feel the same.

Kane is more like a brother than a romantic partner. I can't explain it, but from the second we met, we shared a unique emotional connection, like we were friends or lovers in a previous life. I trust him implicitly, and it's not just because he saved me from the megaraptors. Kane is the only person I have confided in about my nightmares.

I don't know how long we've been standing there, but my face is burning with embarrassment. My pale skin must be flushed ruby.

Kane breaks our heartfelt gaze and looks away.

Is he disappointed? I hope I didn't offend him. How was I meant to respond? I've never been romantically interested in anyone before. The academy is quick to stamp out burgeoning romances. Maybe he thinks our instructors won't notice because he's in a different dormitory.

'Have you thought about who you'll choose for your unit?' Kane asks.

'Umm, I have some ideas,' I say, forcing myself out of my thoughts, back into the here and now.

'That's good. I can recommend some cadets from my dorm if you need help.'

'Sure.'

I notice Avi pushing his way through the crowd, heading straight for me. Abby catches my attention and raises her eyebrows; I know where her mind is at. My heart races. I'm not used to attracting this much male attention all at once.

'Congratulations,' Avi says, ignoring Kane.

'Thanks, ah, you too!' Unfortunately, my flustered response sounds like a polite afterthought. Avi doesn't seem to notice or care – he's one of the few cadets who understands my introverted personality.

Kane quietly steps away, as if to leave.

I sense he's a little intimidated by Avi's confident persona. Avi's one of the most popular male cadets in the academy, after all, and I'm yet to see Kane with any other friends. Like me, Kane is a bit of an enigma that way.

Avi finally acknowledges Kane and offers his hand. 'Kane, isn't it? You were on stage with Zaz at assembly.'

Kane shakes his hand. 'Yeah.'

'Glad to see you're all patched up. That pack of megaraptors you bonded with are easily the best in the academy. Well done.'

Kane nods. His rigid, defensive posture relaxes, proving Avi's personable demeanour is disarming, even to the wary.

'Congrats on leading the votes,' Kane says. 'You get the pick of the academy now.'

'I wish it was that easy. First, I need to team up with someone from the top six I want to work with.'

'Any thoughts on who you might choose?'

Avi looks at me. 'I was about to ask Zaz the same thing.'

'How long have you known each other?' Kane asks.

'Since the Bonding,' Avi says. 'We helped each other escape a pair of tyrannosaurs.'

Kane nods, looking preoccupied and slightly concerned, like he wants to ask more but is holding himself back. He glances between us with an air of insecurity. *Is Kane jealous?*

'We should think about teaming up,' Avi says.

My stomach does a flip. I had a feeling he was going to ask me that.

'Uh, okay. What about Reeva?' I say, peering over his shoulder towards her group. 'I thought you might want to team up with her.'

Avi raises an eyebrow, acknowledging Kane in his response. 'Between us, I think we all know she's high-maintenance.'

I laugh. Kane chuckles and his mood lightens.

'What about the other four cadets?' I ask. 'Don't you want to speak to them before making a decision?'

'I'm sure Wynne and Maia will pair up. They're old friends. They shared the same barracks before the Bonding. That just leaves us two, Seong and Reeva.'

'Reeva won't be happy if she doesn't get to choose.'

'So what?' Avi says. 'We don't always get what we want. Anyway, just putting it out there. We can talk more about it later. I just wanted to speak to you first.'

Avi returns to his friends and they disappear in the crowd, leaving Kane and me alone for another awkward moment. I don't know what to say. Knowing how Kane feels about me makes standing here more complicated than it should be.

Tyson draws the pair of us back into the group conversation and we spend the rest of the morning devising potential units and cadet-dinosaur combinations.

During lunch in the mess hall, an unexpected message illuminates on my subcutaneous chip. [ZAYLA-8311 REPORT TO BRIEFING ROOM 4505 14:00 HRS] *Where's Briefing Room 4505? I've never heard of it before.* I keep the message concealed from my friends. Afterwards, everyone heads for the monorail platforms to depart for the next round of dinosaur sessions, but I slip away in a different direction.

I have no idea where I'm going. Thankfully, my forearm chip vibrates and illuminates with directions, leading me through a maze of interior passages and outdoor areas I've never explored. Mirrored windows and heavy steel doors keep me from observing the legions of personnel working behind the scenes to keep our academy functioning. I often wonder why the Union keeps so much hidden from us.

A winding, open-air walkway leads me through the treetops to a sheer cliff draped with vines and ivy. The roar of distant, breaking waves resonates up the rock face. I turn around and look down upon my island. The view is breathtaking, I can see all the way across the atolls, reefs, and islands that comprise the archipelago. Networks of monorails link the islands and glisten like silk spider webs over the cerulean ocean. Mag-lev trains packed with cadets propel silently along the strands, windows glinting in the sunlight like droplets of morning dew.

The chip in my forearm vibrates, alerting me I've arrived at my location.

I'm standing at a junction where the walkway diverts to a steel door recessed into the cliff. I approach the door and place my forearm over the chip reader. Nothing happens. That's strange. I don't have the security clearance. Voices echo around the cliff.

Reeva, Avi, and Seong round the bend in the walkway and join me. I've never met Seong, but recognise her holophoto from the voting results. She's a little shorter than me, with straight black hair cut into a perfect bob.

Reeva looks surprised. 'How'd you get here so fast?'

Her question doesn't warrant a response. I'm so sick of pandering and reacting to her every comment so I just shrug.

'Hey, Zaz,' Avi says brightly. 'This is Seong.'

Seong smiles, closes her eyes, and lowers her head, bowing in a traditional Korean greeting. I return the gesture. As I raise my head, Seong clasps my hands in hers.

'It's a pleasure to meet you, Zayla. I've heard a lot about you.'

I'm tired of hearing that! I've done nothing to deserve the recognition. But Seong is so warm and accommodating, I don't want to offend her. So I lie. 'I've heard a lot about you, too.'

Reeva brushes past us. 'What are we doing here?'

For once, something comes out of her mouth that doesn't insult me. It will be hard for Reeva to maintain her self-aggrandising persona in our small group. Avi and Seong are too sensible to buy into her crap.

'It must be important,' Avi says. 'They pulled us out of our session with our dinosaurs for this.'

The steel door slides open. Brigadier Ramsey emerges from a starkly lit passage with a stern, troubled gaze. 'Cadets, follow me.'

His no-nonsense demeanour makes me nervous. We hastily follow Ramsey inside and traverse a long passage. A pair of Union guards emerge from the alcoves and follow, rifles gripped tightly across their chest, not slung over their shoulders like we're used to seeing. The heightened security is unusual and seems reactive, feeding my suspicion that something dire has transpired. Ramsey didn't even acknowledge our success in the command selections.

We enter a large lift and descend into the depths of the island. *Maybe I'm about to see what goes on behind those closed Union doors.*

The lift door opens to another bright steel passage. Ramsey sets a brisk pace – any faster and we'll be jogging to catch up. The passage ends at another sealed door. Ramsey turns around and checks his watch as we line up and stand at attention.

'Cadets, you're about to enter a classified briefing. Candidates from the other islands who were voted into command positions will join you. Once seated, scan your identification chip into the chair, and your holographic workspaces will become available. Don't activate them until asked. We have given you updated clearance codes for this briefing. Everything you learn on the other side of this door is for your eyes and ears only. Do you understand?'

'Yes, sir,' we respond in unison.

'Good. Any questions?'

Nobody speaks. I want to ask the obvious. *Is this about the Wraith?* But I shake my head like the others and remain silent.

I don't even need to ask – Ramsey's troubled demeanour speaks volumes. He opens the door and leads us into a darkened theatre. A ring of tiered seating slopes down to a spotlighted 360-degree podium in the centre of the circular space. Cadets from the other islands enter from adjacent doors and silently file inside. I follow Avi down the steps, with Reeva and Seong close behind. An unnerving silence pervades the shadows.

The guards escort us down the steps and instruct us to sit in the front row. Our comrades from the other islands do the same, each one a stranger to me. I count 36 of us, all spread around the first row of seats. Of the entire academy, we represent the chosen few voted into command.

Brigadier Ramsey sits in the row behind us, as do the brigadiers from the other islands behind their cadets. The Union guards form a ring around the centre stage, facing us, weapons ready.

Avi leans close and whispers, 'Seems excessive.'

I acknowledge him with a subtle nod but keep my eyes ahead like an obedient cadet. Avi's right. There's no threat here. The Wraith can't reach us on Earth – they're over 1,000 light years from our solar system.

Earth's international anthem plays and we rise, saluting. The guards watch us with cold, suspicious gazes, giving me a terrible, sinking feeling. The anthem concludes and we sit down.

A silvery-haired man ascends the steps onto the stage. It's Galen

Thoms, the leader of the Union! I've never seen him in person, and doubt any cadet has.

Avi and I share looks of surprise.

Galen takes centre stage. 'Good afternoon, cadets. I wish we were meeting for the first time under better circumstances.' He speaks with a warm, Austrian accent.

'Congratulations on being voted highest for your island. We started this program 18 years ago with 10,000 cadets.'

Galen wanders around the stage as he speaks, making deliberate eye contact with every cadet.

'There are now 7,206 of you left after today, spread across this remote but very important archipelago. Many of your brothers and sisters were lost along the way. But their sacrifices, and the sacrifices of their biological parents on Daxma-5, were not in vain. Without them, we would not be in a position to launch our first offensive against the Wraith. The 36 of you sitting before me now represent the culmination of our program.'

Galen returns to the middle of the stage. He raises his hands to the ceiling and lowers them, summoning a massive hologram of the universe from the shadows.

'Approximately nine hours ago, deep space sensors bordering the Constellation of Nyra detected movement in Daxma-5's solar system.'

The hologram zooms in to the orange dwarf star at the heart of the system and orients itself to reflect Galen's brief.

'For the last 53 years, we have consistently tracked the 17 ghost vessels orbiting Daxma-5. We call them *ghost vessels* because their crews have been dead for centuries, leaving the Wraith as the only inhabitants. Twelve military warships and five civilian transport cruisers. None of them have moved during this time. Suddenly today, we counted 14 vessels. At first, we suspected a meteor shower or asteroid collision destroyed three of them. But our monitoring stations detected warp drive signatures leaving the system, which subsequently vanished. We cannot send in Union forces for fear of infection by the Wraith over our communications frequencies.

Therefore, we can only assume that the Wraith are up to something. We have shut down all long-range scanners in nearby systems as a precaution, effectively blinding us to their movements. The three missing warships contain un-deployed platoons of military robots, full armouries, heavy artillery, and land, air, and sea attack vehicles, all of which can strike us anywhere in the galaxy.'

A cadet on the other side of room raises his hand.

Galen motions him to speak. 'Yes?'

'Why are the Wraith acting now? After all these years?'

'Good question. To be honest, we're not sure they even perceive time the same way we do. Fifty-three years to us could be 53 seconds to them.'

A cadet to my left raises her hand. 'If the Wraith have control of our vessels, does that mean they've accessed our navigational data? They would know where our colonies are.'

'They could find Earth,' someone else interrupts.

Galen addresses the outspoken cadet. 'We encrypt all navigational data to safeguard a scenario just like this. Once we discovered the Wraith had infiltrated our systems, we sent a directive to all vessels to erase all nonessential programs and terminate communications.'

Avi raises his hand. Galen looks in our direction and points to him.

'If the Wraith can infiltrate our technology so easily, how are we expected to land on Daxma-5 before they infect our dropships? They could disable our life-support systems or crash us into the planet's surface.'

Galen narrows his eyes on Avi and crosses the stage, walking through the hologram, disturbing the stars and nebulae like ripples in a pond. They shimmer across his face like he's some kind of omnipotent being.

I shrink back into my seat, intimidated by his larger-than-life presence: the most powerful man on Earth.

'Union scientists have been working on a solution to this problem ever since the massacre. We have devised a way to get our ships into the system and land safely on Daxma-5.'

'How?' Avi asks.

I can't believe how bold Avi is, asking such a direct question to the head of the Union. Every cadet looks at us and I shrink further into my seat.

Galen stands on the edge of the stage and stares down at Avi. I can't tell if he's annoyed or impressed.

'The plan is classified,' Galen says with a tone of finality. He observes us with more than a passing curiosity, then addresses everyone. 'You won't learn about it until you're about to deploy. Considering the recent developments surrounding Daxma-5, we assume the Wraith are moving our vessels into strategic positions to strike against us. If the Wraith were to discover our world, the results would be catastrophic. This rising threat has forced the Union to accelerate our plans.'

We all sit there in silence. My heart is racing. We knew we were going to war, but that always felt like years away. Part of me wished it would never happen, that the Union would figure out another way to defeat the Wraith before deploying us. But the day has finally come, thrust upon us without warning.

Galen raises his hands, and the hologram ascends into the shadows. 'Please, activate your holographic workspaces.'

I slide the projector arm out from the side of my seat and activate my workspace. It projects in front of me just like in class and a timetable of classes and training exercises flow across the screen.

'We have adjusted your curriculum,' Galen says. 'The Union plans to deploy the first platoons of cadets in one month, meaning the next six months of training will be condensed into four weeks.'

We all look up from our holograms and gawk at each other in disbelief.

Avi raises his hand again. *I wish he'd stop doing that!* Galen motions for him to speak. 'How is the command curriculum being reduced to reflect our limited time?'

'It's not.'

'How can six months of training fit into four weeks?'

'Since lieutenants work in pairs, you can divide the curriculum between one another once you've partnered up. It's expected that over time, you will catch up.'

'When is there time to catch up if we're being deployed to Daxma-5?'

'The fastest place to learn is on the battlefield.'

A sigh of disapproval rises through the theatre, proving every cadet is as concerned as me. The Union have set us an impossible task.

'I understand how daunting this seems,' Galen says in a calming voice. 'But you're more ready than you realise. For the last 18 years you have been preparing for this day. Your assets are ready. We've been scanning your neural links during the last few exercises and the stem power measurements have exceeded our expectations. That is why we believe you will be ready to deploy to Daxma-5 one month from now.'

I really want to believe Galen, but I'm not ready, and doubtful I should even be in this room at all. I feel like an imposter. I've only had two sessions with Spino, and both were considered failures by the academy. How can I burden the responsibility of First Lieutenant?

'The training exercises with your assets for this afternoon are adjusted to reflect the revised timetable,' Galen says. 'We have combined the problem-solving and riding exercises into one session. Today, you will ride your assets for the first time. Then, after dinner tonight, you will submit your first preference for your command partner.'

'That's insane,' Avi whispers.

I nod, but I'm not listening, just staring blankly at the updated list of exercises streaming through my hologram as negative thoughts bombard my mind. *I'm not ready for this. I should pull out of the command program. Is that an option? What does the Union do with a dropout? It's not like they can just send me home. The academy is my home.*

'Are you all right?' Avi whispers.

His voice saves me from my downward mental spiral. He subtly moves his hand over mine and gives it a reassuring squeeze. His skin is warm and soft. Nobody's ever touched me like this before.

My chest tightens. Breathless, I melt into his brown eyes for an unguarded moment, then subtly withdraw my hand.

Avi acknowledges my discomfort and backs off.

I glance over my shoulder at Brigadier Ramsey, who is watching Galen speak, unaware of our intimate transgression. But our touch didn't escape everyone's eyes. Reeva inches forward in her seat to glare at me.

I turn and face the stage, trying to keep my anxiety under control. It's hard, my chest is heaving with sharp, rapid breaths, dragging me to the brink of a full-blown panic attack. Right now, the thought of fighting the Wraith or being punished by the academy is preferable to Reeva's inescapable wrath.

11

The train ride to our afternoon dinosaur session is unusually quiet. The sun reflects off the ocean and bathes our carriage with bright, cheery light but does little to alleviate the solemn atmosphere. All 36 command cadets that attended the briefing are now on the same train, heading out to regroup with their respective squads for training. Most stand in silence and stare out the windows, lost in thought. Others speak in hushed conversations. The 7,000 cadets that weren't in our classified briefing don't know about the accelerated deployment, which will be revealed at a special assembly tomorrow. We were only notified in advance so we could prepare for the upcoming platoon and command partner selections.

Avi stands on the opposite side of the carriage from me. I avoid eye contact, wary of who may be watching. Now and then I feel him looking at me, but I pretend not to notice as I'm still processing his intimate advance in the briefing. *Am I'm reading too much into it? Maybe that's how close friends behave. I wouldn't know, I haven't had many.* Either way, Avi's a distraction, and that's a dangerous thing when I'm about to go to war.

But it's not that simple. I can't deny I'm attracted to Avi...just like every other girl in the academy, it seems.

Our train careens past the usual islands and continues to a distant cluster of smaller ones. It's the first time I've travelled this far into the archipelago. Out here, the islands are long and flat compared to the mountainous ones I'm used to, and all concealed within gigantic perimeter walls. The monorail veers towards the largest island in the group, placing us on a collision course for the wall of impenetrable steel panels. At the last second, a hatch slides open and our train hurtles inside.

Our carriage plunges into darkness for a moment, then emerges from the wall into a lush tropical rainforest. Shafts of sunlight stream through the dense leafy canopy. The dappled light flickers across the windows in mesmerising rhythm.

The train slows, and we pull to a stop in an open-air station nestled in the shadow of giant trees. I follow the cadets outside to find an abundance of Union guards stationed along the platform, watching over us, rifles in hand. *Are they protecting us or keeping us captive?* At times like this, it certainly feels like the latter. The entire station is housed within an enormous cage constructed of steel beams, spaced tight enough to stop apex predators from squeezing through. The air is humid and oppressive. Inquisitive, oversized insects dart around us, adding to the island's incessant buzz. Strange bird calls pervade the verdant flora. Monkeys, or what sound like monkeys, screech in the distance. The island is teeming with life.

Brigadier Ramsey arrives on the platform with the brigadiers and wranglers from other barracks. He is deep in conversation with Nadja, assessing data on a tablet. Ramsey nods and Nadja rushes off to talk with the other wranglers.

Avi slips in beside me. 'Good luck,' he whispers.

I nod and glance along the platform, hoping the Union guards aren't watching. I'm paranoid. I don't want to receive a reprimand for inappropriate social interaction. Even though Avi initiated the intimate contact, the Union would punish both of us for the transgression.

I'm rudely bumped from behind and turn to find Reeva on my heels, glaring like a starved raptor. 'Watch where you're walking,' she hisses.

I find my place in the line and avoid turning around again. Reeva's intense gaze feels like it's burning a hole in the back of my head.

Wynne and Maia join us, completing the six cadets voted as First Lieutenants on our island. Wynne is a wiry, blond-haired boy with lively blue eyes. Maia has black hair, dark-brown eyes, and light-brown skin. I'm guessing her parents were South American in descent. We all come from different backgrounds and cultures, but we all share the same nondescript accent.

'It's great to finally meet you guys,' Wynne says, bristling with enthusiasm. 'No need for intros, we all know each other from the voting results.'

Avi laughs.

'I can't believe we've never met,' Maia says. 'We live on the same island, after all.'

Wynne and Maia seem nice. Reeva remains quiet through the introductions. If you take Avi out of the group, we're the type of cadets she socially avoids.

Ramsey marches up to us and we promptly snap to attention. He does a quick head count and presses on. 'Cadets, follow me.'

We follow him down a flight of stairs into a neon-lit subterranean station, part of a shuttle system running beneath the island, and climb aboard a driverless transport capsule. It looks like a giant pill and feels just as cramped. There are no seats, just overhead rails for support.

Ramsey grips a rail. 'Hold on tight.'

The door hisses shut, sealing us inside, with the only view to the outside tunnel through a slim horizontal window. The capsule moves slowly at first, like a cork escaping the neck of a bottle, then rockets forward with an explosive burst of energy. I white-knuckle the railing to fight the inertia. Tunnel lights strobe past the window, indicating our incredible speed.

'Listen up, cadets,' Ramsey says. 'Your wranglers updated me on your dinosaur stats, and we've restructured this afternoon's session accordingly. Today you will work together to achieve a shared goal. There are no other members of your platoon in this mission, just the six of you. It's a good opportunity to test your compatibility with each other. Treat it as a trial run for your potential command partner, and remember, your preferences are due at the end of this week.'

The strobing tunnel lights slow and come into focus as we pull to a stop. Ramsey leads us outside, up a flight of metal steps and into a circular observation pod nestled in a remote pocket of jungle. Reinforced glass windows offer a 360-degree view of the terrain, allowing us to observe the area in safety. Years ago, our very first introduction to the world of prehistoric giants was from a pod just like this.

Ramsey accesses the control pedestal in the centre of the room, initiating a topographical hologram of the surrounding terrain.

'Each of you will start in a different corner of this region. Once you locate your asset, you need to direct them through a maze, collecting a section of machinery on the way.' The hologram rotates as Ramsey explains, displaying a series of hidden walls rising from the terrain to form a maze. 'Your assets are fitted with riding saddles.'

I share a concerned look with everyone (except Reeva) across the glowing hologram.

Ramsey notices our unease. 'Is there a problem, cadets?'

Avi speaks up on everyone's behalf. 'We've never ridden our dinosaurs before. Don't we get a tutorial?'

'As Galen said, your training curriculum is condensed in response to the Wraith threat. Consider yourselves lucky to have this time at all. If the situation were any worse, you might be deployed without further training, leaving these skills to be honed on the battlefield.'

'How can the Union send us to war if we're not ready?' Maia says. 'It risks our lives, our assets, and two decades of meticulous military planning.'

Wynne gives an enthusiastic nod. 'Exactly! We're the only force the Union has. We're too valuable to risk.'

'We're not here to debate the decisions of the Union,' Ramsey says firmly. 'It wouldn't be the first time in history a young, inexperienced army is sent into battle. Ready or not, this academy represents our last hope.'

'I'm ready,' Reeva says. 'I can do it. I trust my asset.'

'Good! That's the confidence I expect to hear from each of you.'

Reeva casts me a smug, emboldened look. *She's setting me a challenge, daring me to do better. I can. I'm strong with Spino. I trust him with my life – plus, he could eat her tyrannosaur for breakfast.* I glare back, confident and unflinching, ready to accept her challenge.

Ramsey touches the hologram and presents a new demonstration. 'To make things harder, the maze rearranges every two minutes. Maintain control of your asset. Don't give into the temptation to sprint over the changing walls, because you won't make it in time. Use the changeover to spot your targets and reassess your approach. Once you've collected your piece of machinery, make your way to the central rendezvous. Here, add your parts to a power generator and bring it online. During this phase, you will also have to deal with an aggressive pack of triceratops. The generator will extend a bridge across the ravine to your finish position. All of you must make it across the bridge to complete the mission. Understood cadets?'

We salute and respond with an energetic, 'Yes, sir!'

'Use this session to sound each other out. Work as a team and consider your command partnerships. Now, make your way outside. Transport drones are waiting to drop you off at your starting points.'

The steel door opens, and we file down a short gangway into a clearing beside the observation pod. Six stainless steel drones eject from the wall on racks. They resemble large metal eggs with a pair of handles poking out from the underside. I pick one up by the grips, finding it surprisingly light for the size. My forearm chip vibrates and the drone powers up in response, releasing four sets of compact blades from its casing. We lift our drones above our heads as the blades whiz to life.

Avi winks at me. 'See you there.'

I look down as my boots leave the ground. All six of us levitate several feet in the air and suddenly shoot off in separate directions. The observation pod shrinks beneath me as I fly over the treetops, wind blasting my face, free as a pterosaur. In that fleeting moment, I'm free from the war, from Reeva, and all my troubles. It's exhilarating.

I relax and enjoy the ride, hands locked to the drone. I couldn't let go even if I wanted to because my subcutaneous chip has locked the muscles in my hands around the grips as a safeguard. Some cadets need it because they're afraid of heights, ensuring they don't panic and let go mid-flight. Not me. Drone drop-offs are a favourite part of my academy training.

I take the opportunity to memorise the landscape. I spot the central rendezvous point, as displayed on the hologram, nestled in a wide clearing on the edge of a rocky ravine.

My drone dips low enough for me to run the tip of my boot across the palm tree canopy. I'm several kilometres from the rendezvous point when the drone swoops into a clearing and deposits me close to Spino. He circles about and watches me land, head tilted, eyes alight with amusement and curiosity.

My chip deactivates, releasing my grip on the drone, and it whizzes off like a large prehistoric insect back to the observation pod.

THUMP... THUMP... THUMP...

Spino lumbers over, leans down, and sniffs me. I give his snout a firm rub. 'It's good to see you too.' He snorts and nuzzles into me in a sign of affection. I dig my boots into the ground and hold steady. 'Hah! I missed you too.'

Spino raises his head and shakes his neck in a way I haven't seen before. I sense his discomfort. He cranes his head around and pokes at something on the other side of his body. I notice a pair of thick leather straps wrapped tightly around the base of his neck, digging into his skin and aggravating him.

I walk around to his left side and run my hand across his chest to settle him. 'What's the matter?'

Spino nips at the saddle which is slung around the base of his neck and juts out like a sidecar. It's an odd position for a saddle, but his spiny sail prevents the mounting straps from fitting over his back. At least the length of his neck remains free to allow a full range of movement. I'm one of the few cadets to ride side-saddle on their dinosaur, with Abby and her stegosaurus being the other exception.

'I know, I know. It's uncomfortable,' I say, rubbing Spino's side. 'Let me on. I'll try to loosen it.'

Spino raises his head and shakes his neck. I don't think he understands what I mean. I close my eyes and send my thoughts to him, keeping my hand pressed against his skin. I visualise myself sitting in the saddle to help him understand. Spino releases a long breath through his nostrils. *Is that a sigh of understanding or resignation?* I open my eyes and find him crouched, offering the saddle to me. *I hope it's understanding.*

I tenderly pat his side. 'Thanks buddy.'

I grip the base of the saddle and awkwardly swing my leg over, attempting to hoist myself into the seat. My boot slips and I flail about like a rag doll, one leg stuck in the saddle. Spino peers down at me and snorts in rapid succession – I never knew dinosaurs had a sense of humour.

'Hey! This isn't funny!' I say, trying to drag myself upright. *This is not the way to do it!*

Spino suddenly boosts me up with his snout and I land on the saddle backwards, facing his tail. He straightens up as I slip into the seat and strap the seatbelt around my waist.

'I need to get better at doing that!'

Peering over the saddle, I find myself roughly two metres off the ground. Looking ahead, I realise we're facing the wrong direction. *Now what?* We're just standing here, not moving. There are no reins or other direct way to instruct Spino where to go, which means everything is achieved by thought, or as our instructors call it, *stem power.* I place my hand on Spino's neck and feel the blood rhythmically pumping beneath his skin, gushing through his veins like an underground river. Spino has a plenitude of raw, untapped power. We've barely scraped the surface of what we can accomplish together.

I focus on turning Spino in the direction we need to go. He repositions his right foot, as if responding to my thoughts.

'That's it! Turn around. You know what we need to do.'

Spino's heavy footfalls vibrate through his body and shake the saddle as he lumbers into position. The surrounding shrubs and grass crunch flat beneath his massive, webbed feet. We are now facing the direction of the ravine and our final rendezvous point.

'Go forward!' I call.

Spino takes a thunderous step forward, then another. As we pick up speed his heaving body jostles me in the saddle. His footfalls become lighter the faster he goes, and within a few strides we are pounding our way towards the jungle at full speed, like nothing in the world can stop us.

'Woo-hoo!'

Spino embellishes my excitement with an almighty...

ROOOAAAR!

His roar resonates through every fibre of my being, charging me with confidence and a sense of invincibility. I've never felt so powerful. This session is going to be a breeze.

12

My confidence is short-lived as Spino charges headlong into the jungle. If he isn't careful, he'll sideswipe a trunk and rip me off, saddle and all. But he's not slowing down. I stand in the saddle, one hand on my belt buckle, ready to unlock it and jump to safety.

'Spino! Watch out!'

At the last second, Spino swings his head around and shields me, flattening the tree about to wipe me out. Leaves and debris shower the saddle as we burst into a field of long grass. Spino slows to a walk and shakes the loose foliage off his body. Several paces into the open expanse, a sequence of steel walls eject from the ground, tearing through roots and displacing huge mounds of soil. The panels equal Spino in length, from tail to snout, and rise in organised right-angled patterns across the field. *CLUNK!* The monolithic walls lock into position, enclosing us within the shadows of a newly formed maze.

'Whoa!'

I rub Spino's neck as he ambles between the walls, sniffing the air and shaking his head with uncertainty. I share his apprehension. The claustrophobic space reminds him of his harsh upbringing in the cramped Union enclosures.

'It's okay,' I say, patting him. 'They're just walls. We'll find a way out.'

Spino stops at the first turn and cranes his head around the corner, sniffing the enclosed space with caution. The path is only wide enough for one-way travel, allowing no chance to turn around. If we reach a dead end, we'll need to wait for the walls to reconfigure before we can move on. Spino would hate that.

'Let's wait and see how it changes.'

Spino exhales a deep breath. He seems relieved by my decision.

The ground rumbles and the interior maze walls descend. But the outer perimeter panels remain in place, locking us in the maze until we solve it. I spot the piece of machinery we need to collect, a large power cylinder with charging couplings on each end, roughly 20 spinosaurus-paces ahead of us in the centre of the field.

Spino senses my excitement and grunts, eager to sprint straight for the cylinder.

'No, no. Not yet. Hold on. We have to wait for the walls.'

Fresh walls rise at different speeds from the grid-like megastructure hidden beneath the field and configure a new maze. I lean forward in the saddle and watch the paths form, memorising as many turns as I can before the walls reach full height. *Times like this, I love my photographic memory.* The panels lock into position and cast us into shadow again. I place a reassuring hand on Spino's neck. 'Okay, I know the way.'

Spino hesitantly trudges forward.

I keep the image of the maze foremost in my mind and relay those directions to him. 'Straight ahead...left...right... Straight ahead again...right...'

We're making good progress into the centre of the field when a distant roar breaks my concentration.

Spino halts and growls, unhappy with me for breaking our rhythm. His growing panic filters through me to create an anxious knot in my belly. I can sense something else – his temptation to run straight for the power coupling next time the walls reset. His flight-or-fight response is getting harder to suppress.

I'm not sure I can hold him back much longer.

The ground reverberates with the rumble of gears and machinery. The walls shudder, shaking loose the piles of soil along their tops, and descend. I concentrate on keeping Spino calm, but his urge to sprint is overpowering.

'Not yet. One more cycle and we can get the power coupling.' Spino grunts and scrapes his foot in the dirt. 'I know you hate it. But I'm here. Remember?'

I stroke his neck and he settles. The walls retract into the grass and reveal the coupling, just two or three strides away. Spino tenses up, anxious to lunge for it.

'No! Hold on. We're almost there.'

The maze resets and I memorise the new pattern, determined to make this our last cycle for Spino's sake. This time we're off before the panels return to full height.

'Turn right...go straight ahead...turn right again... Follow the left wall.'

I stand in the saddle and cheer as we race into the centre of the maze to stand over our prize. 'We did it!'

Spino releases an excited high-pitched roar. It echoes off the walls and bounces straight back at us, reverberating through my head like a giant bell. I cover my ears before I go deaf and allow the noise to subside.

'Okay, pick it up and we can get out of here.'

Spino locks his jaws around the coupling and picks it up. The maze walls descend in response and leave us gazing across an open field once again. I guide Spino in the direction of the ravine, which I memorised to be concealed behind the trees on the far side. He lumbers across the grassy expanse and forges between the trees to emerge in a gravel clearing that runs alongside a deep rocky ravine. Further along, an octagonal metal column stands close to the edge of the ravine. Chunky power conduits protrude from its base and wind across the gravel to a retracted bridge.

'We're the first ones here! I head for the power generator.'

Spino's webbed feet crunch heavily across the gravel. I keep my eyes on the nearby jungle, half expecting a triceratops, or *trikers*, as we call them, to come charging through.

The six-metre-high generator has six empty power slots, one

for each cadet's component. Sensing my intentions, Spino rotates his head and lowers the coupling into an upright position. The generator's magnetic latches lock onto it with a satisfying clunk and the machine whirs to life.

I pat Spino. 'Great job! Now we wait for the others.'

Behind us, the retracted bridge remains idle and won't extend until all the power couplings are in place. On the far side of the ravine, an observation pod awaits–our final rendezvous.

Spino smells something and swings around. I hear it, echoing off the ravine walls like distant, rolling thunder. The rumble intensifies and vibrates through my body like the heavens are about to open.

The trees at the opposite end of the clearing burst apart. An allosaurus charges through the maelstrom of leaves and branches with a power coupling locked in its jaws. Avi sits atop the carnivore, a third of the way along its back in a saddle. He sees me and waves.

I wave back but Spino rears up, all set to confront them. I don't blame him for being anxious, as this is the first time we've been in the company of other cadets and their dinosaurs. It makes me nervous too. *How will different species of apex predators interact?* That's a huge factor in our upcoming selections. No point picking someone to command with if your dinosaurs can't work together.

'It's okay, they're friends,' I assure Spino in a calm, comforting tone.

Spino cranes around and casts me an uncertain eye. I lean forward and scratch him behind his jaw. He relaxes and steps aside, allowing Avi and his allosaurus room to approach, sniffing the air as they pass.

Avi's fully-grown allosaur sports dark-grey skin along its back that tapers off to a light-grey across its underbelly. Flecks of royal-blue and purple shimmer momentarily, depending how the sunlight catches his skin. His bright orange eyes observe us as he lowers the coupling onto the generator. The allosaur is similar in size and build to an adult tyrannosaur except for the bony, horn-like protrusions above its eyes – a devilish feature unique to the species.

Avi shakes his head. 'Ah! You beat me!'

'Stop being so competitive.'

'I could say the same about you.' Avi says with a grin. He admires my dinosaur. 'Your spinosaurus is incredible.'

'So is yours.'

'I like that side-saddle thing you've got going on. Classy!'

I laugh. Avi manoeuvres his allosaur around to stand beside me and Spino. Our dinosaurs sniff each other with curiosity and settle, content to stay close together. The entire ridge begins to vibrate, subtle at first, then quickly grows in intensity. Avi stands in his saddle and peers into the jungle. 'We've got company.'

'I hope it's friendly.'

The rumbling drowns out the hum of the generator. Birds scatter from the leafy canopy and fly over us, screeching. *This isn't good.*

Avi manoeuvres his allosaur around to face the unseen forces cracking and crunching their way through the shadowy foliage. The noise reaches a crescendo and three dinosaurs burst into the clearing, power couplings locked in their jaws. Spino digs his feet into the gravel, lowers his head, and growls, ready to attack.

I jump up and pat his neck. 'Don't worry, they're friends too.'

Maia approaches riding a majungasaurus with striking yellow skin littered in mottled black patches. We call them *jungas*. Wynne rides alongside her on an ochre-coloured gigantosaurus with dark brown stripes. Seong appears behind us on her carcharodontosaurus, a cunning shark-toothed predator species that has earned the academy nickname *sharkies*. Seong's has glossy green skin similar in shade to a palm leaf, with light green stripes accented by white edges down its flank.

Our collection of large bipedal carnivores share a common appearance, with powerful legs, small arms, and devastating jaws, but each species represents a diverse, beautiful spectrum of colours. We acknowledge one another with a nod and appreciate our lineup of impressive new pets. Maia, Wynne, and Seong, give each other space to load their power cells into the generator.

Avi looks down at me. 'We're just waiting on Reeva now.'

'Hmm.'

I couldn't sound more disinterested if I tried. I know it's wrong to think this way, but life would be so much easier if Reeva didn't make it through training. My dark thoughts are short-lived as a blood-red tyrannosaur with a power cell in its jaws crashes through the trees to my left. Bright-yellow patches of skin rise from its underbelly like flames. *How apt! It's like her T-rex was coloured specifically for her fiery personality.*

Reeva stands high in the saddle and checks us out.

I can see the flare of frustration in her eyes from here – she's not happy being the last one to arrive. This doesn't bode well for me. If anything goes wrong from here, she'll make sure I pay for it.

Maia's junga lowers the coupling into the generator and the hum of electricity intensifies. The machine is now equipped with half the power cells required to activate the bridge. Maia directs her junga towards Avi and me, allowing our carnivores to sniff each other out and size one another up.

'This seems too easy,' Maia says. 'Where's the pack of trikers?'

Avi reins his allosaur back to the ravine and keeps a lookout. 'We're not across the bridge yet. We should spread out, protect the others while they load the power cells.'

'Good idea.'

I guide Spino towards the trees while Maia heads to the far end of the clearing to guard the area behind Reeva and her T-rex.

CLUNK! Wynne's gigantosaurus loads a power cell and moves aside.

Seong manoeuvres her sharkie around the generator to the next empty slot. Her dinosaur leans forward and angles its head down to load the cell – that's when I see the brown horns emerge from the ferns behind them.

'Look out!' Spino roars as I scream, drowning out my warning.

Seong glances over, confused and unaware of the danger. The incoming horns rip through the foliage to reveal an enormous triceratops, charging straight at her. She sees it at the last second and reels back her carcharodontosaurus. The triker barrels past them, accidentally dislodging the power cell from the generator with its mighty horn.

Another two trikers thunder into the clearing. One targets Reeva and her tyrannosaur as the other charges towards Avi and his allosaur. Reeva's tyrannosaur steps aside and swipes the triceratops with its tail. The triker raises his horns and nicks a hole in his tail. Her T-rex winces, drops the power cell, and bellows in pain. The cell rolls across the gravel, right in line for the ravine. If it drops over the edge, we all fail.

I point after it. 'Grab it!'

Spino sprints along the edge of the ravine and stomps on the cylinder before it's lost for good. Looking back, everyone is busy avoiding the raging herd of trikers. Their unprovoked aggression isn't normal behaviour for the species. Being herbivores, they only charge other dinosaurs if they feel threatened or to protect their territory. This is neither. I notice each one is tagged behind their bony head frill with an electronic receiver. *I hate this – innocent creatures being controlled and manipulated by the Union to attack us.* But there's no time to be remorseful. I force the negative thoughts from my mind and focus on the task at hand.

I rub Spino's side. 'Okay, pick up the cell. Let's finish this.'

Spino snatches the power cell in his jaws and runs towards the generator. We dodge a frenzied fray of spiked tails and deadly horns as the dinosaur battle topples trees and kicks up a choking cloud of dust. We clear the chaos and approach the generator. Spino slots the cell into the magnetic latches and they snap in place, leaving Seong's dislodged power cell the last one to activate.

'Push that one in as well.'

Spino nudges Seong's cylinder back into the couplings. CLUNK! The generator builds to full power with a satisfying hum.

'Well done! Okay, let's get everyone out of here.'

Spino charges through the battle as I stand in the saddle, screaming over the ruckus. 'Get to the bridge!'

Spino reaches the ravine just as the bridge finishes extending. One catch, it's only wide enough for one dinosaur to cross at a time. I turn around and discover nobody heard me. They're too busy saving their own skins from the trikers.

'Spino, let 'em know.'

ROOOOOOOAR!

I cup my ears, but it does little to block the noise. If not for my seatbelt, Spino's thunderous bellow might vibrate me out of the saddle.

Everyone turns around.

Avi is the closest to me and the only cadet not in immediate danger. His allosaur sprints over to join us. 'Go across, Zaz. I'll wait here and help the others.'

'I'm no help on the other side. I'll cross when we're all safe.'

Avi gives me a nod of admiration and grins. 'All right, then, let's create a distraction. Give everyone a chance to get across the bridge. Got any suggestions?'

CRUNCH!

Another palm tree slams to the ground nearby, giving me an idea. 'We can use the fallen trees to herd the trikers back, staying clear of their horns while everyone crosses the bridge.'

'Excellent idea. We'd make a great command team.'

'You think?'

'Of course. Don't you?'

I give Avi a smile and set Spino to work. Avi and I sprint in opposite directions along the ravine, flanking the perimeter of the battle. Shredded foliage and fallen trees now carpet the gravel. Some trees have snapped at the trunk, others uprooted altogether. I direct Spino to the thickest, longest trunk, confident he can lift it. He crunches through the wood with his teeth and pries the entire tree from the entangled vines. The tree's root ball is caked in a gigantic clump of soil, making the whole tree one giant club. Spino is slower and heavier with the extra weight, but charges into the fray nonetheless, brandishing the tree.

WHOMP!

We pummel the largest triker from behind. The ball explodes across its flank in a burst of soil and shattered roots. The triceratops tumbles across the gravel and rolls to a stop. Dazed, it lays there, bloody wooden splinters protruding from its side like a porcupine.

The distraction gives Maia and Wynne a chance to make for the bridge. They wave in thanks and sprint to safety on their dinosaurs.

Across the clearing, Avi and his allosaur shield Seong and her carcharodontosaurus from a pair of trikers. His dinosaur wields a mid-sized tree, barely enough to keep the deadly horns at bay. To my left, Reeva and her tyrannosaur stand in place, watching me and Spino.

I point to the bridge. 'Go!'

'You go,' she yells. 'I'll help Avi.'

'No, Avi and I have a plan. Head for the bridge.'

Reeva stands defiant, her brow scowled with disgust. I know exactly what she's thinking. *Who am I to be giving her directions?* In hindsight, I should never have said Avi and I had a plan – it's just throwing fuel on a fire.

'Don't tell me what to do, Zaz.'

'Fine, suit yourself,' I say, directing Spino after Avi.

Reeva's T-rex sprints after us and rams Spino in the side, squishing my saddle between our dinosaurs. My saddle tilts up and jams me against Spino's ribs until all I see is dinosaur skin. The pressure forces the air from my lungs and prevents me from taking another breath. *I'm being crushed to death!* Each second feels like an eternity. Reeva's tyrannosaur finally pulls away and my saddle drops back into position, leaving me stunned and gasping for air.

Reeva glares down at me from her elevated position. 'Consider that a warning.'

'For what?' I gasp, pretending to have no idea what she means.

Reeva wants me to stay away from Avi. In her mind, she's already chosen him as her command partner, and nobody will stand in her way, especially me. Spino senses my discomfort and rounds on the pair, throwing the tree down at their feet and roaring in my defence.

Reeva squirms in her saddle and her T-rex pulls his head in – a response you would expect from a startled juvenile, not a fully-grown war machine like hers.

Spino's reaction wasn't an instruction from me, which means our neural link goes beyond normal stem power and reaches into my feelings and emotions. He senses my desire to fight back, even though I never consciously considered it. *We could take them in a fight.* The thought just pops into my head, but it didn't originate from me. It was Spino telling me not to worry and that we're in control of the situation. I smirk at Reeva, confident I can do whatever I want while Spino has my back covered.

I sit back in the saddle and pat Spino. 'Come on, let's go help.'

Spino picks up the tree and pounds across the gravel to aid Avi and Seong. For the first time I can recall, I don't care what Reeva does. *Cross the bridge, or don't cross the bridge. It's on her.* The Union watch everything we do. Maybe this will show them how disruptive she is and force their hand to bring her belligerent attitude into line.

One of the trikers charges Avi and drives his allosaur close to the ravine. His dinosaur teeters on the edge, rocks crumbling out from beneath his feet. The other triker charges from the dust cloud, head down, horns directed at Avi's allosaur.

We'll never reach them in time!

Seong's dinosaur intercepts and pummels the triceratops with its tail, knocking it off-balance. The triker collapses onto its front knees and rolls over the edge of the ravine, metres away from Avi and his allosaur. The remaining triker scrapes its front foot across the gravel and lowers its trio of horns, like a bull ready to charge. Seong is oblivious to the danger behind her. The triker bursts forth, tearing up the gravel, moments away from impaling them. Seong might survive the impact, but her carcharodontosaurus would be dead.

I whack Spino on the neck, hoping he understands. 'Throw it!'

Spino doesn't hesitate. He hurls the tree over Seong and her dinosaur, showering them with dirt and leaves. *THUMP!*

The tree lands behind them and the triker. The triceratops barrels into the trunk at full speed and impales its three-metre horns deep into the wood, stopping it dead in its tracks. The stunned triker writhes about, but can't pull itself free. Seong stares at me and nods in appreciation, wide-eyed and pale with shock.

'Great work!' Avi cries. 'Let's get over the bridge.'

I'm the last to cross the bridge. Reeva and her tyrannosaur wait near the edge on the far side, watching me and Spino. Her revulsion is palpable. Spino grunts at them. *I totally agree.* Reeva's T-rex lowers his head and growls back. If nobody was watching, I'm convinced they'd ram us off the bridge. There's no way Reeva and I can command together. Our dinosaurs loathe one other as much as we do.

13

It's hard for me to act normal at dinner that evening. Abby, Tyson, Rosa, and Kane have no idea we are one month away from being deployed. They will learn about the new Wraith threat in assembly tomorrow, but tonight they're sharing their experiences from their first group sessions. I listen, nod, and smile when necessary, adding little to the conversation. It appears I've fooled everyone except Kane. He watches me with curiosity from the corner of his eye. What is it that makes him different to everyone else?

A quick survey of the mess hall confirms I'm not the only one from the command program wearing the burden. Avi is sitting with Seong and his friends tonight, and both seem quieter than usual. I made a wide berth around his table after collecting my dinner tray to avoid any attention from Reeva. Ironically, I think I'm coping better than her in this situation.

Reeva is usually the centre of attention, but tonight she is just like me, quiet and reserved, while everyone talks around her.

Spino helped me realise something crucial today: I don't need to live in fear of Reeva. If I want to sit next to Avi, I will when I feel like it. Tonight, I don't. I'd rather blend into my group and avoid trouble.

It doesn't stop Reeva from glaring at me. It only happens twice, but that's enough to make it feel like she's been scrutinizing me all night. She's probably wondering who I will choose as my accompanying First Lieutenant.

As dinner draws to a close, I excuse myself and stand, keen to avert any probing questions. I don't have the energy to hide what I know about our impending deployment.

Abby sits upright, as if suddenly realising I hadn't spoken a word the entire time. 'Zaz, where are you going?'

'I'm going to put in my selection for a command partner. I want to get it in early and beat the rush.'

'Who's top of your list?' Tyson says.

His booming voice draws attention from Avi and Reeva. I stand in the middle of their expectant gazes, like I'm caught between spotlights.

'I bet it's Avi,' Rosa whispers under her breath.

Kane freezes, mid-mouthful, and looks up to see how I respond.

'That's classified information,' I say with a smirk, brushing off the comment.

I head for the food station, place my tray in the pile, and cast a solitary eye over my shoulder. Avi acknowledges me with a subtle nod, indicating he intends to follow through on his comment during today's session. *'We'd make a great command team.'* Reeva witnesses our interaction and freezes like a stunned ichthyosaur. The hurt and shock plays across her reddening face for all to see.

I should feel ashamed for taking satisfaction in her embarrassment, but for once, Reeva knows what it feels like to be the outsider.

Outside, the humid night air blankets the island with a velvety mist. A recent downpour has left large puddles on the walkways. The lampposts and retaining wall lights reflect in the perfectly still water, like a window into an upside-down world. I splash through them and arrive at the quadrangle to find a single voting station set up in the middle of the space. The holographic screens emit a vibrant blue glow, illuminating a group of cadets hanging around and chatting.

I approach the opposite side for privacy and hold my forearm up to the panel. My subcutaneous ID chip flashes, and the hologram presents me with a selection of five names.

[MAIA-4756]
[REEVA-6333]
[SEONG-6914]
[WYNNE-8219]
[AVI-0995]
[SELECT FIRST CHOICE COMMAND PARTNER]

The new text flashes in red beneath their names.

I peer over my shoulder, feeling as if I'm about to do something wrong. This is so stupid. I should be able to choose who I want without feeling guilty or pressured. Reeva has a habit of getting under my skin, even when she's not around. *I'm so sick of it.*

I select Avi's name, and the screen presents me with a second option.

[SELECT SECOND CHOICE COMMAND PARTNER]

Not much to think about here. Wynne and Maia are bound to be nominating each other and I'm never going to select Reeva. That leaves Seong. I promptly select her and scoot off as more cadets arrive to observe others make their choices. I'm glad I got in early and avoided the attention.

I detour the cadets migrating from the mess hall to the quadrangle and take an isolated walkway through the jungle. The growing crowd of voices follows me through the trees. It sounds like everyone has moved outside, keen to use up their free time watching the votes before it's lights out.

'Hey, Zaz!' Kane calls from behind me.

Without turning around, I hear Kane jogging to catch up. I'm not in the mood to talk, a well-promoted impression I wish he'd picked up on at dinner. His ignorance instantly switches me into frustration/defence mode.

'Everything all right?'

'Yeah. Why?'

'You looked disinterested at dinner.'

'I wasn't disinterested,' I snap, sounding harsher than intended.

'Sorry, I didn't mean to pry. I just thought if something was bothering you, you might like to talk to me about it.'

'Just because I told you about my nightmares doesn't mean I'm going to open up to you every time I have a problem.'

Kane goes quiet and lowers his head. 'I'll leave you alone.'

I don't respond, even though a big part of me wants to. Kane walks off, leaving me with an overwhelming sense of guilt. I stop with a sigh and turn around, expecting to find him behind me. Nothing, just an empty walkway. *Where did he go?* I glimpse a shadow move between the trees that border the path. I hurry back and discover stairs leading down to a lower section of the island. *Is Kane's dormitory this way?* I'm compelled to apologise and race down the steps after him.

I have no idea where I'm going. Kane has never told me what dorm he's in or where it's located. I arrive at a junction point. The stairs continue on the opposite side of walkway and descend deeper into the darkening jungle. Kane is neither to the left or right, so I continue downwards, picking up speed, leaving the bright lights of the academy high up the mountain. I reach a lower level and find myself deep in the unknown. A shadowy wall of imposing vegetation looms over me, humming with an army of unseen insects. Down here, the distant rumble of crashing waves reverberates up the slope like a waking volcano. I've never ventured this low on the island, even during my early-morning runs.

Kane is nowhere to be seen. I catch my breath and sigh. *Where did he go?* He's always been an enigma to me, and this just compounds my suspicions. Considering the little I know about Kane, he sure seems to know a lot more about me.

I resign myself to losing him and head back. After such a tiring day, it's going to be an arduous trek to the top of the island. I reach the first junction and stop to catch my breath. A sudden movement to my left draws my attention.

THUMP!

Next thing, I find myself rolling across the hard metal walkway, wondering what hit me. I control my tumble and come to a stop on my hands and knees.

A figure looms over me, face silhouetted in the darkness, a halo of blond hair illuminated like flames in the light of the lamppost. Reeva!

'Get up!' Her voice is cold and uncompromising. I cautiously to rise to my feet, noting Lani and a couple of cadets watching from the stairs. 'What are you doing down here?'

'None of your business,' I say.

'Wrong answer.'

Reeva punches me in the stomach. I hunch over and drop to my knees, cradling my gut, straining to draw air back into my lungs.

'I said get up!'

'Why?' I gasp.

'Because I'm not fighting you on your knees.'

I take a sharp breath and rise gingerly to my feet. It feels like my ribs are broken.

'You think you've got everyone fooled with this innocent shy thing you have going on. Your friends only like you because they feel sorry for you. They pity you. If they knew what you were really like they'd never talk to you. The only reason you were voted third for command was because of your spinosaurus. I can't believe the academy wasted one of their best apex predators on you.'

I take shallow breaths between clenched teeth, trying not to look so vulnerable. There's no arguing my way out of this. Our inevitable confrontation has been brewing for years.

'It's only a matter of time before Avi finds out you can't be trusted.'

'If that's true, why do you keep asking me to stay away from him?'

Reeva glances to her friends on the stairs. I hit a raw nerve there. Deep down, I think she's afraid of me, of what I can achieve. What happened between us all those years has only proved one thing: her hatred for me will never wane and only grows stronger over time. Reeva doesn't want me to succeed.

'You've forgotten your place in the academy,' Reeva hisses. 'You're an outsider. Always have been.' She edges towards me, fists raised. 'When it comes to choosing a partner, you're going to leave Avi's name off the list. Understand?'

Too late for that, I think. She has no idea I've already visited the voting station and made my selection. 'What if I've already chosen?'

'Then you'll regret it.'

'What if he chooses me?'

'You tell him you don't want to work with him.'

She has no idea how out of touch she is. Confidence swells inside me and surges through my body like adrenalin. I felt the same positive burst of endorphins riding Spino, that I could take Reeva and her T-rex in a fight. I'm drawing upon that connection right now, as if I'm feeding off Spino's energy, even when we're apart.

I straighten up, ready to fight. 'You can't force people to like you. If Avi chooses me, it's because he doesn't want to work with you. Can't you tell? He's been doing everything he can to avoid you.'

Reeva's expression turns feral. She lashes out with lightning speed. I block the first blow and immediately flick into self-defence mode. Reeva keeps swinging. I lose ground and shuffle backwards, barely defending myself against the ferocious onslaught. I cop a fist on the side of the head, then one across the ear. Then a boot in my side. My combat training takes over and at the first opening I retaliate with a kick, catching Reeva square in the stomach.

She staggers back, clutching her sunken waist.

I assume a fighting stance, fists ready.

Reeva raises her head. There's a fire burning in her eyes, one that can never be extinguished. She comes at me again. We parry blows, tangle arms, and stagger around the walkway, trying to force one another to the ground. I manage to get a leg behind hers and flip her onto her back. She lands hard. Her fist catches me across the mouth, splitting my lip. Specks of blood scatter across her face.

I hold her arms and drive my boot into her neck. Reeva squirms, attempting to kick me off. Somehow, I keep her down. Storms of adrenalin rage through my body. I feel unstoppable. Reeva's face turns red, then purple. I dig in, committed to hold until she passes out.

I'm suddenly grabbed from behind and yanked away.

Lani and the other cadet have me in their grip. I struggle, but it's no use. I'm too spent to fight two at once.

Reeva staggers to her feet and feels her neck. 'You bitch!'

I steel myself and prepare for anything.

Reeva hits me with a solid gut punch, forcing the air from my lungs again. This time around it's impossible to breathe in. I panic, feeling like I'll never take a full breath again. I buckle over, eyes bulging. Reeva grabs my hair and lifts my face to the light, fist poised to strike.

'Three against one,' a male voice interrupts. 'That's not a fair fight.'

I gaze past Reeva's bloody fist and see Kane on the stairs.

'Let her go, or I'll report the three of you.'

Reeva squeezes clumps of my hair between her fingers. I grit my teeth, expecting my burning scalp to rip apart at any moment. She shoves my head in frustration, then releases me and leaves with her friends. I drop to my knees and regain my breath.

Kane helps me up. 'You can't go back to your dorm looking like that. Come on.'

I'm too sore to protest as Kane guides me down the stairs. We follow a winding walkway to a single-storey barracks nestled near the base of the island. The waves are so close they sound like they're breaking just beyond the surrounding trees. We enter a brightly lit corridor and pass several cadets, all of whom stop their conversation to watch me. I feel like an intruder.

Kane guides me into a dark infirmary and assists me onto a gurney. The lights automatically flicker to life, illuminating a sterile room of glass and stainless steel. I gingerly touch my swollen bottom lip with my fingers and look around, surprised to find we're alone.

'Where are the Union officers?'

'Things run a little differently down here,' Kane says. He pulls a mechanical arm down from the ceiling and lines the x-ray scanner up to my ribs.

'Where is *down here* exactly?'

'That's classified.'

I stifle a laugh. Smiling splits my lip and hurts my ribs. I cradle my side and caress my lip with the tip of my finger. 'Oww!'

Kane assesses my scans on a nearby screen. 'Nothing's broken or fractured.'

'Except for my lip.'

'Don't worry, we can fix that.'

Kane retracts the mechanical arm and selects a small tub of dermal gel from the adjoining workbench.

'I can do it,' I say, reaching for the tub.

'It's all right, I got it,' he says, unscrewing the lid.

There's no arguing with Kane, he's determined to look after me. He puts a small dollop on his index finger, raises it to my lip, and gently rubs the gel into my cut. I can't resist staring into his blue eyes. He is so focused on my lip, as it's the only thing in the world. His caring touch sends a warm, tingling sensation through my body. I feel the urge to lean forward and kiss him. Kane suddenly looks me in the eye, as if he read my thoughts.

I pull back, feeling the heat of embarrassment rush to my cheeks.

Kane takes my hand in his, dips a finger in the gel and rubs it across my grazed knuckles, acting as if nothing happened.

'Why does Reeva hate you so much?'

His question sets my heart racing. I stare blankly at him, wondering where to start. It's been in my head for so long, festering away like an infection, seeping into every part of my conscious and subconscious mind.

'It's okay. You don't have to tell me.' Kane resigns.

There I go, drifting off into my thoughts again, not realising how much time has passed. I must stop doing that. Kane offered me a safe opportunity to unburden myself from years of guilt, and I'm doubtful a chance like this will come again.

'It's okay,' I blurt out. 'I should've spoken about it ages ago.'

Kane finishes rubbing the dermal gel into my knuckles and sits beside me, ready to listen. I lean forward and bury my face in my hands, emotions ready to boil over. I could burst out crying, but instead, I lift my head and draw a deep breath.

'Reeva's never forgiven me for leaving her alone.'

Kane remains silent and waits patiently for me to continue. No pressure. He's been a good listener in the past and my heart tells me I can trust him.

'We were six years old when it happened, on a class excursion to the raptor nursery. We split into pairs to feed the juvenile raptors. I was paired with Reeva. We were friends back then, or at least, we were supposed to be.'

'What do you mean?'

'We were feeding the raptors from an elevated cage, dropping chunks of meat into their pen. It was perfectly safe. The instructor was called away to another raptor pen. He told us to stay in the cage and not do anything until he returned. But I couldn't resist, I wanted to see the raptors from the gantry, without the bars obscuring our view. Reeva told me not to go, she pleaded with me to stay. But I didn't listen. Somehow, I convinced her we'd be all right. We weren't.'

'What happened?'

'We climbed onto the gantry for a bird's-eye view, not realising the blood on our hands would drive them into a frenzy. We got halfway across and stopped to look over the railing. They started jumping for us. We didn't know juvenile raptors could jump six or seven feet in the air. At first, they were several metres away from us. There was no way they could get us. But one of them figured out it could scale the wall and jump from higher up. It caught the gantry on its first try and hung there, barking at us, claws scraping on the metal to get up. I can still hear that sound.

'We ran back to the cage, screaming at the top of our lungs. That only excited them more. Because one raptor had made it to the gantry, the others followed its lead. I made it back to the cage before Reeva, she slipped and fell. One of the raptors scaled the railing and ran after me. I was terrified. I slammed the cage shut, not even thinking about Reeva.

'I still see her panic-stricken eyes, staring at me through the metal bars. She was lying on her stomach, with raptors landing all around her. I closed my eyes, convinced she was about to die. I didn't want to watch. I was to blame. I heard the screeches. My eyes were shut but all I could see was red. In my mind, she was being ripped apart. Then my cage door swung open. I screamed, thinking the raptors figured out how to turn handles. It was our instructor, carrying Reeva. She had a gash on her forehead, but she was alive. The raptors had been sedated by a swarm of emergency drones.

'Then, to make matters worse, I didn't own up to my mistake. I was petrified. I didn't want to get into trouble with the Union. Reeva took the blame because she was the one caught outside the cage and did a month in detention, all because of me. Since then, she's never been the same. She'll never forgive me.'

'You were young. We all make mistakes at that age.'

'But mine was bad enough to affect us for the rest of our lives. The way she treats me, that's made me the person I am today. Shy and weak.'

'You're not weak. Don't underestimate yourself. And there's nothing wrong with being shy. If that's who you are, then you can't change it.'

'Maybe I deserve everything she's done to me since.'

'The way she treated you a few minutes ago? You don't deserve that, regardless of what you did in the past.'

I look at Kane. An intense feeling of familiarity rushes through me. I can't shake the feeling that I know him from somewhere. 'Are you sure we don't know each other?'

Kane stares into my eyes. There's something behind his gaze, like he's desperate to tell me a secret, but sworn to silence.

'I have this feeling, every time I see you. It's like I know you from somewhere. Are you sure we didn't share a dormitory in the past? Or a class?'

'I'm sure.'

'The academy is so big; how can you be certain?'

Kane looks around the infirmary with a suspicious gaze, like someone afraid of being watched.

'What's the matter?'

'Nothing,' Kane shoots back. His abrupt tone is laced with frustration. His face softens and he continues in a quieter voice. 'We can't talk here.'

'About what?' I whisper back, my paranoia growing.

Kane stares at me. I can't tell if he's terrified or excited. He looks at my lips and leans forward. I don't pull away. Instead I close my eyes and allow his warm, soft lips to meet mine. I ignore the sting of my split lip and let him kiss me. He is gentle, tender, and somehow manages to kiss me without hurting my lip. My body tingles all over, and for a moment, I forget everything that's troubling me and give myself to him. When I open my eyes, Kane is sitting beside me with a troubled look etched across his face.

'I'm sorry. I shouldn't have done that,' he says.

'It's fine.'

'Are you sure? You didn't kiss me back.'

I suddenly realise my error, and right on cue, the heat rises to my face. But rather than sit there in embarrassment like I usually do, I'm determined to explain my reaction. 'It's just, well, I've never kissed anyone before.'

Kane smiles. 'Neither have I.'

'Why now? I'm all beat up and hardly kissing material.'

'I wanted to be the first to kiss you.'

'What do you mean?'

'It's no secret Avi likes you. Everyone sees it.'

'He's just a friend.'

'For now. I've been thinking about you since the first day we met. I wanted to make sure you understood how I feel before we go to war.'

A sudden panic rises inside me. If the other cadets can see how Avi is attracted to me, they must be able to see how Kane feels as well. If their intentions are so obvious, the academy will see it too. No wonder he's being so nervous. He doesn't want the academy to know. I don't want to be reprimanded or end up in detention for a personal relationship. This can't go on.

'I have to get back to my dorm before its lights out,' I say, hopping off the gurney. Kane attempts to follow me. 'Don't, I can show myself out.'

I'm half out the door when Kane calls my name. 'Zaz?'

I pause with hesitance.

'Next time Reeva corners you like that, don't wait for her to make a move. Strike first.'

I nod and leave Kane alone in the room, looking more worried than I've ever seen him. I keep my head down and hurry past the cadets in the passageway. Once outside, I gasp with relief, half expecting to be nabbed by Union guards for breaching intimacy rules. Cadets are not allowed under any circumstances to form affectionate relationships. The Union deny us that simple human right and hold it ahead of us like a carrot on a stick. If we fight the war, survive, and protect humanity, we're promised a life of freedom. Most cadets don't look that far ahead, never truly believing they will live long enough to enjoy a life beyond our military walls. But regardless, it's a nice dream and something to aim for.

I sprint up the stairs, nursing my aching ribs. By the time I reach the top the last few cadets are heading back to their dormitories. I return to mine just as the lights turn off and slip into bed, boots on and fully clothed. My heart is pounding, my thoughts racing. Between Kane's advances, Reeva's bullying, Avi's obvious – but unsaid – attraction to me, command training, and our impending deployment, it feels like the world is closing in to suffocate me.

If I don't surface for air soon, I'm certain to drown.

14

I wake in the morning to the protest of my battle-weary body, but feel a measure of relief. Every cadet outside the command program will be told about our deployment to Daxma-5 during morning assembly. Thank goodness; that's one less burden on my conscience. It was unfair of the Union to tell us in advance. They should have told everyone at the same time. I find it hard to keep secrets from my friends, especially one as important as this.

Nobody notices I'm already dressed as we jump out of bed and prepare for the morning run. Our instructors march through the dormitory, screaming orders. 'You have one minute to get dressed cadets. Move it!'

'Assembly at zero 700 hours,' yells another. 'Last ones back from the run will have less time for breakfast.'

I'm the first to follow the instructors out the door, determined to avoid any repercussions from last night. Reeva and Lani are bound to insult me and say I needed Kane to save me from a fight. It's inevitable.

My ribs ache with every step, but I run through the pain, feeling like a knife is stuck in my side. We traverse the network of walkways and bridges that dissect the jungle. Morning mists rise from the undergrowth and meet the sun, forming a golden haze that envelopes the soaring cliffs and treetops. I keep up with the leading pack of runners for the first time, driven by a desire to avoid my enemies. I glimpse over my shoulder and find Reeva several cadets behind me, determined to catch up. *Not today!*

Forty-five minutes later, the first of us arrive back at the dormitory, red-faced and sweating profusely. The instructors stand by the entrance and mark our times into their data pads.

'That's your best time yet, cadet,' the instructor says, singling me out.

I give a subtle nod and slip by, avoiding any more attention. Once inside, I waste no time in showering and make my way to breakfast. The mess hall fills up fast.

Abby sits at my table, looking flustered. Her hair is still wet from the showers and has left a dark water stain on her shoulder. She runs her hand along her ponytail and flicks it over her back. 'Talk about rushing. What do you think this assembly is for?'

I shrug my shoulders and scoop a mouthful of tasteless protein porridge.

'We never have assemblies mid-week. There's a rumour going around that Galen Thoms is addressing us.'

'Really?' I say, trying to sound surprised.

Abby is too preoccupied with everyone arriving for breakfast to notice my atrocious acting skills. I'm glad I don't have to keep up this charade for much longer.

'Maybe we're being deployed.'

I swallow my last mouthful with an audible gulp. Abby has no idea how right she is. I collect my tray and stand. 'See you there.'

The outside quadrangle is half full by the time I arrive. Enthusiastic conversations add to the excited ambience.

'I wonder what this is all about?' says a familiar voice. Avi stands beside me and observes the crowd. 'I guess we have to get used to this.'

'What's that?'

'Knowing things in advance is part of serving in the command division.' He leans closer and whispers, 'We have to be good at keeping secrets.'

I smile and nod, doubting he found it as hard as I did. Avi has enough confidence and charisma to mask any secret.

'What happened to your lip?'

I touch my lip without thinking. It's mostly healed from the dermal gel but there's still a slight bump. Of course, Avi had to notice. He's put me on the spot and I can't think of an excuse. My mind's eye replays the fight with Reeva, followed by Kane's kiss. The familiar tingle of excitement rises from my chest and I feel the warmth of a blush spread across my face. *I'm so bad at hiding what's on my mind.*

'Nothing,' I mumble. My tone couldn't be more unconvincing.

Avi gives me a curious, unsatisfied look and nods. It's like he sees right through me. He squeezes my arm in a friendly, but secretly affectionate way.

'I'll speak to you afterwards,' he says, heading into the crowd.

I watch him leave, relieved he didn't push it further. Avi has an innate ability to read people and will make an outstanding First Lieutenant. Me, on the other hand? I can't see how that's going to work when I can't even get out of my own head half the time.

The last few cadets file into the quadrangle and we all line up to face the stage. A gathering storm of Union guards and officials in their dark-grey uniforms watch us from the perimeter. I catch Reeva's predatory gaze from further along the line and it sets my heart racing. I look away and focus on the Union's holographic logo hovering over the stage.

Brigadier Ramsey steps up and addresses the assembly. 'Good morning, cadets. The leader of the Union, Galen Thoms, is standing by to address you via hololink.' His sombre tone foreshadows the proceedings with a dreaded sense of urgency and importance.

Ramsey steps aside and the Union hologram transforms into Galen Thoms. He approaches the front centre of the stage. 'Cadets, the time for your deployment has arrived faster than we anticipated. The Wraith have made their first move against the Union in over 18 years. We must counter their action with a swift and proportionate response. Within a month, you will fight for the future of humanity on Daxma-5, in the very heart of enemy territory.'

I've heard all this before. I'm more interested how the cadets are taking the news. I keep my head forward but let my gaze drift across the rows of grey uniforms. Everyone reacts in silent but telling ways. Feet shift slightly. Hands fidget behind backs. Some cadets bare clenched fists and white knuckles. The more edgy cadets break their rigid stance and glance about, eager to share their discomfort with others. *I wonder how long they'll survive on the battlefield. Probably not long.*

I draw my attention back to Galen's opaque hologram.

'This accelerated timetable means you begin squad exercises today,' Galen says. 'Based on your progress so far, your instructors have divided you into squads. There will be some minor adjustments over the next couple of weeks as we fine-tune your divisions, but any personal requests to change squads must be made via a formal application with your head instructor. We will only approve a transfer in rare circumstances. For the majority of you, the squad you train with today will be the same one you deploy with on Daxma-5... unless, of course, you are maimed or killed during training.'

Now I'm the one glancing about, nervously eyeing the surrounding cadets. I have no concerns about my command partner as the Union are bound to team me with Avi. We selected each other as a first preference. Reeva will end up with Seong. I'm more concerned about the other cadets assigned to my stealth and infantry divisions. Hopefully my friends are among them.

'But fear not,' Galen continues. 'Your training and resilience have brought you this far. We will prevail. And never forget, you have the support of every living soul in the Union behind you. I leave you with some heartfelt messages from the people and families you are protecting.'

Galen's hologram shimmers and vanishes.

A family appears in his place, a mother and father with their three young children standing in front of them, two boys and a girl in the middle, holding a crayon drawing of a dinosaur roaring at a Union flag. 'Thank you, cadets,' the mother says in a warm, paternal voice. 'Your efforts ensure our family has a future.' The girl proudly raises the drawing. 'Roar!'

A few laughs arise from the assembly.

The family are followed by messages from an eclectic mix of people throughout the Union, everyone from clean-cut doctors to greasy-faced mechanics to interstellar pilots to regular people in mundane jobs. They wish us well and remind us of why we fight. These brief glimpses into the outside world are all the Union gives us, and they always know just when to present them. It momentarily distracts us from the dangers on Daxma-5 and fills us with hope – hope that we too may one day live a normal life like them.

The messages finish and Brigadier Ramsey takes centre stage. 'We will reveal your command partners and squads upon the completion of this assembly. Training begins immediately. All squads have designated departure platforms for transport to your training island. Trains will leave at 09:30.'

I'm not sure why, but my heart starts racing. I should know what to expect. At least, I think I do. Today will be my first proper test as a leader, but even though I'll be sharing the responsibility with Avi, I'm still anxious. I'm glad he asked me to team up with him. It takes a layer of unnecessary pressure off me.

I find it hard to concentrate through the remainder of the assembly. Union strategists and brigadiers run through a mundane list of protocols, timetables, and expectations during the lead-up to our deployment. Like me, most cadets fidget and glance about, eager to learn who they are going to war with. The assembly finally ends and the cadets mill into familiar groups, creating an atmosphere of anticipation.

Avi pushes through the sea of grey jackets and joins me. 'No need to be nervous. We'll be fine.'

'Nervous? What do you mean?' I blurt out, surprising myself. *I sound way too defensive.* I was aware of my anxiety, but didn't think I was showing it. 'You kept to your word, didn't you?'

'Of course. The Union would be crazy not to put us together... But –'

'But what?'

'They can be unpredictable. Even though we selected each other, it's up to them to make the final decision.'

'Oh, great!' I sigh.

Four giant holographic screens project into the air, one along each side of the quadrangle. Columns of names populate the screens and the crowd jostles for a clear view of the ranks and squads. I skim across the names but can't read quick enough. Finally, two names stick out that I recognise: [MAIA-4756/WYNNE-8219]

'Damn it!' Avi hisses under his breath. 'Bloody Union bureaucrats.'

'What?' I whisper, heart pounding.

Avi points me towards to the opposite screen, shaking his head. I find his name straight away, but neither of us expected the one beside it.

[AVI-0995/SEONG-6914 PLATOON CODENAME: IGNITE]

An icy hand reaches inside my chest and squeezes my heart, then I discover two names I never thought I would see together.

[REEVA-6333/ZAYLA-8311 PLATOON CODENAME: FLAME]

Our faces appear alongside one another, future command partners, glaring across the quadrangle for all to witness. The solid ground beneath my feet suddenly vanishes and I sway with shock. *How can this be?* I gawk at Avi, lost for words. All he can do it stare back at me, eyes wide as mine.

'It must be a mistake,' I gasp. 'Why would they do that?'

Avi curses under his breath and glares at the Union officers with contempt.

My initial shock fades and I focus on the names making up my squad list, picking out several straight away:

[KANE-000]
[ABBY-2758]
[TYSON-8832]
[ROSA-1486]

Why would the Union place all my friends in the same squad but not allow me to share the First Lieutenant position with Avi? It doesn't make sense.

My subcutaneous ID chip vibrates and I check my forearm. [ASSEMBLE AT PLATFORM 5] illuminates through my skin.

Every cadet receives their orders at the same time and the crowd disperses to their designated mag-lev platforms.

'I guess I'll see you tonight,' Avi says. I've never seen him look and sound this despondent.

'Yeah.'

'Watch your back around Reeva, all right?'

The utterance of her name sends butterflies racing through my stomach. 'I will.'

Avi gives my hand a reassuring squeeze and storms off. I'm frozen in place, staring across the blur of grey uniforms, feet reluctant to move. Of all the people in the academy I could have been teamed with, the Union pairs me with the one person I can't stand to look at. *It's a nightmare.* I reach the train platform in a dazed state, without remembering how I even got there. My body is operating on autopilot while my mind processes the incomprehensible – I'm sharing command duties with Reeva!

The train doors open and everyone files inside. I merge with the crowd, trying not to focus on any one face. I sense the expectant looks from those around me. Most of them know who I am now thanks to the Union splashing my face across their gigantic holographic projections. The slightest eye contact is sure to trigger a conversation, so I keep my head down, hoping that Reeva is on a different carriage. The doors close, and the train departs with a gentle push.

Somebody jabs me in the side and I yelp like a juvenile brontosaurus. Every cadet in the carriage gawks in my direction. *What the hell?* I spin around to find Tyson and Rosa behind me, faces full of surprise. Tyson suddenly bursts into laughter and stifles it with his chunky fist. Rosa elbows him in the ribs. 'Idiot, I told you not to jab her.'

'Sorry,' Tyson spurts, swallowing his laugh. 'I didn't expect that.'

Now I realise how tense my body is. If someone had merely bumped into me, it would have elicited an unexpected overreaction.

'Are you okay?' Rosa asks.

'Some brutal selections, huh?' Tyson adds. 'Never would've picked you and –'

Rosa elbows Tyson harder this time.

I take a deep breath and glance about, concerned with who may be listening. 'Not much we can do about that now.'

'Don't worry,' Rosa says. 'Whatever happens, we've got you covered.'

'I appreciate that,' I whisper.

Their support helps, but I feel a growing sense of urgency. Reeva and I must find a way to work through our differences. It seems impossible, but we need to reach a common ground for the safety of everyone on our squad. Our train emerges from the shadow of the island and zips effortlessly across the ocean atop the mag-lev monorail. Several trains run parallel to ours, then divert off to different island destinations.

My stomach feels tight, like someone is twisting and squeezing my insides. The unusual silence pervading the carriage just fuels my nerves. Even Tyson and Rosa, who are naturally chatty, remain unusually quiet. This war has suddenly become a real and present danger for all of us.

Our train speeds towards an island hidden behind gargantuan steel walls. Sea mist sprays over the carriage windows as we pass through the rugged cliffs that rise from the ocean to meet the wall. We enter a cavernous tidal water grotto and draw to a stop alongside a subterranean platform nestled within the ancient volcanic stone. From here, a maze of escalators and well-lit corridors branch out and burrow deep into the island interior. We file onto the station and stand to attention as Union officers assemble along the platform. Everyone is so quiet, I can hear the water lapping against the grotto walls.

A stern-faced female officer marches by and addresses us with a powerful voice. 'When you hear your platoon's name called, assemble and follow the instructor to your training zone. You will be briefed on location before the session begins.'

The platoon names echo through the grotto, starting from the far end of the platform.

'Ignite... Flame... Blaze... Torch... Burn.'

As each platoon is called, the instructor holds up a holographic sign with the name emblazoned in vibrant yellow letters.

Boots scuffle as cadets push to reach their designated instructor. Tyson leads me and Rosa through the crowd, parting the bodies like an unstoppable ice-breaker. Kane squeezes through the chaos and walks alongside me. He smiles and I force myself to smile back, even though it's the last thing I feel like doing.

'We'll be fine,' he whispers. 'Remember, we've been through worse.'

Is my anxiety that obvious? Regardless, Kane's optimistic approach puts me at ease and the knot in my stomach loosens. A hand reaches through the bustle of grey jackets and grabs my arm. My mind flashes back to last night, being held by Lani as Reeva punches me. I flinch and clench my fist. Kane clutches my wrist and prevents me from swinging a devastating punch.

'We're all together. How cool is this?' Abby says, oblivious to how close she came to losing a tooth.

Her lively eyes are brimming with excitement and trepidation. I nod, doing my best to share her enthusiasm, and give Kane a surreptitious nod of thanks. It's nice to know he's got my back. *Seems to be a common theme.* Surrounded by friends, I should feel more supported than ever, but nothing can save me from the inevitable pandemonium of commanding with Reeva.

We line up in front of our instructor, a youthful-looking female who doesn't appear much older than us. Her dark hair is tied back neatly in a ponytail and juts out from the back of her grey beret. It's so hard to judge anyone's age outside the academy, as every cadet is the exact the same age. The surname PEREZ is embroidered on her jacket with small colourful ribbons of rank and service adorning the patch below her name.

'How's the lip?' whispers a voice from behind.

A chill races up my spine. I peer over my shoulder to find Lani and Reeva standing behind our group. Lani pushes out her bottom lip, rubs it, and gives me a pitiful look. Reeva just stares into my eyes, cold and void of emotion.

'First Lieutenants Reeva-6333 and Zayla-8311, step forward,' Perez says.

Reeva and I approach and stand at attention.

Perez eyes us over. *How much does she know about us? Who am I kidding? This is the Union – they know everything about us. They probably know about the beating I took last night. If so, why'd they put us together?*

'Do we have a problem, lieutenants?'

'No, ma'am,' Reeva replies in a loud voice, drowning out my softer response.

Perez focuses on me. 'Do we have a problem, Zayla-8311?'

'No ma'am, we don't.'

Perez furrows her brow and assesses me with her piercing hazel eyes, then scrutinizes the cadets standing in line behind us. 'Flame platoon, follow me.'

Perez leads us through the station, up several escalators, and onto a travelator that tunnels beneath the island. Every so often a shaft of light from the surface shines down through a maintenance hatch or access point, accompanied by a distant thump. The deep rhythmic thumping sounds like a giant heartbeat. Muffled roars penetrate the metres of soil and bedrock between us and the jungle above, indicating our dinosaurs are on the island and waiting to join us for our training session.

Reeva says nothing to me in the presence of our new instructor. *At least she has the sense to do that.* Our platoon keeps just as quiet and follows close behind.

The travelator ends at yet another escalator, which emerges on the surface inside a bustling dome-shaped outpost. The expansive space comprises tiered levels equipped with sprawling holographic workstations manned by Union scientists, officers, strategists, and dinosaur handlers. A dome of thick glass panels invites sunlight into the airy space while maintaining a safe barrier to the dense jungle outside.

Perez directs all 30 of us to stand around the central holographic station, a large circular pedestal dominating the middle of the space.

'Listen up, cadets!' Perez yells. 'I will only run through this briefing once. The rest will be up to you.'

A large hologram materialises over the pedestal, depicting a collection of modular buildings sitting in the shadow of an enormous satellite dish, all of which are encompassed within a triple layer of impenetrable concrete walls laced with razor wire along the top. Combat marine robots patrol the spaces between the walls while several tyrannosaurs stalk the outer perimeter between the walls and the surrounding jungle.

Our platoon gathers and jostles for an unobstructed view of the hologram. We're all standing shoulder-to-shoulder, eager to take in every detail. I try to keep my distance from Reeva, but the crowd forces us together.

'We have constructed a replica of a communication station on Daxma-5 in the nearby jungle.' Perez swipes her control panel and the hologram zooms in to the tyrannosaurs. 'The T-rexes are placeholders for the local titanoids, a species that share a similar size and level of aggression. They are highly territorial. Between the walls, the robots are programmed to defend the base and will imitate being controlled by the Wraith, meaning there will be high levels of unpredictability in their actions. Be prepared for anything. Your mission is to subdue the tyrannosaurs, penetrate the outer walls, take out as many robots as necessary, infiltrate the station, and shut down the satellite dish.'

Tyson raises his hand and Perez nods.

'Excuse me for asking, Sergeant Perez, but what good are our dinosaurs against that kind of firepower?'

'We will fully equip you and your dinosaurs with battle armour for this exercise. The robots will fire stun rounds, enough to take down even the biggest dinosaurs in your platoon. Remember, don't just attack them head-on or rely on brute force. Take advantage of your ranks.'

I look down the line of cadets, all glowing in the hologram's light, faces filled with fear and apprehension. Their tension is palpable.

Perez eyes us over and softens her demeanour. 'Rely on your lieutenants. They will get you through this.'

That's the worst thing she could have said. I dare not look at the faces of our platoon now. The only thing Reeva and I have ever agreed on is an intense disdain for one another and everyone knows that. This is going to end badly.

15

Following the briefing, Perez directs Reeva and I into a private meeting room away from our platoon. The cramped, soundproofed space has no chairs or windows, just a solitary blank table lit from above by a stark spotlight.

'Your ID chips will activate the strategic command console,' Perez says, motioning to the table. 'You have ten minutes to devise a strategy before suiting up and joining your platoon. This room is not monitored, so anything you strategise remains confidential. You'll have a couple of minutes to brief your platoon before deployment. Understood?'

'Yes, ma'am,' we both reply.

Perez leaves and the door seals shut behind her, muting the outside world. *Oh crap! Locked in a small dark room with Reeva is my version of hell.*

We stand on opposite sides of the table and stare one another down, like a pair of apex predators protecting their territory. We haven't been this close and alone in over a decade, not since childhood. Her steely-blue eyes assess mine with calculating precision. *What's her game plan?* The harsh overhead light emphasises the faint raptor scar on her forehead. Unlike our memories of that fateful day, it has almost faded to nothing, reminding me it's my fault we're standing here like this: despising one another.

'I have no idea how we ended up together,' Reeva says, 'but I'm sure it's your fault.'

I'm so tired of bearing the guilt for something that happened years ago. I know I deserve it, but enough is enough. A surge of bravery rises through me. 'Maybe it's your fault.'

'What?' Reeva hisses. 'You wanna go there?'

I do, actually. A sharp pain shoots through my injured lip, reminding me of last night. My sudden burst of courage evaporates and suppresses my knee-jerk response behind a more rational response. *We have a job to do.*

'So how are we gonna do this?' I say, looking at the console, ready to get down to business. I press my forearm against the glass surface and it displays my details.

[ZAYLA-8311/SPINOSAURUS-B010 COMMAND PROTOCOLS ACTIVE]

Reeva watches me with an air of suspicion then scans her ID chip.

[REEVA-6333/TYRANNOSAURUS-B010 COMMAND PROTOCOLS ACTIVE]

A 3-D holographic map materialises over the table displaying the communications station, our adversaries, and available platoons. I examine the layout of the buildings, walls, and control panels that operate the steel gates into the complex.

'Getting past the T-rexes shouldn't be an issue,' I say. 'We have a 30-strong platoon against four of them. But the gates can only be opened from the inside. That means we need someone to get over the walls and let us in.'

'We can use our largest infantry to breach the wall.' Reeva says reasonably, dragging a pair of two holographic dreadnoughtuses up to the wall. 'The dreads can drop their cadets over the top. The only problem is the robots.'

I position several pterodactyl units over the first wall. 'Use the pterodactyls to draw their fire and lead them to the back of the compound while the dreads open the gate.'

Reeva nods and moves several units inside the first wall. 'Once we're inside, we send infantry and stealth divisions to permanently disable the robots. Then we can send in the dreads and begin working on the inner gate.'

'Okay, so we just do the same again. What about the robots

behind the inner wall? We can't draw them out of sight like we did for the inner wall. The compound is one open space except for the buildings. They'll be waiting for us as soon as the gate opens.'

Reeva stares at the hologram for a long moment, then positions a unit of megaraptors on the outer gate. 'We hide out of sight when the gate opens and use a decoy to draw them out. Then we ambush them from behind.'

Ambush! Her choice of words makes my traumatised lip tingle. *Yeah, I know you're good at that.*

Reeva frowns at me, as if she knows what I'm thinking. 'Something wrong?'

'Nope, nothing.' I focus on the hologram, keen to get past the momentary distraction. Our units are in the best positions available, like pieces on a chessboard, ready to checkmate. 'I think our plan will work.'

Reeva persists drilling into me with those piercing eyes. I put up with it until I can't stand it a moment longer. 'What is it?'

'Just because we figured this out together, don't think it changes anything between us. I'm not putting my life on the line for you on the battlefield. I don't trust you, and never will.'

Fair enough, I think. *I don't trust you either.*

We leave the meeting room to find Perez waiting for us. 'Your platoon has suited up and awaits you in the departure bay. Follow me.'

Perez leads us through the outpost. We pass a group of concerned-looking scientists gathered around a malfunctioning hologram. The schematic flickers, dematerialises, then reappears, and I catch snippets of their conversation over the chatter.

'It's not a mainframe glitch...there's something disrupting the code.'

'We can't fix it from here.'

One of the scientists looks at me and we lock eyes. His anxious expression fills me with dread. *Something's wrong.*

'Cadet?' Perez holds a lift door open, waiting for me to join her and Reeva.

I hustle inside. Reeva gives me a sidelong glance and shakes her head. The lift descends multiple levels beneath the outpost. We then traverse a long corridor, through a fortified steel door, and into an armoury stockpiled with pulse rifles, high-voltage dinosaur control staffs, handheld tasers, and other weapons. We enter an adjoining room where armoured exosuits hang from rows of conveyor belts like sleeping robots, waiting to be woken up.

The first exosuit in each row hangs over a circular podium in an open state, awaiting a human occupant.

'Time to suit up,' Perez says.

'I've never worn a full exosuit before,' I say.

'There's nothing to be concerned about. Just step onto the podium. The robotic arms will automatically adjust the armour to fit your height and body weight. Consider it a second skin – one that will keep you alive on Daxma-5. They are devoid of microprocessors to avoid infection by the Wraith. The suit interfaces with the neural processor embedded in your skull, the same one that links you to your dinosaur. It won't be long before you forget you're even wearing it.'

I huff to myself. *Easy for you to say. You're not the one wearing it.*

'Your compressed schedule means you never had time to complete your exosuit training. So now it's integrated into your first group exercise.'

Reeva leaps onto the podium like she's done it a million times, keen to beat me to the mark.

I step up and turn my back to the armour, then press my heels into the boot stirrups and lean back. The plating closes around me and forms a perfect protective shell. The elbow, knee, and ankle joints whir and hum as the robotic arms screw and unscrew the sizing bolts to lengthen and accommodate my tall, lean frame. Gloves slip over my hands and attach to the forearm bracers. *Click.* The chest plate seals around me, and the neck ring snaps into place. The helmet comes down over my head and seals to the ring with an ear-popping adjustment of air pressure.

I take my first step forward and discover the suit is almost weightless and enhances my movement. Reeva steps down from the podium and we face each other through our crystal-clear visors. Her body-hugging dark-purple armour shimmers in and out of view as it camouflages with the room's metallic wall panels. Reeva's outline is highlighted inside my visor with a bright green line.

'The suits default to camouflage mode,' Perez says. 'Their nanoparticle plating automatically changes colour to reflect your environment. Your visor detects other suits in camouflage mode with a green outline. If the line changes to yellow, then the occupant is injured. Red means they are critical and near death.'

'What if they're dead?' Reeva asks.

'Then they're dead,' Perez says matter-of-factly. 'Bodies won't display a highlight colour.'

'What about communications?' I ask.

'Anything you need will be activated by your neural chip and displayed in your visor. Every command is thought activated. There are dozens of comms controls, but you only require two for this training exercise. [OPEN COMMUNICATION] and [PRIVATE COMMUNICATION], followed by the birth number of the cadet you want to speak with. Any time you need to give your suit an instruction, focus your eyes on the two squares in the central grid overlay of your visor. When the squares turn yellow, your exosuit will interpret the next thought as a command.'

'What if we need something else?'

'Like what?' Perez says, narrowing her gaze on me.

'If someone's injured or we need to contact the Union. This is a live exercise. There's bound to be casualties.'

'We're monitoring each one of you. If someone's life signs turn critical, your orders are to leave them and complete the mission. We will intervene at the earliest opportunity, without interfering with your mission, and give them medical attention. Understood?'

I give Perez a halfhearted nod.

This accelerated training program doesn't sit right with me. The Union is rushing us into situations we're not prepared for. I've learned successful militaries of past civilisations had years of training and real-world experience before being sent to war. Every cadet has lived in the academy since birth and learned so many things, but it feels like our most important training is being crammed in at the last minute. We've had no real-world experience in our suits. It's going to be sink or swim.

We follow Perez out of the armoury into the subterranean transport system. A short ride on a travelator delivers us to an underground hub of vast tunnels and shafts. Two Union guards stand in front of a towering steel door. They lower their pulse rifles and salute Perez, then stand aside as the door rumbles open.

'This is where I leave you,' Perez says, gesturing to the shadowy void beyond. 'Inside, your platoon awaits. You have five minutes to brief them before the gangway opens.'

Reeva and I share a look through our visors.

Who takes the lead here? I've gone from avoiding Reeva at all costs to making every decision with her. Before I have a chance to say anything, she forges ahead of me. *I guess that answers my question.*

We enter a sprawling industrial bay. The grubby steel walls and floors are littered with scratches, showing how the Union have used the underground network to move the dinosaurs between islands. Our platoon stands at the far end, camouflaged in the shadows. As I focus on each cadet my visor highlights them with a green outline, along with their name, birth number, and dinosaur. Their suits are not in full camouflage mode as each of their faces remains visible through the visor, illuminated by a halo of white light.

'I've got this,' Reeva announces inside my helmet, startling me.

It sounds as if she's speaking inside my head, and too close for my liking. A small readout appears at the base of my visor: [REEVA-6333 PRIVATE COMS CHANNEL]

'What about me?' I reply.

'I'll brief the platoon.'

'We came up with the plan together. We should take turns explaining it.'

Reeva rounds on me, blue eyes glowering through her visor's halo. 'I meant it when I said I don't trust you. Keep your mouth shut and let me do the talking.'

I freeze, unsure if I should respond. Doing so will only inflame the situation.

'Okay!?' she says, leaning towards me a threatening manner.

I don't want to argue about this now, especially in front of our platoon. Part of me is glad she's taking control of the situation – I never felt comfortable in a command position anyhow. Plus, if she makes a bad decision, then the blame falls upon her more than me. If Reeva wants more responsibility, she can have it.

I feign a sigh of resignation. 'Okay.'

Reeva gives me quizzical look, expecting me to argue the point. She eases off and marches over to the platoon. I follow and stand dutifully by her side, quiet and complicit, as she explains the plan.

Kane stands at the front of the group, watching me through the hologram Reeva is using to break down the mission. I know what he's thinking. *Why is Reeva doing all the talking? Shouldn't they be sharing their lieutenant duties?* For now, I'm not fussed. I've never been great at public speaking. My strength will come on the battlefield. With Spino by my side, I'm confident I'll be more effective there.

Reeva finishes just as red lights flash through the room. Klaxons wail and the metal wall ahead of us parts horizontally through the middle, revealing a replica of a Union drop ship departure bay, complete with dinosaur pens. Our entire platoon of dinosaurs are secured in individual holding pens, barely wide enough for them to move. They thump against their enclosures, grunting and snorting, anxious to be set loose. The slender necks of a pair of dreadnoughtuses rise from their pens like gigantic tree trunks. Their tiny heads and pointed craniums brush the ceiling a dozen floors above. Beside them hang cages housing a pair of pterodactyls and a quetzalcoatlus. They sit hunched in their enclosures, wings folded, beaks sticking out through the bars. A cacophony of distressed roars, barks, and screeches echo through the bay.

I feel Spino's anxiety. The sooner we get out of here the better. Our dinosaurs are not used to being confined to such cramped spaces, especially the larger carnivores like mine.

Spino's sail rises from the top of a pen beside the main bay door. His outline flashes in my visor. [ASSEST LOCATED: MOUNT FOR DEPLOYMENT]

Nearby ladders and stairs lead to rows of gantries that service the pens, allowing cadets who ride their dinosaurs to mount them safely from above.

[DEPLOYMENT IN 60 SECONDS] flashes inside my visor and the countdown begins. [59... 58... 57...]

Our platoon splits up and races off to join their assets. I sprint over to the first stairway and climb two flights to the second level. The clang of our exosuit boots resonate through the bay and upset our dinosaurs even more. Racing on, I have a bird's-eye into the fierce lineup ready for battle: allosaurus, gigantosaurus, majungasaurus, and tyrannosaurus, all suited up with armour-plating and saddles.

I approach Spino's pen and leap onto the platform alongside his saddle. He rears up in fear and slams his flank against the enclosure. His mental discomfort surges through me in a shared wave of panic and nausea. *I understand.* Going from the freedom of an island to being locked in a strange steel cage is a big shock.

'Hey, Spino, it's me,' I say, running my glove along his armoured flank.

My presence doesn't settle him like it usually does. He can't feel my hand through the glove or hear the natural resonance of my voice behind my helmet.

[30... 29... 28...]

The countdown is half done. If I don't soothe Spino's nerves before deployment I might not be able to control him. I focus on the faint grid displayed inside my visor and think [DETACH HELMET]

[WARNING: NOT ADVISED] flashes across my visor. [DEPLOYMENT IN 20...19...18...]

Screw it!

[COMMAND NOT RECOGNISED]

'Stupid suit. That wasn't a command,' I say aloud, reaching for the automatic release mechanism on my neck ring.

HISS! The securing ring releases my helmet. I jump into Spino's side-saddle, detach my glove, and reach through the gap in his armour to stroke his neck. I feel the mighty torrent of blood gushing through his veins with each beat of his heart.

'No need to fret. I'm here.'

Spino jerks with excitement at the sound of my voice but his neck is secured through the gate, preventing him from craning his head around to face me. His luminous green eyes focus on me through the bars and his panicked snorts become slower, more relaxed breaths.

'That's it. Good boy. You're okay. We'll get used to each other with our amour on.' I hold up the helmet. 'See this? I have to put it back on, but it's still me.'

Spino grunts and raises his head.

I'll take that as a yes. I slip on my glove and place my helmet onto the locking ring just as the visor countdown completes.

[2... 1... INITIATING DEPLOYMENT]

Every dinosaur pen springs open at the same time. Spino lunges forward and I topple backwards into the saddle. Reeva and her tyrannosaur emerge from the pen opposite and all four of us stare one another down for a tense moment. The platoon assembles behind us, cadets and dinosaurs ready for battle.

The gigantic departure bay doors open outward and lower to form a ramp into the jungle. Bright, natural light spills into the bay. A lush deep-green jungle awaits. The satellite dish denoting our destination is visible, rising from the mists hovering above the treeline.

Reeva's voice appears in my helmet. 'I'm assigning all units to their attack formations now.' She uses a holographic map projected from her saddle to assign the cadets and their dinosaurs to positions around the target.

'Everyone knows what to do,' she says. 'Deploy!'

Spino lumbers forward. I don't need to vocalise my directions as he perceives them on a subconscious level, acting as an extension of my mind and body. We stomp down the gangway and head towards the palm trees. The rumble of an earthquake builds and follows us, so deep and powerful it resonates through Spino and vibrates my saddle.

I turn around and find our full platoon charging after us, thundering across the ground in all their primal power.

The massive bipedal carnivores guard the flanks while the smaller species stick to the middle. Just behind me is an allosaurus, followed by a carcharodontosaurus, with a majungasaurus and second tyrannosaur rounding out the pack. They stomp after me and Reeva, roaring, carrying the cadets atop their saddles. Between the giant carnivores are megaraptors, velociraptors, a mapusaurus, and tiny packs of troodons and compys, all running alongside their cadets. Two massive dreadnoughtus bring up the rear, plodding along with their tree-trunk–sized legs. Their long slender necks and small heads rise high above the trees.

I recognise the stocky cadet riding in the saddle of a dread. It's Tyson!

The entire platoon plunges into shadow. Overhead, a magnificent quetzalcoatlus, the biggest flying dinosaur in the Union, swoops after a pair of pterodactyls. Their wings momentarily blot out the sun and blast us with a gust of wind. They zoom ahead and skim the treetops, then arc upwards to a higher altitude as their cadets remain low in the saddles, leaning forward into the wind shear.

Wow! This is the first time I've seen everyone together and working as a platoon.

I spin around just in time to confront a fast-approaching row of palm trees and hazardous vines. Riding side-saddle is dangerous, and I must remain vigilant. One careless detour could leave me impaled on a branch or strangled in the vegetation. Spino senses my concern and slows, allowing the smaller units to overtake us.

'Watch out! Coming through!' a voice blares through my helmet. [KANE–000 PRIVATE GROUP COMS] appears in the lower left of my visor.

Kane and his pack of megaraptors cut past and swerve through the jungle, with him atop the largest raptor, riding it like an upright horse.

Abby, Tyson, and Rosa's names appear beneath Kane in the private channel.

'I hate taking orders from Reeva,' Abby says.

'Yeah,' Tyson chimes in. 'When are you gonna start calling the shots, Zaz?'

'I'm not worried. I prefer she makes the mistakes on the first mission.'

'Good call,' Rosa says.

'Although we both came up with the plan.'

'Do me a favour, Zaz.'

'What's that?'

'Just do one thing on this mission to remind her and everyone else that you're both in charge.'

'I second that!' booms Tyson.

'I third that,' Abby says.

'If you don't, it'll be harder next time,' Rosa says. 'You know what Reeva's like - a power rush like this will go straight to her head.'

'Keep the chatter down, guys,' Kane says. 'Save it for the mess hall.'

'Kane's right,' I say. 'I'm closing the private channel. Good luck everyone!'

[CLOSE PRIVATE CHANNEL] I think. The names disappear from my visor. I enjoyed talking to my friends. They gave me a welcomed confidence boost, but Kane's right - this isn't the time for idle banter. And Rosa made an excellent point: I need to keep Reeva in check to earn trust from our platoon.

Our first group exercise is more important than I realised. If I don't prove myself now, I'll be forever living in Reeva's shadow.

16

Startled flocks of birds take flight from the treetops as Spino smashes through the jungle at full tilt, swiping the dangerous foliage clear of me with his snout and showering my saddle with stripped leaves and vines. Around us, every dinosaur bigger than a megaraptor is ploughing headlong for the target, knocking over trees, flattening the undergrowth, and disturbing every living thing within a one-kilometre radius. Lucky this isn't a stealth mission. Our raucous platoon can be heard across the island.

We burst through the trees and charge into a clearing. The impregnable outer wall of the compound looms over us and casts the area into shadow. Beyond the gigantic panels of grey steel, I spot the central spire of the satellite dish, rising high into the blue sky like a shiny needle.

Kane's megaraptors and the other mid-sized platoon units work their way around the edge of the clearing, camouflaged by the trees.

Reeva emerges from the jungle on her tyrannosaur, hands in front of her helmet, fending off a barrage of low hanging branches. I can't hear her; but can easily see her cursing into her visor. I chuckle to myself. *I guess riding side-saddle has its advantages. Easier to get a dinosaur to turn its head than duck.*

'Look out, Zaz! Rogue T-rex incoming left,' screams a voice in my helmet.

ROAR!

I look left and find my visor enveloped by stained yellow teeth and a glistening pink tongue. The gaping dinosaur maw threatens to devour me and munch a hole in Spino's side. I flinch away from the jaws and Spino does the same, imitating my movement with the added bonus of his powerful tail.

THWACK!

Spino's tail smacks the T-rex across the snout and the dazed predator stumbles away to end up nose-first in the dirt, snorting and whimpering. The remainder of our apex carnivores enter the clearing and attack the T-rex while it's down. The unfortunate creature is no match for the onslaught of claws and teeth as its olive-green flesh is torn into meaty chunks. Bright-red blood spills across the ground.

I turn away, sickened by the carnage. One part of the academy I will never be able to stomach is the heartless slaughter of living creatures.

A pair of scarred and mottle-skinned tyrannosaurs stomp into view at the far end of the clearing, with a third appearing from the opposite direction, flanking us from both sides. The salivating theropods kick up huge plumes of dirt as they raise and lower their heads, hungrily sniffing our scents on the breeze. The poor creatures look like they haven't been fed in days.

Open communications. I wait for [CHANNEL OPEN] to appear in my visor before giving the order. 'Dreadnoughtus units advance to the wall. We'll take care of the T-rexes.'

Tyson's response echoes through my helmet. 'Copy that, Lieutenant.'

The ground shakes with the ferocity of an earthquake as Tyson's dreadnoughtus stomps past us. For a big guy, Tyson looks surprisingly miniscule on the back of his humungous sauropod. A second dreadnoughtus runs alongside them. My visor highlights the cadet riding it with a green outline and displays the name, [RENAE-0965/DREADNOUGHTUS-B014], a cadet I've never met. I only know six cadets out of the 45 on my platoon, and some of them may die before I ever speak to them one-on-one. It seems wrong to fight alongside cadets we don't even know, but maybe the Union want it that way, to keep our emotional attachments to a minimum.

'Zaz, what are you doing?' Reeva yells. 'Fall into formation.'

I'm overthinking things, like usual. Every time I stop to think Spino does the same, placing both of us in jeopardy. I must remain focused. Keep moving. Spino lumbers into position beside Reeva and her tyrannosaur, ready to face the advancing T-rexes.

Tyson and Renae pull their dreadnoughtuses to a stop before the wall. The sauropods twist and lower their impossibly long necks so their heads are level with the saddles. Tyson and Renae grab hold of the bridles and their dinosaurs lift them skyward, like living cranes.

At the same time, our flying units swoop the outer wall. My visor highlights Rosa leading the pack atop her pterodactyl. Glowing pink tracer fire lights up the sky after them, bursting like fireworks from inside the base. Rosa and her pterodactyl bank hard to avoid the dummy rounds.

[SHOW MAP] I think. [TRACK HOSTILES] A topographical map of the entire base displays inside my visor. The robots between the walls are chasing after our aerial units, leaving a section of the space between the walls unguarded. *Our plan's working!*

The first two T-rexes lower their heads and charge me and Reeva.

'Defence formation!' Reeva calls.

I steer Spino in beside her as a gigantosaurus rushes over to assist. The cadet's name flashes across my visor [JED-5768]. Another cadet I've never met.

'Stand fast, Jed,' I say. 'We need to protect the sauropods while they lower Tyson and Renae over the wall.'

'Affirmative,' Jed replies. 'Those tyrannosaurs won't get past us.'

The beasts bear down on us, jaws agape, eyes fierce and insatiable. This is not normal T-rex behaviour, especially considering they're outnumbered in numbers and size. They didn't become apex predators by being this stupid... The Union must be doing more than starving them, and are probably provoking them with neural implants.

Spino sidesteps the attack, almost throwing me from the saddle as he locks his jaws around the bigger T-rex's neck, driving the beast headfirst into the ground. Columns of dirt and rocks spew into the air.

Reeva's T-rex spins about, smashing the other T-rex against the wall as Jed's gigantosaurus sprints in and swipes its exposed flank with his clawed foot. A torrent of blood gushes from the divots like a crimson waterfall.

I teeter in the saddle as Spino struggles to hold down his catch. Our pinned T-rex uses its mighty hind legs to drive itself forward, leaving huge mounds of upturned soil behind its muscular heels. With each push, its head burrows a little deeper into the ground.

'Need help here!' I call to no one in particular. 'We can't hold this one down.'

The trees to my left burst open and Abby bounds towards us on her stegosaurus. 'Coming! Just keep him there.'

The T-rex's nostrils snort through the soil like a whale's blowhole as it inches forward, trying to break free. Its tails swishes through the air, whistling and snapping like a giant whip.

'Watch out for that tail,' I scream.

'Affirmative!'

Abby's stegosaurus charges in, swings about, and lashes its spiked tail into the T-rex's hindquarter, penetrating deep into its flesh with a loud *squelch*. The effect is instant. The T-rex loses all power and slumps to the ground, legs paralysed. It whimpers like a hatchling and collapses sideways as Abby's stegosaurus releases its spikes.

'Whoa! That tail is lethal,' I say.

'Glad I could help.'

Renae's voice sounds over the comms. 'We're inside the walls and hotwiring the main gate now –'

Tyson talks over her. 'A few more seconds and... There we go!'

The first immense gate parts down the middle and slides open.

Reeva's T-rex stomps towards the opening. 'All units convene at the main gate,' Reeva announces. 'We've breached the outer wall.'

Of course she has to be the first inside, I think. I wouldn't put it past Reeva to take all the credit if this mission is a success. Our platoon converges on the gate, leaving the mortally injured tyrannosauruses to suffer until the Union put them out of their misery. Aside from the heartless carnage, so far, so good. No casualties and everything's gone according to plan.

Our platoon assembles around the gate as it slowly slides open. The tiny compys and mid-sized raptor units move in first, while the bigger species stand aside and wait their turn.

[TRACK HOSTILES BETWEEN THE WALLS] I think, and my visor displays the request. The robot patrols are now on the far side of the compound, firing at our flying units swooping the walls. This is working better than expected.

CLUNK!

The massive gate retracts all the way and our remaining platoon moves inside, filing along the space between the walls. It's a tight fit and we jostle for standing room.

'Stealth units procced between the inner walls and take out the patrol robots,' Reeva orders. 'Dreadnoughtus units prepare to breach the inner wall.'

'Copy that,' Renae snaps back.

The pair of dreads are the last dinosaurs to enter the gate. They lower their heads and invite Tyson and Renae to grab hold of the bridles, then lift them up and over the wall. Meanwhile, four raptor units race off, two in each direction. I watch Kane and his megaraptors disappear and feel a knot form in my stomach. It's not the time to feel anxious about my friends, but I can't help it. [TRACK RAPTOR STEALTH UNITS]

The raptor units display inside my visor, each outlined in green, like an X-ray peering through the compound walls. Kane leads the charge. Within seconds his raptors encounter the first robot and leap onto it, tearing through the pneumatic tubes and energy cables powering its arms and legs. The robot flails about like a broken toy. The trailing raptor unit overtakes Kane and attacks the next robot while the other two units approach from the opposite side to finish the job.

BOOM!

My visor flashes white and displays the message [TRACKING SIGNALS LOST] A fireball erupts on the far side of the compound, followed by a dark mushroom cloud, which casts an ominous shadow over the satellite dish.

'Kane! What was that?' I cry out. There is no answer, just the crackle of static. 'Raptor units respond. What's happening?'

[RESUME TRACKING] My visor sensors adjust and locate several bodies on the ground. Kane is one of three highlighted in green, while the fourth body, [YOLANDA-8374], is pulsing between an orange and red outline.

'Comrade down! Yolanda's critically injured.'

[REEVA-6333 PRIVATE COMMS] appears in my visor. 'What are you doing, Zaz?'

'The raptor units need medical assistance.'

Reeva's bright-red T-rex moves in front of Spino, blocking our path forward. She glares at me across the space. 'Focus on the mission.'

'There wasn't supposed to be live rounds during this exercise. Something bad's happened.'

'Forget about it. We were told to complete our objective, no matter the cost.'

'You continue. I'm going to check on them.'

'You're not a medic,' Reeva snaps. 'Stay on mission.'

'You can't order me to stay. I'm going to help our comrades. You stay on the mission, but I'm going to help.'

I give Spino a pat on his neck and he lurches forward, pushing past Reeva and her T-rex. [OPEN PLATOON COMMS] 'I'm assisting the raptor units. All other units stay with Reeva and complete the mission.'

I forge on between the compound walls, my insides a churning bundle of nerves, well aware my decision will only drive a bigger wedge between me and Reeva. The mushroom cloud is now twice as high as the satellite dish and the path ahead is choked with smoke. Spino slows and starts wheezing.

'It's okay,' I say, sharing his apprehension. 'We're almost there.'

Our entwined senses make my lungs feel heavy, as if I'm breathing in the smoke as well, even though my suit's air filtration unit makes that impossible.

I stare blindly into the smoke, watching the cadet's green outlines grow larger in the haze. We're almost upon them, yet I can't see a thing. An orange glow emanates from the gloomy fog of grey, hinting at a hellish scene beyond.

'Okay, stop here,' I say.

Spino needs little coaxing to follow my instruction, more intent to raise his head and sniff for clean air. *I don't blame him.* He finally kneels to accommodate me and I dismount. My visor indicates Kane is only metres away, but I still can't see him. His startled raptors suddenly dash past me, barking and screeching, disoriented in the smoke.

'Zaz, I'm over here,' says a familiar voice.

I discover Kane sitting on the ground against the wall, pale-faced and staring at me with glazed eyes though his cracked visor. He lethargically reaches for me and I help him stand.

'What happened?'

'I think the robot fired a live missile, destroyed itself in the process.'

'They're meant to be using dummy rounds.'

'It looked like it was malfunctioning.'

'Malfunctioning?'

'Yeah, it was ramming its head against the wall. Then punching it. Over and over, like it was trying to break through to the other side. One of our raptor units attacked it the same way we took the others down, but the way the robot reacted was unpredictable, I swear it was...'

Kane's eyes glaze past mine and focus on the burning debris. His voice trails off to nothing.

'Swear it was what?'

Kane's eyes return to mine. 'Behaving like it had a mind of its own. Like it was trying to escape.'

'But they're automatons, devoid of self-awareness. They fight until they succeed or die trying. They're not programmed for self-preservation.'

'Unless they're being controlled by the Wraith.'

'What do you mean?'

'Either the Union programmed the robots to imitate the Wraith and didn't tell us, or we've been infiltrated by the Wraith.'

'I saw something before we left the outpost, a problem the techs were trying to fix. What if it was the Wraith?'

'The Union would never have approved this exercise if they thought their computer systems were compromised by the Wraith.'

'Maybe they didn't know. What if the Wraith are already here, lurking in our networks, waiting for the perfect moment to attack?'

'I hope you're wrong, Zaz, and it's just a malfunctioning robot –'

'That desperately needs to escape? I doubt it.'

Kane's megaraptors emerge from the smoke, barking and hissing, their light green eyes flitting about nervously. They settle as he gives them a reassuring rub on the snout. 'Hey boys, come here. It's okay.'

The outline of a cadet appears inside my visor with the name [JASON/0945]. I can't see him, but he's coming towards us. A moment later, he staggers from the smoke in a blackened and smouldering exosuit. If not for the high-tech protection, he'd be dead.

I rush forward and help him. 'Are you hurt?'

'Huh?' Jason replies, louder than necessary.

'Are you okay?'

'I'm fine, just a little deaf,' Jason says, tapping his helmet as if that might fix his problem.

His raptors appear behind him and bark sharply at the sound of his voice. They fared a lot worse, with cuts and burns to their exposed skin.

'I lost a raptor in the explosion,' Jason says. 'What's going on? I thought this was a training exercise.'

'We're not sure.'

[REEVA-6333 PRIVATE COMMS] flashes in my visor. 'Zaz, what's going on over there? We're about to open the second gate. We need you back here.'

I peer through the haze and target Yolanda's body 30 metres from our position. Her outline is still pulsing between orange and red, meaning she's critically injured and needs immediate attention. 'We're about to reach Yolanda. Hold off for a minute.'

'What do you mean hold off?'

'Don't open the gate.'

'Why not?'

'The robots are malfunctioning. One of them was acting weird, then fired a live round.'

'You're acting weird!'

'I'm serious. We've got a casualty.'

'Wake up, Zaz. Danger goes with the training. I can't believe you don't know that by now.'

'It doesn't feel right.'

'We're not basing mission decisions on a hunch. The Union are watching everything we do. They'd know if something was wrong. If there was, they'd shut us down. It's all part of the exercise – they're adding real-world danger.'

'But this doesn't fit the brief.'

'That's the point, Zaz. It's a test. War is unpredictable and messy. They want to see how we respond under pressure. The Union needs every cadet they have, so why would they risk their best assets right before deployment?'

'Please, Reeva, just hold off until I see what's going on here.'

'I'm not waiting.'

'If you open those gates, you're putting us all at risk.'

After a long pause, Reeva replies, 'I'll give you one minute.'

The private comms channel cuts off before I have a chance to respond. I can't believe I was almost about to thank her.

'What's wrong?' asks Kane.

'Reeva's given us one minute to find Yolanda and assess the situation before they open the next gate. If there's something wrong with the robots, we need to abort the mission before she unleashes the rest of them.'

'Whatever you need, I'm here for you.'

'I'm with you too,' Jason says loudly.

'All right,' I say, heading for Spino. 'Let's get our dinosaurs moving.'

Spino tilts his head and watches me approach with a curious, concerned gaze.

'Don't tell me you're having second thoughts!'

Spino shakes his head and snorts as if to say *no*. He lowers his body and I mount the saddle. Kane and Jason round up their raptors and assume tactical diamond formations ahead of me. We press on through the clearing smoke.

The mangled, burning remains of two robots rest in the bottom of a fresh crater. We step around it, scraping along the blackened walls, to find the charred raptor from Jason's unit laying in a death pose, neck curled back, tail extended with its mouth wide open. The force of the blast was so strong it stripped the raptor's battle armour from its body. Spino clears the carnage in a single stride while Jason's raptors whine and bark at the sight and smell of their fallen pack member.

My visor tracks Yolanda's outline through the haze. Spino's elongated gait covers the remaining distance in seconds. Fifteen metres, ten, five. My heart quickens upon seeing Yolanda's prone body.

'Okay, Spino, that's close enough. Stop here.'

I dismount and stumble over the rubble towards her. Yolanda's helmet is scorched, clouding the visor and making her face hard to see. I rub off some of the soot and find her semiconscious and struggling to breathe.

'Yolanda, can you hear me?'

She moans something unintelligible.

I check her suit. No signs of a puncture or shrapnel wound. [CHECK VITAL SIGNS] I think and her stats list inside my visor:

[YOLANDA-8375/HEALTH STATUS]
[FRACTURED RIGHT FEMUR]
[FRACTURED RIGHT HUMERUS]

[THREE BROKEN RIBS]
[PUNCTURED LUNG: TRAUMATIC PNEUMOTHORAX, REQUIRES IMMEDIATE MEDICAL ATTENTION]

No wonder she can't breathe. Every breath Yolanda takes is escaping her punctured lung and filling her chest cavity with air. The build-up of pressure will eventually squash her heart and send her into cardiac arrest.

Kane and Jason join me. Their raptors form a defensive ring around us.

Jason kneels beside me and detaches a medipack from his suit. 'I've got this,' he says, withdrawing a long heavy-duty needle.

'I'm scanning the robot that malfunctioned a few metres ahead,' Kane says, pointing to the haze. 'It appears to be offline.'

'Appears to be?' I say.

'It's hard to get a definitive reading. There's interference.'

'From what?'

'Unknown source.'

[REEVA-6333 PRIVATE COMMS] interrupts me. 'You've got 30 seconds,' Reeva says, then abruptly terminates the channel.

'We can't wait,' I say to Kane. 'We need to move. Now!' Spino grunts and raises his foot, ready to follow me. I hold my hand up to stop him, 'No, stay here! Protect them, okay?'

Spino lowers his foot with a whimper.

'I'll be okay, I promise. Just look after Jason and Yolanda.'

He grunts in agreeance and lumbers over to stand astride them. Nothing will harm them while they're protected beneath his underbelly.

Kane follows me into the smoke. Several paces in, we find ourselves stepping over Yolanda's raptors. Each one is charred to a crisp and smouldering like a log after a bush fire. Further on, we find the robot responsible for the carnage slumped against the wall. A close-range blast has obliterated its right arm and peeled back its chest plating to expose crucial circuits and hardware. The robot whirs and clunks, attempting to stand up, yet it doesn't register on my sensors. [SHOW ROBOT STATUS] I think and my visor displays [UNIT-90253-INOPERATIVE]

'Why I can't get a reading on it?' I say.

'I don't know – neither can I,' Kane replies. 'But it's active, we can see it moving.'

'It's masking its functions.'

'That's not possible.'

The robot goes limp.

'It's stopped.'

A ripple of luminous blue energy materialises from the processor cores deep inside its chest and travels across the robot. The wave moves with an organic, almost purposeful motion, as if probing the damaged components for something, then suddenly disappears.

'Whoa! Did you see that?'

'I did,' Kane says, stepping back. 'What the hell was it, a Wraith?'

I can't answer, I'm too curious. *There's no way it could be a Wraith. The Union would have told us if we'd been infected.* Yet I can't explain it, for some strange reason I don't feel intimidated by the anomaly. Instead of moving away, I lean closer, eager to see the manifestation again. [SCAN ALL ENERGY FREQUENCIES] I think and my visor displays a reading of zero.

'Watch it,' Kane says. 'Don't get too close.'

The energy reappears from the robot's internals and flows over my glove. It curls up and around my arm like a glowing blue snake.

Kane's panicked voice fills my helmet. 'Zaz, what's happening?'

A gentle buzz begins in my chest, like a swarm of humming bees, then spills across my arms, legs, and head like warm water.

'Zaz, your time's up. We're opening the gate,' Reeva announces.

I'm too enthralled by the ethereal sensation to respond.

'Zaz, do you hear me?'

My visor's energy frequency reading suddenly climbs exponentially. 0 volts... 300 volts... 1000 volts... 2000 volts... 10,000 volts... 50,000 volts.

I should be panicking, but I'm not. The energy swirls around my exosuit and pulses across my visor in a rhythmic heartbeat.

Every inch of my body tingles with waves of goosebumps and I feel weightless, as if I'm floating inside my exosuit. *This is incredible!*

'It's all over you,' Kane yells. 'I'm reading a massive build-up of energy...the frequencies are off the charts.'

His warning falls on deaf ears. I'm spellbound by the out-of-body experience, as if I'm being touched by some greater power, on the verge of something profound. The energy abruptly leaves and returns to the robot, swirling into its power couplings like water down a plughole, and terminates our connection. My goosebumps fade and the blissful feeling twists into gut-wrenching fear.

The robot's head clunks to life. Its cracked ocular lens focuses on me with an unsettling red glow. *This is bad.*

[MISSION TERMINATED] flashes across my visor in bold flashing text. [UNAUTHORISED PARAMETERS EXCEEDED]

Reeva's scream pierces my ears. 'Zaz, what did you do?'

Kane grabs my arm and yanks me away. 'Get back! It's initiated self-destruct mode.'

We run for safety as a swarm of emergency drones whiz overhead and swoop upon the robot, forming a protective barrier to smother the blast.

BOOM!

The muted shockwave knocks me and Kane off our feet and we roll to a stop in front of Jason.

'What the hell was that?' Jason asks as a wall of smoke and dust rolls past.

I wish I knew. I sit there, shell-shocked, trying to comprehend what I experienced. *Did I just encounter a Wraith, or a simulation designed to emulate one?* Either way, the Union are bound to reprimand or punish me. But even worse than that, Reeva will make sure I pay for this failure until my dying day.

17

Kane and I are swiftly removed from the training session and flown over the compound in an aerial evacuation pod. Down below, our platoon and their dinosaurs depart through the gates and start their journey back to the original mission location. I'm not pleased to leave Spino in such a frantic state. He's obviously anxious with the herding drones, constantly smelling the air and searching for me. I wish I could ride him back and calm him down, but the Union has other plans for Kane and me. They want to keep us separated so we don't talk to the other cadets about what happened.

We sit opposite one other in silence, terrified to utter a word, aware the Union is monitoring everything we say.

A glowing red message flashes in the bottom of my visor. [ZAYLA-8311 REPORT TO BRIGADIER RAMSEY] *This isn't good at all.*

Our pod lands outside the observation dome. Inside, the Union workers rush about like a colony of obedient grey ants, safely contained behind thick panels of glass and steel. Four armed guards assemble by the exterior hatch as Brigadier Ramsey and Sergeant Perez emerge, their faces wracked with concern. A group of scientists laden with scanning equipment joins them.

I jump out of the pod beside Kane and we remove our helmets to greet our superiors.

Ramsey raises his hand. 'Stop right there, cadets.'

The scientists keep a safe distance and mill around us, scanning our exosuits with their devices. They take our helmets and place them in magnetically shielded metal cases. Another scientist approaches the pod and sweeps his scanners over the hull.

Ramsey looks us over. 'How do you feel?'

'Okay,' I say.

'Fine,' Kane cuts in. 'Why was our mission terminated?'

'That's classified.'

'Did we do something wrong?' I ask.

Ramsey's piercing gaze makes me uncomfortable. His decades of military service have helped to hone a stony-faced, impenetrable mask that gives nothing away.

The head scientist approaches Sergeant Perez and holds out a data tablet. 'Scans are complete. No signs of infection or malfunction.'

'Good, then the exosuits worked as expected,' Ramsey says.

Perez nods and turns her attention to us. 'Head inside cadets, remove your exosuits, and report for debriefing.'

The guards escort Kane and me into the observation post, where everyone has stopped what they're doing to watch us pass.

Kane glances at me over his shoulder and whispers, 'What the hell is going on here?'

'Stop talking, cadets,' Ramsey snaps.

I keep my mouth shut and follow the guards, confident we're about to find out. We're taken through an airtight hatch into a windowless room that has two full-body bio-scanners and a couple of sterilization cubes. Freshly pressed fatigues and brand-new black boots await us on separate steel benches.

'Leave your exosuits in the steri-cubes,' Perez says. 'Stand inside the bio-scanner before you dress in your fatigues. Once cleared, you can come out.'

Perez, Ramsay, and the guards leave and the door closes with a hiss of pressurised air. I face Kane, embarrassed that we need to strip down in front of each other. I can already feel the heat rising to my face. No male or female change rooms here. *Well, this is awkward!*

'Don't worry, I won't look if you don't,' Kane says, shooting me a cheeky grin as he turns his back to me.

I turn away, blushing to myself. I've never been comfortable with nudity, whereas most cadets don't even think twice about it. We've been sharing change rooms our entire lives – a fact that should make me care less, but I've always shielded myself from prying eyes, making sure I showered at the quietest times to avoid the embarrassment. I click and release my exosuit in chunks and drop the pieces into the cube, trying to keep up with Kane. I don't want to be left undressing with him standing around waiting for me.

Kane removes his final chest plate and *plonks* it loudly into the cube.

I can see his naked reflection in the stainless steel walls as he enters the bio-scanner. His strong back and muscular arms make my heart race. I hurriedly break down my suit and scurry over to the scanner, resisting another peek. Moments later, my subcutaneous chip lights up green with the message: [SCAN COMPLETE: CLEAR]

We dress in our fatigues and exit the room. Ramsey and Perez have already departed, leaving the guards to escort us to an underground transport system. We all load into a shuttle pod that carries us deep beneath the island. Tunnels of jagged rock whiz past, giving way to vast subterranean caverns and luminous grottos.

Our shuttle slows and stops alongside an underground platform. The guards direct us into a glass elevator and we rise through a thicket of jungle undergrowth into rays of glorious sunlight. I squint upwards. Our elevator ascends a clear tube constructed up the face of a cliff, heading straight for an outpost atop the peak. We climb high above the treetops to find the breadth and might of the Union unveiled across a cluster of islands. Dense jungles, rocky beaches, and towering mountains give rise to fortified buildings, landing pads, satellite dishes, and a myriad of land, sea, and air vessels.

'This is the Union's main command island,' I whisper to Kane. 'Must be important if they've brought us here,'

'I don't know any cadet that's ever been here.'

'Me either.'

We swiftly ascend into darkness and bright white lights flash down the window. I feel queasy as the elevator slows and opens to a sprawling foyer of polished steel and glass. Massive walls of tinted windows overlook the entire archipelago.

Brigadier Ramsey rushes over to meet us. 'Hurry up, cadets. Galen Thoms is due to arrive in a couple of minutes.'

I share a look of surprise with Kane. No cadet has ever met the leader of the Union in person, and judging by Ramsey's anxious demeanour, I'm guessing it's a first for him as well.

We follow Ramsey through the foyer and into a private room. The hushed space looks more residential than military, with chairs, lounges, buffets, and tables spread across the sparse, open plan design. A group of faceless officials watch us from the shadowy alcoves along the walls. Ramsey ignores them. He motions for us to stop at a long glass dining table lined with grey leather chairs embroidered with the Union logo.

'What's this about?' Kane asks. 'Are we in trouble?'

'I don't know any more than you. My orders were to have you brought to Galen Thoms for a personal interview.'

'Is that unusual for a cadet?' I ask.

Ramsey gives me an odd glance. 'It's unusual, period. He rarely speaks with anyone in person.'

My attention is drawn to a sleek craft docking on the outside of the building. The streamlined, elegant design is unlike any Union vessel I've seen. Ramsey straightens his uniform and pulls back his shoulders. Funny, he appears more nervous than me. The interior docking door slides open and Galen Thoms emerges, in the flesh!

He looks just like his hologram...maybe a little older. His grey hair has more of a silver hue and his wrinkles are more defined. His navy suit and black dress shoes are less military and more civilian clothes, a rare sight in the academy, as cadets never interact with anyone outside the program. Our instructors are always dressed in drab grey Union uniforms. Galen strides towards us with his arms behind his back, a friendly and welcoming smile on his face. His intelligent blue eyes assess Kane and me as he stops and salutes. We salute back.

'Thank you, Brigadier Ramsey, I'll take it from here,' Galen says without batting an eyelid towards Ramsey.

Ramsey nods and gives us curious, sideways glance. 'Of course, sir.' The brigadier scurries off like a child told to leave the room.

Galen addresses the officials in the shadows. 'Give us the room, please.'

The shuffling sound of shoes is followed by the hiss of a closing door. A heavy silence envelops the three of us, leaving me unsure how to behave in the presence of the Union leader. *Do I stare straight ahead or look Galen in the eye?*

'Relax, cadets. Inside this room, you're outside the academy and its restrictions. Normal rules do not apply. I've brought you here for an informal conversation.'

I remain rigid, eyes focused on the windows. How do I act casual and informal? It's something I've never been asked to do.

After an extended pause, Kane speaks up. 'I thought this was an official debriefing, sir.'

Kane's bolder than me; I'm too nervous to utter a word.

'In a way, but our discussion remains between us. Nobody is to be told what we talk about, including your superior officers. Understood?'

'Yes, sir,' we reply in unison.

Galen nods and observes us in silence. I feel small and inconsequential before such a powerful figure, like a microbe being scrutinised under a microscope.

'You may have noticed the outpost was experiencing some technical glitches before your training exercise.'

I nod, a little too eagerly.

Galen focuses on me. 'Those glitches were coming from Union Central Command. They were shutting down systems and servers to prevent a Wraith infiltration.'

I knew it!

'But you already suspected as much, didn't you, Zayla-8311?'

'Yes, sir.'

'Your platoon is the first to encounter a live Wraith.'

'How did the Wraith make it through Earth's defences?'

'We're still tracing their signature back through our satellites and starships. Our current theory is the Wraith sabotaged an encrypted communication subsystem, allowing them to travel undetected from Daxma-5 all the way to Earth, bouncing from one computer system to the next.'

Kane speaks up. 'If the Wraith are here, shouldn't we deploy for war straight away?'

'We should be Code Red!' I add.

'To the best of our knowledge, only a single Wraith made it through. Our communications network was shut down the moment we detected the anomaly and every encryption algorithm rewritten to enhance security.'

'It's not enough,' Kane says.

'You're right,' Galen replies. 'But it's the best we can do in the short term to buy us time.'

'Why did you need to bring us here? We should be preparing for war.'

'You two were the closest to Unit-90253, the Wraith-infected robot, and that makes you unique.'

'In what way?' I ask, apprehensive about his potential questions. I've barely had time to process my close encounter and wouldn't even know how to explain it.

'Your first hand experience is invaluable. You're the only humans to survive such a close encounter. We understand the Wraith to be a sentient form of energy with an intelligence that is equivalent, possibly superior to ours. I want to know what happened when you approached Unit-90253.'

Kane looks at me. 'Zayla got a lot closer than I did.'

Galen steps into my personal space, intense and eager, impressing upon me the pressure to answer honestly.

'The Wraith came out of the robot like a burst of raw energy, but it moved gracefully, like a living thing. It swirled around my glove and moved up my arm. I think it was trying to enter my suit, but couldn't.'

'Did you experience anything unusual?'

'Like what?'

Galen draws a hesitant breath, as if he's about to give away some top-secret information. 'Did it feel like it was trying to communicate with you?'

His question jumpstarts my heart. *That's it!* The blissful, out-of-body experience makes sense now. The Wraith was attempting to communicate with me, yet it never felt threatening or dangerous.

'Yes, sir, it wanted to kill us,' Kane cuts in. 'There was no doubt it had malicious intent.'

'Did you sense that in some way?'

'I thought that was obvious. It tried to blow us up.'

Galen is only mildly interested in Kane's response and drills his eyes into mine. 'What about you, Zayla–8311? Did you experience anything unusual?'

What do I say? My loyalty to the Union dictates I should tell Galen the truth, but every fibre of my being warns me not to. Am I betraying humanity by keeping it a secret? We could lose the war because of my inaction, a silence that could lead to the downfall of our civilisation. But something deep inside me compels me to keep my life-changing encounter a secret.

'Zayla–8311, I asked if you experienced anything unusual.'

I'm sure he can see my pulse pounding up my neck. Galen's eyes suddenly feel dark and hostile, like a storm brewing on the horizon.

'No, sir. The only thing I experienced was fear and the urge to protect my platoon.'

Galen scrutinises me, as if expecting my façade to falter. *Did he just sigh under his breath?*

'Your vital signs and visual feed suggests otherwise. Let's take a look.'

Galen withdraws a palm-sized holoemitter that projects the view as seen through my exosuit visor. My pulse, blood pressure, and breathing are highlighted as the recording replays the moment the Wraith made contact with me.

'At this exact moment, your vital signs settle to what could only described as a state of extreme relaxation, as if you're at peace with your encounter,' Galen says. 'This is highly unusual considering what you were facing.'

'I didn't know what I was facing, sir.'

'But you're in the middle of battle. Your comrades are injured, one of them mortally. You're facing an unknown threat, yet you enter a trance-like state while your suit is scanning rampant energy signatures. Something profound is occurring here.'

'Like what?'

'I was hoping you could tell me.'

I stand my ground, determined to look strong. *I'm in this far – I can only continue the lie.*

'I'm not sure... It's possible the electrical activity disrupted my exosuit's operation.'

'What are you suggesting happened?' Kane says to Galen, admirably rising to my defence.

Galen turns off the holoemitter. 'In all previous encounters with the Wraith, nothing like this has ever been reported.'

'Do you think they were trying to communicate with me?'

'No. As you know, the Wraith can embody the indigenous creatures of Daxma-5 and override our technology, but if they were to take control of a human being, this war would be over before it's fought. Always remember, opening your mind to them can only lead to catastrophic repercussions.'

Now I get it. The only reason we're here is because Galen thinks I have some insight into the Wraith. I don't, but I think I was close to communicating with it. Strange that I sensed no threat, just harmony and an urge to submit myself to the Union. Maybe that's how the Wraith gain control of a living creature, by lulling the host into a false sense of safety. The prehistoric creatures on Daxma-5 would not have the mental capacity to know any better, so it's no surprise they can be controlled so easily. I can't explain it, but I feel compelled not to speak or doubt my feelings.

'I will watch the two of you with great interest,' Galen says. 'Your efforts have not gone unnoticed.' He salutes us and we salute back. 'That will be all, cadets. You may return to your barracks.'

Kane leaves, but I can't: not until I learn one more thing. 'Excuse me, sir, what happened to the Wraith I encountered? Was it destroyed in the blast?'

'It was contained.'

'What does that mean?'

'It won't pose a threat to the Union again.'

The finality in Galen's tone warns me not to push it any further. An odd sense of relief falls over me as we leave, not because the Wraith can't harm us, but because it survived. *Why do I care what happens to a Wraith? We're about to go to war and kill thousands of them.* My conflicting emotions are disconcerting and there's nobody I can speak to. I keep quiet on the return to our barracks, leaving the small talk to Kane and Brigadier Ramsey. For once, Ramsey is the one asking all the questions, but his curiosity is cut short when Kane reveals we can't discuss our meeting with Galen. We arrive in time to join the cadets heading towards the mess hall for dinner.

'This'll be interesting,' Kane says. 'What do we say if someone asks where we were?'

'Nothing.'

'We can't say nothing. We were obviously somewhere.'

'Just say we can't speak about it.'

'Really?'

'Just tell them we were in a classified briefing. Simple.'

'It won't cut it with our group – you know what they're like.'

I'm not in the mood for this. I can't stand Kane's wishy-washy resolve a second longer. 'Don't say anything or we'll both be punished. Okay?'

'Sorry.'

'Stop apologising for everything!'

It's the first time he's frustrated me, but it's not entirely his fault. I feel the weight of everything piling up and it's becoming too much to handle. We join the queue, collect our dinner trays, and sit opposite Abby, Tyson, and Rosa, steeling ourselves for the inevitable barrage of questions.

'Good to see both of you in one piece,' Tyson says. 'Where were you? The infirmary?'

Rosa shakes her head. 'They were evacuated from the training mission by an evacuation pod, not a medical one, you doofus.'

'Oh! Excuse me for not taking notice,' Tyson retorts. 'I was trying to fend off a squad of robots on the inner wall. Waiting for the platoon to catch up.'

'Stop arguing,' Abby interjects. 'I've had to listen to Reeva and Lani complain all afternoon.'

I gulp down a mouthful of food and almost choke on it. 'What are they saying?'

'Reeva hasn't stopped bad-mouthing you since our mission was terminated. She blames you for our failure. I'd stay out of her way.'

'Bah! Don't do that,' Tyson says. 'Get in her face, tell her to shut up.'

Rosa bangs her knife and fork down on her plate. 'Your ham-fisted approach doesn't work with everyone. Zaz will deal with Reeva on her own terms.'

'I didn't hear you give any useful advice.'

'Maybe Zaz doesn't want advice. Did you consider that?'

'Stop it!' I cry. My voice draws the attention of the cadets sitting at the nearby tables. I freeze, fists clenched around my knife and fork, surprised by my outburst. I didn't mean to be so loud. An unpleasant heat rises to my face, yet this time it's not embarrassment. It's anger.

I wait for the adrenalin rush to ease and speak in a measured tone. 'I can deal with Reeva myself.'

Abby, Tyson, and Rosa stare at me, gobsmacked. Abby's gaze drifts over my shoulder to someone standing behind me.

'What did you say?'

Reeva's voice sends a shiver through my body. I'm half expecting her fist to slam into my head as I warily rise to face those icy-blue eyes. Reeva is so close she's almost stepping on my toes. Lani stands behind her, goading her, itching for a fight, while every cadet in the mess hall has stopped eating to watch. Their faces sway, like I'm looking at the room from a moving boat. I'm giddy with fear and remind myself to breathe. I support myself against the table with clammy hands, heart pounding through my chest.

Reeva leans close until her face is all I can see. 'I asked you a question.'

I swallow loudly. I'm so terrified I couldn't respond if I wanted to. Reeva shoves me back and I fall against the table, knocking over everyone's drinks. My plate of food slides across the table and lands in Abby's lap.

Tyson rises, ready for action. 'Hey!'

I momentarily lock eyes with Kane. His advice rings through my brain like a gigantic bell: *Next time Reeva corners you like that, don't wait for her to make a move. Strike first.*

'You said you were going to deal with me yourself,' Reeva says.

I grip the edge of the table to hide my trembling hands. This isn't good, I need to respond and prove to everyone I'm not a pushover.

'Yeah, just what I thought,' Reeva snickers. 'You're weak. No wonder we failed our first training mission. You're not fit to command a platoon.'

I feel like I'm dissolving into the floor with embarrassment and need to do something drastic to escape.

'You're as spineless as your overhyped spinelessaurus.'

That's it!

My right hand tightens into a fist and swings. CRACK! Knuckles meet jaw in a sharp, ear-splitting collision. Reeva stumbles back, hand clasped over her mouth, as a collective gasp sounds around the mess hall.

'Whoop!' Tyson bellows.

Reeva removes her hand and a drool of blood oozes over her lip. Then I see the gap in her front teeth and the pearly white blobs in her bloodied palm.

I just knocked out her front teeth!

Reeva stares at the remains of her once-perfect smile and looks up, blood glistening across her chin like a voracious carnivore. She tosses the teeth aside and lunges for me. I dodge her first swing and collapse backwards onto the table. Reeva jumps on top of me and we roll over the table, crashing through everything. Cutlery, plates, and glasses fly in all directions. Warm food squishes onto my back as we tumble over the other side, bounce off the bench seat, and hit the floor. Reeva lands on top of me and sits astride my chest, one hand on my collar, the other drawn back in a fist to strike.

I grab a dinner tray off the floor and deflect her punch. *DONG!* Reeva cradles her fist and lets go of me.

I swing the tray and smash her across the side of the head, sending her rolling over the floor. Lani rushes around the table, takes one look at Reeva rubbing her bright-red ear and lurches for me. Abby sticks out her foot and trips her up. Lani lands heavily, grunts, and spins around to see who was responsible.

Abby steps forward and raises her fists. 'If you wanna join the fight, you have to go through me first.'

Cadets crowd around us, cheering and shouting. Their enthusiasm electrifies the air. I don't feel any pain, just a heady rush of adrenalin, as if I'm channelling Spino's energy. Reeva scrambles to her feet and I rise to meet her. We rush towards one another and collide awkwardly. She grabs my hair and yanks it back. A searing pain shoots across my scalp. I dig my fingernails as hard as I can into her face and we stumble sideways into the crowd. They bounce us back into an empty space.

My hair feels like it's about to rip from the roots. I drag my nails across Reeva's cheek and catch the soft squishy corner of her eye. She yelps and releases me.

We both take a second to assess our injuries.

My head feels like it's on fire and I can barely touch my scalp. Reeva fingers the ruby welts developing across her cheek. Her injured eye glistens with tears and she struggles to keep it open.

I make use of the advantage and strike first. She deflects my first punch with one arm and swiftly sends her other fist into my stomach. The hit empties the air from my lungs and Reeva swings for my head. I raise both arms and block the punch, but I'm running on zero oxygen. I can't breathe. We grapple one another and stumble out of control. The crowd parts and we crash into another table. The cheers are so loud, I can't hear anything else.

I'm desperate for air and struggling to inhale through the fear and exertion.

Reeva throws me across the table, climbs on top of me, and digs her knee into my chest, denying me that precious gasp. I'm on the verge of fainting.

Reeva grabs a dinner tray and raises it above her head with both hands, ready to sever my face like a guillotine. Her eyes are consumed by a frenzied, insatiable bloodlust, like a carnivore about to devour its prey. Reeva wants me dead.

'That's enough!' announces an authoritative voice.

Union guards push through the crowd and grapple Reeva, ripping the tray from her grasp and saving me from a mangled face. I inhale life-giving air as the guards yank me to my feet, keeping me and Reeva out of arms reach.

Brigadier Ramsey pushes the guards aside, takes one look at us, and shakes his head. 'I expected more from you two.'

'But, sir...' Reeva says with a lisp through her gappy mouth.

'Don't say another word!' Ramsey yells. 'It's illegal for commanding officers, training or otherwise, to strike one another. This transgression warrants a tribunal. Until then, you've lost your cadet status and will remain prisoners of the Union.'

My brain refuses to process what my ears just heard. Abby and Rosa watch on, tears in their eyes. Tyson stares at me with, his jaw hanging wide open. Kane pushes through the throng of cadets, eager to get near me. I can see he wants to speak up in my defence, but now isn't the time.

'Get them out of my face,' Ramsey says.

The guards forcibly escort us from the mess hall. I lower my head in shame, unable to bring myself to look at anyone. *Did I just end my career?*

18

The guards shove me inside a small holding cell and the barred door closes with a resounding *clang*. I lean against the wall and slump to the cold concrete floor. This is my new reality: a prisoner of the Union, with all my rights and privileges stripped away. One uncontrollable outburst of anger has cost me everything. But it shouldn't come as a surprise – my tension with Reeva has been building for years. I allowed that negativity to fester like an infected wound and I became socially withdrawn and avoided confrontations. The injuries inflicted in that raptor pen all those years ago run deep, and to this day, we're still suffering.

The timing couldn't be worse. We were about to be deployed as humanity's last hope against the Wraith. My bond with Spino was stronger than ever, and as First Lieutenant, I had a chance to overcome my introverted personality and make a difference in the war.

CLANG!

Reeva stumbles into the cell opposite mine and paces like a caged animal, face scratched, blond hair wild and messy. It's a shock to see her so dishevelled, as she always takes great pride in her appearance. She senses my presence and stops, glaring at me through her straggly fringe.

My will to fight has escaped me and so has Reeva's, it seems, as her eyes quickly lose their fire. She turns her back to me and sits on the bench seat, head slumped between her shoulders. I hear what sounds like a sniffle, then a sob.

Is Reeva crying?!

My heart sinks. There was a time when we were inseparable friends. I'm conflicted with hatred, guilt, sympathy, and regret. Sitting here, with my nothing but my thoughts, I recount the laughs, hugs, and good times we shared as if they happened yesterday. After all these years, and the chasm that's opened between us... Could Reeva still feel the same about me?

The cell lights flicker.

It's not something I usually take notice of, but my close encounter with a Wraith makes me suspicious. What if more than one Wraith made it through Earth's defences? Now I feel guilty for not telling Galen the truth about my close encounter, and it could cost the Union deeply. The euphoria I experienced may have been the way the Wraith takes control of their hosts, by lulling them into feelings of bliss and contentment. Those feelings have since passed, and I feel like I've woken up. Maybe the Wraith are learning how to control humans, and I was the first guinea pig in their experiment. It's frightening being locked up and unable to help.

The sound of marching boots echoes down the passage. Two guards arrive outside my cell and the door slides open. One of them steps inside my cell. 'Zayla–8311, turn around, place your hands behind your back.'

I comply and feel the cold magnetic cuffs snap around my wrists. The guard places a firm hand on my shoulder and directs me into the passage to join Reeva, who is also handcuffed. Seeing her bloodshot eyes and missing teeth makes me feel sick with guilt. We never should have let things get this bad. The guards march us through the detention centre. The empty cells are a sober reminder of how rarely cadets end up here.

We enter a dimly lit courtroom and stand before a long judges' bench with five chairs. The Union seal hangs on the wall behind, illuminated by a spotlight. This is my first visit to a military courtroom. The guards stand behind us and leave us cuffed. Five figures dressed in grey suits and berets file in through a side door and sit along the bench. I recognise Brigadier Ramsey and General Astrid Fowler, but the other three stern-faced officials are new to me.

Ramsey acknowledges me with a fleeting glance.

General Fowler sits in the middle seat, activates a hologram, and assesses the information in a hasty manner, as if this situation is one huge inconvenience. Her grey-streaked hair is drawn into a tight ponytail, which accentuates her high cheekbones, broad forehead, and dark brown eyes. She makes me nervous. Fowler is regarded as the toughest woman in the Union and is renowned for her unforgiving, no-nonsense nature.

'Are the handcuffs necessary?' asks Ramsey.

Fowler ignores his query and scrolls through the information, pausing every few seconds to read specific details. I tiptoe, attempting to see what information has piqued her curiosity and glimpse an image of Spino and Reeva's T-rex, accompanied by stats and text.

Fowler finishes and deactivates the hologram. 'Until we work out how to punish these cadets, the cuffs stay on, Brigadier Ramsey. They've broken the code of conduct for an acting lieutenant.'

'Technically, they are not lieutenants,' Ramsey responds in a cautious tone. 'They are cadets with a provisional lieutenant ranking and should be dealt with as such.'

Fowler leans forward and trains her unsympathetic gaze on us. 'You two have quite a history, don't you?'

Silence follows. Reeva is uncharacteristically quiet, giving the impression she wants me to do the talking.

'We do, General,' I say.

'Tell me about it, Zayla–8311,' Fowler says. 'How did we all end up here?'

All eyes in the room focus on me, including Reeva's, and my opportunity for atonement has been thrust upon me without warning. I swallow nervously and take a deep breath to begin.

'Twelve years ago, I made a terrible mistake. Reeva and I were feeding raptors in the nursery. When our instructor was called away, I convinced her we should climb outside the cage for a better look. It drove the juveniles crazy. They almost killed us. Afterwards, I let Reeva take the blame. She did a month in detention because of me. I betrayed my best friend.'

I look to Reeva, hoping my admission might have helped bridge the void separating us. Her teary eyes offer no consolation, and she shakes her head in disgust. My stomach sinks. *I'm stupid. One apology won't solve our problems.*

I face the judgement panel, content to accept responsibility. 'This is all my fault.'

'Not entirely,' Fowler says. 'You didn't force Reeva onto that gantry, she decided to follow you. Your actions after the incident are the root of this problem. Your inability to own up to the truth shows a weakness of character –'

'They were children,' Ramsey interjects.

'If that were the only problem, Brigadier Ramsey, this would be less of an issue.' Fowler reactivates the hologram. 'Zayla-8311's psychological evaluations leave a lot to be desired. Reports show an inability to communicate her thoughts and emotions. She is shy and withdrawn in class and social situations. Her friendships rarely last and she's overlooked by other cadets for group activities. Quite frankly, I'm shocked that she was even selected for a First Lieutenant position.'

Fowler's damning description cuts me like a knife. The worst part is she's right: the reports are accurate.

'And the evaluations for Reeva-6333 are just as bad, albeit on the opposite end of the spectrum. Her tutors describe her as belligerent, entitled, and a bully. My assumption is she's popular among the cadets, not because she's liked, but for fear of falling on her bad side. There have been dozens of complaints over the years from cadets and tutors alike. It surprises me she was nominated for command at all.'

Reeva's hands squirm in the cuffs. Like me, her faults have been laid bare for all to see and sound far worse when said aloud.

'As lieutenants in training, you are required to set a standard for other cadets,' Fowler says. 'Your display in the mess hall tonight was a disgrace. How will your comrades ever respect you if you don't respect one another?'

I feel like I should answer, but that was clearly a rhetorical question.

Reeva and I wait nervously as Fowler, Ramsey, and the panel members decide our fate in hushed tones, backs turned to us. The general listens to their comments, nods, and swivels on her chair to face us, ready to deliver the verdict.

'Given the urgent situation regarding the Wraith and the fact both of you bonded with apex predators, two of the Union's most valued assets, we've decided 12 hours of hard labour in the dinosaur pens will suffice for now. Your lieutenant positions are hereby suspended pending an official review.'

Fowler stands as the guards lead us out. 'A parting piece of advice to both of you: focus on your future, not your past. The Union depends on you.'

Reeva glances at me and moves on. Bad things aside, a spark of hope has formed. I feel a shred relief and renewed purpose as we march through the detention centre. After years of hatred, there may finally be a light at the end of the tunnel – a chance for forgiveness, or at the very least, understanding.

I don't see another option, because should we fail, we have no future in the Union.

The guards escort us to a subterranean platform and we board a mag-lev train. Reeva shuffles along, head hanging between stooped shoulders, deflated and beaten. I think General Fowler's dressing-down made her realise her popularity is not all it appears to be. It would be hard for Reeva to hear the truth when she's turned a blind eye to it for so long. *I guess she has a conscience, after all.*

A Union medic joins us and sets to work replacing Reeva's retrieved front teeth with a specialised dental kit. Minutes later, the medic finishes and hands Reeva a small mirror. She assesses the result and tests the strength of her teeth with her fingers. Her renewed smile seems to perk her up a little.

We arrive at a subterranean industrial-style platform and the doors, unleashing an overpowering stench of sewerage. No pristine windows or polished steel floors at this stop, just stark neon strip lighting, dark tunnels, and rusty steel girders framing walls of rough-hewn rock. Everything is covered in a thick layer of dirt and grease. Workers dressed in filthy overalls gawk at us as they trudge by, the whites of their eyes beaming like spotlights from their grimy faces. Reeva and I have stepped behind the scenes of the Union's dinosaur program, an area rarely seen by cadets.

We arrive at a caged elevator and the guards unlock our handcuffs. The mesh door rattles open, revealing a burly unshaven worker in plastic overalls and boots caked in dinosaur poo. The smell is unbearable. I peg my nose shut, but the odour is so pungent, I can taste it on my tongue.

'Get in,' the worker says.

Reeva and I reluctantly step inside as the guards scurry back to the mag-lev train, coughing and spluttering. *Lucky them! We're stuck here. All we can do is block our noses.*

'You'll get used to the smell quicker than you think,' he says. 'Once you do, you won't forget it. Stays with you wherever you go.'

Reeva bites her fist and gags, tears welling in her eyes from the effort. Watching her just makes me want to wretch even more, but I hold tight and force down the surge of rising nausea. The door *clunks* shut and the lift jerks up the rocky shaft.

'Name's Russ, I'm in charge of dino sanitary,' he says, rubbing the greenish-brown smear off his name badge with pride. 'Never seen your kind down here before.'

'Our kind?' I gasp.

'Cadets. You must've done something pretty bad to be sent down here to the bowels of the facility. Especially now, with all the equipment failures.'

'Failures?'

'Yeah, we've had maintenance drones and robots failing left and right. Something to do with Union Central Command shutting down, rebooting systems. We can't clear the pens, not without some good ol' fashioned muscle. That's why you're down here, to help us shovel the shit.'

'Us?' Reeva blurt outs. Her ashen face takes on a hint of green and she gnaws her fist, resisting the urge to vomit.

'Sure. Do you know how long it takes a dreadnoughtus to drop two tonnes of excrement?'

I shake my head. *I really don't want the answer.*

'Less than thirty seconds. And the smell!' he cackles. 'You ain't smelt nothin' like it. I got 50 workers up there shifting the mess with shovels and we're barely scrapin' the surface. We been countin' on some serious help.'

'You must be expecting someone else,' I gag.

'Nope, you two are just the muscle we need.'

I doubt it!

Our lift shudders to a stop. Reeva and I wait for the doors to open, like runners at a starting line, hands glued over our mouths. I swear Russ is grinning with amusement under that filthy beard. We dash from of the lift, down a ramp, and exit the mouth of a cave into a jungle and glorious fresh air. A misty volcanic peak looms over the treetops, and beyond that, a domed megastructure that encircles the island. We're back where we completed our first bonding and training sessions with our dinosaurs.

Russ emerges from the cave and points to a clearing behind the trees. 'I forgot to mention, you're not working alone.'

To my delight, I see Spino's distinctive sail rising through the treetops. His luminous jade eyes target me through the foliage, and he cranes his head over the leafy canopy. I'm disappointed to find him muzzled and restrained by giant electrified shackles that keep his legs from moving. Spino tries to roar but barely manages a muffled growl. Reeva's T-rex is locked down beside him and sniffs the air excitedly as his tiny forearms wave about. Both dinosaurs pull against the shackles, anxious to be freed, as me and Reeva run over.

'Now that's the muscle I'm talkin' about,' Russ calls after us. He holds up a remote control and deactivates the shackles, releasing our dinos.

Spino looms over me and lowers his head so his eyes are level with mine. He swishes his massive tail about like a dog and jigs his hips from side to side in excitement, showering the area in leaves and branches.

I reach through the muzzle and rub his snout. 'Hey, boy. I wasn't sure I was going to see you again.' Spino whimpers and snorts through the metal bars gagging his mouth. 'I know, I know. I hate it too,' I whisper.

'Ready to get to work?' Russ says.

Reeva pats her T-rex through the muzzle, but he's not as easy to settle as Spino. 'We need these muzzles off,' she says.

Russ shakes his head. 'Not on my watch. I got a full cleanup crew out here. They won't work anywhere near apex predators without a muzzle.'

'He won't harm your crew,' I say. 'Not while I'm around.'

'Uh-uh. Union regulations stipulate that any carnivorous species must be muzzled when working alongside humans. No exceptions.'

Spino senses my displeasure and growls at Russ. Russ takes a nervous step back and holds up the remote, threatening to reactivate the shackles.

I settle Spino with a pat. 'It's okay. Let's get the work done and we can get this muzzle off afterwards.'

Russ strides over to a row of palm trees. 'Mount up, cadets. Your work area is through there.'

I hoist myself into the saddle and Spino rises to full height. Reeva joins me atop her T-rex, and we ride side by side in silence. We haven't spoken since the fight in the mess hall, and Reeva has remained unusually quiet ever since. No snide or biting remarks – nothing at all. This could be an opportunity towards reconciliation.

'Have you given him a name?' I ask.

Reeva flashes me a suspicious eye and looks ahead, ignoring my question.

I also stare ahead, embarrassed by my attempt to bridge our divide. *Who am I kidding? We've been enemies for years. As if one fight and punishment would change all that.*

'Argo,' Reeva says without looking at me.

Her response catches me off-guard. 'Cool name,' is all I can add. I hadn't thought this far ahead and didn't really expect to begin a conversation. Now I'm stuck, I don't know what to say. Then Reeva does the unthinkable: she asks me a normal question.

'What did you call yours?'

'Spino.'

Reeva chuckles. 'Original name.'

A nervous chuckle escapes my mouth. I was half expecting her to make another *spinelessaurus* joke. 'I know. I couldn't think of anything else, plus, it suits him.'

'Don't worry, you're not the only one with a lack of imagination. I almost called mine Rex.'

We laugh, the first together time in over a decade.

I fend off a bunch of palm leaves as Spino squeezes between the trees. We enter a clearing and are suddenly hit with an overwhelming stench of dinosaur poo. Spino shakes his head and groans – even he can't stand it. Argo lumbers up beside us, craning his head away from the smell, snorting and huffing while Reeva squishes her face and pegs her nose.

Upwind, a hill of dinosaur crap dominates the grassy clearing. A team of Union workers toil around the edges, barely making a dent as they shovel poo down a slope into huge antigrav bins. The workers cheer and wave their shovels upon seeing us.

Russ catches up to us, panting. 'Dreadnoughtus poo is great compost. We ship it from here to the other islands. It's full of nutrients. The prehistoric flora thrives on it.' He points to the heavy-duty earthmoving equipment parked on far the side of the clearing. 'All our vehicles, sanitary robots, and drones are down because of the system-wide shutdowns, leaving us to shovel shit the old fashioned way.'

'What do you want us to do?' I ask.

'Push it into the bins,' Russ says, walking over to two large metal scoops. 'Your dinosaurs can use these earthmoving blades. We've attached an interlocking mechanism to the front of their muzzles.'

'Don't we get a mask for the smell?' Reeva asks.

Russ laughs and walks over to join his team, who are now congregating for a well-earned break. I'm more worried about Spino than myself, since he needs to bury his head in the stinky mound.

I guide Spino over to the scoop and he reluctantly bows down, hooks his muzzle into the attachment, and nudges it towards Poo Mountain. Reeva and Argo manoeuvre their scoop into position and we shovel the humongous droppings down the slope. The firmer ones roll into the bins and land with wet-sounding *plonk*. Reeva swaps between holding the saddle and blocking her nose, while Argo nudges the scoop in short bursts and continuously raises his snout for fresh air. Their shared discomfort doesn't surprise me – tyrannosaurs have the strongest olfactory sense of all apex predators. If they can smell fresh blood from kilometres away, then I hate to imagine what sensations he's sharing with Reeva.

So far, Spino and I are coping a lot better.

'Is this a punishment for us or our dinos?' I say. Reeva doesn't answer. 'At least the dreads are herbivores. I'd hate think what we'd be shovelling if this was carnivore poo.'

Reeva is too overwhelmed to answer. Argo gives a muffled roar and steps away from the mound, disengaging his muzzle from the scoop. Reeva tries to coax him back into position, but he's having none of it. Argo stomps off and shakes his head, barking in protest through his locked jaws. His human-sized arms claw for the muzzle but aren't long enough to reach it.

Russ waves across the clearing. 'Hey, get back to work!'

Reeva wrestles with the reins but can't turn Argo around. He lowers his head and raises his tail, a sign he's ready to fight.

'Turn around or we're both in trouble,' Reeva snaps. Argo growls, and she whips the reins harder.

She's not going to win this fight. I've never had to use reigns with Spino, but T-rexes have a different temperament. Maybe their neural link isn't enough.

Argo defiantly stomps towards the jungle, proving he's just as stubborn as Reeva, and crashes haphazardly through the trees. Reeva is caught in the timber and knocked off her saddle. She rolls along his back and drops several metres to the ground as Argo disappears.

I swing Spino around, dismount, and run over to help.

Reeva waves me away. 'Leave me alone! I don't need your help.' She stands and swipes the slurry of mud and poo off her clothes. 'Don't think I'm your friend now just 'cause I talked to you. I still hate you.'

I stare at her in shock, feeling the blood drain from my face. All the progress I thought we'd made evaporates in an instant.

'Admitting your guilt to the Union doesn't change the last 12 years. You should've said something when it mattered.'

'We were kids, I didn't –'

'That's no excuse!' Reeva snaps, voice wavering with emotion. 'You betrayed me. I'll never trust you again.'

Tears well in our eyes and I give Reeva a moment to calm down, hoping this is just a knee-jerk reaction due to her frustration with Argo.

'How are we supposed to command together?'

'We don't need to be friends to give orders. Just do what I say and we won't have a problem. Got it?'

'What the hell's going on here?' Russ yells.

Reeva and I round on him in unison: 'SHUT UP!'

Spino growls and stomps down between us. Russ stops dead in his tracks and peers over Spino's giant foot, shock turning to frustration. 'Get your dinosaurs under control. This ain't some cushy academy drill – you've got a job to do here. How are you supposed to win this war for us if you can't even shovel shit?'

WHOOSH!

The three of us peer skyward as a pink flare rockets through the dome's opening and explodes into an umbrella of crackling fireworks high in the atmosphere.

'That's a warning flare,' I say.

'For what?' Russ says.

My subcutaneous chip vibrates and flashes a message in bright-red: [INCOMING WRAITH THREAT]

Reeva looks up from her forearm, wide-eyed with shock 'We're under attack from the Wraith.'

'That's impossible,' Russ says. 'The Wraith are nowhere near Earth.'

Tracer fire whizzes from the rim of the dome and criss-crosses the sky like a giant net.

'It looks like the Union are firing blindly, hoping for a hit,' I say.

Several specks appear in the upper atmosphere, far above the tracers. Bright halos of light erupt around the incoming objects.

'Look! Something's entering the atmosphere.'

Russ unclips a pair of electronic binoculars from his utility belt and focuses on the anomaly. 'They're Union ships. Military transport vessels. Looks like off-world robot troop transports. Why would they be returning?'

Reeva snatches the binoculars from Russ and looks for herself.

'Why are we firing on our own vessels?' Russ asks.

'Because we're not in control of them,' Reeva says. 'The Wraith have turned our robot platoons against us.'

Reeva hands me the binoculars. I watch the vessels clear the atmospheric turbulence and begin to dive. The binoculars pinpoint their trajectory to a single island. *Oh my God!* My heart skips a beat. 'They're heading for the barracks!'

Emergency klaxons wail across the island. Spino rears up in fear of the unnatural noise and pants through his muzzle. Dinosaurs across the island roar and stomp through the jungle, desperate to escape the unsettling sound. Several dreadnoughtuses' necks rise above the canopy and their tiny heads holler in discomfort, adding to the cacophony. The ground shudders and rumbles as if the volcano is about to blow. Trees rustle and sway, shaking loose leaves and scaring flocks of birds into the air.

'We'll be trampled to death if we stay here,' Russ says.

Argo bursts through the trees and heads straight for Reeva, head low to the ground and whimpering like a juvenile. She strokes his snout through the muzzle and consoles him. Russ backs away from us, slipping and sliding in the mud.

'Where are you going?' Reeva snaps. 'Release their muzzles.'

'What for?'

'Because the Wraith want to wipe out the academy.'

Russ gives us a double-take. 'What are you talking about?'

'She's right,' I say. 'The Wraith wants to end this war before it starts. We're the only cadets with dinosaurs, which means we need to get over to our barracks and protect our friends.'

Russ throws me the controller. 'Fine, take it. Just wait until I'm a safe distance away before you release your weapons.'

'There's no safe distance if the Wraith are here,' Reeva says.

Russ runs off, one eye on us, the other on the sky, tripping and scrambling across the grass like a freshly hatched gallimimus. I'd laugh at his ineptness if I wasn't so terrified.

I compliment Reeva with a nod. 'Well said.'

She nods back with a hint of a smile. 'What now?'

'We need to find a way off this island.'

19

I click the controller button and unlock our dinosaur's muzzles. Spino's detaches and lands in the mud with a heavy *splat*. Relieved to be free, he shakes his body and kicks the muzzle out of sight, roaring after the device like it's a living thing. I don't blame him. They should ban muzzles on dinosaurs that have bonded with cadets. Argo swings his head and launches his open muzzle over the clearing, narrowly missing Russ and his crew on the far side. They scream at us in protest.

'How do we get off this island?' Reeva asks as we mount our dinosaurs.

'Honestly, I hadn't thought that far ahead.'

Reeva cocks her head at me.

I look around, determined to find solution. The island is enclosed within a gargantuan wall that's too high to climb and too thick to penetrate, specifically designed to keep every dinosaur on land or air from escaping. I guide Spino around the mound of dreadnoughtus poo and check the line of antigrav containers at the base of the slope.

'Russ said they ship the manure to other islands as fertiliser. If we track where those containers came from, it might lead to a way through the wall.'

'Argo can do that. I'll lead the way.' Reeva settles into her saddle and snaps the reins.

Spino doesn't need coaxing like Argo. His instincts are synced with mine and he tracks Argo without physical instruction on my part. There's no path through the jungle, just Argo's supersensitive tyrannosaur nostrils to lead the way.

Thunderous blasts boom across the island like volcanic eruptions. The noise vibrates my chest and fills me with dread as I look up. Fresh tracer fire streaks across the blue sky, which is now littered with smoke trails and fiery blasts. The Union is throwing everything at the incoming vessels to stop them from releasing the robot marines upon the academy. They probably never expected the Wraith to attack the heart of their operations.

Argo pushes through the jungle perimeter and stands before the giant metal wall. 'This is as far as we can go,' Reeva calls over her saddle.

Spino stomps up beside them and I look for myself. A dark service tunnel large enough for our dinosaurs stands before us, blocked by a steel portcullis. Deep inside, the far end of the tunnel glows with daylight but is blocked by several more portcullises.

'We can't break through one of those gates, let alone several of them,' Reeva says.

'Stand down! Dismount your assets,' booms a male voice.

The announcement startles Spino and he whips around. A squad of eight Union soldiers dressed in head-to-toe battle armour stand behind us, tranquiliser rifles aimed at our dinosaurs. One dart is enough to drop them in their tracks.

'Wait!' I raise my arms. 'We're trying to help. Those dropships are heading for the barracks. We need to defend the academy.'

The lead soldier presses his earpiece into his ear, listens and nods, then holds out a holocommunicator. Brigadier Ramsey's hologram materialises, but shimmers and distorts. He strains to see us through the interference. 'Zayla, Reeva! Can you hear me?'

'Yes, we're here,' I call back.

'What are you two doing?'

'Trying to defend our barracks. Let us off the island.'

'We're shutting down all nonessential systems to limit the Wraith invasion, including maintenance. I'm afraid you're locked in there until the attack is over.'

'Release us before you shut it down,' Reeva says.

'Negative. We're hoping our surface-to-air defence systems can take out the dropships before they land.'

'Hope isn't enough!' I yell. 'If one of those dropships gets through, the academy is unprotected. We're your last line of defence.'

Ramsey is distracted by someone offside and argues with them. His hologram breaks up, then reappears momentarily. I can't make out anything he's saying in the garbled signal.

'Brigadier, we're wasting time,' Reeva yells.

'Sir, they're our friends,' I add. 'We have to do something.'

Ramsey's hologram stabilises, then drops in and out. 'Communications systems... temporarily shutting down...you have authorisation to –'

The hologram disappears.

An unsettling silence follows, and I share a tense look with Reeva. The portcullises blocking the service tunnel suddenly rattle to life and ascend in unison.

The lead soldier gives his squad a hand signal to stand down. 'Let them go.'

I give Spino a supportive pat on the neck and direct him into the circular tunnel. His sail scrapes along the ceiling, but it bends to accommodate the curved ceiling. The dank, humid space makes me claustrophobic. Spino senses my discomfort and scrambles towards the light, panting just like me, motivated by the promise of clean air and open space. We emerge from the end of the tunnel atop a rocky, windswept coastline, with the immense wall looming behind us. Powerful waves pound the shore below, throwing up a dense mist that blankets the coastline.

I lick the saltwater from my lips. *So, this is what freedom tastes like.* For the first time in my life, I have ventured beyond the confines of the academy, free as any normal person living in the Union. The ocean stretches out before me, inviting me to explore the world.

Argo exits the wall with a dissatisfied grunt, crouched awkwardly on his hind legs to give Reeva headroom in the tunnel. He stands upright and stretches one leg after the other.

Reeva pats Argo on the neck. 'Well done, Argo. What's next, Zaz?'

I round Spino into position and grip the saddle. 'This way!'

Spino charges along the ridge, his webbed feet propelling us forward with astonishing speed. The wind and sea mist blast my face and the waves crash alongside us, reverberating up the wall like rolling thunder, feeding my exhilaration. We leap off the ridge and land on a sandy beach. Argo follows, kicking up great plumes of sand, and we race on, around a point, and emerge from the shadows of the wall to a panorama view of the archipelago.

The sky is ablaze with air-defence missiles and tracer fire. One of the incoming vessels takes a direct hit and spirals into the ocean in a blazing fireball.

I watch in awe, a knot of terror growing in my gut. *This is war!*

A plume of whitewater erupts from the impact zone, sending mini-tsunamis towards the islands. The remaining two vessels weave undeterred through the onslaught, on target for the academy.

'We can use the mag-lev track like a bridge to get our dinosaurs over there,' Reeva says.

The island with our barracks is ten kilometres from here, linked by the elevated mag-lev tracks used by our trains. Spino cranes his head around, barks at me, then edges towards the water, telling me exactly what he wants to do.

'Spino can get there faster by swimming.'

Reeva looks at me like I'm crazy. 'Swim?'

'Spinosauruses evolved to hunt in the water.'

'Yeah, but humans didn't.'

'He can swim it faster than he can run.'

'How long can you hold your breath?'

'Don't worry, he'll look after me,' I say, patting Spino's neck. 'See you over there.'

Reeva stares at me for a beat and nods. *Is she worried about me?* It could be my imagination, but she looks genuinely concerned for my wellbeing.

Spino powers into the water and drives through the metre-high waves like they are mere ripples in a pond. Meanwhile, Argo stomps across the beach to the rocky headland that supports the mag-lev pylons. He climbs the rocks until he's level with the track and leaps onto the polished steel. The structure creaks under his 15-tonne weight, but Reeva rides him well and guides Argo on track towards the island.

A wave of cool seawater washes over my legs. Spino is almost neck deep. The next wave catches me off-guard and I swallow a mouthful of seawater. Spino tucks his arms into his side and launches into the ocean, giving me a fleeting chance to fill my lungs with air.

We dive beneath the surface. I close my eyes and hold my breath. *How long will we be under?* The force of the water almost rips me out of the saddle – I wasn't expecting such relentless pressure. I white-knuckle the saddle, hoping my feet can stay planted. My heart is pounding. *How long until I can breathe?* My lungs feel like they're going to burst. I can't even open my eyes. *I need to breathe. Does Spino realise?*

I have no clue how deep we are or how long it will take to reach the surface. I'll need to let go if he doesn't surface soon. My lungs are burning. I can't keep my mouth shut any longer, the urge to breathe is impossible to resist.

I loosen my hold on the saddle, ready to let the water drag me free.

Spino suddenly bursts from the ocean and I fill my lungs with lifesaving air. I open my eyes as Spino splashes down and paddles with his head above the water, giving me precious seconds to catch my breath. His sail juts out of the water and reaches high above me like a gigantic shark fin. I should never doubt our connection – he knows exactly when I need to breathe.

We're a third of the way to the island now and I can see my barracks atop the mountain peak. The aerial battle rages overhead. Burning shrapnel plummets into the ocean, leaving streaks of black smoke hanging in the air. The first mini-tsunami impacts the coastline ahead in a raging wall of white, stripping and flattening the palm trees.

Spino arches up and dives again, but this time I'm prepared.

I take a deep breath and nestle into his shoulder like an extension of his body. The water pressure reduces by two-thirds, and he swims faster than ever.

The oncoming tsunami drags us up and inside the wave, then drops us down a steep slope. We plummet to sea level and encounter a turgid onrush of island debris being sucked out to sea. Spino changes his swimming angle to protect me with his body and powers through a smaller succession of waves to arrive on the beach. The tsunamis recede, leaving a craggy coastline stripped of vegetation. I look over my shoulder and see Argo several kilometres behind, slowed by the monstrous waves swamping the mag-lev track. Reeva sits low in the saddle, clutching the reins to ride out the inundation.

VROOM!

High above, the pair of approaching vessels activate their reverse landing thrusters and prepare to touch down on the barracks. A steep, 300-metre-high mountain smothered in dense foliage stands between us and hundreds of vulnerable cadets.

'We have to get up there, Spino.'

Spino charges headfirst into the arduous ascent. He ploughs through the low-lying jungles, toppling trees while protecting me from the debris with his snout. His clawed toes dig into the soil and find purchase between the roots while his hands grapple the vines. Spino's small but muscular forearms help leverage us upwards in a near-vertical climb, one precarious foothold after another.

I wrap the saddle straps around my wrists and look down. The beach is a dizzying 100-metres below. Argo and Reeva have become mere specks on the track, minutes away from reaching the island. *We're on our own for now.*

Spino's breathing is now loud and laboured, pushing my saddle outwards with each cavernous breath, to drop inwards as he exhales.

This is the hardest I've ever seen him work, but he is determined to succeed.

A glint of glass and steel flickers through the foliage above. We've almost reached the main section of the barracks.

'Keep going! We're almost there.'

Spino hyperextends his neck and chomps onto an exposed root, then uses the leverage to hoist us over the ridge and into the academy grounds. He flattens a wire fence and bursts through a dense thicket, half-tripping over an elevated path.

Screams sound all around us. Union guards and cadets scatter to avoid being trodden on as Spino stomps along the main path, slipping and sliding on the smooth flat surface.

'Look out!' I cry, waving like crazy. 'Get out of the way!'

We approach the main stairs to the quadrangle and Spino leaps off the path and careens through the jungle. It's a congested route through the trees, but easier for Spino's clawed toes to get a foothold in the dirt than the steel-plated paths. Cadets dive in every direction to avoid the falling branches and barely miss being trodden on. My stomach is in my mouth the entire time, I can barely watch. *Spino, please don't step on anyone!*

A gust of wind rips through the trees ahead and the vessels land. Spino leaps over the last flight of stairs into the quadrangle, narrowly sidestepping a group of cadets. Union soldiers swarm into the area, pulse rifles aimed at the vessels. Our unexpected arrival confuses them and they swing their aim between us and the vessels, unsure which threat is worse.

Brigadier Ramsey pushes through the platoon, pulse rifle in hand, dressed in full combat gear. 'Zayla, what are you doing?'

'What I trained for! Get the soldiers out of here. They're in our way.'

The vessels deployment ramps open with a hiss and exhaust fumes billow across the quadrangle, camouflaging the Wraith threat. Ramsey holds his ground.

We're running out of time. He must know his men don't stand a chance against Wraith-hijacked combat robots. I stand in my saddle to get his attention, mustering all my confidence and authority. 'We can take it from here. Reeva's not far behind.'

Ramsay looks between me and the encroaching smog, then waves to his troops. 'Fall back! Escort all cadets to safety and lock down the barracks.'

The soldiers retreat, giving me and Spino a chance to assess the situation. The nearest vessel sits on the edge of the quadrangle, metres from a steep slope leading down to the cliff we just climbed. Spino flicks his snout at the vessel, suggesting he can knock it over the edge.

'I was thinking the same thing. Do it!'

Spino lowers his head and charges. I loop the straps around my wrists and dig my boots against the saddle walls, anticipating the collision. *BOOM!* We hit with such force I'm thrown clear and left dangling over the side of the saddle, wrists caught in the reins, flailing about. The vessel slides sideways. Two of its landing legs slip off the edge and the craft teeters in position, jamming the deployment ramp half shut and locking the robots inside.

CLUNK... CLUNK... CLUNK...

The march of mechanical feet reverberate across the quadrangle.

Dangling here like bait, I'm an easy target.

I swing and kick at the saddle, desperate to climb aboard. Spino cranes his head around and nudges me back in with his snout. I untangle the straps around my wrists and look up as a row of glowing yellow eyes materialise from the haze.

CLUNK... CLUNK...

A column of Earth robot marines march towards me in perfect unison. The mechanical titans stand eight feet tall, with shiny titanium alloy endoskeletons plated in camouflaged armour. Their gun barrels, shoulder-mounted rocket launchers, and machine guns whir into position and lock on me. Spino lowers his head in a defensive posture, making a guttural growl.

I wish I could block my negative thoughts for Spino's sake, but I can't help thinking the obvious. *We're in trouble!*

ROAR! Argo majestically thunders into the quadrangle with

Reeva high in the saddle, waving to me. I've never been so happy to see her.

Argo drops his head and barrels into the robots side-on, knocking them over like a row of dominoes, throwing off their aim. He picks the first robot up in his jaws and hurls it into the greenery. Spino and I use the distraction to dart for cover as stray rockets and bullets whiz over our heads.

BOOM! BOOM! BOOM!

A volley of blasts erupt around us, sending a gust of superheated air across the quadrangle. Spino sprints away and leaps between the trees as the fireballs consume the sky behind us. We turn around as the maelstrom clears to find the dropships still standing, but even worse, the robots march – unscathed from the flames – scanning for us.

I direct Spino deeper into the jungle and call to Reeva. 'Follow me.'

Argo trudges heavily behind us, ploughing through the foliage at breakneck speed to escape the robot's targeting range. Once clear, it takes intense willpower to convince Spino to stop. His fear and adrenalin is palpable, but if I get my own flight-or-fight response under control, it will help manage him.

'Where are you going?' Reeva yells in frustration, fighting a similar tug of war with Argo. 'Why are we running from the fight?'

'I'm not. We need protection. The robots can't match our speed and agility out here.'

'Do you have a plan?'

'Yeah, we need to push the dropship off the edge of the quadrangle before the other platoon deploys. It should roll down the hill, over the cliff, and away from the academy. Then we only have half the robots to deal with.'

Reeva pauses for a moment to think. 'We can take your idea a step further.'

'How?'

'We split up. You draw as many robot marines as you can to the cliff, keeping in line with the dropship. Argo and I will go back to the quadrangle and push it over the edge. If we time it right and you get clear, the dropship should take a few of those marines with it.'

'Why are Spino and I the bait?'

'You're faster, plus Spino doesn't have the strength to push the dropship off in one go. Argo does.'

Spino waves his snout at Reeva and grunts, unappreciative of the insult. Argo opens his muscular jaws and roars in response.

I give Spino a steadying pat and give Reeva the nod. 'All right, let's do it.'

'Zaz!'

'What?'

'Just make sure you get out of the way. Okay?'

I give Reeva one final nod and race off with Spino, feeling surprised by her parting message. *Is she concerned about me? Maybe we're making progress after all.*

The robots close in around us. I can't see them, but I can hear them crunching through the foliage, snapping timber with their metallic limbs. A loud whistle pierces the jungle canopy, getting louder, more intense by the second. *Oh no!* I duck. Luckily, Spino imitates me.

WHOOSH! Two short-range rockets fly over his head and explode deeper in the jungle. *Lucky! That was too close.*

RARGH!

A third rocket punches a hole through Spino's sail and detonates nearby. He winces and blindly changes direction, crashing through a clump of vines and almost ripping me from the saddle. My scream only elevates his urgency. In the water his sail is an advantage, but on land, it's a handicap among the trees. Bullets whistle after us, shredding the foliage. I hear the pitapat of bullets impact his flank. Spino's thick skin and dense muscles can take some hits, but too many will prove fatal. I focus my thoughts and guide Spino downhill, towards the cliff. *Good boy. That's it – you know where to go.*

VROOM!

The surrounding trees thrash under the thrust of jetpacks. *Oh, great!* Three robots drop through the treeline 50 metres ahead of us, then another four to our left. Add the ones coming up behind us, and we're running straight into a classic, triangular kill zone.

'Whoa!' I scream. 'Get the ones behind us first.'

Spino slides to a stop and whips about, toppling a palm tree with his tail. He lifts it with his jaws and charges back the way we came, straight in line with a pair of robots. Their machine gun forearms lock on us and open fire. Bullets whistle by. One rips through the saddle, shaving my thigh. I see blood but don't feel a thing. *Is that Spino's blood or mine?* Spino hurls the tree and scatters the robots like bowling pins.

'Yeah!'

I suddenly realise we're in the perfect spot, with the dropship uphill from our position and the cliff below us. But Spino doesn't have much energy left. He's panting heavily and each step is more lethargic than the last. Jetpacks roar over the trees, but I can't see them through the leafy cover.

'Don't worry, it's all downhill from here,' I say, patting Spino's neck. 'Now they're the ones running into a trap.'

I withdraw my hand and find it covered in blood. Spino's neck is riddled with bullet holes and glistening bright with crimson. A knot of anxiety builds in my stomach, but that's not just me – I'm sharing Spino's dread. He doesn't want to die.

'We're almost done. Just hold on a bit longer. We'll get you fixed up.'

Spino plods on, half stumbling down the slope.

'That's it, you can do it. Just get to the cliff.'

There's no sign of any cadets or Union guards as we retrace our steps along the path and over the collapsed fence to arrive at the cliff. We teeter on the precipice. Spino feels so weak, I'm convinced the wind might blow us over.

The robots descend from the sky and land behind us in a semi-circle, cutting off any chance of escape.

Spino backs up and slips on the cliff's edge, sending a shower of rocks to the beach hundreds of metres below. The robots train their weapons on us. I hug Spino's neck as best I can and rest my head against his body, feeling his laboured heartbeats vibrate through me. He's given me all he can. There's no more fight left in him.

'Just close your eyes,' I whisper. 'You did awesome.'

Spino cranes around to check on me. His luminous green eyes give me a parting look of sadness. *I know, I understand.* In an ultimate show of dedication, he shields me from the unavoidable hail of bullets.

CRASH! The sound of twisting metal and falling trees echoes down the mountainside. It's so loud, it drowns out the roar of the waves below.

'Reeva did it!'

My elation gives Spino one last spurt of energy. He spins and leaps off the cliff as the robots open fire. All I see is sky and ocean as we sail into the air, with nothing but a sheer drop to the rocks below. *What are you doing?* We suddenly jerk to a stop and swing upwards. I grapple the saddle and look up to find Spino's jaws locked around the exposed tree root that helped us on our first climb.

'Our lucky tree!'

Spino grunts and holds tight.

The dropship rolls over the precipice, dragging the robot marines and half the jungle along with it. Everything appears to sail past us in slow motion. *I can't believe we're alive.* Seconds later, a thunderous explosion reverberates up the island.

Spino clambers up and over the edge and falls in a heap. I stagger from the saddle and collapse, clutching my thigh. One of the bullets hit me after all but I was too full of adrenalin to feel it. My pants are soaked in blood and cling to my legs. I feel dizzy as I crawl over to Spino's head and lay my arm across his brow. He whimpers and nudges me affectionately, with barely the strength to open his eyes.

A trail of destruction stretches up the mountainside. Snapped tree trunks and flattened undergrowth littered with shrapnel leads back to the quadrangle. Argo and Reeva stand proudly at the top, peering down at us, flanked by Ramsey and a platoon of soldiers.

'We did it,' I whisper in Spino's ear. 'We did it.'

20

I spend the afternoon in the infirmary and lose count of how many Union officials visit to check on my progress with the medics. None of them talk to me, but they all seem concerned. That means one thing: the Wraith invasion is escalating faster than expected. The medics fuss over me and continuously check the status of the healing band wrapped around my thigh. I hope the veterinarians are taking as much care with Spino. He was riddled with bullets and semiconscious when we parted and I pleaded to remain at his side, but Brigadier Ramsey assured me he would be taken care of.

Beep. Beep. Beep.

The healing band vibrates and the orange progress light switches to green, indicating my tissue and muscle has regenerated. I sit up, swing my legs off the bed, and a doctor rushes over.

'Don't worry, it's okay,' I say, waving him off.

I've worn enough healing devices to know how to remove them. The metal band clicks open and I separate the two halves. My skin displays a pink blemish where the bullet went in, and that's it.

The doctor presses his finger on the spot. 'How does it feel?'

'Fine,' I say, hopping off the gurney. The moment I put pressure on my leg a shooting pain penetrates my thigh. I conceal a grimace and ride out the pain as it subsides. I don't want to spend any more time in here than I have to.

Ramsey enters the infirmary. 'Good to see you up and about.'

'What about Spino? Is he okay?'

'The vets are operating now, doing everything possible to return him to full health. He's expected to make a full recovery.'

'I want to see him.'

'In due course. We have an urgent review meeting with General Fowler at 17:00 hours.'

'What for?'

'We're going to war on Daxma-5. The Union is preparing to deploy all cadets and dinosaurs over the next 24 hours. I'm petitioning the general to have you and Reeva reinstated as lieutenants. If not for your bravery, there would be no one to send to war. The Wraith struck right in the heart of our operation and we must retaliate before another attempt.'

'Do you think the general will agree?'

'I hope so. You and Reeva showed great initiative today.'

'If we're reinstated, you should split us up.'

'Why?'

'We fight all the time and question each other's decisions.'

'That's what makes you work so well together. In fact, it's what I was counting on all along.'

'What do you mean?'

'I was aware of your backgrounds when I signed off on you commanding together. You have something to prove to one another. That friction keeps you alert, keeps you questioning each other's decisions. It helped you succeed today. We need that kind of initiative in the battlefield. The last thing I want is a bunch of chummy cadets patting one another on the back. You two came together when it mattered most and I'm counting on General Fowler seeing the same.'

'Thank you, sir.'

'You have one hour to return to your barracks and clean up. Look sharp, cadet. I want you in full dress uniform.'

'Yes, sir.'

'You're dismissed.'

I leave the infirmary and return to the barracks to find it bustling with activity. Cadets dressed in combat fatigues rush by me, duffle bags slung over their shoulders, heading off for deployment. Those that recognise me tip their caps in respect. *Wow! Word travels fast.* Everyone knows Reeva, and I saved the academy, but there's no time to talk or celebrate the short-lived victory. We're deploying for war.

My dormitory is eerily quiet. Most cadets have departed, leaving neatly made beds like they intend to return. Seems odd considering none of us will ever step foot in this room again. The few that are left behind pack their bags in silence, oblivious to my arrival.

'Zaz!' Rosa rushes over, face beaming, arms open to receive me. We embrace.

'I'm so glad you're all right. I can't believe what you did.'

'I can,' Tyson says, sneaking up to wrap his bulky arms around me. 'You and Reeva fight like a pair of starving raptors.'

I laugh, happy to see their friendly faces. 'When are you being deployed?'

'Fifteen hundred hours.'

'What's the invasion plan for Daxma-5?'

'They haven't briefed us yet.'

'Why not?'

'There's no time apparently,' Rosa says. 'We've been told we'll be given our missions after launch. The academy is being split up across a fleet of deep space armoured transports, all with different routes to Daxma-5. The Union want to separate us as soon as possible in case of another Wraith attack. They don't want all their soldiers in one place.'

'Makes sense.'

'Are you and Reeva still our squad lieutenants or what?'

'I don't know yet.'

'The Union would be crazy not to reinstate you, especially now we're deploying for war. There's no time to replace you.'

Tyson puts a hand on my shoulder. 'You're irreplaceable, but they can swap Reeva. We won't miss her.'

I wish I could agree. I never thought I would admit to needing Reeva, even to myself. Brigadier Ramsey was right – Reeva and I need each other to succeed. Spino and I would never have survived the Wraith attack if not for her and Argo.

'We'll see you on the transport,' Rosa says, eyes brimming with hope.

Tyson salutes me. 'Yeah, make sure you're there, lieutenant!'

Rosa straightens her jacket, salutes me, and I salute them back. It's strange being their friend and commanding officer. I don't feel superior, yet they respect my position and look up to me, reminding me of my responsibility. I owe it to my friends and platoon to do my best no matter what Reeva throws at me. The survival of humanity may depend on it.

Over the next hour I pack my bag, shower, and dress in my full First Lieutenant uniform for the first time. The grey material feels stiff and smells of freshly pressed linen. I straighten my collar, don my beret and check myself in the mirror. At first glance, I don't recognise the strong, assured woman staring back at me. *Is that really me?*

By the time I finish lacing my boots there is nobody left in the dormitory and I take one last look around. Life in the academy has come to an abrupt end.

A pair of Union guards wait for me by the exit. I sling my bag over my shoulder and follow them through the deserted hallways and common areas. For a person who loathed crowds and noise, the isolation and silence bothers me now. We step outside and the roar of rocket engines draws my eyes skyward. The first interstellar troop transport to Daxma-5 climbs towards the clouds, leaving a billowing column of exhaust.

The guards lead me into a glass tube elevator and we ascend the side of a cliff. From here, I witness the mind-boggling scope of the deployment. Several rockets take off simultaneously from the surrounding islands, all laden with a precious cargo of humans and dinosaurs.

Atop the elevator, I'm taken inside a tiered control centre with a perfect 360-degree view of the archipelago. Masses of officers, scientists, technicians, and personnel work at fever pitch on their holographic screens, coordinating the movement of cadets, supplies, and the precarious transfer of dinosaurs from their pens to their interstellar transports. I'm directed through the organised chaos to a door on the far side, where a woman with a closely shaved head of blond hair waits to enter. She's wearing the same uniform as me and turns as I approach.

'Reeva!' I gasp. 'I didn't recognise you.'

She ignores my stunned expression and looks me up and down. 'I'm surprised. The dark-grey looks better on you than I thought. You might pass for a lieutenant after all.'

'Thanks, you too.' I grin, noticing she is still assessing me. *Is that a glint of admiration in her eyes?*

'How's the leg?'

'Healed.'

'What about Spino? He was pretty beat up.'

'Okay, I hope. I haven't seen him since I went to the infirmary. How did Argo go in the battle? Any injuries?'

'Just a few bumps and scratches. Nothing serious.'

'That's good,' I say, unable to take my eyes off her harsh new hairstyle. 'Why'd you shave your hair?'

'I thought it was a good time for a change.'

'As good as any.'

'Plus, I don't know what kind of shampoo they have on Daxma-5. This way I don't need to worry about it.'

We share a chuckle as the door slides open. Brigadier Ramsey greets us with a stern expression and we promptly stifle our giggles. 'Follow me, cadets.'

The shadowy meeting room is dominated by a long meeting table. General Astrid Fowler sits in the middle, flanked by a row of familiar faces: Suda Satoshi, our lecturer; the dinosaur wrangler Nadja Schulze; and Sergeant Perez, our training supervisor. Their faces appear to hover in the darkness like spectres, illuminated with a blue glow from their data screens set into the table. Fowler scrutinises us with an air of disdain as we sit.

Ramsey takes a seat beside me, giving the impression it's us three against them. It dawns on me that Ramsey has been on our side throughout academy life, pulling strings when needed, making sure we end up in the best position possible.

'The Union owes you a debt of gratitude,' Fowler says. 'If not for your actions, every cadet on this island would be leaving in a body bag instead of a transport.'

I nod and remain silent.

'For me, one burning question remains. Can you work together like this on a consistent basis? Or was this a one off? Your rocky history suggests the latter. That's why I've invited your former mentors to this meeting – to gain a clear perspective on what to expect from you two. Suda Satoshi, would you please tell everyone what you were telling me?'

'I see two very intelligent cadets with great potential sitting in front of me, but I fear that potential is being squandered. Their ongoing dislike for each other and antagonistic behaviour has been a source of classroom disruption. I don't see how they can resolve their differences in time for it to matter.'

'I concur,' adds Sergeant Perez. 'Their bickering during the first platoon training mission wasted critical time. This is unacceptable and will prove disastrous on the battlefield.'

'Nadja, do you have anything to add?' Fowler says.

'There's no denying their dinosaur bonds are some of the strongest in the Union, and their apex predators are prime examples of our best weapons. But unless Reeva and Zayla can work in harmony, those bonds will suffer, and their dinosaurs will be less effective.'

'Hmm...' Fowler crosses her arms and leans forward. 'I'm still undecided about your futures, but before I make a decision, I want both of you to tell me why you should retain your First Lieutenant status.'

My heart skips a beat. Fowler has put us on the spot and I'm woefully underprepared, feeling like I didn't study for an exam.

'We don't have to like each other to get the job done,' Reeva says. 'I believe we work better that way, as opposed to being good friends.'

Fowler frowns. 'My concern isn't based on how much you

like each other. It's about respect. These reports of antagonistic behaviour don't sit well with me. Successful leadership is built on a foundation of respect, a trait you sorely lack for one another.'

'We act like we don't respect each other,' I say, 'but deep down, I think we do.'

'Think?' Fowler snaps. 'That's not good enough for me. I need absolutes.'

'The most important thing is winning the battle,' Reeva says.

'And we've proven we can do that!' I add. 'Without us, there'd be no one left to fight the war.'

Fowler narrows her gaze, frowns, then looks down and scrolls through her data screen. I wish I could see what's on it, as I'm not confident we've convinced her. She finally looks up and speaks in a sombre tone.

'Respect must be earned. But we don't have the luxury of waiting for you to resolve your differences, which makes your positions a liability. Your actions worked this time, and we thank you for it, but I fear for the next battle. Therefore –'

An incoming alert cuts Fowler off mid-sentence.

She deactivates the beeping and Galen's voice resonates around the room like a god. 'I'll take over from here General Fowler.'

'Yes, sir,' Fowler says.

Galen's hologram appears in the empty chair at the end of the table. 'Cadets Zayla-8311 and Reeva-6333 are to retain their positions as lieutenants, effective immediately. I have designated a special mission for their platoon on Daxma-5, with the potential to accelerate our victory over the Wraith.'

'Excuse me, sir, but I think –'

'We don't have time to think, General Fowler. We must act, sometimes outside the box if necessary. The Wraith threat has never been more prevalent. They are on our doorstep.'

'We have reserves standing by to take their positions.'

'Your concerns are noted, but these two cadets have proven themselves worthy of a second chance. Nobody can argue with that.'

Fowler forces a reply through pursed lips. 'Of course, sir.'

'Now get them on the transports. We have a war to win.'

Galen's hologram dematerialises.

Fowler sighs with exasperation and points at Brigadier Ramsey. 'You heard Galen Thoms. Get these cadets on their transports.'

Ramsey rises from his seat. 'You mean lieutenants?'

Fowler raises an eyebrow. 'Don't get smart with me, Brigadier Ramsey.'

'Yes, General. Apologies.'

Fowler salutes us and marches from the room in a huff. I don't blame her for being angry – it was embarrassing to have the Union leader undermine her decision in front of everyone. The scary part is, Fowler is probably right. Reeva and I have only proven ourselves once, and our dysfunctional relationship may come back to haunt us at the wrong time.

Ramsey escorts us through the control centre, down the elevator, and into the mag-lev station where we board a train and speed across the ocean towards our launch island.

I take a moment to appreciate Earth's natural beauty. It may be my last. The late afternoon sun has started its descent to the horizon and the clear archipelago waters shimmer between turquoise and azure. Schools of fish swirl in brilliant flashes of silver, contrasting against the dark reefs and deeper water.

Reeva's voice draws my attention. 'When will be briefed on our special mission?'

'After launch,' Ramsey says. 'I'm yet to receive an official communication, but I believe Galen will brief you personally on the mission.'

'What about Spino?' I ask. 'When will I see him?'

'The vets had trouble administering his final round of healing patches. The more he recovers, the more unsettled he is becoming.'

The knot in my stomach tightens and I realise it's more than nerves. This uncomfortable feeling has been eating inside me since the infirmary, alerting me to Spino's distressed state. I didn't pay attention. He's only an adolescent, after all, a fact that's easy to forget considering his immense size and power. Our bond has strengthened to a degree where we sense one another's emotional state, even when separated. My stress has only fed into his and exacerbated the situation.

'I need to see him. He'll settle down when I'm with him.'

'You're scheduled to join your platoon and board your transport in 30 minutes.'

'I need to see Spino before they attempt to transfer him. He won't like it.'

'Don't worry, they'll sedate him if there's any trouble.'

'Don't sedate him. I just need a few minutes with him, that's all.'

'Your launch window is set; we can't change it.'

'But there's still time. He's afraid – I feel it. He needs to see me.'

Ramsey shakes his head and pulls out his data pad, makes some adjustments to the schedule, and looks up. 'Reeva, you will rendezvous with your platoon as planned. Zayla, you won't board with them. Instead, head down to the dinosaur loading bay. You can assist escorting your asset aboard, then rejoin your platoon once you're in orbit.'

'Thank you, sir.'

'Your asset is just as valuable as you. My job is to keep both of you healthy and ready for battle on Daxma-5.'

Our train travels into the shadow of an island and pulls to a gentle stop. *I hope Union space travel is as smooth as their mag-lev trains.* The station is empty except for a few Union personnel. We take a long escalator ride up to a vast launch platform set between a lagoon and soaring cliffs. Our sleek rocket stands in the middle of the platform, reaching for the sky in a majestic marvel of modern engineering. The white heat-shielding panels catch the afternoon sun in a glorious blaze of deflected sunlight. Cooling gases stream from the exhaust engines and create a mist across the pad. The lower third of the vessel's loading doors sit open, with the interior bays connected to three levels of retractable gantries attached to a multi-storey tower. Teams of workers shepherd a triceratops, majungasaurus, and stegosaurus along the lower level, followed by a pterodactyl in a giant cage. The middle level is bumper to bumper with forklifts, loading drones, and off-world six-wheel-drives. I spot our platoon assembling on the top level, bags over their shoulders, filing into line and about to board.

'Get going, lieutenants. We're on a tight schedule here.'

'Yes, sir!' we say, saluting Ramsey.

Reeva and I hustle across the pad and do our best to keep clear of the traffic. Forklifts laden with supplies zip past, horns honking, drivers waving in anger. We join the cadets milling around the lifts that service the loading tower. Their subdued chatter does little to mask the underlying tension everyone must be feeling.

'Zaz!'

I look over and see a hand waving at me from the crowd.

'Abby!' I call back.

We force our way through the sea of shoulders and duffle bags to meet halfway in a heartfelt embrace.

Abby looks me over, eyes glistening with tears. 'What happened? Everyone said the Wraith injured you in the attack. I was so worried. Some cadets said you died.'

'I'm fine, just shot in the leg.'

Abby notices my beret and smiles. 'Excellent job, Lieutenant.'

Now the tears well in my eyes. Seeing Abby so happy for me draws all my emotions to the surface. The pressure of everything I just went through has affected me more than I realised. *Commanders should be tougher than this.* I suppress my tears and put on a brave face. 'Thanks. I wish I could join you, but I'm on my way to the loading bay to help with Spino.'

'How is he?'

'Okay, I think. I'll catch up with you after the launch.'

'Avi was looking for you.'

'Why?'

'He wanted to speak to you before take off.'

'Did he say why?'

'No.'

'Where is he now?'

'I'm not sure, somewhere in the crowd.'

The lift doors open and the mob drags Abby along. 'I'll see you up there,' she says, pointing one finger towards the sky with an excited, but apprehensive glint in her eyes.

I'm so lucky to a have friend like Abby. She fills me with strength and confidence when I need it most. I push through the cadets in the opposite direction and force myself clear.

ROOOAAAR!

I know that roar. It's Spino! He senses me nearby. My chest swells with anticipation and excitement, feelings he's sharing with me at this exact moment. I hurry towards the loading bay doors, eager to be by his side, when Avi appears out of the crowd to block my way.

'Zaz!'

He grabs my hand and pulls me out of sight. I'm startled by his sudden appearance, but follow with curiosity. What could be so urgent, and private? A flutter of delight ripples through me, confirming what I've suspected all along. I know what Avi wants. *Is this really happening? Do I want his affection right now?* Avi draws me into a secluded area between a stack of steel containers and palettes then spins to face me, drops his bag, and stares at me with those deep-brown eyes. I've never seen him so uncertain, or determined.

'What is it?' I say, feigning ignorance.

'I didn't want to leave without saying goodbye.'

'You could have said goodbye to me over there.'

Avi doesn't respond. The long, intense silence makes me tremble. His handsome face leans towards me until it's all I can see. I close my eyes as his warm lips press against mine. We share a lingering kiss. My head spins and I become weightless as a feather. Every care, every worry, vanishes in the moment. His hand gently squeezes mine and draws me back to reality. My entire body ripples with pleasure. *I've never felt like this before.*

Avi pulls back but keeps holding my hands. 'I couldn't go to war, not until I showed you how I feel about you.'

I nod, lost for words, mind blown, and my body still tingling.

Avi waits for a response, as if his universe hinges on my next words.

How do I react? I enjoyed the kiss, but moments before, I was in a completely different world, not thinking about kissing someone, let alone admitting how I feel about them. Like usual, I'm lost in my thoughts and forget to respond.

Avi lets my hands go and takes a half step back, his face shrouded with disappointment. I've never seen him so unsure of himself, but weirdly, I find it empowering.

'I'm sorry,' Avi says. 'I shouldn't have done that.'

I can't help empathising with him. I've been in awkward social situations like this more times than I can count. 'Don't be sorry. It was nice but –'

'I get it. You don't feel the same way.'

'It's not that. It's just... I'm not in that headspace. If you understand what I mean.'

Avi brightens a little. 'I do. I shouldn't have expected you to feel what I'm feeling. But I wanted you to know if we make it through this war, I'd like to be with you.'

I smile, but reality quickly wipes it from my face. 'It's hard to plan for the future when we don't even know if we'll be alive tomorrow.'

'That's why I needed to tell you.'

'Can I ask you something?'

'Of course, anything.'

'Why me? You could have had any girl in the academy. But you chose me.'

Avi nods thoughtfully and takes a breath. 'I admire your unassuming nature, your bravery. You show compassion, not just for others, but for the dinosaurs. You treat your friends with respect and stand up to your enemies.'

I shrug my shoulders and grin. 'I won't argue with that.'

'Also...I think you're the most beautiful girl I've ever seen. You look incredible in your lieutenant's uniform – it suits you perfectly.'

My face feels like it's on fire. *I'm blushing, badly.* I should have expected my body to respond with such an intense physical reaction. But this time feels different. I'm not embarrassed, I'm aroused. My reaction means one thing – I'm just as attracted to Avi. But the distraction frightens me and my mind automatically shifts gears. *I haven't got time to think about this now.*

'We should get going,' I say. 'We don't want to miss the launch.'

Avi gives me a disenchanted nod and picks up his bag. I lead the way out and give him a parting wink and smile, suggesting this isn't the end of our relationship, and might just be the beginning of a future one. He perks up and salutes me, then marches for the lifts. A concerned-looking face appears from the crowd and watches us. It's Kane! *How long was he watching me and Avi? Did he see us kiss? No way, we were hidden.* A guilty feeling sweeps over me and I wave to him, acting as normal as possible.

The crowd hustles forward and Kane is swept along before he can respond.

I lose sight of Kane and press on, fretting about what he's thinking. *How much did he see?* It shouldn't bother me, but it does. I'm closer to Kane than Avi and I feel like I owe him an explanation. *Why? He's not my boyfriend, although sometimes it feels that way.* I see Kane more like a brother than anything else, but that's not how he feels. I can't explain why, but there's something mysterious about Kane that keeps me from being romantically attracted to him, as if my subconscious is warning me to stay away.

BEEP!

A forklift swerves to avoid me and the driver shakes his fist in anger. 'Watch it!'

I jump aside, cursing myself for being so distracted. There's only one relationship I should focus on right now, the one between me and Spino.

The dinosaur loading bay is unusually quiet as I pass between the imposing steel doors. Most of the pens and cages are empty. A team of workers wielding electrical prods shepherd a sauropelta and dacentrurus into a steel mesh lift, with a cluster of herding drones hovering as backup. The workers keep a safe distance from the dinosaur's armoured bodies and lethal horns.

'*BUARK!*'

The familiar bark draws my attention to a solitary pen at the back of the bay. Spino's head pops over the steel gate and his vivid green eyes light up upon seeing me. I run the remainder of the way. He watches me until I'm close, then pulls his head back and presses his snout under the gate, sniffing for me. I reach inside and pat him.

'It's okay. I'm here. I'm so glad you're all right.'

'About time,' calls a voice from overhead. 'We were about to sedate him.'

A gruff, overworked wrangler peers down at me from the overhead gantry. He presses a button on his remote control and the gate clunks open.

Spino steps forward and nudges me with his snout, puffing and grunting as happy as I've ever seen him. His budding enthusiasm becomes a game, with him nudging me, and me trying not to fall over. I dodge his snout and run between his legs as he swings around, chasing me in a playful manner like a giant puppy. White healing patches dot his body and the hole in his sail has closed over and healed.

'You need help?' says a grumbly voice.

A sweaty, grubby-faced man approaches us brandishing a high-voltage control prod. Behind him stands a 20-strong team of equally exasperated workers and a hovering swarm of herding drones, all ready to zap Spino into submission.

'I've got this!'

My voice resonates through the bay, surprising me how loud and confident I sound. Spino stays by my side as we stride through the bay. The moment feels surreal, like something from a dream. *Are we really leaving to fight the Wraith on an alien world?* After 18 years in the academy, it's finally happening.

Then it hits me, these may be our last steps on Earth.

ARE YOU READY FOR MORE?
LOOK OUT FOR THE
OTHER THRILLING BOOKS
IN THE EXTINCTION ACADEMY SERIES

A Note From Andrew D. Connell

Thank you for reading my *Extinction Academy* series. Working as a self-published author, the success of my writing relies on you, the reader. Your reviews are the most effective way to introduce new readers to my books. So if you enjoyed this book, please consider leaving a review on Amazon or your place of purchase. A single sentence, or solitary one word review is often enough, but if you're willing to write more I'd love to hear your thoughts.

Subscribe to my author newsletter at *andrewdconnell.com* for the latest news and upcoming releases.

– Andrew D. Connell